COLD MAGIC

did not raise his voice. "I and my kin are bound by hands stronger than my own, by an unbreakable contract. *I cannot help you.* Please go, before you bring trouble to this house, where it is not wanted."

"So be it. I'll take my leave."

The latch scraped on the back window that overlooked the narrow garden behind our house. Hinges creaked, for this time of year the window was never oiled or opened. An agile person could climb from the window out onto a stout limb to the wall; Bee and I had done it often enough. I heard the window thump closed.

Uncle said, "We'll need those locks looked at by a blacksmith. I can't imagine how anyone could have gotten that window open when we were promised no one but a cold mage could break the seal. Ei! Another expense, when we have little enough money for heat and light with winter blowing in. He spoke truly enough."

I had not heard Factotum Evved until he spoke from the office, somewhere near Uncle. "Do you regret not being able to aid him, Jonatan?"

"What use are regrets? We do what we must."

"So we do," agreed Evved. "Best if I go make sure he actually leaves and doesn't lurk around to break in and steal something later."

His tread approached the door on which I had forgotten I was leaning. I bolted to the parlor door, opened it, and slipped inside, shutting the door quietly just as I heard the other door being opened. He walked on. He hadn't heard or seen me.

It was one of my chief pleasures to contemplate the mysterious visitors who came and went and make up stories about them. Uncle's business was the business of the Hassi Barahal clan. Still being underage, Bee and I were not privy to their secrets, although all adult Hassi Barahals who possessed a sound mind and body owed the family their service. All people are bound by ties and obligations, and the most binding ties of all are those between kin. That was why I kept stealing books out of the parlor and returning them. For the only books I ever took were my father's journals. Didn't I have some right to them, being that they, and I, were all that remained of him?

Feeling my way by touch, I set my boots by a chair and placed the journal on the big table. Then I crept to the bow window to haul aside the heavy winter curtains so I would have light. All eight mending baskets were set neatly in a row on the narrow side table, for the women of the house—Aunt Tilly, me, Beatrice, her little sisters, our governess, Cook, and Callie—would sit in the parlor in the evening and sew while Uncle or Evved read aloud from a book and Pompey trimmed the candle wicks. But it was the bound book of slate tablets resting beneath my mending basket that drew my horrified gaze. How had I forgotten that? I had an essay due today for my academy college seminar on history, and I hadn't yet finished it.

Last night, I had tucked fingerless writing gloves and a slate pencil on top of my mending basket. I drew on the gloves and pulled the bound tablets out from under the basket. With a sigh, I sat down at the big table with the slate pencil in my left hand. But as I began reading back through the words to find my place, my mind leaped back to the conversation I had just overheard. *The rising light marks the dawn of a new world*, the visitor had said; *or the end of the orderly world we know*, my uncle had retorted.

I shivered in the cold room. *The war is never over.* That had sounded ominous, but such words did not surprise me: Europa had fractured into multiple principalities, territories, lordships, and city-states after the collapse of the Roman Empire in the year 1000 and had stayed that way for the last eight hundred years and more; there was always a little war or border incident *somewhere.* But worlds do not begin and end in the steady mud of daily life, even if that mud involves too many petty wars, cattle raids, duels, feuds, legal suits, and shaky alliances for even a scholar to remember. I could not help but think the two men were speaking in a deeper code, wreathed in secrets. I was sure that somewhere out there lay hidden the story of what we are not meant to know.

The history of the world begins in ice, and it will end in ice. So sing the Celtic bards and Mande djeliw of the north whose songs tell us where we came from and what ties and obligations bind us. The Roman historians, on the other hand, claimed that fire erupting from beneath the bones of the earth formed us and will consume us in the end, but who can trust what the Romans say? Everything they said was used to justify their desire to make war and conquer other people who were doing nothing but minding their own business. The scribes of my own Kena'ani people, named Phoenicians by the lying Romans, wrote that in the beginning existed water without limit, boundless and still. When currents stirred the waters, they birthed conflict and out of conflict the world was created. What will come at the end, the ancient sages added, cannot be known even by the gods.

The rising light marks the dawn of a new world. I'd heard those words before. The Northgate Poet used the phrase as part of his nightly declamation when he railed against princes and lords and rich men who misused their rank and wealth for selfish purposes. But I had recently read a similar phrase in my father's journals. Not the one I'd taken out last night. I'd sneaked that one upstairs because I had wanted to reread an amusing story he'd told about encountering a saber-toothed cat in a hat shop. Somewhere in his journals, my father had recounted a story about the world's beginning, or about something that had happened "at the dawn of the world." And there was light. Or was it lightning?

I rose and went to the bookshelves that filled one wall of the parlor: my uncle's precious collection. My father's journals held pride of place at the center. I drew my fingers along the numbered volumes until I reached the one I wanted. The big bow window had a window seat furnished with a long plush seat cushion, and I settled there with my back padded by the thick winter curtain I'd opened. No fire crackled in the circulating stove set into the hearth, as it did after supper when we sewed. The chill air breathed through the paned windows. I pulled the curtains around my body for warmth and angled the book so the page caught what there was of cloud-shrouded light on an October morning promising yet another freezing day.

In the end I always came back to my father's journals. Except for the locket I wore around my neck, they were all I had left of him and my mother. When I read the words he had written long ago, it was as if he were speaking to me, in his cheerful voice that was now only a faint memory from my earliest years.

Here, little cat, I've found a story for you, he would say as I snuggled into his lap, squirming with anticipation. *Keep your lips sealed. Keep your ears open. Sit very, very still so no one will see you. It will be like you're not here but in another place, a place very far away that's a secret between you and me and your mama. Here we go!*

2

Once upon a time, a young woman hurried along a rocky coastal path through a fading afternoon. She had been sent by her mother to bring a pail of goat's milk to her ailing aunt. But winter's tide approached. The end of day would usher in Hallows Night, and everyone knew the worst thing in the world was to walk abroad after sunset on Hallows Night, when the souls of those doomed to die in the coming year would be gathered in for the harvest.

But when she scaled the headland of Passage Point, the sun's long glimmer across the ice sea stopped her in her tracks. The precise angle of that beacon's cold fire turned the surface of the northern waters into glass, and she saw an uncanny sight. A drowned land stretched beneath the waves: a forest of trees; a road paved of fitted stone; and a round enclosure, its walls built of white stone shimmering within the deep and pierced by four massive gates hewn of ivory, pearl, jade, and bone. The curling ribbons rippling along its contours were not currents of tidal water but banners sewn of silver and gold.

So does the spirit world enchant the unwary and lead them onto its perilous paths.

Too late for her, the land of the ancestors came alive as the sun died beyond the western plain, a scythe of light that flashed and vanished. Night fell.

As a full moon swelled above the horizon, a horn's cry filled the air with a roll like thunder. She looked back: Shadows fled across the land, shapes scrambling and falling and rising and plunging forward in desperate haste. In their wake, driving them, rode three horsemen, cloaks billowing like smoke.

The masters of the hunt were three, their heads concealed beneath voluminous hoods. The first held a bow made of human bone, the second held a spear whose blade was blue ice, and the third held a sword whose steel was so bright and sharp that to look upon it hurt her eyes. Although the shadows fleeing before them tried to dodge back, to return the way they had come, none could escape the hunt, just as no one can escape death.

The first of the shadows reached the headland and spilled over the cliff, running across the air as on solid earth down into the drowned land. Yet one shadow, in the form of a lass, broke away from the others and sank down beside her.

"Lady, show mercy to me. Let me drink of your milk."

The lass was thin and trembling, more shade than substance, and it was impossible to refuse her pathetic cry. She held out the pail of milk. The girl dipped in a hand and greedily slurped white milk out of a cupped palm.

And she changed.

She became firm and whole and hale, and she wept and whispered thanks, and then she turned and ran back into the dark land, and either the horsemen did not see her or they let her pass. More came, struggling against the tide of shadows: a laughing child, an old man, a stout young fellow, a swollen-bellied toddler on scrawny legs. Those who reached her drank, and they did not pass into the bright land of the ancestors. They returned to the night that shrouded the land of the living.

Yet, even though she stood fast against the howl of the wind of foreordained death, few of the hunted reached her. Fear lashed the shadows, and as the horsemen neared, the stream of hunted thickened into a boiling rush that deafened her before it abruptly gave way to a terrible silence. A woman wearing the face her aunt might have possessed many years ago crawled up last of all and clung to the rim of the pail, too weak to rise.

"Lady," she whispered, and could not speak more.

"Drink." She tipped the pail to spill its last drops between the shade's parted lips.

The woman with the face of her aunt turned up her head and lifted her hands, and then it seemed she simply sank into the rock and vanished. A sharp, hot presence clattered up. The spearman and the bowman rode on past the young woman, down into the drowned land, but the rider with the glittering sword reined in his horse and dismounted before she could think to run.

The blade shone so cold and deadly that she understood it could sever the spirit from the body with the merest cut. He stopped in front of her and threw back the hood of his cloak. His face was black and his eyes were black, and his black hair hung past his shoulders and was twisted into many small braids like the many cords of fate that bind the thread of human lives.

She braced herself. She had defied the hunt, and so, certainly, she would now die beneath his blade.

"Do you not recognize me?" he asked in surprise.

His words astonished her into speech. "I have never before met you."

"But you did," he said, "at the world's beginning, when our spirit was cleaved from one whole into two halves. Maybe this will remind you."

His kiss was lightning, a storm that engulfed her.

Then he released her.

What she had thought was a cloak woven of wool now appeared in her sight as a mantle of translucent power whose aura was chased with the glint of ice. He was beautiful, and she was young and not immune to the power of beauty.

"Who are you?" she asked boldly.

And he slowly smiled, and he said—

"Cat!"

My cousin Beatrice exploded into the parlor in a storm of coats, caps, and umbrellas, one of which escaped her grip and plummeted to the floor, from whence she kicked it impatiently toward me.

"Get your nose out of that book! We've got to run right now or you'll be late!"

I ripped my besotted gaze from the neat cursive and looked up with my most potent glower.

"Cat! You're blushing! What on earth are you reading?" She dumped the gear on the table, right on top of the slate tablets.

"Ah! That's my essay!"

With a fencer's grace and speed, Bee snatched the journal out of my hands. Her gaze scanned the writing, a fair hand whose consistent and careful shape made it easy to read from any angle.

She intoned, in impassioned accents, " 'His kiss was lightning, a storm that engulfed her'! If I'd known there was romance in Uncle Daniel's journals, I would have read them."

"If you could read!"

"A weak rejoinder! Not up to your usual standard. I fear reading such scorching melodrama has melted your cerebellum."

"It's not melodrama. It's an old traditional tale—"

"Listen to this!" She slapped a palm against her ample bosom and drawled out the words lugubriously. " 'And he slowly smiled, and . . . he . . . said—' "

"Give me that!" I lunged up, grabbing for the journal.

She skipped back, holding it out of my reach. "No time for kisses! Get your coat on. Anyway, I thought your essay was..." She excavated the tablets, flipped them closed, and squinted her eyes to consider the handsomely written title. "Blessed Tanit, protect us!" she muttered as her brows drew down. She made a face and spoke the words as if she could not believe she was reading them. "'Concerning the Mande Peoples of Western Africa Who Were Forced by Cold Necessity to Abandon Their Homeland and Settle in Europa Just South of the Ice Shelf.' Could you have made that title longer, perhaps? Anyway, what do kisses have to do with the West African diaspora?"

"Nothing. Obviously!" I sat on a chair and began to lace up my boots. "I was thinking of something else. The beginning and ending of the world, if you must know."

She wrinkled her nose, as at a bad smell. "The end of the world sounds so dreary. And so final."

"And I remembered that my father mentioned the beginning of the world in one of his journals. But this was the wrong story, even though it does mention 'the world's beginning.'"

"Even I could tell that." She glanced at the page. "'When our spirit was cleaved from one whole into two halves.' That sounds painful!"

"Bee! The entire house can hear you. We're not supposed to be in here."

"I'm not that loud! Anyway, of course I spied out the land first. Mother and Shiffa are up in the nursery where Astraea is having a tantrum. Hanan is on the landing, keeping watch. Father and Evved went all the way out into the back. So we're safe, as long as you *hurry*!"

I plucked the journal from her hand and set it on the table. "You go on ahead to the academy. I just need to write a conclusion. It's the seminar the headmaster teaches, and I hate to disappoint him. He never says anything. He just *looks* at me." I excavated my slate tablet and pencil from beneath the coats and caps.

Bee shoved my coat onto one of the chairs, searching for her cap. After tying it tight under her chin and pulling on her coat, she swung her much-patched cloak over all. "Don't be late or Father will forbid us the trip to the Rail Yard."

"Which handsome pupil do you intend to flirt with there?"

She launched a glare like musket shot in my direction and strode imperiously from the parlor, not bothering to answer. I wrote my conclusion. Her little sister Hanan clattered down the stairs with her to bid her farewell by the front door. Up in the nursery, Astraea had launched into one of her mulish fits of "no no no no no," and our governess, Shiffa, had reverted to her most coaxing voice to appease her. Aunt Tilly's light footsteps passed down the steps to the ground floor and thence back to the kitchen, no doubt to consult with Cook about finding something sweet to break the little brat's concentration. I wrote hurriedly, not in my best script and not with my most nuanced understanding.

That is how those druas with secret power among the local Celtic tribes, and the Mande refugees with their gold and their hidden knowledge, came together and formed the mage Houses. The power of the Houses allowed them to challenge princely rule while—

I heard footsteps coming up the stairs, and a key turned in the office door. I paused, hand poised above the slate. Men entered the office; the door was shut.

Uncle spoke in a low voice no one but me could have heard through the wall. "You were supposed to come at midnight."

A male voice answered. "I was delayed. Is everything here I paid for?"

"Here are the papers."

"Where is the book?"

"Melqart's Curse! Evved, didn't you get the book?"

"It must still be in the parlor. Just a moment."

I wiped the "while" from the slate and pressed a hasty, smeared period to the sentence. It would have to do. I scooped up the slate tablet and my schoolbag, bolted for the door, and got out just as the door between the study and the parlor was unlocked.

I halted on the landing to listen. Aunt Tilly was back upstairs, speaking with Shiffa about the girls' lessons for the day while Astraea whined, "But I wanted yam pudding, not this!" Meanwhile, Hanan had gone back to the kitchen and was chattering with Cook and Callie in her high, sweet voice as the three began to peel turnips. Pompey, with his distinctive uneven tread, was in the basement. I fled down the main stairs and out the front door, and it was not until I was out of sight of the house that I realized I had forgotten my coat, cap, and umbrella. I dared not return to fetch them.

Yet what is cold, after all, but the temperature to which we are most accustomed? It is cold for half the year here in the north. However pleasant the summer may seem, the ice never truly rests; it only dozes through the long days of Maius, Junius, Julius, and Augustus with its eyes half closed. I stuffed the tablet in my schoolbag between a new schoolbook and my scholar's robe, and kept going. To keep warm, I ran instead of walking, all the way through our modest neighborhood and then up the long hill into the old temple district where the new academy had been built twenty years ago. Fortunately, the latest fashionable styles allowed plenty of freedom for my legs and lungs.

As I crossed under the gates into the main courtyard, a fine carriage pulled up to disgorge a brother and two sisters swathed in fur-lined cloaks. Though late like me, they were so rich and well connected that they could walk right in the front through the grand entry hall without fearing censure, while I fumbled with frozen hands at the servants' entrance next to the latrines. The cursed latch was stuck.

"Salve, Maestressa Barahal. May I help you with that?"

I swallowed a yelp of surprise and looked up into the handsome face of Maester Amadou Barry, who had evidently followed me to the side door. His sisters were nowhere in sight.

"Salve, maester," I said prettily. "I saw you and your sisters arrive."

"You're not dressed for the weather," he remarked, pushing on the latch until it made a clunk and opened.

"My things are inside," I lied. "I can't be late, for the proctor locks the balcony door when the lecture starts."

"My apologies. I was just wondering if your cousin Beatrice…" His pause was so awkward that I smiled. I was certain he was blushing. "And you, of course, and your family, intend to visit the Rail Yard when it is open for viewing next week."

"My uncle and aunt intend to take Beatrice and me, yes," I replied, biting down another smile. "If you'll excuse me, maester."

"My apologies, for I did not mean to keep you," he said, backing away, for a young man of his rank would certainly enter through the front doors no matter how late he was.

Inside, as I raced along a back corridor, all lay quiet except for a buzz of conversation from the lecture hall. I had a chance to get to my seat before it was too late. In icy darkness, I hurried up the narrow steps that led to the balcony of the lecture hall. The proctor had already turned off the single gaslight that lit the stairwell and had gone in, but I knew these steps well. With the strap of my schoolbag gripped between my teeth, I tugged my scholar's robe on over my jacket and petticoats. I shrugged the satin robe up over both shoulders and smoothed it down just as I felt the change of temperature, from bone cold to merely flesh-achingly chilly, that meant the door loomed ahead.

Had the proctor locked it already?

Blessed Tanit! Watch over your faithful daughter. Let me not be late and get into trouble. Again.

3

My hand tightened on the iron latch, the metal so cold it burned through the palm of my writing gloves. I applied pressure, and the latch clicked blessedly free. Catching my breath, I listened as female voices gossiped and giggled, schoolbook pages turned, and pencil leads scratched on paper. A heavy tread approached, accompanied by the jangle of a ring of keys. Straightening, I opened the door and crossed the threshold into the proctor's basilisk glare.

She lowered the key she had been about to insert into the lock and attempted to wither me with a sarcastic smile. "Maestressa Catherine Hassi Barahal. How gracious of you to attend today's required lecture."

I opened my mouth to offer a clever reply, but I had forgotten the schoolbag gripped between my teeth and had to grab for it as it fell. The neat catch allowed me to sweep into a courtesy. "Maestra Madrahat. Forgive me. I was discommoded."

Some things you could not fault a respectable young woman for in public, even if you wondered if she was telling the truth. She favored me with a raised eyebrow eloquent of doubt but stepped aside so I could squeeze past her along the back aisle toward my assigned bench. "Button your robe, maestressa," she added, her parting shot.

As I hastened along the aisle, shaking from relief and shivering from the cold, I heard her key turn in the lock. Once again, I had landed—just barely—on my feet.

A few of the other pupils glanced my way, but I wasn't important enough to be worth more than a titter, an elbow nudge, or a yawn. At the back of the balcony's curve, I slipped onto the bench beside Beatrice. Her schoolbook was open to a page half filled in with an intricate drawing, and she was shaking a broken lead out of her pencil as I sat down.

"There you are!" she whispered without looking at me, intent on her pencil lead. "I knew you would make it here in time."

"Your confidence heartens me."

"I dreamed it last night." She slanted a sidelong look at me. "You know I always believe my dreams."

Below, on the dais at the front of the lecture hall, two servants rolled out a chalkboard and hung a net filled with sticks of chalk from its lower rim.

I bent closer. "I thought you dreamed only about certain male students—"

She kicked me in the ankle.

"Ouch!"

The headmaster limped out onto the dais and we fell silent, as did every other pupil, males below on the main floor and females above on the balcony. The old scholar was not one to drag out an introduction: a name, a list of spectacular experiments accomplished and revolutionary papers published, and the title of the lecture we were privileged to hear today: *Aerostatics, the principles of gases in equilibrium and of the equilibrium of balloons and dirigible balloons in changing atmospheric conditions.* Then he was finished, although a surprised murmur swept the hall as the students realized the lecturer was a woman.

"So, did you complete the essay?" Bee demanded, the words barely voiced but her expression emphatic. "I know how you love the headmaster's seminar. It would be awful if you couldn't go."

Under cover of the measured entrance of the dignitary in a headwrap and crisply starched and voluminous orange boubou, I made a business of extricating my schoolbook from my bag and arranging it neatly open before me on the pitted old table with my new silver pencil set diagonally across the blank page. Meanwhile, I spoke fast in a low voice as Bee fiddled with her broken lead.

"I finished but not quite how I wanted it. It was the strangest thing. Some man had come in through the window and was waiting in the study."

"How did he manage that?"

"I don't know. Uncle wondered the same thing. That's why they'd gone out to the garden when you came down. Then another man came after that. Uncle had to get a book from the parlor for him—I had to run so Evved wouldn't see me. Blessed Tanit! I left the journal I was reading on the table. He'll wonder why it was there!"

"He's been very absentminded and more snappish than usual these days. I think he's anxious about something. Something he and Mama aren't telling us. So perhaps he won't notice or will forget to ask."

"I hope so. What else could I do? I grabbed my schoolbag and my essay, and I ran all the way to the academy, only I forgot my coat, so I was very, very cold." I was still cold, because a third of the long underceiling windows were propped open with sticks to move air through the otherwise stuffy confines of the cramped balcony tiers. "One exciting thing did happen, however," I added coyly. "As I ran into the courtyard, a very fine carriage rolled up and who should step out but Maester Amadou and his twin sisters."

Bee's hands stilled. Her rosy lips pressed tight. She did not rise to the bait. Not yet, but she would. Instead, she said in the most casual voice imaginable, "I saw the twins come in." She gestured to a pair of girls seated in the front row by the balcony railing, resplendent in gold-and-blue robes cut to emphasize their tall figures, their hair wrapped in waxed cotton scarves whose sheen might have given off more light than the poor gas illumination. They recorded dutiful notes, writing in unison, as the esteemed professor sketched the lines of an airship on the chalkboard. "How did they get up here faster than you did?"

I smiled, luring her closer. "Maester Amadou stopped me. To ask a question."

"Oh. A question." She sighed wearily, as if his questions were the most uninteresting thing in the world to her.

"He asked about *you*."

Sprung! I gloated expectantly, but she turned her back on me, her attention flying away to fix on a spill of movement in the hall below us. Certain male pupils were coming in fashionably late and now settled into their assigned places. It seemed likely she would stare at Maester Amadou's attractive form and excellent clothes for the next century just to thwart me of the chance to annoy her, or perhaps she would stare at him because she had been doing so from the first day he and his sisters had arrived as pupils at the academy college, right after the Beltane festival day almost six months ago at the beginning of the month of Maius.

Two could move pieces in that chess game.

I rearranged my skirts, careful to fold back the front cut of the outer skirt so as to reveal the inner layers of petticoats, and tugged on my jacket to make sure it fit properly down around my hips. Then I buttoned the academic robe to conceal it all and folded my hands in my lap.

I tried to listen as the distinguished guest lecturer abandoned the introductory remarks to begin devouring the meat of the talk—the principles of aerostatic aircraft popularly known as airships and balloons. An interesting topic, especially in a time when the new technological innovations were very controversial. It was particularly interesting because the scholar was female and from the south, from the famous Academy of Natural Science and History in Massilia, on the Mediterranean, where female students were, so it was rumored, allowed to sit on the same benches as male students.

Because I had run from our house to the academy, a significant distance and much of it uphill, and because of my late essay, I hadn't had time to eat my morning porridge. So now, despite the unpadded bench pressing uncomfortably into my backside and the chilly draft wrapping my shoulders, I began to doze off.

A body immersed in a fluid is buoyed up by a force equal to the weight of the displaced fluid. Likewise, by this same principle, a craft that is lighter than air will be buoyant . . . gases expand in volume with a rise in temperature . . . by creating a cavity filled with flammable air . . . if pigs could fly, where would they go? . . . Will there be yam pudding for luncheon? . . .

I am sailing across a blinding expanse of ice in a schooner that skates the surface of a massive ice sheet, and a personage stands beside me who I know is my father even though, as happens in dreams, he looks nothing like the man whose portrait I wear in a locket at my neck—

A jab to my ribs brought me to my senses. I jerked awake, grabbing for my pencil, but it wasn't lying on my open schoolbook where I had left it. Bee's right hand gripped my right wrist and pinned my hand to the table we shared. Idly, I noted the smeared gray of pencil lead on the tips of her thin white wool gloves.

"What did he ask about me?" she whispered. Under the gloomy hiss of the gaslights—we female pupils stuck up here in the balcony got only half the light afforded the male pupils in the main hall below—I could see her flutter her eyelashes in that obnoxious way she had, the one that never failed to demolish the objections and reproaches of any adult caught in the beat of those dark wings. "Cat," she added, her voice warming, "you have to tell me."

I yawned to annoy her. "I'm bound by a contract not to tell."
She released my wrist and punched me on the shoulder.
"Ouch!"

Heads turned. Though she might look like a dainty little thing, Bee was a bruiser, really pitiless when she got roused. I glanced toward the curtained entrance where the proctor stood at guard as stiff as a statue and as grim as winter, staring straight ahead. The industrious pupils returned their attention to the lecture, and the bored slumped back to their naps.

"You earned it!" Bee knew precisely how to pitch her voice so only I could hear her. "I've been in love with him forever."

"Three weeks!" I rubbed my shoulder.

"Three months! Ever since I had that dream of him standing, sword drawn, on earthen ramparts while fending off soldiers wearing the livery of a mage House." She pressed a hand to her chest, which was heaving under a high-collared dress appropriate for the academy college's proper halls. "I have kept the truth of my desperate feelings to myself for fear—"

"For fear we'd wonder why you so suddenly left off being in love with and destined to wed Maester Lewis of the lovely red-gold hair and turned your tenacious heart to the beauty of Maester Amadou with his piercing black eyes."

"Which you yourself admit are handsome."

She bent forward to look over the rows of benches and the female pupils seated in pairs at study tables. Given that we were seated in the cramped back row of benches with the other female scholarship students, we could see only the front third of the spacious main hall below us. Maester Amadou lounged in the second row in a chair placed at a polished table close to the podium. His fashionably clothed back was to us, but I could see that he was rolling dice with his tablemate, the equally well-connected Maester Lewis, a youth of high rank who had been fostered out to the court of the ruling prince of Tarrant whose territory included our city of Adurnam. The young men were both so strikingly good-looking that I wondered if they sat together the better to display their contrasting appearances, one milk white and gold haired and the other coffee dark and black haired. On the dais, pacing back and forth in front of the chalkboard and waving a hand in enthusiastic measure, the esteemed natural philosopher launched into an explosive digression on the natural laws pertaining to the behavior of gases, words scattering everywhere.

"Yes, he's almost as pretty as you are," I retorted, "and well aware that his family's wealth allows him to walk in late *and* then to game in the front of the hall, all without repercussion. He's the vainest young man I ever met."

"How can you say so? The story of how he and his three sisters and aunt escaped from the assault on Eko by murderous, plague-ridden ghouls—forced to call their good-byes to their parents and cousins left behind on the shore as the monsters advanced. It's a heartbreaking tale!"

"If it's true. The settlement and fort were specifically established at Eko because it is an island, and ghouls can't cross water. So how could ghouls have reached them? Anyone can say what they like when there are no witnesses."

"You just have no heart, Cat. You're heartless." Her scowl was meant to pierce me to the heart, if I'd had one. With an indignant flounce of the shoulders, she turned away to furiously sketch on a blank page of her book, using *my* good silver pencil with its fresh lead.

"If by that you mean I don't fall head over ears in love with every handsome face I encounter, then I thank the blessed Tanit for it! Someone needs to be heartless. His family is well-to-do and well connected, that's certain. His elder sister married the younger brother of the cousin of the Prince of Tarrant. His aunt is known to be very clever at business, with contacts reaching across the banking houses of the south. All points in his favor.

Especially given the always impoverished state of the Barahal finances. Now I want my pencil back."

"You're going to tell me what he *asked* about *me*," she murmured without looking up or ceasing her drawing, "because otherwise I will pour a handful of salt into your porridge every morning for the next month—"

"Catherine! Beatrice! The Hassi Barahal cousins are again demonstrating their studiousness, I comprehend."

Distracted by the sound of Beatrice's voice, I hadn't noticed the proctor's slithering approach along the back aisle. She came to rest right behind us, close enough that her breath stirred the hair on my neck. Her gaze swept the balcony. The other female pupils were all intent on recording the formula $V(1)T(2) = V(2)T(1)$, which was shedding chalk dust on the board as the venerable professor repeated Alexandre's law: *At constant pressure, the volume of a given mass of an ideal gas increases or decreases by the same factor as its temperature increases or decreases.*

The maestra grabbed my schoolbook off the table and flipped through its blank pages. "Is this a new schoolbook, maestressa? Or the sum total of your knowledge?"

Cats always land on their feet. "Flammable air is fourteen times lighter than life-sustaining air. It can be produced by dissolving metals in acid. Gas expands as its temperature goes up. No wonder the mage Houses hate balloons! If it's true that proximity to a cold mage always decreases the ambient temperature of any object, then wouldn't a cold mage deflate any balloon sack just by standing alongside it?"

Her narrowed gaze would have flattened an elephant. But the gods were merciful, because instead of sending me off to the headmaster's office for impertinence, she turned her attention to Bee. My dearest and most beloved cousin hastily set down my pencil and attempted to close her sketchbook. The proctor slapped a hand down, holding it open to the page where Bee had just sketched an impressive portrait of a personage obviously meant to be me. With a cackling death's-head grimace and denarii for eyes, the caricature gazed upon an object held out before it in a bony hand.

"I see you have been paying attention in anatomy, at least," remarked the maestra as icily as the draft that shivered over us through the high window slits. "That is a remarkably good likeness of a four-chambered heart, although is a heart not meant to reside in the chest cavity?"

Bee batted her eyelashes as her honey smile lit her face. "It was a moment's fancy, that is all. An allegory in the Greek style, if you will. If you look at the other pages, you'll see I have been most assiduously attending to this recent series of lectures on the principles of balloon and airship design." She kept talking as she flipped through the pages. The babble pouring mellifluously from her perfect lips began to melt Maestra Madrahat's rigid countenance. Buoyed up by a force equal to . . . gases expand in volume with . . .

Soon pigs would fly.

"Such fine draftsmanship," the proctor murmured besottedly as Bee displayed page after page of air sacs inflated and deflated and hedged about with all manner of mathematical formulae and proportional notations, balloons rising and slumping according to temperature and pressure, hapless passengers being tossed overboard from baskets on high and falling with exaggerated screams and outflung arms—

The maestra stiffened, breath sucked in hard.

Bee swiftly turned to a more palatable historical sketch of the Romans kneeling in defeat at Zama before the newly crowned queen, the *dido* of our people, and her victorious general Hanniba'al. And she kept talking. "I am so very deeply anticipating our outing to the Rail Yard next week, where we will be able to view the airship for ourselves. How incredible that it propelled itself all the way across the Atlantic Ocean from

Expedition to our fair city of Adurnam! Not a single human or troll lost in the crossing!"

"Imagine," I added, unable to control my tongue, "how the cold mages must be celebrating its arrival, considering that the mage Houses call airships and rifles the reckless tinkering of radicals who mean to destroy society. Do you suppose the mages mean to join the festivities next week as well? It's said half the city means to turn out to see the airship, if only to stop the Houses from attempting something rash."

Every pupil sitting near enough to overhear my words gasped. Hate the Houses if you wished, or kneel before them hoping to be offered a trickle from the bounteous stream of their power and riches and influence, but everyone knew it was foolish to openly speak critical words. Even the lords and princes who ruled the many principalities and territories of fractious Europa did not challenge the Houses and their magisters.

The proctor snatched Bee's book from the table and tucked it under an arm. "The headmaster will see you both in his office after class."

Half the girls on the balcony snickered. The other half shuddered. The twins kept taking notes, although I didn't know them well enough to say if they were that oblivious or that focused. Maestra Madrahat took up her guard post at the entrance, her keys hanging in plain sight to remind us that no one could sneak out and down the stairs and that no venturesome young male could sneak up and in. None of that *here*, in the abstemious halls of the academy.

The headmaster will see you both.

"Oh, Cat, what have we done now?" Our hands clasped as we shivered in a sudden cold wind coursing like a presentiment of disaster down from the high windows.

Bee and Cat, together forever. No matter what trouble we got into, we would, as always, face it as one.

4

When the lecture ended, we all dutifully snapped fingers and thumbs to show approval. Afterward, some students stood to offer praise, one male pupil raising a song while a chorus, scattered through the hall and balcony, clapped a rhythm and sang the response:

To the maestra of learning, heavy with wisdom.
On this day we greet you.
Our ears like maize grow ripe with knowledge.
On this day we greet you.

Bee hummed and tapped along, offbeat and out of tune. The academy's head of natural history offered a mercifully brief speech thanking the eminent visitor for gracing us with her presence and illuminating insights, and afterward reminded the gathered pupils of the academy-sponsored trip to the Rail Yard to view the airship, coming up next week, and the public lecture to be offered on this very evening by the very same visiting scholar on the very same subject.

Bee sighed as she returned my pencil. "Father will make us go. It's hopeless. We're doomed to the dreary gray of Sheol for another evening of hearing the same lecture all over again."

"I thought you'd given up believing in the afterlife after last year's lecture series on natural philosophy."

"Reason is the measure of all things. It's perfectly reasonable to assume I will die of boredom if I have to sit through the same lecture all over again."

"You just said that."

"Exactly my point. I won't even be allowed to draw."

"Say you have a headache."

"That was my excuse last week when the eminent scholar from the academy in Havery was speaking on the origin, nature, range, function, and persistence of ice sheets."

"That one was actually interesting. Did you know that glacial ice covers all land north of fifty-five degrees latitude and once covered the land as far south as Adurnam—"

"Quiet!" She dropped her head into her hands, strands of black hair curling around her fingers. Her elegant silver blessing bracelet, given to her by her mother seven years ago when she made twelve, glimmered like a dido's precious keepsake in the amber light. "I'm devising a desperate scheme."

I slipped my schoolbook into my bag beside the essay and buttoned the pencil into its pocket, from which Bee could not easily steal it. We waited for the balcony to clear: The back-row students always descended last. When our turn came, we rose in order and filed out past Maestra Madrahat. The proctor still clutched Bee's sketchbook, and I wondered if Bee would snatch it out of her hands, but the fateful moment passed as we pushed into the narrow stairwell, following the other whispering girls down the steep steps while the last of the row clipped at our heels. The gaslight's flame murmured.

The young woman ahead of us turned her head to address Bee, who was in front of me. "Was that the book with the naughty drawings?" she asked.

"Yes." Bee's whisper hissed up and down the stairwell, and other girls fell silent to listen. "Ten pages drawn after the lecture on the wicked rites of sacred prostitution practiced in the ancient

Phoenician city of Tyre according to the worship of the goddess Astarte."

More giggling. I rolled my eyes.

"Those are just lies the Romans told," said our interlocutor, who, like us, was the daughter of an old and impoverished Kena'ani lineage. Unlike us, Maestressa Asilita had been given a place at the academy college because of her genuine scholarly attainments. In addition, she had a remarkable gift for coaxing Bee off the cliff. "Like the ones about child sacrifice. Do you have drawings of that, too?"

"Bee," I warned.

"Grieving parents wailing as they scratch their own faces and arms to draw blood? Priests cutting the throats of helpless infants and lopping off their tiny heads? And then casting their plump little bodies into the fire burning within the arms of the Lord of Ba'al Hammon? Of course!"

Girls shrieked while others, sad to say, giggled even more.

"What is that you said, Maestressa Hassi Barahal?" demanded the proctor's voice from on high.

"I said nothing, maestra," I called back as I ground a fist into Bee's back. "I spoke my cousin's name only because I was tripping on her hem and I wanted her to *move faster*."

The light at the end of the stairs beckoned. We surged out and down the wide corridor in a chattering mass of young women soon joined by a chattering mass of young men. The actual children, the pupils under sixteen, were herded away to the school building in the back of the academy, but we college pupils spilled into the high entrance hall to await the summons to luncheon.

The academy had been erected only two decades before with funds raised from well-to-do families who resided in the prosperous city of Adurnam and its neighboring countryside, all ruled over by the Prince of Tarrant and his clan. Those families came from many different backgrounds, and some had fought bitter wars or engaged in blood feuds in the past. The prince had clearly instructed the architect to placate everyone and offend no one. Therefore, the inner stone facade of the entrance hall had been carved with a series of reliefs depicting plants: princely white yams, hardy kale, broom millet, poor-man's chestnut, jolly barley, honest spelt, humble oats, winter rye, broad beans, northern peas, sweet pears and apples, stolid turnip, quick radish, and even the newcomers brought over the ocean—maize and potatoes. Something for everyone to eat!

"Luncheon smells so good," whispered Bee, licking her lips.

Yam pudding. My favorite! The assembly bell rang.

She pulled me around the outside of the milling crowd, whose fashionable clothing brightened the hall with so many bold colors, including intense stripes of red that matched my mounting irritation at being dragged along like baggage.

"Bee!"

"We have to get my sketchbook back. Look! There goes the old basilisk. Blessed Tanit save me. She's giving it to the headmaster! Cat, do you have any idea—"

"I have an idea that I'm very hungry. Unlike you, I missed my morning porridge."

"He's seen us!"

Maestra Madrahat saw us, too, and she beckoned like an angry Astarte, goddess of war, summoning malingering troops to battle. Bee hauled. I lagged. Why ever could I not keep my mouth shut?

The headmaster was a tall, elderly black man of Kushite ancestry who had a scholarly background in the newly deciphered hieroglyphics of ancient Kemet, which the Romans felt obliged to call Egypt. The headmaster was the one person who the various monied factions in the principality of Tarrant had all agreed would, like the plants, offend no one because of his impeccably distinguished and noble Kushite lineage. Even though the great wars between Rome and Qart Hadast—called Carthage by the cursed Romans—had been fought two thousand years ago, what Kena'ani mother would actually want a son of Rome teaching her precious daughters? Our ancient feud was far from being the only dispute or duel raging in the private salons and mercantile districts of Adurnam with its many lineages, clans, ethnicities, tribes, bankers, merchants, artisans, plebeians, and lords living all smashed together in the city's stately avenues, crowded alleys, busy law courts, and the narrow parks where hotheaded young men fought duels.

Adurnam, city of eternal quarreling!

The great port city was built along the banks of the Solent River, downstream from the vast marshy estuary we in Adurnam called the Sieve. As many rivers and tributaries and streams flowed into the Sieve as peoples, lineages, languages, gods, rhythms, and cuisines flowed into the city. So it was no wonder that the academy had chosen for its headmaster a man who could claim relation to the Kushite dynasty, whose scions had been peacefully ruling venerable but decaying Kemet—Egypt— for the last two thousand five hundred years. Even the Roman Empire had lasted only a thousand.

"Now is not a convenient time, maestra," murmured the headmaster in a low voice I could hear, although I certainly was not meant to. "Does this matter really warrant my attention?"

"If you'll just speak to them, maester."

He looked toward me, as if to say with his gaze that he knew how well I could hear although we were still a thrown book away and they were speaking softly.

Bee leaned her whole body into tugging me, and we crossed the gap out of breath and staggered to a halt before him. Bee pulled off her indoor slippers, and this impulsive gesture of respect—removing shoes before an elder—made him smile. We kept our gazes humbly lowered.

"The Barahal cousins may attend me," he said as he tucked Bee's schoolbook under an arm. He offered a courtesy to the maestra and, leaning heavily on his cane, made his way across the hall.

Bee tugged her slippers back on and cast *such* a look at me. "Are you going to help me or hinder me?" she murmured.

I sighed, knowing I had no choice. Like obedient handmaidens in the old tales, we followed him out through the marble portico into the chill of the inner court, a central garden covered by a glass roof. The courtyard was surrounded on three sides by a two-storied stone building that housed classrooms, workshops, and tutors' offices. No sun shone through the glass today; flakes of snow powdered the sloped roof. The noise of the hall behind us receded as a waiting servant opened the door to the library wing, and we entered a somewhat less chilly marble corridor. The headmaster took the wide stairs toward the upper floor, slow progress because of his infirmity. Bee's gaze was fixed on the schoolbook under his arm in the manner of a stoat waiting for the prime instant to steal an egg.

His office was behind the first set of doors in the upper corridor. The servant, who had paced us up the steps, moved around to open these doors so the headmaster could enter without altering his steady advance. The office was spacious, with one wall of windows facing the rose court, a door into an adjoining chamber, and the rest of the wall space lined with bookcases. Mirrors hung on the back of each door, creating corridors of reflecting vision that revealed most of the chamber before and behind me.

The chamber was neither oppressively tidy nor unpleasantly messy but rather graced a middle ground between cluttered and neat. A chalkboard had been pushed in front of one bank of bookcases, facing four chairs. The large fireplace had been refitted with a circulating stove whose warmth radiated through the room. His desk had not a scrap of paper on its polished surface while the big table set beneath the windows formed a topographical masterpiece of stacked books, open books, two globes set on pedestals, and several half-unrolled maps with corners weighted down by scarabs carved out of green basalt. A longcase clock faced the table, its glass door revealing the steady motion of pendulum and weights within. Glass-doored bookcases held carefully labeled papyrus scrolls in cubbyholes classified according to chronology and subject matter.

On a pedestal in one corner was fixed the severed head of the famous poet and legal scholar Bran Cof. A scan of the chamber, as I saw it reflected within the mirrors, showed me a glimmer of magic like a cowl around the poet's sleeping head but no other sign of magic's presence. I caught the headmaster watching me in the mirror, though. Could he see chains of magic in mirrors, as I could? It was said that mirrors reflect the binding threads of power that run between this world and the unseen spirit world, but the truth of that statement is a secret hoarded by the sorcerers who have the power to manipulate such chains of power, people like cold mages, fire mages, druas, master poets, and the bards and djeliw. I was not one of them. I could not manipulate or handle the chains of magic except on a purely personal level: I could use them to conceal myself, to hear better, and to see in the dark. And, of course, I could see them in mirrors.

There was only one thing I remembered my mother saying to me, long, long ago, when I was five years old: *Don't tell anyone what you can do or see, Cat. Tell no one. Not ever.*

I had obeyed her. I had never told anyone, except Bee, because Bee knew everything about me just as I knew everything about her.

The headmaster smiled gently at me in the mirror's normal reflection. I looked away, because it was proper that I look away, being the student and he the elder.

"The cousins Hassi Barahal," he observed in his dry voice, "certainly know of my admiration for the Hassi Barahal brothers."

Naturally we knew of it, since his admiration paid our tuition.

"Your father, Beatrice, has done the academy board certain favors on whose basis your tuition is excused by the board of directors."

"Favors" being a more palatable word for less palatable activities.

"Obviously your father's journals, Catherine, to which your uncle has provided us full access, have proved invaluable in the academy's quest for a deeper understanding of natural history. Daniel Hassi Barahal understood that scholars seek to unravel, explain, and explicate from scientific principles the workings of the natural world out of purely disinterested motives. That includes the mysteries of mage-craft and its ties to a spirit world said to lie athwart our own. He was something of a scholar himself, if not precisely educated in the academy. Given the mage Houses' notorious and hostile secrecy, which they can back up with actual retribution, such attempts to uncover the worlds' workings seem bound to fail." He paused to glance at the mirrors.

I said nothing. Neither did Bee.

"Yet we scholars are a stubborn crew. It is these circumstances— the information provided by your fathers, each in his own way—that have led me to turn a blind eye to certain reports of your behavior that are not what we would prefer to see in our female students. Allowing girls into the academy at all is controversial, so those young females who study here must conduct themselves at all times with prudence—"

A bell tinkled.

My stomach growled softly in response, but it was not the luncheon bell but a lighter handbell rung from the adjoining room. For an instant, that aged and solemn face looked startled, then concerned. As swiftly as a curtain is swept closed, he concealed his feelings beneath a meaningless polite smile.

"Wait here, maestressas."

Still clutching Bee's schoolbook beneath an arm, he limped to the door and, as the servant opened it, vanished into the adjoining room. We caught a glimpse of close-packed shelves of books before the servant closed the door behind both of them. Bee and I stood alone in the headmaster's office, except, of course, for the sleeping head of Bran Cof. A rumble of voices drifted from a far chamber, but I wasn't close enough to the inner door to pull apart the words.

"Do you think he just forgot he had it? Now what will happen?" Bee said in a low, fierce voice.

"He'll page through and see the seven hundred small and large portraits of Maester Amadou's pretty eyes and perfect jaw and braided hair. And before him, Maester Lewis with his red-gold hair and elevated brow and narrow chin. You've filled up reams of paper and ten or twelve schoolbooks with sketches of the best-looking young men in the academy."

For once she did not spit fire. "I don't care if people laugh at me for that. I've never cared what other people thought."

True enough. "Then what matters so much to you?"

Her gusty sigh shuddered in the room, and for an instant I caught an echoing shudder of movement, eyes drifting as in dreams, beneath the closed eyelids of the poet's head. I tensed, a shiver of cold crawling down my back, and stepped closer to Bee to clasp her hand.

What if he opened his eyes?

"I don't know how to explain it," she murmured, squeezing my hand. She hadn't been looking at the head. Maybe I had imagined what I had seen. Bran Cof's enchanted head had last been known to speak over one hundred years ago, on some arcane legal matter.

"Bee, we promised to always tell each other everything. What worries you so much about what's in your sketchbook?"

The door into the adjoining room opened. We both jumped like children caught by the cook with honey cake stolen hot from the pan. As the headmaster's assistant walked into the room, we offered a hasty courtesy to cover our embarrassment. His cheeks pinked—easy to see because he was albino—as he offered a more elaborate courtesy in return.

"Maestressas, I did not know you were here." We called him the headmaster's dog, not kindly. He hailed from a distant eastern empire beyond the Pale, and indeed one could discern his Avar heritage in his broad cheekbones and the epicanthic fold at his eyes. Rumor whispered that as a child, he had been rescued by the headmaster from death under the spears of the Wild Hunt that rode on Hallows Night. If true, the story explained his utter devotion to the old scholar.

We folded our hands politely before us and smiled at him.

For a moment, he looked ready to faint, for I am sure we appeared like two vultures biding our time until the dying cease their inconvenient thrashing. Then he glanced at Bee, his face curdling to such an unseemly shade of red that I conceived the horrible notion that the poor young man believed himself in love with her. Naturally such an infatuation was utterly forbidden between any of the teachers or their assistants and one of the academy's prudent and virtuous female pupils, even if she was going to turn twenty and reach the age of majority in just under two months. Even if she had a mean left hook. Even if she had shown the least interest in him, which she had not.

"I beg your pardon," Bee said so sweetly the words stung. "The headmaster instructed us to wait for him here. Will he return shortly?"

Her smile was too much for him. He croaked out a garbled word and bolted back the way he had come, wrenching the door closed behind him.

"Bee! Was that necessary?"

She stared at the door as if her gaze alone could splinter it into a thousand shards. "You know how I have always had such vivid dreams. I've started drawing them out to help remember them by."

"How can you draw a dream?"

Her color was high, and her hands were clenched. "I had to try to make some sense of them because the details haunt me! I don't even know why, and it doesn't matter, but I can't bear to have people looking— I can't explain it. I didn't even show them to *you*!" Tears welled in her lovely eyes. I knew when Bee was bluffing, and this wasn't it.

I grasped her hands. "When he comes back in, you cause a distraction, anything to get him to put the book down and shift his attention elsewhere. I'll sneak it into my schoolbag."

Nodding, she let go my hands and wiped her cheeks. The longcase clock's pendulum ticked. Ticked. Ticked. Ticked. Bee stared at the poet's head as if daring Bran Cof to open his eyes. I couldn't bear looking in case he did, so I let my gaze wander to the chalkboard. It had been recently erased, but I could still read traces of figures and words as a geologist can read down through layers of sediment and rock. *The Hibernian Ice Sheet Expedition: Lost, no bodies or wreckage recovered. The Alps Ice Cap Expedition: Turned back by ice storms. The First Baltic Ice Sea Expedition: Remnants rescued after a year missing. The Second Baltic Ice Sea Expedition: Lost, no bodies or wreckage recovered.*

"I wonder who *that* lesson was for," said Bee. "It's strange to look at that and remember that both your father and your mother were members of the First Baltic Ice Sea Expedition. That they were the 'remnants rescued after a year missing.' Them and, what, ten others?"

"Three others. Only five survived out of the twenty-eight who set out. I think I've read my father's account of the opening months of that expedition a hundred times. 'No man has ever crossed the tempestuous Baltic Ice Sea or set foot on the towering and inhospitable Skandic Ice Shelf.' No woman, either, for that matter. Fifty-four journals he wrote and numbered. That's the only time he mentions my mother."

She made a face. "Probably because the next two volumes are missing."

"Yes," I said peevishly, "the very ones covering the rest of the expedition, when any idiot who can do math—"

"That would be you."

"—can draw the conclusion that I was conceived in the latter months of that very expedition."

"It is curious," she agreed. "You would think a man falling in love would write paeans about the fine eyes of his beloved. But perhaps it was later, in the midst of the crisis on the ice, that they—"

A tremor in the floor alerted me. I lifted a hand to warn her. I heard, as she did not yet, the halting *step-tap* of the headmaster approaching the door. We composed our faces and pretended to be looking out the windows at the bare branches of autumn trees in the rose court. The door opened. The servant entered first, holding the door for the headmaster, who limped in with a preoccupied frown on his face. He seemed surprised to see us.

"Are you still here?" he asked. "Forgive me. I meant to dismiss you. Did I speak to you about the wisdom of not antagonizing the mage Houses, maestressas? Even in so small a way as imprudent speech?"

Bee's eyes had gone wide as china plates, and her chin trembled. The headmaster was no longer carrying her sketchbook.

"You did, maester," I responded promptly, seeing Bee was in no condition to speak. "I'll guard my tongue. It was ill-considered of me. I beg pardon."

"Ah, well, then. Best you go down to luncheon." A smile flitted and vanished on his seamed face. "I believe there is yam pudding. My favorite!"

The servant had crossed the chamber already and opened the outer door for the headmaster. We had to follow him down the path offered.

5

But that did not mean that, once out in the corridor, I could not feign a broken ribbon on my slipper, pretend to lose my footing, and therefore be obliged to kneel and fuss to make things right. Bee, leaping at once into the gaps between my beat, begged the headmaster to go on ahead and we would catch up as soon as the torn ribbon had been jury-rigged.

He and his servant went on, leaving us behind just as we'd hoped.

"We *have* to get back in and find it." Bee used the tone of voice that, like a stake, always impaled me to the wall.

"Both the headmaster's office and the formal library are specifically off-limits to unchaperoned pupils. We already know that the headmaster's dog is roaming loose among the books." I rose. With my height, I towered over her. "Can you imagine what will happen if we're caught in either place?"

"I'll go alone." She pressed her left hand to her bosom but fixed her right around the door's handle and misquoted the famous words of the great general Hanniba'al: " 'I will either find a way, or make one.' "

"Very pretty," I muttered. "Too bad the even more decorative Maester Amadou is not here to admire your fetching pose. Only, you should have your right hand raised in the manner of an orator declaiming."

She looked at me, all honey. "It's not locked."

I could smell luncheon's distant promise. I was so hungry. But there was no one in the corridor. Either find a way, or make one.

"It will be on your head," I muttered.

I adjusted my schoolbag's strap so it wouldn't shift. Then I bent to listen at the keyhole, hearing no sound from the chamber beyond except the ticking of the clock like the swing of fortune: triumph, disaster, triumph, disaster. I lifted a hand, she turned the handle, and we slipped inside. She closed the door and let the handle rise with a faint *snick.* The chamber lay eerily empty. The poet's head looked merely like a remarkably lifelike carving. Even so, I kept thinking its eyes were about to pop open and spot us sneaking where we weren't allowed. We slid quietly across the polished floor—many years of fencing practice had honed our ability to move smoothly—and at the far door, I again listened at the keyhole.

At first hearing: nothing.

I shut my eyes and listened more deeply, letting my cat's hearing creep through the unseen room on the other side of the door to the shift of air and temperature that betrayed a larger chamber beyond, in which one male voice asked a curt question and another replied in a cramped monotone I was sure belonged to the headmaster's dog. I could not *quite* hear distinct words: a map of Adurnam? The Rail Yard? Gas?

Was everyone in the academy discussing the newly arrived airship?

There was no point in waiting. We must be as bold as the didos of our people, the queens who had founded cities, battled the Romans to a standstill, and commanded voyages of discovery across the Atlantic Ocean and around the horn of Africa. I nudged Bee's foot with my own. She slid the door open a crack, wedged a foot in, peered inside. Like lightning, she flashed through the gap and vanished. I slipped after her, and she shut the door behind us.

Fiery Shemesh!

We stood in a chilly chamber of aisles, alleys of shelves that reached floor to ceiling, all crammed with books of every height, width, and thickness, some old and others new, more books than I had seen in one place in my life: This was a storage library. The polished wood floor caught streaks of light from the courtyard windows rising to our left, but mostly the light was broken up by the high shelves. We stared straight down a central aisle lined with pillars, each of which marked a side alley of shelves running perpendicular to the shadowed edges of the room. At the other end of the space, one side of a double door had been propped open against a stack of books so new their leather bindings gleamed. The vast formal library beyond had a vaulted ceiling and ample sunlight.

A man spoke, a brusque request for "that document you mentioned." Although we could not see him, I heard, almost felt, his feet shifting on the floorboards. Another pair of feet *clip-clapped* toward the open door.

I yanked Bee into the shadows to our right. We shivered like mice while the headmaster's dog walked briskly down the central aisle and into the headmaster's office. Its door closed behind him. We darted along the back aisle to the other end of the room. Creeping, we ventured up this alley, books leering at us from either side, to the door that opened into the library hall. From this angle, we could get a look only into the left-hand sweep of the huge chamber.

Five towering windows took up most of the outer wall facing the rose court, running from cushioned window seats all the way up to the crown moldings that joined wall to high ceiling. Long, heavy curtains of a dutiful gold fabric swagged down on either side of each window, tied back by braided gold cords. I nudged Bee and pointed to the gathered drapes. She nodded.

We crept to the left until we could see the rest of the chamber.

The inner three walls were lined floor to ceiling with book-shelves. A rolling book ladder rested beside the far doors. In the half of the chamber nearest us, settees and side tables were arranged in handsome groupings flanked by braziers to allow scholars to read and converse in comfort. On the far half of the chamber, three long tables were set crosswise so as to take advantage of the full length of the natural light streaming in through the tall windows. Oil lamps rested by tables and couches to provide light in the evenings. None were lit now. Even the massive fireplace lay cold, despite the chill.

A man stood with his back to us, bent over one of the tables as he examined papers spread before him. He was dressed in a magnificently starched, polished, and embroidered green boubou, the voluminous sleeves and folds of the robe marking the old-fashioned style. But if his muscular shoulders; vital posture; short, almost shaved, black hair; and restless hands were any indicator, he was young, not old.

Behind us, the headmaster's office door snicked open.

We skated over the polished floor and slipped behind the nearest draperies just as the headmaster's dog trotted back into the chamber. The visitor had not even turned; he was impatiently tapping a hand on the table, the driven pattern of the beat familiar to my ears, because it was one of the drum dances popular on festival days. Bee stood crushed behind me. I tweaked back an edge of the drape.

The assistant hurried to the table, set down a long tube, and uncapped it. He unrolled a schematic busy with lines and curves, then secured the corners and the sides with iron paperweights molded in the shapes of Kemet's gods and goddesses.

As this precise ritual unfolded, my gaze wandered across the chamber.

On a side table by one of the couches, Bee's sketchbook lay

beneath a slender leather-bound book set thoughtlessly atop it. I could retrieve it as long as neither of the men turned.

Everyone says that the West African Mande lineages and European Celtic tribes were together able to establish the mage Houses, because they possess more conduits to the spirit world than any other peoples known to the natural philosophers, but that does not mean other peoples do not have a few tricks up their sleeves.

We who call ourselves Kena'ani made our fortunes and solidified our sea-trading networks because there were a few things we did particularly well with the aid of the gods—back when our people believed in gods—and with the connivance of the natural world, which must be understood and manipulated so as to harness its power. Some say the Kena'ani are a godless, spiritless, magicless people who will sell our swords and souls for money and will trade anything, even our honor, as long as we make a profit by doing so. They can say what they want. We know how to keep our secrets. We know what information we are willing to share, what we're willing to sell, and what we will never reveal.

Bee and I learned that lesson young: It's easier to get away with things you're not supposed to be doing if no one suspects you can even attempt them. *Tell no one. Not ever.*

Bee twisted her silver bracelet as she took in a deep breath to fill a false voice she could cast elsewhere as a distraction: an ancient woman's craft she'd learned from her mother's mother that I'd never gotten the knack of. As for me, I bent my gaze not inward and not outward but between in and out, into the space where things exist but are not noticed by those who walk past them without seeing that which is not important to them. I drew a veil out of the frail threads of magic inhabiting this space and wrapped myself in it.

A strong word, or a knock—hard to say which—resounded at the far double doors. As both men looked that way, I stepped out from behind the drape and skimmed smoothly across the shining floor toward the table where the books rested. I did not look directly at the two men—the gaze of one person on another can be as hot as fire—but I kept track of their movements in my peripheral vision. The headmaster's assistant hastened over to the door and opened it while the visitor bent back to his perusal of the papers spread before him on the table. My knee bumped the low side table just as the assistant muttered, "I'll be burned," and he turned.

I froze, as still as the table, as silent as the couches, as unexceptional as the floor he stood on and never noticed because it never need be noticed. His gaze flowed right over me without a flicker. He shrugged, closed the door, and returned to the table, again turning his back as he settled in beside the visitor.

"I haven't much time. I'm late already," said the visitor in the impatient tones of a man of high status who expects deference. "You said you possess a recently published volume on the subject of aerostatics."

I dared not risk shifting the top book to get the one beneath. Instead, I swiped up both books and skated straight for the open library door, my back to the men, my skin tingling as with the arrows of discovery pinioning my body. But neither called out. Neither looked. Neither noticed me, someone who was no more important than the other furniture in the room.

At the door, I slipped into the dim alleys of shelving. Bee glided in after me. We skittered to the back aisle and froze there as the headmaster's dog walked straight down the central aisle and into the headmaster's office. We saw his figure flash by, but he never looked down the side alleys to see our shapes huddling in the shadows. Bee touched my wrist to claim her sketchbook. I handed it to her. As for the other book, the one I'd been forced to pick up, I felt all I could do was place it on a shelf and hope the headmaster and his dog and servant would think it had been misfiled.

As I raised it, I read its boldly stamped title: *Lies the Romans Told.*

Was there truly a book written on the venerable theme of lying Romans? Here, all along, I had just thought it a figure of speech, as one might say *hot-tempered Celts, sharp Fula bankers, war-loving Iberians, fashionably rude Parisi*, or *noble Kushites.* Obviously only a person of Kena'ani ancestry would even have bothered to write an essay on lying Romans, because out of all their ancient enemies, the Romans had hated and maligned us the most. The memory of Rome's empire was revered in histories today, even among the descendants of the many Celtic peoples and nations that had battled the imperial legions so fiercely centuries ago. After all, what would Europa be without Roman roads, the public sewers, and extensive aqueducts? Here in Adurnam, as most everywhere in Europa, we spoke a mixed language whose roots were Old Latin. Driven by curiosity— what else could you expect from a cat?—I flipped open the cover to the title page, bold black print on white paper repeating the title and recording the author's name.

Daniel Hassi Barahal.

My father's name.

Bee pinched me back to earth.

The headmaster's assistant clip-clapped briskly back along the central aisle without seeing us and out into the formal library. He shut the door into the library hall behind him.

I knew I ought to leave the book, but I could not bear to. I dropped it into my schoolbag and grabbed Bee's sketchbook to thrust in beside it. We hurried down the back aisle and crept into the headmaster's office. The clock ticked faithfully on. At the door leading into the corridor, I bent to listen at the keyhole.

No one moved in the corridor beyond.

A hoarse voice behind us whispered, *"Rei vindicatio."*

We bolted out of the office, shutting the door behind us, and stood panting and trembling in the empty corridor.

"That couldn't have been the poet's head!" Bee touched the door, as if to make sure it separated us from whatever had spoken inside.

A rush like streaming water poured through my body, the sensation of dizziness and drowning so strong I could not speak. Bee's face was shining from exertion and triumph and nerves, and suddenly I knew I was about to start laughing hysterically. I ran to the marble stairs, Bee right behind me. We had to clutch the wooden railing as we descended at a stately pace simply to stop ourselves from keeling over with the weight of the guffaws we must hold inside. I could not look at her. Meeting her eye would be fatal. From the stairs, we dashed across the glass-roofed inner court and tumbled into the high, haughty vault of the entrance hall with its carved plants.

"There you are! Late for luncheon. Running about unattended! What has the headmaster had to say to you?"

Maestra Madrahat uncoiled herself from the proctor's bench placed to survey the entrance hall; one teacher or attendant was always stationed on the bench when college was in session to watch for pupils sneaking about where they weren't allowed.

I leaped into the breach, not needing to feign the breathless fervor of a chastened penitent who has barely escaped the lash, because my heart was pounding so hard I could scarcely suck in enough air to talk, and my pulse was rushing in my ears like a whispering voice: *Had the head of Bran Cof spoken? Did my father write that book?*

I could babble with the best of them. "He spoke to us, maestra. See poor Beatrice's tears! He said to accompany him down to luncheon. But a ribbon on my slipper broke, and I had to pause to see if I might fix it. So he came ahead and we stayed behind. Now we are here."

This stream of words made her frown, but my statement was so unexceptional she could not protest. I stared at the stolid turnip adorning the wall relief, avoiding Bee's face altogether lest I entirely lose my composure and burst into uncontrollable snorts of laughter fueled by excitement, relief, and the frightening memory of that disturbing whisper.

A huge crash, plates dropping and smashing on the floor, splintered the air, followed by shrieks of surprise and shouts of startled laughter from the dining hall. Even the maestra flinched at the tremendous sound. Bee hid her face in her hands, shoulders quivering. Hot tears started out of my eyes as I bit my lower lip. Hard.

In the dining hall, everyone began talking at once.

I had not taken three breaths before two figures appeared at the dining hall entrance.

The maestra muttered, "Clumsy cow! How long have I been telling them they must hire a better class of servants rather than these used-up, unsightly widows of crippled soldiers!"

Bee sucked in her breath as hard as if she'd just been knifed under the ribs. I thought she meant to ruin everything by spitting in the maestra's bitter face, but instead she looked toward the arched entrance. Her expression altered, brightened; indeed, she positively glowed like the spring sun rising.

Maester Amadou emerged from the dining hall at a slow walk, supporting an elderly serving woman. The old dame was clearly rattled and unsteady on her feet; one of her hands was streaked with blood from where she had taken a gash.

He guided her across the room toward us. Bee became practically refulgent. No trading vessel's captain could have appeared as ecstatically delirious at seeing land in the wake of a mast-ripping storm.

But he was not looking at *Bee*.

"You are just the one to know what to do, Maestra Madra-hat," he said in a mild accent tuned with a musical soporiferous-ness. "The ancilla needs medical attention. She has cut her hand on the crockery."

The old woman turned a glazed look up to his face. I wasn't sure if she was infatuated or in shock from blood loss. Yet, after all, she looked old and weary and pale, and if Bee had known what I had just been thinking, she would have kicked me and I would have deserved the kicking.

"If she had not clumsily dropped the tray, she would not have cut herself," said the maestra ungraciously.

Maester Amadou smiled the comment into oblivion. "While it was indeed she who dropped the tray, it was not the ancilla's fault, maestra. I had a leg stretched out in an inconsiderate fash-ion. The ancilla stumbled over my rude foot."

The old woman gave him a startled look, which only I noticed because both Bee and the maestra could not take their eyes off his smile. He was not a particularly tall young man—he was barely taller than I was, although it was true I was tall for a woman—and he looked extremely well in his fashionable clothes, a tailored dash jacket of indigo cloth and a patterned kerchief tied at his neck in the informal style known as "the Buccaneer."

"If a physician could be called, maestra? Perhaps someone to sit with the ancilla until the physician arrives so she does not faint? I would do it, but I think it is not allowed for men to enter the kitchen, is it not?"

"It is not, indeed!" said the maestra. "To mingle so freely! Well, I will just take her back there and let one of the cooks sit with her until a physician can be brought from the women's hospital."

"In recompense for my inconsiderateness," he added, "my family will reimburse any fees required by the physician as well as the cost of replacing the broken dishes. I am sure the ancilla will be back at work as soon as she is able and that her position will be held open for her given that the fault was all mine."

Bee sighed audibly.

The serving woman flushed to the roots of her silver hair.

Even I was mildly impressed by this daunting performance, beneath which Maestra Madrahat was entirely drowned. She retreated as if on an inexorable outgoing tide, bearing the injured ancilla with her.

Maester Amadou politely addressed his comments to both of us.

"Are you coming in?" he asked without a trace of self-consciousness in the face of Bee's smile, which would have rendered unconscious any other young man. "There is room at the table with my sisters, if you would have in your heart the willingness to share our benches with us."

I saw by Bee's blush that we would accept and we would be pleased and we would eat our luncheon sitting at the table of Maester Amadou and that afterward, for the next week at least, I would hear his praises sung and spoken all day and whispered of into the late hours of the night in our shared bed until clawing off my ears would seem a less agonizing fate.

However, as I was the eldest Maestressa Hassi Barahal, even if by a mere two months, it was my place to accept or reject the invitation on behalf of myself and my dearest cousin.

"How kind, but"—Bee's dainty foot pressed down on my left slipper and began to really squish my little toe—"ah! Of *course* we would be delighted to join you." She eased off. I forced a smile as my toe throbbed. "Is there still yam pudding? It's my favorite."

6

Bee was floating, and I was brooding, when we departed the academy midafternoon after our seminars. My shoulder ached under the emotional weight of the purloined book within the schoolbag. Its pages were silent because closed, but my mind was howling with questions.

Did my father write this monograph on lying Romans? And if so, why had no one ever told me of it? Why was there no copy in our house? But these were only stepping-stones to the brink, where the edifice on which my tender life trembled as on a knife's edge. One question rose time and again whenever I was troubled enough to brood over the man whose miniature portrait nestled in the locket I wore at my neck and whose journals graced his brother's parlor, or over the woman who had left no portrait and only a handful of remembered words in my heart.

My parents had drowned during a river crossing along with a hundred other people, yet the only detail my uncle had ever given me when he spoke of the gruesome task of identifying their water-soaked corpses days later was that beasts had done damage to their features, so he had had to identify them by other means: the locket and greatcoat my father wore, my mother's red hair still coiled in a single thick braid, and a silver brooch later sold to pay the burial costs.

But if that were true, how could we be sure those were *their* bodies? Lockets and brooches could be given away or stolen.

Other people had red hair and coats. So how could we be sure they were really dead, not just run away, kidnapped, or somehow lost?

We hurried along the high street that led past the academy grounds and the adjacent temple sanctuary. Kena'ani temple gates never closed, no matter day or night, winter or summer, storm or fair weather, not that many people in these enlightened days ventured inside those gates except as sightseers. Every guidebook to Adurnam noted that this temple, dedicated to the goddess Tanit, was the ancient center of the Phoenician trading settlement founded two thousand years ago on the banks of the Solent River.

I glanced in now, as I always did when I passed, wondering if the goddess would summon me to the court of truth at which all my questions about my parents would be answered. Our ancestors marked sacred ground with a lustral basin for washing at the entrance, an arcade of pillars, and a marble altar whose ceiling was the blessed heavens. The sign of Tanit, protector of women, face of the moon, both bright and dark depending on Her aspect, was carved on the gates, on each pillar, and on the altar stone.

In one corner of the enclosure, a pair of elderly priests in shabby robes shivered on the raised porch of the winter house. A veiled woman stood at the base of the steps. She held a birdcage in one hand and a basket covered with a scrap of linen in the other.

Bee kept striding, but the woman's tense posture drew my gaze, so I paused to watch.

The supplicant set the laden basket down on the porch. The priests accompanied her to the altar stone. Their feet squeaked on the afternoon's dusting of fresh snow. Their shaven heads and exposed ears looked shiny with cold. The drape of the woman's loose robes hid the identity of the bird, but when they reached the altar and withdrew a turtledove from the cage with gentle hands, I knew the woman had come to ask for the blessing of a child.

Their bodies blocked the brief ceremony. One of the priests would break the bird's neck; his arm moved sharply as he afterward cut off the head. Blood would be spilling on the stone, but the wind was blowing both smell and sound away from me. Probably the cold air was already congealing the blood. Feathers, bones, and flesh would be consumed in fire, while the priests would eat as their evening's meal whatever provender the supplicant had brought in the basket.

"Cat!" Bee had stopped lower down on the walk.

Four street sweepers worked on the intersection beyond her. As I hurried toward her, my hands began to stiffen and my lips felt blue.

"What happened to you?" she asked, falling into step as I strode up.

"A woman in the temple made a burnt offering. Probably hoping for a child."

"She'd be better served asking her physician to examine her husband for signs of pox."

"Who's heartless now? My father wrote…let me see…" I dredged words out of my memory. " 'Until the scholars can fully explicate how our actions in this world echo in the spirit world, we ought to assume any action may have repercussions we can't predict.' "

She glanced at me, then veered toward the street sweepers— thin children younger than Hanan and as ill dressed for the cold as I was—and pressed a bronze *as* into the gloved hand of each startled child.

When she caught up with me, she spoke in a low, firm voice. "I admit there are forces in the world we do not understand. But the priests of our people are relics of another time. Still, even relics have to eat. I suppose there's no harm in the offering if it comforts her and feeds them. So, do you think Maester Amadou likes me?"

"Why do you even ask?" I demanded, laughing.

She flashed me a triumphant smile as she linked her arm in mine. Her cheeks were bright with the cold. She'd pulled off her hat to give to me, and her hair spilled in unruly black curls to her shoulders. The afternoon's dusting of snow made our passage easier as we walked downhill, but without coat or cloak, I was, like the impoverished priests, shivering deeply.

Where we passed the remains of the ancient town walls, the land dropped away into a wide hollow. Now filled with buildings, in ancient times it had been a harbor and marshland shore. The eastern hills lay smeared with a smoky pallor of coal haze in the failing afternoon light, but I could easily see the triple spires to the west that housed three of the mighty bells whose music made the city famous. A single high plinth, visible across the distance, marked the site of the village founded by the Adurni Celts when they had come to do business with foreign traders on the marshy banks of the Solent River.

"Look!" shrieked Bee, pointing.

Other students, walking in the same direction, halted and stared, then began to clap and cry out to alert others. For there sailed the airship over the eastern district of the city, visible from here because of the contour of the land. Like a bird, it moved in the air without plunging to earth, but it had such an astonishing shape, not like a balloon at all but rather like a balloon caught at opposite points and drawn out to an ovoid shape. Half cloud and half-gleaming fish, it floated against the sky as might a lazy, bloated creature so well fed it has no need to look for supper. A huge basketlike gondola hung beneath, and to our shock and delight, lines were tossed—barely visible as faint threads at this distance—to unseen people below. We watched as, hooked and caught, it yanked up against the tautening ropes, and the process of winching it down into the Rail Yard commenced.

"Best we hurry," said Bee. "You're cold."

We made our farewells to the other pupils and turned left at the high walls of the long-abandoned tophet, whose gates were always locked. A coal wagon rumbled past. Serving women walked with baskets weighing heavily on their arms.

"That was the most amazing thing I've ever seen!" cried Bee. "I can't wait to draw it! Only I'll give it a fish's eyes and a mouth and tail. As if it were really alive!"

From the main thoroughfare and its shops, we turned into a residential district populated a hundred years ago solely by families of Kena'ani lineage and built to their preferences: balustrades along the upper-floor windows and colonnaded front doors. These days, a diverse group of households with common mercantile interests shared the district. It was a clean, prosperous neighborhood, safe even in the evening because of the recent installation of gaslight on the major streets. Fenced parks with handsome trees and shrubbery ornamented the small squares, each centered around a carved stone monument. After a brisk fifteen-minute walk in which Bee remained oddly silent, no doubt distracted by her memories of Maester Amadou's dark eyes and the magnificent airship, we arrived at Falle Square and home.

When we reached the gate of our once-grand four-story town house, we closed the wrought-iron gate behind us and climbed the steps to the stoop. The door opened before we reached it. Aunt Tilly ushered us in with kisses and, after dusting the baking flour off her hands, helped us shed our boots and Bee her coat.

"Your cheeks are ice! Cat, how could you be so foolish as to run out without your coat?" She gave me a grave look. "I discovered them in the parlor this morning before anyone else was the wiser. Well, you're just fortunate you never get sick."

She herded us past the public rooms, which we rarely used

once the cold weather set in, to the small sitting room in the back over the kitchen. The stove shed heat through the floor. The abrupt change in temperature made me sweat. After stepping downstairs into the kitchen to ask Cook to heat milk for chocolate, Aunt returned and sat between us on the threadbare settee. She chafed our stiff hands between her own warm ones.

"You're looking bright, Beatrice," she said to her daughter.

"We saw the airship, Mama!"

"Did you? And you, Catherine? You look darkly menacing, as if you are tumbling sharp-edged rocks through that busy mind of yours. Did the airship please you not so well?"

"No, it was spectacular. Bee is going to draw it but call it an airwhale, a mythical creature of the heavens."

"But that frown is still there. What subject has set you thinking so hard?"

I tucked my schoolbag against my legs, trying desperately to bring back the sharp, excited way I had felt on seeing the airship, but my thoughts were not air-bound but rather moored to the past.

"Lies the Romans told," I blurted out.

Bee shot me a startled look.

Aunt did not even blink. "The academy directors fought for ten years over the proper syllabus to be used in presenting the history of the wars between the consuls of Rome and the didos of Qart Hadast. To broach so volatile a subject! I wouldn't have expected that, now the controversy has died down."

"There is a book written on the theme."

"Is there?" Her sly grin was far more subtle than Bee's honey smiles. "I must admit, it would take up at least three lengthy volumes, don't you think?"

"What is '*rei vindicatio*'?" I asked, and found myself tensing, as if Bran Cof's head were likely to materialize in the sitting room and chastise me for having disturbed it.

"Oh, dear, are you studying law in your seminar now? It's a complicated Roman legal action to do with a difference between ownership and possession—"

"Tilly!" Uncle bellowed from the floor above. "I can't find my hat!"

She rose. "Cook and Callie are busy, so just run down and fetch the pot and cups yourself. You can take dinner at lamp-lighting in the nursery with the little girls, or wait and share a collation with us at evening's end when we get home from the academy. For the lecture tonight, you'll need to change into something more"—she frowned at my jacket and petticoats, a style I had assiduously copied from the plates of a very up-to-date fashion magazine Bee and I had seen in the window of a milliner on High Street last year—"more sober."

"Tilly!" Uncle called again.

She hurried out the door.

"Do you think it was the poet's head that spoke?" Bee whispered. "We'll never be able to tell anyone that we heard the famous Bran Cof declaim! Even if it was only two words. Now, I'll get the chocolate while you get that bag up to our room before Papa decides we must display our day's academic work at dinner for his delectation. That would be a disaster! He'd see my sketches. *And* you'd have to confess you stole a book from the academy."

"A book my father wrote!"

"A book whose author's name is the same as your father's. That doesn't prove anything."

She was right, so I retraced my steps to the entryway. Our governess was still up in the nursery with Hanan and Astraea; Cook and the hired girl Callie were busy with dinner; and our man-of-all-work, Pompey, would be stoking the evening fires or preparing trays to carry up to the nursery for their early dinner. I climbed the stairs to the first floor with the bag clutched against me. At the top of the stairs, the huge hall mirror showed me myself—yes, that was me, as always, my face, my body, my long-fingered hands, my wishfully fashionable jacket and petticoats sewn as well as Bee's and my skill could manage. In the mirror, a ragged nimbus like a storm cloud fringed my form; it sparked in the mirror's reflection only if I was particularly annoyed or upset, and I knew how to furl it in, like binding back one's hair.

As I slunk along the first-floor hall past the closed doors of the front parlor and Uncle's office, Aunt's and Uncle's voices traded rhythms from behind the office door. Their knack for talking over each other without quite getting in each other's way reminded me of festival drums. Our factotum's bass rumble interposed an unexpected counterbeat, followed by a silence.

I hurried past the rack of fencing sabers and up the stairs to the second floor. I slipped through the fourth door, the one at the back of hall, into the room Bee and I had shared for the almost fourteen years I had lived in Uncle and Aunt's house.

The curtains were open, and the stove had been recently kindled. I threw myself across the wide bed and pulled out the book. After wrapping the feather coverlet around me, I shifted to catch what light remained from the windows that overlooked the back garden with its frosted earth and leafless trees. A twig scratched at the windowpane as the wind rattled it: Bee called that branch "the skeletal hand." It was an old friend from the tree that grew down past Uncle's office window, and its presence made me comfortable.

I opened the book and found the publication date: Most people across Europa used the Augustan year, dating from the installation of the first emperor of the Romans.

The year of my birth was 1818.

A man bearing my father's name had published a monograph the year I was born.

I flipped through the pages in the fading light, but the flare for the dramatic and the self-deprecating turn of phrase displayed by my father in his journals was absent here. This was an awkwardly written tome filled with dry recitation of ancient Roman accusations, taken from quotes by tedious Roman writers of ancient days and refuted with the usual unassailable truths.

The first lie: that our name for ourselves is Phoenician, when in fact we call ourselves Kena'ani.

The second lie: that the rulers of "Carthage" engage in the barbaric practice of child sacrifice to propitiate bloodthirsty gods.

The third lie: that "Phoenician" women are all whores.

The fourth lie: that "Phoenician" traders will lie, cheat, and steal to get a bargain.

Fifth, seventh, eleventh... There was nothing new here. Wasn't there any scrap in this volume that might reveal something new about my father?

A tap on the door roused me. I stuck the book under the pillow, but it was only Bee with the chocolate. I let her in and, closing the door behind her, unbuttoned my jacket, shifted out of my overskirt and petticoats, and asked Bee to lace me into a simple chemise with a sober, respectable overdress of evergreen-dull wool.

"What's your hurry?" Bee asked, sipping at her chocolate.

"You go up to dinner," I said. "Tell Aunt I'll eat later. Come down to the parlor and warn me when it's almost time to go."

She set down the cup. "It will be on your head. Can I have your share of the chocolate?"

"Yes. Will you help me dress?"

First, she hid her sketchbook in the base of the wardrobe. Then she finished my chocolate. After that, with her accomplished fingers, she laced up the back of my clothes and arranged my hair pleasingly with clips and combs. She was more careless with her own dress, possessing that knack of making any piece of clothing look fashionable just because she was wearing it.

By the time the dinner bell rang, she, too, was ready in her soberest finery to go up to the nursery and give my excuses. Callie and Pompey stamped up the back stairs with trays while Aunt and Uncle climbed the front stairs, Bee in their wake. I shut my eyes and listened down the threads of magic: Cook and Evved were talking quietly in the kitchens. Something about codebooks? Our governess, Shiffa, was in the nursery, pouring water into a basin for the girls to wash their hands as they said the blessing.

Aunt and Uncle would spend some time with the little girls over the nursery dinner before repairing to their rooms to dress. One had to dress carefully in our circumstances. Appear too obviously impoverished, and folk would avoid us. We had to keep up appearances in order to attract the business that supported us.

I had time to hunt. I grabbed the book on lying Romans and padded downstairs and into the empty parlor where at dawn I'd finished my hasty essay. It was the custom in Aunt and Uncle's house to take an early dinner and after it a session of necessary sewing and mending accompanied by reading aloud. We were sent to our beds soon after the sun set. Aunt often said that she chose to follow the ancient Kena'ani tradition of rising and falling with the sun, but I supposed it to be not a "traditional" but rather a cost-saving measure, because oil and candles and coal and wood were expensive. Shivering, I lit a single lamp, all I needed, and drew my hand along my father's journals, which were shelved in numerical order. The physical books came in various sizes and widths, some cheaply made with crude stitching or a poor grade of paper, others with calfskin bindings so creamy my fingers lingered on them. Some had been battered and stained in the course of their individual journeys, while others remained pristine.

Daniel Hassi Barahal had begun his travels, and his journals, when he turned twenty, as I would in a mere eight days. From that time until my birth, he had always been traveling, and he had always been writing. When one book was filled, he would start another and leave the finished volume at any Kena'ani trading house to be shipped through to the Hassi Barahal mother house in Gadir. After the death of my father and mother, the journals had come into my uncle's possession.

I pulled down the journal numbered 46, his account of the opening weeks of the Baltic Ice Sea Expedition, and opened it to the final entry. First came a vivid and lengthy description of the aurora borealis. Then, a detailed accounting of my father's political debate with Lt. Tara Bell, a young lieutenant from the Amazon corps of the army of the infamous Iberian general Camjiata, known most commonly as the "Iberian Monster." Twenty years ago, Camjiata had tried to conquer Europa while claiming he was only trying to restore the glorious days of the early Roman Empire. It was he, or his council of advisors, at any rate, who had funded the expedition. Lt. Bell had been assigned watch with Daniel Hassi Barahal for the brief span of gloom that passed as night.

When my father argued that an empire was a violent and unjust form of government, she retorted that the Romans had created peace among warring tribes. When my father pointed out that anyone can make a desert and call it peace, she replied that there is just as much, if not more, injustice among the multitude of principalities and duchies and independent city-states that had arisen throughout Europa after the empire finally fractured into pieces in the year 1000. Certainly the Celtic peoples loved their petty feuds and cattle-raiding wars; her own Belgae people did, and they were Celts, weren't they?

When my father objected that an empire could not be natural because no one after the Romans had managed to build one, she laughed and told him the Celts were simply too quarrelsome to unite on any endeavor. And, anyway, she went on, Camjiata was, on his father's side, descended from the Mande lineage called Keita, who had ruled the Mali Empire. Any fool, she added, knew that Mali's armies had once spanned West Africa. That was before the salt plague had released the ghouls that had driven out much of the population. Just because an empire had not been achieved again in Europa did not mean it could not be achieved elsewhere by others or ought not be attempted for the benefits it offered. What might those be? my father had wondered sardonically. Security and prosperity, she had replied with, he wrote, "the heartwarming blind certainty of a loyal soldier."

Was my father disputing with her out of his own fiercely held beliefs, or just to play his part in a friendly debate in order to pass the time? Perhaps argument was his way of flirting.

The volume closed with the argument.

The parlor door opened.

7

I jumped, but it was only Bee, slipping inside.

"So much for working in secret. If it hadn't been me, you'd have been caught." She picked up *Lies the Romans Told* from the table, flipping through it casually. "No illustrations! Bah!"

"The dates don't make sense," I said.

She raised dark eyes to examine me, then set down the book. "I'm cold. Let's go sit under the blanket in the window seat."

In the window seat overlooking the square, we tucked a wool blanket over us to keep off the chill and closed the heavy curtains behind our backs to hide us from anyone who might wander into the parlor. We did not worry about someone from outside looking up and seeing us there because of the cawl knit into the glass as a screen against prying eyes.

Our breath made steam flowers on the windowpanes. Winter's cold had truly settled, although it was still eight days away from year's end according to the common year: Hallows Night, as they measured such things here in the north. Outside, snow glittered in the square and in the canopies of trees; the streets had been swept clean.

"Go on," Bee murmured, leaning against me.

I frowned. "I wondered that if my father wrote that monograph on Roman lies, I might find some trace of its being written in his journals. Interviews, stories, chance encounters, notes. But the last entry from the ice sea expedition is dated in the summer of 1816. The next two numbered journals are missing."

"The record of the rest of the expedition."

"So we must suppose. There stands my father on some benighted barren island in the Baltic Ice Sea, in the summer of 1816, debating with my mother over the legality of Camjiata's war while watching the aurora borealis. Journal forty-nine opens eighteen months later in the final months of 1817. He is drinking and dining in the city of Lutetia."

"The city of light, as its Parisi inhabitants call it. I'd love to visit."

"Yes. So there he is, acting as a secretary to the legal congress presided over by Camjiata before the general elected himself permanent first consul of the restored Roman Empire. How my father got a post as secretary in Camjiata's court is never explained. I'm sure that would be much more interesting reading than five volumes recording fifty-eight days of debate and discussion over law and legal codes."

"Tell me the utter truth. Have you actually read every single word in those five volumes?"

"I have! Once. But only to see if he ever mentioned the ice expedition, its rescue, and what happened between him and Lieutenant Tara Bell. He never does."

Bee sighed as with unfathomable sorrow, pressing her forehead into the glass and shutting her eyes, making me wonder if she really did have a headache. The square's stone monument was visible by the light of the streetlamps: a proud female figure standing between pillars, facing the viewer, her right hand raised in the orator's style and her left hand clutching the sigil of Tanit, protector of women. At the full moon, Bee and I left flowers, or a smidgeon of honey, or a tiny cup of wine at the base of the stele, in honor of those who had come before us, the Kena'ani women who had lived and died in Adurnam, far from their ancestral home and yet tied, always, to their ancient roots. Maybe they watched over us, as mothers watch over their precious children, those children fortunate enough to have living mothers.

"Go on," she said into the glass.

"Eight days before the turn of the year, he is summoned. It's the last entry, just those two words: 'Am summoned.'"

"Summoned to what?"

"It never says. That's the last journal. Doesn't that all strike you as odd?"

Bee straightened as she shook off whatever melancholy possessed her. "Cat, listen. The most reasonable explanation is that he returns in haste to his wife, who bears a child, which is you. With a young wife and a new child, I don't think it at all odd he might not have written more journals. He wrote them when he traveled. Couldn't it be that this was the one time in his adult life he stayed in one place? By the hearth with his beloved wife and newborn child?"

"But that doesn't explain—"

"Cat. You are making too much of this. I know you want the story to be more romantic than it is, although it's romantic enough. Everyone knows the Amazon soldiers were not allowed to marry on penalty of death. Yet she did marry, and she did leave Camjiata's army, and she did come with your father to Adurnam to live with his family. So that means she lived in fear of being arrested as a deserter and a law-breaker by the agents of Camjiata. Meanwhile, she must also have feared that the agents of the Prince of Tarrant—who was, after all, one of Camjiata's most bitter enemies—would arrest her as a spy."

"Aunt and Uncle are so ashamed of what she was that they've forbidden us to even speak of her. I can't even ask questions about her life. Is that fair?"

"I don't think it's fair. But if we Barahals are touched with any possible stigma of association with the Iberian Monster, we'll lose all our business."

"That's your father talking."

"People must eat. That's why your parents came to live with the family in Adurnam, isn't it? What else could they do? Your father had to go to work again for the family. Yet his heart wasn't in it. He fought with everyone. The reports he prepared were useless. He did not want to leave your mother and you alone, and your mother could not travel with him into those regions that lay under the rule of Camjiata's empire where the family needed your father to travel."

"To spy for them," I muttered.

"Nor did your mother like living in this house, in Adurnam, where she felt vulnerable and maybe disliked. After a few years, the brothers quarreled. Your father and mother left, taking you with them. Then there was that terrible accident when the ferry crossing the Rhenus River capsized, and they drowned with a hundred others, and you survived, pulled out of the water, and so you came to us. Don't try to make the story more than it is, dear Cat. It's not a trap. You don't have to gnaw off your paw to get out of it. It's just sad that they died, that the two brothers remained unreconciled, that you were left an orphan at six years old. But at least you came back to us—"

"Hush," I whispered through my tears.

Bee froze with her right hand clasped to her chest and her face raised, posed unmoving like one of the living re-creations of the honored ancestors in a tableaux at the Feast and Festival of the Sun Sacrifice, which here in the north the locals called the winter solstice.

Put a saber in her upraised left hand, and she'd have run me through, just to put me out of my misery. Because she was right. Everything she said was right. It's just I didn't want the story to end that way.

"Beatriz? Catarina?" Our governess, Shiffa, had been imported all the way from the Barahal motherhouse in Gadir to teach us girls deportment, fencing, dancing, sewing, and how to memorize large blocks of text so we could write them down or repeat them later. All of which she did, and always with a rigid smile. Her giddily cheerful voice rose in volume as she entered the parlor. "Girls! It's time to leave for the lecture."

We did not move. In the square outside, a trio of men barged out of Ranwise Close at a strong clip. I recognized Banker Pisilco's stoop. He reached the park gate opposite our window, waved a farewell to his companions, and opened the gate into the park. The other two forged on with heads bent together, deep in conversation, but the banker struck out across the lit path past the monument and through the park toward the houses on the far side of Falle Square. It was odd to watch his shadowy form pass from shadow into the aura of gaslight and back into shadow, from light into shadow, light into shadow, and all the while, whether in light or in shadow, his hat glimmered as though dusted with tiny stars.

"Girls?" Shiffa stumbled among the couches and rattled the journals I'd left lying open on the table. "Oh, dear," she muttered in a grating tone of fond exasperation. "What are these doing out again? That child!"

Abruptly, her breathing shifted. Her fingers fluttered pages, and she sucked in a hard breath and whispered to herself in a tone so steely it was as if a different person were speaking, "Melqart's Curse! We were assured every copy of the codebook had been burned."

Bee lowered her hand to grasp my wrist, her fingers tightening until I thought she would crush my bones. We had left *Lies the Romans Told* on the table. *The codebook?*

"Have you found the girls, Shiffa?" My aunt's voice rose from the direction of the stairs. She sounded as if she were trying not to laugh.

"No, they're not in here, maestra," called Shiffa in her fussy, happy voice, which now sounded utterly false to my ears. "They weren't in the nursery or in their bedchamber, those mischievous creatures!" She moved out the door, and Bee let go of my wrist as I grimaced.

"I told you, Tilly!" My uncle's voice rumbled from farther below. "They're hiding in the attic."

Aunt moved down the staircase to the ground-floor foyer, still speaking. "It's your own fault for trying to force them to attend a lecture that they assured me they already heard once today."

"We are not attending to hear the lecture, but to be seen. The girls have made excellent connections at the college. Tonight's lecture is more about politics than aerostatics. It's a bold step for the Prince of Tarrant and his court to agree to tether an airship in the Rail Yard, much less hold a public exhibition of it for all to see. He and his clan are declaring through this act that they do not support the mage Houses' opposition to the new technological innovations."

"As I am well aware, dear. Yet we must be careful never to show an inclination to any side. You know we must not draw the attention of the mage Houses."

"Yes, yes," he said impatiently. "They've forgotten about us. That was a long time ago. Camjiata has been safely locked away in his island prison for over thirteen years. Anyway, those rich Fula bankers will be at the lecture."

Bee stiffened, but not because she had heard this mention of Maester Amadou's family. She was looking outside.

"Which is the only reason I am attending," said my aunt. "You know there will be trolls."

"Trolls are clever creatures in their own way, Tilly. This unreasoning prejudice serves you ill."

Bee grabbed my sleeve and tweaked it to get my attention. With a lift of her chin, she indicated the twilit streets beyond the ice-rimed panes. An unmarked black coach rumbled down the west side of the square, pulled by four horses as pale as cream. As it passed down the street, each lamp it passed flickered and faded and, once the conveyance had rolled on, flared back into life. The coach turned the corner left onto our street, its journey traced by the dying and rising of light.

The lamp standing beside the park gate dimmed to a sullen shell of orange-red. The coach halted in front of our house. The coachman swung down to hold the reins of the two lead horses. Their breath rose out of their nostrils like smoke. A footman, dressed in a heavy black flared coat, climbed down from the brace between the back wheels, bumped out a pair of steps from the undercarriage, and opened the coach's door.

Bee squeezed my fingers so hard I actually grunted in pain. In a swirl of flared fashionable jacket so saturated a red you could faintly discern its color against the dusk, a personage descended from the coach, leaning on a gilded cane, and walked up the front steps. From this angle, we could not see him arrive at the front door, located under cover of the stoop and concealed by the entry pillars. Three sharp knocks rapped the heavy door, delivered by a blunt instrument. The entire house, all four stories and set back, shuddered like a cornered animal.

"I don't like this," Bee muttered in her serious voice, nothing like the blabbering light-minded aether-head she often pretended to be. "It reminds me of a dream I had last month. Twilight brings bad tidings. . . ." She released my hand.

I shook out the ache in my fingers. "Ah! That really hurt!"

"We've got to hide," she said in an altered tone. She shoved away the blanket and pushed out from behind the curtain. "Hurry, Cat!"

The way she looked, with her entire body tense and a scared heat pouring off her, flooded me with cold fear. I slid off the window seat. My feet touched the chilly floor just as the front door below was opened, as though the opening door caused the floor's exhalation of cold.

Evved could talk down his nose at anyone. "I'm sorry, maester, the family is out for the evening."

The personage pushed past our steward without a word. Of course, I couldn't see him, but I felt that presence enter the house in the same way your hair rises and your neck tingles before a storm. I felt it in the joints and eaves of the house, straining to protect us against a presence powerful enough to enter without an invitation.

"If we move fast . . ." Bee made a little humming noise, a buzzing through her teeth, and hurried to the open door, past the open journals. Shiffa had taken the Roman lies book.

From below rose voices.

"What manner of intrusion disturbs our evening?" demanded Uncle in the voice he used to dismiss the pretensions of social-climbing trolls. "We have not given you leave to enter. We are not at home."

A male voice, reeking of mage House privilege, replied, "That is an odd sort of lie, because here you are."

"As you can certainly see by our dress, we are in the act of departing the house for an evening engagement. Please be so good as to call tomorrow."

We slithered out the open door into the passage that ran back from the wide first-floor landing. The door to Uncle's office was closed, but the latch clicked down, pushed from inside. I shoved Bee behind me and dug deep for a concealing glamor as Shiffa emerged from the office. She walked right past us, past the full-length mirror in which our reflections clearly showed, to *me*, and halted at the railing beside the potted dwarf orange tree at the top of the grand staircase. She bent forward to observe what was going on in the entryway below.

The voice continued. "I hope I need not remind you to what manner of person you are speaking. I am here now, so you will attend me now. I will be done with my business and gone within the hour."

"Fiery Shemesh!" cursed Uncle, his voice tingling with suppressed fury—and fear. "You're from Four Moons House. A magister from the Diarisso lineage."

A cold mage in our house! Behind Shiffa's back, we skated soundlessly across to the foot of the upper stairs.

"Did you not get the message I was meant to arrive today?" His words and accent were cultured and elegant, yet his indignation soured them. It was almost enough to make my straight hair curl.

"We received no message, no warning." The tight way Aunt Tilly choked out the words really frightened me. The house vibrated with sympathetic anger. "You can't possibly still maintain you have a claim."

"Indeed, we can and we do. The contract clearly states that Diarisso ownership extends until the twentieth birthday. Ownership reverts to the Hassi Barahal family only at sunset on the evening that begins the natal day, when the subject attains her legal majority."

Bee tugged on my wrist, having more self-possession than I did. We set foot on the stairs, creeping toward the next floor.

"I believe the proper legal term is *rei vindicatio*," he went on. "I am here to reclaim ownership of what you have been generously allowed to keep possession of."

There was a man whose pretensions wanted slapping down!

How he could make those words come out with such conde-
scension was beyond my understanding. We kept climbing,
working around the boards that creaked.

"You'll have to come back tomorrow," said Aunt even more
briskly, "because she's not here."

We stopped, Bee and I. We just stopped, as though an unseen
hand with fingers of ice had fastened itself on our shoulders and
pulled us to a halt.

"I understand you may not be in charity with the terms of
the settlement that were forced upon you thirteen years ago, but
please do not attempt another bald-faced lie. I know she is in
the house. In fact—"

I heard an even tread mounting the grand staircase. A chill
mist exhaled from the surface of the mirror. Bee was ahead of
me, farther up the stairs, so I braced myself, hoping my body
would hide hers. For on the very first day I had come to live
with Aunt and Uncle, Aunt had solemnly told me that I was to
look out for my little cousin Beatrice, even though Bee was only
two months younger than I was and already, at six, a complete
hellhound with a temper just as bad as Uncle's and a mean sting
that she hid behind her honey face.

*You know we love you for yourself, Cat. You're never to think
otherwise. This is your home now. But I lay this charge on you, that
you must protect Bee, if there comes a time when she needs your
protection.*

Right now, with that Four Moons personage and his powerful magic climbing the stairs, with the mist rising, I was certain
those words had been meant for this day out of all days.

Shiffa took a step back from the railing and raised her hands
theatrically, like a dido sighting her warrior hero onstage.
"Blessed Tanit! Such a good-looking young man!"

He marched into view, framed by the fading gold wallpaper
on one side and the polished black balustrade on the other.

He wasn't as handsome as he clearly thought himself to be. He was just well turned out, nothing you wouldn't expect from a pampered son of Four Moons House. Also, he was much younger than I had taken him for from his voice.

When he spotted me, his eyes widened as if he were astonished, likely by the regrettable dullness of my soberly unfashionable dress. I shoved Bee up another step, hoping she would bolt for the door to the attic, and I took each step down with a drawn-out measure worthy, I am sure, of the great principessas of the theater.

"Yes, Aunt! I'm coming," I said brightly. "I do apologize for taking so long to dress. You know how I've been wanting to attend a lecture as engrossing as one on the principles of aerostasis! Especially since we just this morning were fortunate enough to listen to a lengthy lecture on aerostatic aircraft by the very same esteemed professor we are engaged to hear tonight. Perhaps it will prove to be exactly the same lecture delivered verbatim! I can't believe that it's finally time to leave. Oh! I beg your pardon, Magister. We haven't been introduced."

We hit the first-floor landing at the same time, he coming up and I coming down. He said, "Don't try your luck at the theater, maestressa. You may have the looks, but you don't have the skill."

He had a mustache and a beard trimmed tight along the line of his jaw, and he kept his hair cropped short against his dark head in the manner of professional boxers. It was the kind of style you saw in paintings brought to life fifty years ago when the scions of the House had ruled fashion. There was something very bad about a young man who dressed in such an old-fashioned and overdone style and who had such a particular way of looking down his nose at a well-brought-up girl whose lineage was acceptable in polite company, even if her family could not move in elite circles because of a few problems with money.

I opened my mouth to retort with scathing words that would cut him to the heart, figuratively speaking, when Bee, the utter fool, bumped up against me. Anger streamed off her like heat. I stuck my hands to my hips, elbows akimbo, to stop her from grabbing a sword off the rack and skewering him.

Red-faced, Aunt reached the landing behind him. As she halted beside the personage, she smiled in an absolutely false way. My tongue smarted, as if I'd just licked a block of ice.

"Come down, girls," she said, and I knew then that she'd known all along we were hiding in the window seat. The house was hers, after all; very little escaped her notice. "Are Hanan and Astraea with you?"

Bee popped out beside me, and I grabbed her upper arm and held on like I meant it, which I did. She loosed a glare at me, but she stayed where she was and fulminated.

"I'm sure the little dears are asleep," I said. "They were quite exhausted from their day's studies, for we are a studious family here, are we not? Are we leaving soon for the academy, Aunt?"

"I haven't much time. I'm late already," said the personage in the very same arrogant voice I had heard earlier today in the headmaster's library.

I was sure it was the same voice—hard to get quite that much biting pride into such otherwise innocuous words—but his clothes were less traditional and more fashionable. Because I hadn't seen his face in the library, I examined him dubiously. It seemed unlikely in the extreme that a magister, scion of a prominent mage House, would have entered the very academy of natural historians and scholarly philosophers that the cold mages were known to scorn and distrust.

My expression, meant to be disdainful, must have impressed him, if not in a good way.

"*She* is the eldest Hassi Barahal girl?" he asked, indicating me. How he stared!

"She is the eldest of the girls," agreed Aunt, indicating me.

Uncle puffed up beside her, looking as enflamed with anger as Bee, and at these words he cast such a look at Aunt that I knew something was up. Something bad. Something very, very wrong.

8

"You are the eldest Hassi Barahal girl?" the personage asked me, an odd question given that he had just asked Aunt the same thing.

"So I have always been told," I retorted.

"Cat," murmured Aunt warningly. "Silence is better than disrespect."

He ignored her and glanced almost slightingly at Bee. Bee was shorter, dainty with a plumpness that made her seem a year or two younger than she really was, and, of course, she was beautiful. His gaze fixed back on me. "It must be asked and answered three times. You are the eldest Hassi Barahal girl?"

Aunt sucked in a sharp breath. "Catherine!" she said warningly.

Uncle shut his eyes.

I just found the cold mage irritating. "As we said twice already. I am the eldest."

"So be it. The contract was sealed with magic. You cannot lie to me." He stared at me a moment longer, gave an abrupt, infinitesimal shake of the head as with utter disdain, and turned to Aunt. "The clothing she is wearing is simply not acceptable. You need pack only a small trunk for the journey. The House will provide all she needs once we arrive."

"Once we arrive *where*?" I looked at Aunt for clarification, but she was quite deliberately not looking at me, so I looked toward Uncle instead, but *he* wasn't looking, either; he'd already steered Bee toward the stairs.

"Darling, up you go. It's well past bedtime."

Bee caught my gaze, but we kept our mouths shut. That was the code of Bee and Cat: Keep your mouth shut and don't say anything until you know what's going on and how much trouble your cousin, who is also your best friend in the world, is in.

Aunt sailed past me and kissed Bee on the cheek. "Yes, darling, just kiss Catherine good night and be gone." Trembling, Bee gave me a kiss on each cheek while Aunt kept talking to the personage. "The dear girl may wish to choose some of her clothing for herself, what she likes best. You know how girls are. They like to have special things with them, very sentimental—"

The magister whistled sharply, a piercing sound that made us all flinch. As Uncle pulled Bee away, she twisted off her bracelet and thrust it into my hand. Then Uncle dragged her up the upper stairs, him hauling with the desperation of a man in pain and she stumbling up backward as she watched me. I didn't move. I was too stunned, her bracelet the only solid weight that fixed me to earth. The personage set a hand on the railing. A wisp of mist rose from the polished wood as he leaned on it, canting head and shoulders to look down into the foyer.

I wondered what would happen if I shoved him over.

"Bring him in," he called to an unseen servant, perhaps to the footman who had been riding beside the coachman.

Aunt tried again. "I am sure she would like to bring a few chosen items with her, if you would just let her go up to her chamber and choose—"

He turned back. "She will not leave my sight. You will supervise the packing of a *small* trunk, as I have indicated, and she will remain on the landing with me until the trunk is packed. That way she can't *vanish*."

I am not a Cat for nothing. I'm really very friendly, but there comes a time when people cross a line and must be put in their place.

"You are being rude, Magister. What gives you the right to speak to my—"

"*Catherine!* That is enough."

I flinched. Aunt's tone was just as proud and snappish as his, only hers hurt, for she never spoke to me that way.

"Catherine, you'll mind your manners and remain silent while I'm gone. Shiffa, come with me."

Head lowered, Shiffa followed Aunt up the stairs. I clenched my hands and breathed in and breathed out and said nothing, for so Aunt had commanded. Silence I would keep if I was held over a fire and my toes roasted. Nothing would make me talk now.

"Catherine," he said. "Catherine Hassi Barahal."

I slanted a withering glare at him, but he wasn't looking at me or trying to speak to me. He was only trying out the name, as the schoolmaster at the beginning of term repeats the names of new pupils in order to remember who he has in his class. If I knew what was going on, it would be so much easier to keep my mouth shut, but I had to trust Aunt and Uncle and do what they told me. They had never treated me differently from their own three girls, not even considering how my uncle and father had fought before my parents' untimely death. I knew my duty. I knew they loved me.

He measured the scalloped wallpaper, the spindly legged sofa in the Galatian style set against the wall, the gilt ornament painted on the lintels over the doors, and the parquet flooring, with its mosaic pattern meant to echo the mazelike stone mosaic of the ground floor, where visitors were supposed to stay, blocked by the pattern of the stones from ascending to the upper private floors where the family resided. He fingered the dwarf orange, and the green leaf at once frosted as if caught in winter's grip. It cracked into dust against his skin. With a grunt of disgust, he rubbed his fingers, then blew on them. White flakes drifted to the floor. He sighed as though to say that every passing breath endured in this plebeian house was more than he could take.

In the flecked depths of the huge first-floor-landing mirror, I studied him. His height, his dark brown complexion and symmetrical features, his hands and that part of his throat revealed above the embroidered collar of his jacket: all matched in the mirror the way he looked on the landing. His magic was hard for me to see, although faint tendrils snaked out from him. Either he was so powerful that magic exhaled from him, as misty breath is expelled from the lips on a winter day, or he was actually using his magic to search the house, as if he sought to uncover our secrets. How could he just march into this house as if he owned it? I wanted to claw that disdainful expression off his face. But I did not. Because he looked into the mirror and saw I was watching him.

"What do you see in there?" he demanded.

"Your boots are scuffed."

Men who stand in that arrogant way with their backs straight, their shoulders tight, and their chins lifted the better to sneer at those lower than them can be neither comfortable nor happy. But that doesn't mean they know it. His gaze flicked down to his polished, perfect boots, then up again.

He said, "You have no idea of the privilege and honor being shown to you this day. You are ill prepared and ill mannered and ill suited. But a contract is a contract, sealed, bound, final. I will do my duty, and you will do yours."

He rapped his cane twice on the floor. A chill wind gushed in from outside. Another presence entered the house, one that wheezed as it mounted the grand staircase step by effortful step until an old gray man climbed into view, leaning heavily on the balustrade. He wore gold earrings, the mark of his profession as either a bard or a djeli, although in these days the two were often indistinguishable. He was otherwise dressed in a threadbare dashiki in the old style, loose and ankle length; he had thrown over it a humble clerk's long wool coat. No fashionable flares added dash or mystery to its lines, and it was patched at the elbows. Snow dusted his shoulders and the silver coils of his hair. When had it begun snowing again?

The old man looked at me, looked at the personage, and heaved a sigh as of grief. He saw the mirror at once, of course, but the mirror did not see him. Bards and djeliw had the ability to manipulate and respect the essence that flows through the spirit world. For them, so scholars believed, mirrors were a conduit into the spirit world that lies intertwined with our own. I was shocked at his lack of vitality and the poorness of his clothing. Bards and djeliw were often feared and sometimes only grudgingly tolerated, but it never paid to scant on the offerings you made to a person who could mock you in the street for your miserliness.

"You can use that mirror," said the personage.

"It will do, Magister," said the old man, "for you can be sure I can make use of any mirror. Naturally a man of your exalted inheritance—child of Four Moons House, descendant of the sorcerers and their warriors who crossed the desert in the storm, those from whom Maa Ngala, Lord of All, removed all fear so they could guide and protect the weak and the helpless—knows what he is about, and he has decided already what it is he means to do. Is this the one?"

"Heard you a lie in what they said?" demanded the personage with an edge to his voice that made me shudder.

The old man merely shrugged as he looked at me and then away. "I heard no lie."

"Then do what you were hired to do. Certainly you've been recompensed handsomely enough."

"So I have, Magister." He reached into a pocket and pulled out a ball of yarn.

Once or twice in your life the iron stone of evil tidings passes from its exile in Sheol into that place just under your ribs that makes it hard to breathe. That makes you think you're going to die, or that you're dead already, or that the bad thing you thought might happen is actually far worse than you had ever dreamed and that even if you wake up, it won't go away.

Uncle trudged down the stairs with shoulders bowed. He wouldn't look at me. Aunt sailed down in his wake with her head high and her expression so drawn I knew she was trying not to cry. Shiffa halted at the top of the stairs beside a trunk.

In the mirror, the humble ball of yarn appeared not as yarn but as a glimmering and supple chain of gold. Now I was shaking. Aunt walked up to me and embraced me tightly, pressing her lips to my ear and mouthing words in an unvoiced voice I alone could hear.

"For now, you must endure this. Speak no word of the family. Say only that you are eldest. Give away nothing that might give them a further hold on us." She drew back, kissed me on each cheek, and said audibly, her voice a tremolo, "My dear girl."

"You'll stand as witnesses for her," the magister said to Aunt and Uncle.

"Legally, *you* are required to provide two competent witnesses as well," said Aunt, her expression sharpening as with hope of a reprieve. Uncle said nothing. He would not even raise his head to look at me. "As you have no witnesses, the ceremony cannot proceed tonight. Very well, feel free to return tomorrow—"

He rapped his cane on the floor three times. An echo resounded, the house throwing the spell back at him, but it wasn't any use. We heard a tramping and stamping before the door burst open and slammed against the wall.

"Gracious Melqart protect us!" Evved croaked from below.

Up they thumped as my heart galloped until I became dizzy with dread. And just as quickly I was crackling with indignation, for he had summoned his coachman and his footman to be his witnesses. The coachman was a burly fellow with white skin and spiky white hair, and the footman, who rode in the back and opened the door for his master, was a perfectly ordinary man of Afric origins.

Then I looked in the mirror, and all my indignation vanished, even my dread. I was simply too stunned to feel anything.

There stood the coachman, exactly the same. But the footman was not a man at all, not when you could see what I could see in the mirror. He was a woman, first of all, so tall and broad-shouldered and powerfully built that a glamor disguising her as a man would be easy to bind. In the mirror, she was limned by a phosphorescent glow, bright orange and flaring blue, and she had a third eye, a mystic eye of light in the center of her forehead, that allowed her to see from this world into the spirit world.

An eru she was, for the evidence in the mirror told me she could be nothing else.

My father had transcribed in his journals the tales old people told him in their villages. He recorded the words of scholars as they debated what they knew and did not know. He observed; he described; he speculated. The eru were servants of the long-vanished Ancestors. They were powerful spirits that could cross from the spirit world into this world and back again. They were born out of the ice and, like winter, were too potently magical for any mere human to control. The eru were masters of storm and wind; they need bow before no mere earthly creature.

So how had an eru come to serve humbly at the beck and call of a cold mage?

"Is there any further objection?" asked the personage with a kind of weary sarcastic scorn.

"There is a matter of documents we were forced to place in the keeping of Four Moons House as a surety," said Uncle hoarsely.

"I have them." He beckoned to the old man. "Do as you are bound. Make it quick! I'm late already!"

Scholars distinguish between three kinds of contracts: a flower contract composed by a handshake and a few words, that blooms and dies according to the will of the makers; an ink and vellum contract written and sealed with the force of the law courts behind it; and a chained contract, sealed by magic and never lightly undertaken because it cannot be broken or altered except by death. Bards and djeliw, the masters of speech, can thread words of power into the webs of seeing that are the essential nature of mirrors, and by this action can chain certain contracts into the spirit world itself, making of them a binding spell, an unshakeable obligation, an unbreakable contract.

Uncle was weeping softly. Aunt wore a face of stone, cold and forbidding as she stared at the personage with a force that would have congealed a lesser man.

The old man sang under his breath, but the power of the whispered words made the air hum. With a wordless shout, he flung the ball of thread into the mirror while holding on to one end. With a sound like a latch opening, the uncoiling thread penetrated the mirror and at once could be seen as glittering links in an unrolling chain. As it rolled, I began to see the shadows of another landscape, the hills and forests and rivers of the spirit world. All our weak images faded to nothing as the mirror turned smoky with power as he chanted words in a language I did not know. Ghostlike sparks spinning off the eru could still be distinguished, but even these sparks were blurred as the chain of binding was fixed and the mirror became opaque.

What were they doing to me?

"In this world, one hand is given into another, one house opens its door to a stranger who will enter and become no stranger. In this world, one hand is given into another, and the other house opens its door to a stranger who will enter and become no stranger. This is the chain of obligation bound into the family of Hassi Barahal in payment for what they have owed the House of Four Moons. As it was agreed in the year... The eldest daughter is the payment offered in exchange for..."

The words flew too swiftly now for me to understand them. It took all my energy to not collapse to the floor and start in on a screaming fit that would put Bee's tantrums to shame. It took all my energy not to drop to the floor and sob with choking fear.

In this world, one hand is given into another.

There are three kinds of marriages legally recognized in the north: a flower marriage, which flourishes while the bloom is still on it and dies when it withers, which no respectable northern woman in these days could ever consider contracting; an ink and vellum marriage, hedged about with provisions and obligations and mutual agreements and legal and economic protections; and the binding marriage, more common in the old days and retained almost exclusively, according to my academy masters, among the Housed because of the raft of legal and magical complications at risk when two children from different mage Houses seal a betrothal.

We Barahals were assuredly not members of any of the thirty-six mage Houses, nor did we suffer under their patronage or owe anything to any House. Or so I had always believed, until now.

"Dua! Dua! Dua!" The old man tugged on the thread, and suddenly there was a click like a door closing. A ball of perfectly ordinary yarn nestled in his hand, and the mirror reflected nothing but the landing and the people standing there in various stages of impatience, grief, boredom, and shock. All the magic woven into the mirror had been sapped out of it by the grip of the spell, so even the eru appeared as a perfectly ordinary man with black skin, black hair tied back in a dense horse tail, and the distracted smile of a person whose thoughts wander elsewhere.

Or maybe I had dreamed that vision in the mirror. Maybe I hadn't seen an eru at all. Maybe Bee was right, and I was seeing only what I *wished* were true because it was easier that way than accepting what I didn't want and could not understand: that the world was cruel and had ripped my parents from me just because it happened that way sometimes.

The personage rapped his cane twice on the floor. The house seemed to groan, and there came a shout from upstairs, like a girl waking from a nightmare.

"Now, Catherine, Four Moons House has taken possession of you," said the personage to me. He produced a large envelope from his jacket and held it out.

Aunt snatched the envelope from his hand. "You make it sound as if she's your slave, but she is your wife. That was the agreement."

He regarded her with an expression very like contempt. "What difference these hair-splitting words make to the truth of the matter I cannot see."

Uncle burst into wrenching sobs. "Please forgive us, Cat."

"Enough! We knew this day might come!" snapped Aunt with such anger that even the personage startled and took a step back, bumping into the railing. If only the railing might give way and he plunge over … but it held fast.

The coachman and the footman sprang up the stairs to grab the trunk between them as Shiffa backed away. They clattered past us, down again to the front door.

"Aunt Tilly?" My voice trembled.

"Yes, dear one."

Still sobbing, Uncle hugged me.

"Come along!" said the personage.

What was his name? I hadn't even heard it.

Aunt extricated me from Uncle's despairing sobs and, clasping my hands, kissed me on the forehead, then on either cheek. She was still not crying, but that was only because—I could see—she refused to release precious tears. *Give away nothing that might give them a further hold on us.*

"What am I supposed to do?" I asked, and my voice was more the wail of a hurt child than that of a young woman accustomed to twisting out of any fall so she landed on her feet. But the world was twisting away under me, and I couldn't find the ground.

She released my hands, as dying people release their soul when death arrives. She let me go, and the personage took hold of my wrist in an unyielding grip.

"Go with your husband," she said.

9

Flakes of spinning snow burned my cheeks as I stumbled down the steps, remembering at last to twist Bee's bracelet onto my right wrist, as though I were daughter to her mother, embraced by her heart and her protection. I had no bracelet of my own.

At the coach, the cold mage offered me an elbow to balance on so I could mount the stairs into the interior like a respectable person, but I grabbed the handles and clambered up gracelessly without touching him. We Cats are particular, don't you know? I wanted to hiss at him, but I knew I must not. I must not dishonor the Barahal name. I must give him no further hold over me, beyond the fact that I was now the property of his house.

As Bee would say, "Don't kick unless you can really hurt them."

I sat next to the far door, facing the back. The coach shifted under his weight as he settled onto the opposite seat by the open door, facing forward. The footman closed the coach's door. I glanced out the window still open beside him, but the door to the house had been shut and the curtains were all drawn. I bent in order to see the nursery windows on the third floor, and I was sure I saw a face staring out through the misty panes. The cold mage shuttered the window with a snap. Tears stung my eyes. I blinked repeatedly to drive them away.

The coach rocked as the coachman and the footman heaved on my traveling chest and settled themselves. I heard the clink

of coin or other objects changing hands as the old man was
given a final offering and dismissed to find his own way home
through the bitter night. The coachman slapped his whip
against wood and then whistled. More smoothly than I imagined possible, the coachman eased into the carriage court and
turned the bulky equipage around. Then we rolled out onto the
street, wheels rumbling on stone, returning the way they had
come.

He opened the window on his side. I looked onto the square.
The streetlamps gleamed, fading as we passed them and flaring
back into life. Snow swirled over the grass and the familiar trees
of the park: the oak tree we called Broken Arm because of the
time Bee fell while climbing; the five groomed cypresses all in a
row, like children in uniform lined up at school; the drowsing
cherry tree, dreaming of next year's fruit. The stele showed her
back to me, plain stone. Maybe I would never see the votive's
serious face again. I shivered.

"Such gaslight will be outlawed soon enough," he muttered,
twitching a shoulder as if in discomfort as we passed yet another
streetlight, which flickered. He closed the shutter, leaving us in
the dark.

Or him in the dark, anyway. I could use the faint threads of
magic that were stitched through the world to enhance my
vision in the dark, just as I could listen for the hiss of the streetlight spurting back to life behind us.

He fingered his left cuff and drew out an object from the
sharp creases, maybe a key or a scribe's knife, something formed
out of one of the noble metals and small enough to fit length-
wise within the palm of his hand. He fiddled with it, then began
tapping it against one thigh to one beat while he drummed
lightly with his other hand on his other thigh to a different beat,
three against two.

The coach rolled through unseen streets. The journey dragged

on for so long that my anger and fear began to congeal into a
dreary sort of resentment. Yet run as it would, my mind could
not come up with any reason why Aunt and Uncle had sold me
to Four Moons House. My thoughts ticked over with the revo-
lution of the wheels; ideas and bursts of anger and fear clattered
in time to the fall of hooves on stone in counter-rhythm to the
faint patter of the cold mage's hands. What disaster had forced
their hand? What contract had they sealed? What documents
were in the envelope? Why had they done it, and why had they
never warned me? Had the head of Bran Cof tried to warn me?
Or maybe Aunt and Uncle weren't the responsible ones. Had
my parents got into trouble and used me as surety to get out of
it? Did this have anything to do with their deaths?

Fiery Shemesh! Had I really seen an *eru*?

The personage sat there in the dark, silent but for the play of
his hands, until I began to wonder if he even knew he was
drumming.

A hundred cunning retorts and cutting stage lines lilted
across my tongue, but I bit them down. Let him not believe me
to be so cowed, or grateful, or *honored* that I would beg for any
scrap of pity or kindness or, for that matter, some idea of what
was going on and what might happen to me now.

I would not speak until spoken to.

We left the residential streets and entered a commercial district where I could hear the popping race of goblin chatter and
conversations in a dozen variants of Latin. His hands stilled,
and he seemed to be listening. A Greek demanded directions in
his choppy diction. On the other side of the street, a man
declaimed in stentorian tones, "We must stand together. We
must raise our voice. We must demand a seat on the city's ruling
council. Our own councillors, *elected* by us, not appointed by
the prince." The Northgate Poet! Now, at least, I knew where
we were.

I smelled the luscious aroma of coffee and heard the rumble of masculine conversation from inside a coffeehouse, where brew and the company of like-minded raconteurs could be imbibed, a place where a woman would never dare set foot. Farther away, handbells rang a rhythm and abruptly ceased. Close by, a peddler called, "What do ye lack? What do ye lack?"

Answers, I thought. *Questions.*

The cold mage coughed into a patterned kerchief.

I sat up straighter, waiting for the words I was sure would come.

He lowered the handkerchief and resumed his drumming.

The coach rolled along thoroughfares that stayed alive after the fall of night. Beggars clacked for alms. Bells conversed: first an opening from the sharp tenor of the bell that guarded the temple dedicated to Komo Vulcanus, answered by a scolding bass out of Ma Bellona-Valiant-at-the-Ford, and the high, excited response of the sister temple towers, Brigantia and Faro by the river.

He brought the handkerchief up to his face again, but this time to cover the reek of urine and vomit off the street. I was made of sterner stuff. A flood of noise marred our passage down a street filled with lively evening life, the scent of spilled beer and the off-key singing of drunken men.

"Away with the oppression of mages! Why should they break our gaslights just 'cause they don't like 'em?"

"Nay, it's princes and their greedy kin who trample us!"

"You take your choice: taxes or fetters!"

"Nay! Nay! Let's call, like the Northgate Poet says: *freedom* or fetters!"

"Oi! There's one of them bloody House coaches now. As you please, boys! As you please! We're many, and they're few."

A heavy object slammed into the side of the carriage. I grabbed the seat to keep my place as a roar of voices mobbed around us and began, with the weight of their bodies, to rock the vehicle back and forth. If my heart thundered, it was no more than what I hoped the horses would do: gallop out of there.

"Clear off! Clear off!" shouted our coachman, although how I could know it was his voice I can't say. It carried so.

Jeers and curses greeted his cry.

"See how you like the mud when you freeze yer pale white arse in it!"

"Tip 'em over! Tip 'em over!"

Maybe my teeth were chattering. "What are you going to do?" I demanded.

His hands stilled. He'd shut his eyes!

Even cats can't see through wood. Nor could I. But I saw a spray of sparks, like Han fireworks spitting gloriously in five colors. A blue sizzle landed in my glove, as if it had spun right through the carriage walls, and it burned not hot but deadly *cold* as it seared my skin. Men screamed, more in fear than in pain, and the mob scattered as the vehicle lurched forward, throwing me sideways so I hit my shoulder and bit down a yelp. I would not cry in front of him.

My husband said, quite clearly, in his precise, cultured voice, "A pox upon that cursed wraith!"

We rolled on. The blue sizzle *popped* and vanished.

"You are uninjured?" he asked stiffly. A spark pricked the darkness and expanded into a wan cold light by which he examined me with a frown.

I was shaking, and my shoulder ached, and I clung to the seat strap, wanting Bee beside me to face him down and wishing Aunt was there to smooth my hair and offer me a cup of hot chocolate, but...

But.

But.

But the truth was that I was trembling too hard to get anything out of my mouth.

I heard a chant rise in our wake like a nest of hornets mad-
dened by smoke:

"Better to perish by the sword than by hunger!"

"Let princes and lords rot in their high castles with none to
serve them!"

"Into the mire with them magisters and their foul cold
magic!"

"I trust you are not too rattled," he said in a clipped voice.
"Once we are out of the city, it's unlikely we will have to endure
any more such unfortunate disturbances."

I thought of a hundred terribly clever and scathing rejoinders
I might make to a man who could sit there thinking of nothing
but his own comfort. Instead I kept my expression as detached
as that of an actress returning flowers sent her by an unsuitable
beau.

"Yes," I said, managing an airy tone of unconcern. I could
speak as pedantically as he did! "Some say the trolls have con-
taminated the restless city laborers with their peculiar ideas. I
suppose that out among the bucolic fields and villages ruled by
the Houses, we need fear no unpleasantness."

"Is that what you think?"

Since it was not, I said nothing; I had already said too much.

"I've never met a troll," he remarked, "nor even seen one close
up." He looked thoughtful, and as his face relaxed, it was as if I
glimpsed a different man. Then he realized I was staring at him,
and his expression closed and the light snapped out.

"Was there something else you wanted to say?" he asked
behind the veil of darkness.

"No."

We clattered on, swung hard around a corner, and rolled
through a quiet neighborhood where I heard the splash of water

tossed onto stone, a kitchen maid emptying the wash water, perhaps. We rocked to a halt amid the balm of calm voices. His door was opened from outside and he disembarked. Shaking and aching, I emerged blinking into the pleasant courtyard of a compound lit not by gaslight but by the unmistakable hard white glow of cold fire oozing from ceramic bowls hanging from brackets set under the eaves and from pairs of elaborate stone cressets mounted on stands beside the doors and gates.

A pair of men armed with crossbows and swords shut the gates behind us. Two exceedingly well-dressed and proud-seeming personages—one male and one female—met us with cups of water, which we drank, then handed empty to waiting servants.

"We expected you before this, Magister," said the man without preamble, in the manner of an equal.

My husband looked taken aback by the baldness of this greeting. "I was delayed."

"We were told to expect the mansa's sister's son," said the woman, looking him rudely up and down, "but you do not resemble him whatsoever, so I suppose you must be that other one we've heard spoken of."

"I must be," he said icily.

I shivered, as if it had actually gotten colder, and maybe it had.

"I suppose that explains the delay," she added. "Have you ever traveled to a city before? It must seem very strange to one such as you."

"I trust the inconvenience has not disturbed the smooth running of this establishment." His always-arrogant expression shaded toward anger.

"Of course not!" she retorted with the indignation common to the proud. "We know our duty and will discharge it and maintain the highest degree of quality appropriate to Four

Moons House, as is expected of and understood by those who grew up within the family."

These deadly currents I could not navigate or even comprehend, so I was grateful when the male attendant indicated a waiting ancilla, who led us down a corridor and past a flight of stairs. I was ushered into a parlor that overlooked a garden through expensive paned windows and was shown to a well-made chair placed next to a side table polished to a fearful gleam. The woman followed, bringing warmed water in a basin and a warmed cloth so I could wash my face and hands. An open door on the far side of the room revealed a sleeping chamber beyond, fitted with a capacious bed draped with hangings.

I knew what marriage entailed, but at that moment, with the cloth squeezed so tight in my hands that drops of water stained my dress, I comprehended that, in fact, I knew nothing that mattered.

What had the Hassi Barahals owed to Four Moons House that Aunt and Uncle must pay in the coin of my flesh?

My husband had not come in after me.

Despite the cold outside, the chamber breathed warmth, but of course I saw no hearth, no fire, no coal-burning stove.

"You will want to change for supper," said the woman.

"I will?"

Her smooth countenance slipped, and she looked at me as if I had turned into a toad. Then she smiled without a sliver of sincerity and, with the same frigid courtesy, indicated the sleeping chamber. I rose, trembling, and followed her past the bed and into a closet almost the size of the bedroom I shared with Bee. There lay my trunk. An unknown hand had opened the lid to reveal the hastily packed garments within. Two dinner dresses lay draped over the back of a dressing chair.

She considered my perfectly respectable clothing as she might a serpent. "You will have to use one of these garments. And no time to iron out the wrinkles. Still, with such a costume, wrinkles are the least of the offense. I will send a girl to help you dress."

She left before I could punch her with the strong left hook noble young Maester Lewis of the red-gold hair had taught to Bee and me. Tears pricked and burned, so I thought of ice and did not cry. Waiting, I tugged off my boots to stand barefooted on the plank floor, expecting its cold pinch to shock away the last of the tears. But the floor oozed heat. Ah! It was glorious.

The door clicked open, and I turned with a start.

The girl had strawberry hair and blue eyes, a blandly pretty face as uninteresting as the blandly tasteful décor, and most importantly she had deft hands with buttons and laces. I tried to draw her into conversation, since she looked about my age, but she might as well have been mute. Or she might actually have been mute. Given what Bee and I heard about the cruelties and whims of the Houses, it would not have surprised me if they had cut out her tongue. I chose the celadon crepe, my best dinner gown. It was not perhaps at the height of fashion, but it had good line, as Aunt would say.

Aunt, who had handed me over without blinking.

The woman entered and shooed the girl away. She eyed me critically. "I suppose that is the best you have. I can see why the mansa did not wish to saddle his nephew with you."

Better not to reply. I stared at her, hoping she thought I was stupid.

"We will take supper now," she added.

I kept silent as I walked behind her through the sleeping chamber and the parlor, into the hall, and across it to a finely appointed room whose windows looked out onto the lit courtyard. She sent me in ahead of her, alone.

A table set for four with china, silver, and glass graced the center of the room. Two bowls hanging from brass tripods poured cold light on the scene, and two pairs of candlesticks bled threads of cold light from their placement on each sideboard. A small side table placed beside the window held a platter on which rested an unusual, large-veined stone and a glazed earthen vessel scored with a geometric pattern in whose belly rested a spray of white flowers.

I turned as my husband walked in. He now wore a long dinner coat tailored from stunningly expensive "king's cloth," the color so rich a gold that the eye melted in ecstasy just to look upon it. According to my father's journals, a mystic symbology was woven into the very pattern of the cloth, but because the Houses guarded their secrets with firmly closed mouths, no outsider knew what these signified. He sported also a knotted kerchief at his neck in the style known as "the diaspora," so complicated in its magnificent folds and falls that I blinked in admiration.

His dark eyes narrowed. "I thought you brought appropriate clothing."

"I did!"

"Why are you wearing this, then? To appear so, when they already think me—"

He broke off before I could further lose my resolve not to speak, for the two proud attendants—I knew no one's name here except my own—entered the supper room, looking, like him, as pleased as if they had been asked to drink salt water. He walked to the sideboard, where we all washed our hands in a bronze basin. He poured from an open bottle into five cups, then took the offering cup to the window, poured a few drops onto the stone, and set the cup on the table beside the vessel. Returning to the sideboard, he handed out the other cups, first to me and then to the others.

We drank. The mead was honeyed and rich, burning down my throat to my empty belly.

"Not promising. I expected better." He set down his cup and, before I realized what he meant to do, plucked the cup out of my hand. "You won't want that, Catherine."

My mouth opened, and then I remembered Aunt's words and closed it. Our companions pointedly said nothing, but neither did they drink more.

A young male servant pulled out the chairs. We sat. The first course was carried in by four silent servers: a clear-broth fish soup, several lamb and chicken dishes swimming in bright sauces, platters of gingered beans, gingered rabbit liver, roasted sweet potato, and a pair of savory vegetable stews fortified with millet. How I wanted to display my offended dignity by spurning the food, but I was so very, very hungry, and it smelled so very, very good.

They set down the plates, and the woman spooned lamb in red sauce onto his plate for his approval. He tasted it and winced.

"Absolutely not."

The chicken with an orange sauce.

"I can't be expected to eat this."

"I would be willing to try it," I said in a low voice, but although the woman glanced at me, my husband ignored my words.

The lamb in gravy, the gingered rabbit liver, the beans, and the vegetable stews met with the same scorn.

"Is this all your kitchen can manage? It is not what we are accustomed to at the estate, but perhaps you've been so long away tending house here in the city that you've forgotten."

I winced, trying to imagine what Aunt would say if she ever heard me speak so ungraciously. The servers carried away the offending dishes. I wanted to weep. I would have scraped the smears of sauce off his plate, just to get some flavor on my parched tongue. He considered the clear soup and the bland orange potatoes with disdain.

"These are so simple they can, one hopes, offend no discriminating appetite. Very well. Can I hope there might be a suitable wine, a vintage better than that sour mead? A cheese, perhaps, and sliced fruit?"

The woman's expression was as emotionlessly correct as his was disdainful. "I will ask personally in the kitchens, Magister."

She deserted the chamber.

"I have certain things I need," said my husband.

"All that was requested is ready," said the man in a tight voice.

"Is it?" my husband replied in a tone thoroughly insinuated with doubt. "I'm relieved to hear it, after this supper."

The room lapsed into an awful silence. For the longest time he merely sat, looking out the frost-crackled windows into a dark courtyard. The heat rising from the floor warmed my feet and legs, but my shoulders were cold as I stared at the bright slices of potato and the cooling soup with its pure broth and moist, white fragments of fish floating among scraps of delicate cilantro. I thought I might really and truly start crying when my stomach rumbled.

"But after all," said the man abruptly, as if his chain had finally snapped, "I'll just go to the workshop and make sure." He rose and left.

Without looking away from the window, my husband hooked the bell and rang it.

The young man who had maneuvered the chairs entered the chamber, quite flushed, and touched the fingers of his right hand to his heart. "Magister?"

His voice softened slightly. "Serve the soup and potatoes to the maestra, if you please."

"Yes, Magister." The attendant looked relieved.

So I supped on potatoes and on soup, which even lukewarm

was spectacular, subtle and smooth and perfectly seasoned, although my husband did not deign to touch it. Afterward, the woman returned wearing a mulish expression and carrying a tray with six bottles, eight varieties of cheese, and fruit. He sampled the wines—pouring a few drops into the offering cup before each tasting—and the cheeses and rejected them all, while finally accepting a single apple, sliced at the table and shared between us, and one precious hothouse mango, prepared likewise.

Yet when he rose, thereby announcing that our supper was complete, I was still famished.

"If you'll show me to the workshop," he said to the woman.

"Of course, Magister."

They left the dining chamber as if they had forgotten I existed. I sat there too tired to rage, and just as I had begun to contemplate actually stealing the bits of food placed as an offering on the platter next to the stone, the girl appeared to save me from an act so disrespectful I was ashamed even to have thought of it. She escorted me through my parlor and into the sleeping chamber, where she helped me out of my celadon supper dress and into my nightdress.

"Maestra," she said at last, an utterance that offered neither question nor answer except to remind me bitterly that I was now a married woman, with all that implied.

She left me sitting on the edge of the bed with a bowl of light to keep me company. Heat drifted up from the floorboards. My toes were warm, and my heart was cold. In all the years I remembered well, I had never gone to sleep without Bee beside me to whisper to before slumber overtook us. Now I was alone.

The light dwindled, and when its glowing dome dulled and collapsed into a wisp, I tucked myself under the bedding.

I lay there in dread for hours, hearing the rumble of carriages gradually fade as the city fell into its late sleep, hearing the occasional cry of the night guard on his rounds: "All quiet! All quiet!" I recognized the droll bass of Esus-at-the-Crossing and Sweet Sissy's laughing alto as they sang the changeover, the death of the old day and the birth of the new. The beat of festival drums rolled faintly and was quickly stifled, or perhaps that was when I fell asleep and dreamed of happier times, dancing koukou.

I woke from an uneasy doze with my forehead wet with sweat. Somehow, the chamber had grown horribly warm. I got out from under the heavy covers, swung my feet to the floorboards, and padded over to the shutters. I found the clasp, turned it, and pulled the shutter aside, then unclasped the expensive paned window and opened it to take in a lungful of blessedly cold air. Then I coughed, having sucked in a huge breath of wood smoke, coal dust, and sewage stink. My eyes stung as I caught a whiff of ammonia.

The door behind me opened.

I gasped, turning, my hand still grasping the window's handle. A figure moved into the chamber; light formed into a luminous globe beyond his left hand. After a moment of complete incomprehension, I realized I was staring at my husband.

My husband! Come at last and very late to the marriage bed. Possibly drunk. Probably appalled at the necessity of consorting with an unwanted and unfashionable wife. I wanted to throw myself out the window, only I remembered Aunt's parting words: *Go with your husband.*

My duty was clear.

Strangely, he was fully dressed in practical traveling clothes that were dirty and torn. A moist substance streaked his cheek. He looked as if he'd been in a fight.

"Catherine, close that window," he said in an angry voice, as if by opening the shutter I had done something to personally offend him. Me! Torn from my home, hauled through the city, and then starved and left to cower like a beaten dog in a trap!

There came on the wind a sound, or maybe just a tremor in the air, a bitter kiss on my lips. My Cat's instincts flared. I turned to the window, wondering if I really was going to have to throw myself out and run through the garden to get away from his cold fury, now sparking.

"Down!" he shouted.

A huge explosion flashed mere blocks away, and the entire inn shuddered as the boom hit. Glass cracked; panes shattered. I was flung backward and lay stunned on the floor as I watched through the window, now above me, sheets of flame rise into the night sky above a bedlam of screaming men and barking dogs.

10

"Get up! Get dressed! Riding gear, if you have it."

He made no move to help me. Instead, he strode to the doorway and called impatiently back into the parlor. "No! You must *all* leave. You should have left already, as your masters have evidently abandoned you. Hurry."

I staggered up and stumbled to the dressing closet. His mage light followed me but he did not, so I had light and privacy as I stripped out of my nightdress and fumbled into fresh undergarments, a chemise and a soft wool tunic that fit close against my torso, and after that a split-skirted riding skirt and a blouse. I hurried back into the bedchamber, buttoning my jacket so fast I came up with one extra at the top and the jacket askew.

The conflagration rumbled like thunder that never faded. The reflection of flames flickered in the shards of broken glass strewn over the floor. Acrid smoke made my eyes water. There was blood on my hand, but I felt no smarting cut. I swiped my eyes and began to undo the buttons.

"Leave it!"

In the inn's courtyard, a cacophony of voices howled in concert. A splintering crash raised shouts of triumph. Then a woman screamed, but the sound was brutally cut short.

"Out the window." His voice was curt. "If they catch you, they'll kill you."

"Won't they kill *you* first?" I retorted.

A weight thudded against the closed parlor door, throttling my anger into fear. I bolted for the bed, yanked off the coverlet, and threw it over the lip of the window to protect against splinters and glass. I swung my legs over. The inn was raised considerably off the ground, so I had to jump, but cats land neatly, knees bent.

"Move!"

I ran into the garden, looking over my shoulder in time to see him drop to the ground. He pulled the coverlet down behind him. Cloth ripped where it caught on jagged glass, but he shook it free. Trampling through dead flower beds, I raced toward the far wall, measuring its height with my gaze. It was too high to clamber over, so I scanned for footholds or anywhere I could grip with my fingers. A tree grew next to the wall with a bench resting beneath the canopy. I jumped up on the bench seat, gathering myself to make a leap for the upper branches.

"Don't," he said, grabbing my wrist to stop me. He wasn't looking at me; I followed his gaze with my own.

Sweet Tanit in her bower!

A man with a rifle stood framed by the broken window, taking aim.

I tried to make a sound; at first no word came out. Then they flooded. "That's a *rifle*! Those are illegal!"

My husband raised his other hand as though flicking away a fly.

I tugged, but he did not release. He just stood there, as if we were poised in a park on a peaceful night to breathe in the scented air. "Rifles are far more accurate than muskets, or didn't you know that?" I pointed out.

"I'm surprised you do, since rifles are illegal."

I have good vision, even in the dark. The man in the window tensed and released. Fire!

There was no sound. No flash. No percussion.

The man turned and shouted into the interior. "We've got a mage! Bring the crossbows!"

"Up," my husband said.

I clambered over a big branch like I was mounting a horse. He shoved the mass of the coverlet, now shedding feathers, into my face.

"What—"

"Take it! Must you question everything? While it's true the rifle won't fire, I likely won't survive a crossbow bolt."

I took it. He climbed after me. A pair of men appeared in the window, lifting crossbows to sight. On the branch, now at the same height as the window, he ripped the coverlet from my hands and, just as the men released the bolts, flung it outward as if rich fabric and the feathers of a rumpled and now-dirty coverlet, however finely made, could stop two iron bolts.

The coverlet billowed open and began to unravel along the rip. I stared as the cloth unwove, becoming a cloud of threads, some racing out in front while others lagged behind with the mass of downy feathers, all of it slowly drifting toward the window as if on unseen wings. As the two bolts pierced the cloud, they unaccountably slowed and began to wobble. Surrounded by the cloud of feathers, they simply dropped heavily to earth, all their momentum sucked clean away. The threads and feathers meanwhile accelerated toward the men hurriedly cocking new bolts into place, as if they had fed on the speed of the bolts and turned it into their own energy.

A yank on my braid pulled my head around.

"Move!" He went up.

I scrambled after him, easing out on a thick branch to the top of the wall. As he swung his legs over, the branch he was on snapped off and it—and he—dropped out of sight with a thump into the alley. Straddling the wall, I looked back to see the men in the window flailing in a storm of down.

"Catherine!" He was rising, dusting off his clothes with one hand as he raised a cold bubble of illumination in the other.

I lowered myself until I hung from my arms and then let go. Naturally, I landed with perfect grace and straightened immediately to scorn the hand he offered, since he had been expecting me to tumble to earth as clumsily as he had.

"Who are they?" I asked. "Why do they want to kill you?"

"Why do you suppose it is *me* they want to kill?"

My heart was racing and my thoughts were churning and my mouth lost that tight leash Aunt Tilly had bound it with. "How much time do I have to answer the question?"

He took a step back from me. "I was warned that Barahals would have little conversation and fewer manners, coming from a clan of spies and mercenaries. Can we go now? Or must we duel in the Celtic style with more pointless insults?"

On the other side of the wall, men shouted orders. No doubt they were sending men the long way around to cut off both ends of the alley.

"Which way?" I asked.

He measured the sky. I had no trouble seeing in the light made by the fire, hazy and red and tangled with streamers of smoke, but he seemed to be looking for something else. Temple bells came alive, first one and then the others joining in, ringing the fire chase: *Awake! Awake! Awake!* Their thundering rhythm drowned out his answer. With a grimace of annoyance, he gestured more broadly than necessary, as if he thought my vision was as poor as most people's would be: *this way.* As he turned to run, he stumbled over the broken branch lying across the narrow alley. I snorted. Didn't mages possess spirit sight, as I did? He took one dragging step, righting himself with a shake, and took off at a run for the eastern end of the alley, the one that lay farthest from the inn's gated entrance. I ran after him. Maybe the Barahals *were* now spies and mercenaries, if you felt obliged to use those words, but that meant Barahal children, male and female, were trained in the family business. By the time we got to the end of the long alley, he was breathing hard and I wasn't.

Not until I stuck my head around the corner. A mob of torches bobbed along the street, heading toward us from both directions. Men brandished shovels and clubs and swords; behind the front line, crossbows were being leveled. Voices chanted, but fortunately the bells were so loud I couldn't make out what the crowd was screaming beyond "kill!" and "burn!" and "revenge!"—the usual furious shouts that come right before a mob's victims are swarmed and brutally hacked to death.

Fear came in a rush so strong that for an instant I could hear nothing except an indeterminate roaring. It seemed I would choke on terror.

A howl cracked over the mob, muffling the peal of the bells. Every burning torch shuddered and snapped out. Just like that. An icy wind blew through, shattering tree limbs and dropping men as though they'd been punched. Through the crowd rolled the coach, ghastly where the twisting light of the conflagration, still burning strong, caught in its lineaments. The horses no longer looked like flesh-and-bone beasts; they galloped about an arm's span *above the ground*, the white-haired coachman flicking his whip over manes as translucent as icicles. The other creature hung off the riding board in the back, looking no longer anything like a human being but rather a storm of cold magic so powerful it began to pelt ice along the street.

They pulled up alongside us as men wailed in fear, faces pressed into the ground. The eru leaped down from the back, flipped out the stairs, and opened the coach's door, as precisely as would any humble footman serving an exacting household. My husband climbed in without looking back, but I stared at the eru, who paused in the midst of chaos and looked right at me.

"Greetings, Cousin," it said in a voice that sounded so perfectly normal I should not have been able to hear it above the clangor of the bells and the wail of the storm winds and the cries of the mob. "I'll offer you a gift, if you're inclined to accept. For I think you may need this."

It flicked an object off the rack on the roof where boxes were tied and tossed it to me, hilt first. I caught it instinctively, felt its weight and balance mold to my grip. If there's one thing a Barahal knows, it is the sword. For it is true we are born to a lineage long scorned, if necessary, to the rule of the powerful: that of the hired swords and spies who across the centuries have done the dirty work of princes, bankers, guilds, and mage Houses. Djeliw and bards never sang praise to us, although we Barahals had always served honorably, paid the bitter price, and finished the job.

My husband called from inside the coach. "What is taking so long? We must *move*."

The horses stamped restlessly. The cold cut to my bones, and my teeth chattered. The eru turned away, and only then was I able to drag my cold-heavy legs up into the coach. I collapsed onto the seat facing him. He slammed the door shut. The stairs thunked into place beneath the undercarriage. The coach jerked forward once, twice, and a third time, slamming me back each time against the box.

The coachman shouted, "Ha-roo! Ha-roo!"

Blue sparks spun, and then we were rolling with a grinding roar along the cobbled street. I had a blinding headache.

"I didn't see you had a cane," he said, so surprised he sounded neither irritated nor supercilious.

I gaped, for I still felt a sword's hilt molded as if to my hand, but when I looked, it was as if with doubled vision: a ghost sword slim and straight and gleaming, layered within and around a fashionable ebony cane like the one my husband carried, an affectation of perfectly healthy and wealthy young men that Bee and I often mocked. Where was Bee now? Was she thinking of me, sleepless, in the room we had shared for over thirteen years? Had she noticed the distant fire in a far district of the city and wondered what it signified? If it would spread? If the entire city would go down in flames?

Hastily and awkwardly, I changed the subject. "Blessed Tanit! Surely that was a mage storm. I didn't realize you were so powerful." Yet I was shaking in the face of the immense power raging around us, for either he had raised that storm untrammeled and barely out of breath, or he had bound an eru, a creature of the dread ice, which had raised the storm on his behalf.

Vanity blinds even powerful men to blatant attempts at distraction.

He tugged at the neck of his jacket, straightening it where it was rumpled. "My abilities were unexpected, that's true. So unexpected that the masters of Four Moons House did not even recognize what they had until the diviners of five rival houses were caught asking questions in the villages. I was the strongest spirit in a generation, so they said, although diviners have a way of exaggerating to emphasize their own importance."

Glory loosens the tongue! He rattled on in that clipped, arrogant way he had.

"That's why I was given the honor and the privilege of this assignment."

There I sat, an honor and a privilege. The contract sealed by magic. Why on earth did Four Moons House want a daughter of the Barahal clan?

He twisted in his seat, flipped the latch, and slid open the window set into the back of the coach. Behind us, the glare of light made bright the sky, roofs limned as with a painter's knife, licks of flame curling skyward at erratic intervals as skeins of fuel caught. There was an ammonia sting in the air that made my eyes water and a flavor odder still that I wasn't familiar with.

The flames illuminated his satisfied smile. "Done well, if I must say so. Completely destroyed! They were sure I was too inexperienced to manage it!"

He was talking about the conflagration! I wasn't the honor and the privilege at all. To him, I was an afterthought, a mere *task*.

We sloped around a corner and rumbled down a deserted street, its doors and gates shut against the night. He snapped shut the board and sank back into the cushioned seat. The winds had died. The roil and clamor of the conflagration and the hunting, furious mob faded. One by one, the bells ceased their toll as fire horns woke in the distance, calling men to man the water brigades.

"What did you do?" I demanded.

"The airship, of course. Weren't you paying attention?"

"The airship?"

"I destroyed the airship of course."

"You destroyed the airship?"

"Must you repeat everything I say?"

Of course, the mage Houses hated airships. They hated the busy technology of combustion, the scalding power of steam, the schemes and contraptions imported across the ocean by those cursedly clever trolls and their treacherous human allies in faraway Expedition. While foreign engineers were lecturing on design principles in the halls of the academy, a House had sent its agent into the Rail Yard where the huge airship from Expedition was being stabled.

Gracious Melquart! The man had walked arrogantly into the academy library and used their scholarly materials to figure out how and where and when to do it!

"You did it alone?" For I wondered where the eru had been,

and what manner of creature the coachman might actually be. Perhaps he was human, as he appeared to my eye, but perhaps he was not. Unlike the man I had been forced to marry, I wasn't arrogant enough to believe I comprehended everything.

"You doubt I could?" he retorted dangerously.

"Since I know nothing about you or Four Moons House, I'm scarcely likely to have any opinion on that subject, am I?"

"Spoken resentfully! You should be cognizant of the honor shown to you by Four Moons House, established by the Diarisso lineage, who with their sorcery brought so many families and households safely across the desert." For a breath, a sniff, a blink, a humbled tone of awed respect for these ancestors shone in his voice like the glimmer of sunlight on water. Then the tone was gone. "Certainly I did not expect to find myself bound in such a way, to a person—" He broke off.

"I was never told of any sort of contract."

"It falls to the mansa to speak to you of the contract. For now, it would be better if we were silent."

"I don't even know your name!"

"My name?"

"Must you repeat everything I say?" But my embarrassed and pathetic counterthrust sailed right past him, missing its mark.

"It was spoken in the contract to seal the binding. Weren't you *listening*?"

Anger is better than tears. "Did it ever occur to you that I might have been too stunned to listen? That I had no expectation, no warning. Did you even think—" I gulped down tears. I could not go on. I had humiliated myself in front of him, and that was the very last thing I ever wanted.

He exhaled sharply, as at a powerful emotion. The illumination dimmed until the interior was mostly shadow. He settled back on the cushions and closed his eyes. We rolled along. Now and again the coachman's whip snapped, a sound like the crack of kindling fire, although combustion of all things is anathema to the cold magic so assiduously nurtured and cultured and studied for so many generations by the mage Houses that wove their power out of the vast breathing spirit of ice that is the soul of the hidden Ancestors.

At length he stirred, then spoke barely above a whisper, as though he feared the servants outside might hear and thus gain power over him by the rule of naming. "Andevai Diarisso Haranwy."

Still embarrassed, I could not resist prodding him. "You name yourself in the Roman style, I collect. Yet you are obviously not of Roman descent."

His eyes opened. "How can you be sure no one in Four Moons House is of Roman descent? Even the highest patrician's child and the poorest slave woman's whelp may come to the attention of the magisters if such a child has been gifted by the gods with a soul touched by cold magic. Also, we can pick and choose when it comes to marriage, as must be obvious to you today. Anyway, why should it be surprising we use the Roman style of naming? Is 'Catherine' not a derivation from a Roman form with an ancient Greek origin?"

"Do you mean to insult me?"

"How am I insulting you? You misunderstand me. I am only explaining why it is unexceptional for people not of direct Roman descent to use a common style of naming where once the Romans ruled. Perhaps you Phoenicians have a different view on the subject."

"Naturally we do, being contrary according to the nature we were born with, which is one of the lies the Romans told. For one thing, we are Kena'ani, not Phoenicians. We can borrow from the Greeks of ancient days as easily as the Romans could, so it's perfectly normal for children of Kena'ani lineage to take given names derived from the Greeks. We are not restricted to the names of generals and queens from our illustrious history, although people seem to think we ought to be!"

"Are you attempting to convince me otherwise? Anyway, I never heard that 'people' thought anything particular of Phoenicians except—" Abruptly his lips closed hard over unspoken words.

"Except *what*?"

He did not reply.

"I am not afraid to hear whatever you are afraid to say."

That riled him. "Very well. You must know what people say far better than I do. During the siege of Carthage, the queen of your people sacrificed her own firstborn child and that of every household to the god of the city. Who therefore brought down lightning and storm winds to destroy the besieging Roman army."

"And thus Rome's attempt to gain power over the seas was broken by a heartless people who care for nothing except the profits they can make as merchants and who therefore are willing to sacrifice even their own sweet infants to angry Moloch," I finished in a trembling voice. *Keep silence!* my aunt had said. But I could not bear to be passively submissive, to bow my head and let people speak such lies. My ancestors had not battled Rome to a standstill two thousand years ago by bowing their heads and baring their throats. "Are you done maligning my people? It is easy to toss comments and descriptions into the air when they do not fall back upon you but rather paint others— others whose clothes you will never have to wear—in an unflattering light so you can feel better about yourself."

The words were my father's. I felt their truth resonate like power in the closed space.

Blessed Tanit! What an idiot I was. I braced myself for a furious retort, but he remained silent for so long I began to think he had fallen asleep.

At last he cleared his throat and said in an expressionless voice, "You might consider rebuttoning your jacket, for it looks very slovenly. Was there anything else you felt it necessary to say to me?"

My mouth tasted of ashes, the leavings of this tiny victory. "No," I said in a small, tight voice, grateful for and even a bit amazed by his restraint. I could not begin to imagine what thoughts were chasing through his mind. He shifted, turned his head, and closed his eyes. He did fall into sleep then, as if exhaustion had swallowed him whole. His head rocked on the upholstered backrest to the rhythm of the coach, his breathing as light and shallow as if he were running in his dreams from gouts of flame and shimmering crossbow bolts.

The hilt of the ghost sword burned cold against my hand. I saw its dual nature while he saw only a fashionable cane. That meant he wasn't as clever or as powerful as he thought he was, was he? I was still bound, but I was no longer entirely helpless.

And yet, new questions rose like so many spawning fish. Why could I see the threads of magic that knit ghost sword and ebony cane into one object? Why had the eru given it to me?

For as I clutched the hilt, I heard in my memory's ear the chary whisper of the eru's voice that had sounded so clearly despite the noise raging around us.

Greetings, Cousin. You may need this.

11

Long into the night we rolled, and at length I dozed. When I woke shivering in morning's gloomy light, I saw he had opened the shutter on his door. We had left the city behind and rattled through a patchwork of neat townships, gardens, pastures, and farms, all half obscured by a sleeting rain. I wanted a heavy wool shawl or winter coat against the cold but had nothing. I had lost my gloves in that headlong escape, so my aching fingers fumbled as I unbuttoned and evenly rebuttoned my jacket.

Pasturage spread green where hills sloped upward in the distance. A hare sprang alongside the road, heading back in the direction we had come. Cattle grazed meekly under the watchful eye of half-grown lads who turned their heads to watch us rumble past. No doubt we were an unusual sight. Toll roads were traveled only by those who could afford carriages, and in any case at this time of year with winter breathing down off the ice, folk did not like to travel. I was suddenly wishing for Bee, to draw strength from her presence, but I was alone. A black cane bumped against my booted feet. I stared at it, but in daylight it was just an ordinary cane. It is strange what the mind can dream up when it is frightened. Wishful thinking, as Bee would say, will sting you when you stick your nose too deep into a sweet-smelling flower.

For a while we ran alongside a rail track. I leaned forward to get a better look as we passed a tiny depot where a long rail car sat on the siding, a new team of horses being harnessed to the vehicle as passengers paced the station walk. One man, rigged out in an ankle-length worsted coat like a radical, shook a fist in our direction.

CURLING GAP, the depot sign said. I recognized the name of a village on the edge of the outer district of the city of Newfield. If we were passing Newfield, that meant we were traveling northeast on the Adurnam-to-Camlun Pike. I reached to unlatch the shutter, but my husband's sharp gesture checked me.

"You can't open that shutter."

"I just wanted to see if I could see the Newfield round tower," I protested. "It's very famous."

"You can't open that shutter," he repeated, as if I were a simpleton.

I did not want to argue a trifle—I did not want to argue at all, although smacking my fist into his face seemed an attractive option—so I twisted my fingers together to make sure they didn't attempt something I would later regret. Instead, I stared out the open window on his side: rectangular farmhouses flanked by granaries and byres, rubbish heaps at pasture's edge, here and there a village of the distinctive round houses that my father had noted were known especially among the northwestern Celtic tribes and certain of the Mande tribes who had fled West Africa over three hundred years ago.

The man I had to call my husband sat opposite me, arms crossed as he stared out the window. He seemed to be looking inward, mulling deep thoughts like spiced wine. He was still smudged and stained from his night's adventures: a torn sleeve, a streak like mud on his left cheek, a chaff of straw caught in his carefully trimmed beard. He had a proud face more Afric than Celtic and very handsome eyes, of the kind Bee loved to swoon over, so brown they were almost black, thickly lashed and finely formed. He had boasted of destroying an airship. He had been glad to do it, no matter its cost to others in material and labor. Perhaps in lives.

He shifted forward, and I averted my gaze hastily, but he wasn't interested in me. The road was beginning to rise into the chalk hills. Somewhere up here stood the famous windmill, but because it lay on the western side of the road and my shutter remained closed, I had no chance to see it. We drove into a wood of black pine, and soon I saw nothing but pine beyond the ditches that flanked the raised roadbed.

He grabbed his own cane—polished ebony inlaid with gold—and, thrusting it out the open window, rapped the side of the carriage.

"The beacon!" he called.

The coachman cracked his whip, and horses and coach swerved off the road. I braced myself for a jolting fall, but rather than crashing down into a ditch, we rolled along two dirt strips with grass grown between that cut through the pinewoods. The air grew abruptly colder. Under the dark thatch of branches, the rain ceased prattling on the roof. We scraped along dry ground that hadn't seen rain this day and shortly afterward jerked to a halt.

He opened the door without waiting for the footman, leaped out, and strode away. I sat shivering. When nothing happened except for the horses stamping and slobbering, I slid along the seat to the door and jumped to the ground. The dense pine-woods lay behind and somewhat below us. I gazed onto a land-scape empty of human presence, a rolling, open countryside of smooth-shouldered hills and a single high beacon of a hill—Brigands' Beacon, most likely—rising where a pale chalk track wound up its grassy slope. He was walking up the slope toward the crest of the hill.

The carriage rested near a fire circle, a neat ring of stones within which lay the charred remains of branches and, beside it, a small byre sheltering stacked firewood. The coachman walked among the team, offering the bucket to each beast in turn, and although the liquid was clear as water and sloshed in a waterlike manner, I could not help but think there was something strange about the way the cloudy light glinted in the drops that spattered from the horses' muzzles after they'd had their drink.

I had to walk, because I was so very cold, and as I paced, I watched my husband vanish over the hill's horizon. It was as if the sky had swallowed him. Not an unpleasant thought, now that I reflected on it. Yet what would become of me then? How far did our chained marriage actually bind me?

The coachman finished rubbing down the horses and went to the circle, stacking wood and kindling and, with flint and steel, sparked a fire. The flames caught. The wood burned.

No cold mage, he! Nor creature of the breathing ice, like the eru. Fire did not come to their hands, and their presence killed it.

I crept close to the blessed warmth. "Heat is a glorious thing, is it not?" I said. "When winters run long and cold, as winters do, a fire is the best thing of all."

"Maestra," he said, unsmiling but not unfriendly.

He wore his short hair in the lime-whitened spikes traditional to Celtic warriors in ancient days, according to the records of Kena'ani traders and Roman generals. The style had come back into fashion a generation ago among the soldiers fighting for Camjiata and his Arverni-Iberian army during Camjiata's attempt to unite—or, as others said, conquer—Europa. In recent years, the fashion had spread throughout the north among laborers and the poor, even into the territories of the western Celts who had fought hardest to halt the Iberian Monster's advance. After all, now that the threat of war was past, humble laborers who toiled for harsh masters might recall that

Camjiata's revolutionary legal code had offered hope for a measure of emancipation.

After a moment, the coachman walked back to our vehicle and dug into a storage space under the driver's box. Seen from this angle, in the pearlescent light of a cloudy day, the damage the carriage had taken in the night showed vividly: The box was scarred with pits and gouges and was spittled with mud and debris flung by angry hands. Just who the mob hated most I could not be sure: the princely clans that had ruled and feuded, and feuded and ruled, in the eight hundred years since the collapse of the Roman Empire, or the powerful mage Houses that had brought down the Iberian Monster and exiled him to an island prison thirteen years ago.

The coachman walked back to me with a heavy wool coat draped over one arm. "You might wish for this, maestra," he said, offering it politely. "He'll not like its look, but it'll keep you warm."

If the coachman had not already been wearing an outdoor coat, I'd not have accepted it, but he was, so I did, and spoke grateful thanks as I pulled it on over my riding clothes and buttoned it up to my chin.

He stripped the gloves off his own hands. "These, too, maestra. Your hands look like they're turning to ice."

"I can't take those!"

He paused in the act of offering, and I knew the shame of having insulted another person who was trying to give me a gift.

"I meant, I can't take the gloves off your hands when you're out of doors driving. Thanks to your kindness, I at least can now curl my hands up inside these sleeves."

He wasn't a smiler, but the skin around his eyes wrinkled. "Best you do take them, maestra. The weather's turning. I'm accustomed to the cold."

I had to take them or compound the insult. The gloves fit tolerably well. At first my fingers smarted, and then they tingled, and then I began to feel my digits might survive the journey intact.

"You might want to stretch your legs," he added. "We'll not reach the next inn until nightfall."

"Won't you need to change horses?"

He glanced their way. "They'll endure."

Because maybe they weren't mortal horses, but I didn't say that aloud. "Why did we stop here at all, if it's so far to the next inn?"

He looked toward the hilltop. "The magister must pay his respects."

"Pay his respects to, ah, what?"

"His ancestors." With a lift of his square chin, he indicated the fire. "I'll brew tea."

"I'll walk, then."

He was a man who could stand uncannily still and yet seem to be aware of everything around him. His gaze caught mine. He had the blue eyes known in the north as the mark of the ice. "I am obliged to inform you that a powerful spirit inhabits the hilltop."

I looked at him and he looked at me. It was then I realized I had not seen the footman since I had emerged from the carriage.

"Who are you?" I asked.

His expression did not change. "I am a coachman." With a nod, he turned away to his work.

We must be what we are. And right now, I was intensely curious. I strode up the chalk track, whacking at stalks of grass with my cane. The view from the top was astonishing. The crisp autumn air made the sprawl of hills seem as sharply delineated as the tips of cold-whitened grass brushing at my skirts. On the

lowland plain to the south rose a faintly seen tower, likely Newfield's famous Round Tower, beyond which the lowland plain
fell steadily away toward the marshy Sieve. Just ahead, a steep
escarpment marked the east-west line of the chalk ridge; far to
the north, many miles onward, rose another high beacon hill.
The line of the road speared between my feet and that distant
landmark. Only where the pinewoods spread dense below me
did a mist climbing through the branches obscure the view.

I saw no trace of my husband anywhere. Besides the grass, a
ring of tumbled boulders patched with lichen was the only fea-
ture on the broad swell of the hill's crest. At the lower limit of
the stone ring partway down the steeper northern slope stood a
proud oak that had not been visible from the fire circle. A tingling like the buzzing of bees trembled in the air as if an unseen
presence did indeed reside here.

"There stood here once a shrine to Cernunnos the Hunter. In
later years, it served also as an altar to Esus-at-the-Crossing, the
Respected One, and another besides, whose name I cannot tell
you. Yet now it sits neglected."

The eru had walked up beside me. In daylight, her appearance as a perfectly ordinary—if quite tall—woman of Afric origins was so strong that I wondered how I had ever mistaken her
for a man. I wondered if I had also mistaken the third eye seen
in the mirror, or the sparks of her magic, or the storm she had
raised. Yet it seemed unlikely that the Houses, with their strict
adherence to tradition, would allow a woman to perform work
they would consider fitted for men.

"I see only the one track. How can this be a crossroads?"

"Can that truly be all you see here?" As familiar as a family
member, she rested a hand on my forearm.

The knife of sight cut through the foggy veil obscuring the
pinewoods below. Another land lay beyond, smoky within the
mist, a summer woodland vista of stately oak and proud ash in

full leaf. The trees grew along a shallow valley marked particularly by a small lake heady with reed beds on the shore and a grassy hummock jutting up from the glittering waters. Andevai, or a cloudy apparition very like him, stood on the lake's bank. His right arm moved as if he were releasing something. A bright object flashed in the sun—where had sun come from?—and splashed as it struck the surface of the waters. Then it was swallowed beneath.

The footman removed her hand from my sleeve, and all I saw was fog rising in thickening streamers within the black pine.

"What was that place?" I demanded, out of breath, my heart thudding in my chest as heat flushed my cheeks.

"What do you think it was?"

"Was that the spirit world? Are you really an eru? How else could you see from our world into the spirit world?"

"Is that what you think?" she asked with a smile that annoyed me.

"Why did you call me 'cousin'?" I asked.

"Why do you think I did?"

"My mother's people are the Belgae. They live in the far north, in the Barrens. My father wrote that you can see the ice from their villages. The Romans fought them. The mage Houses civilized them. So maybe her forebears had congress with those who live on the ice." Certainly my mother had known there was something a little different about me. She'd warned me to keep quiet about it, as if she thought I had something that must be hidden. "Although as far as I know, my mother was perfectly human."

"That seems likely, looking at you."

I laughed, exhilarated, because I felt I was dueling with forces I did not understand. I could not understand it, but I did not fear her, not at all. "And I am the eldest Hassi Barahal daughter. My father's lineage came out of Qart Hadast in the north of

Africa. His people are Kena'ani sea traders, who in ancient days battled the Romans to a standstill. So that explains nothing. How are we cousins?"

"How are we not?"

"That's not an answer! Isn't it said the servants of the night court answer questions with questions?"

"Do you believe the courts exist?"

"How would I know? I know a lot of village tales about a day court and a night court that rule in the spirit world. I heard a distinguished lecturer once say that the courts are a metaphor, in the Greek style. That they're simply a way for people to explain the cycle of winter and summer. Or that they're a story about the natural reversals of fortune people experience over the course of their lives."

"That is a story," she agreed.

"Do you believe the day court and the night court exist?"

"Do you think I can answer that question?"

"I do think so, but I think you won't. Scholars say the reason they have not been able to explain magic through scientific principles is because those who handle magic are so secretive."

"To which I would answer, trust what your eyes see." She wore no coat, only a flared jacket over loose trousers, all clean and neat and evidently without any susceptibility to the chill air that had now begun to seep even through the wool coat and into my bones because I was standing still.

"Everyone knows House magisters use sorcery to create illusions that appear real. And you've now appeared to me as a man, as a woman, and as an eru. How can I trust what my eyes see? Even you are not what you at first seemed."

"We must be what we are," she said with a laugh. "I have never been anything but what I seem. It is the chief gift of my people." She tilted back her head and shut her eyes, as if listening.

"What do you hear?" I asked.

"Do you not hear the djeli?"

I looked around but saw no one, nor did I glimpse any figure striding below on the misty edge of the pinewoods with a ball of thread or a kora, a bell, or a fiddle in hand.

She left my side and approached the ruined shrine. I did not follow her. The place made me uneasy, and I did not want to enter sacred ground. These were not my gods. Untying a leather bottle from her belt, she poured a clear liquid over the stones. Maybe she said something; the wind chasing the height tore away her words. Then she walked back, her stride easy and loose and strong. Grass rippled as a cold breeze combed through the clearing. Branches swayed in a silent dance. I felt in my bones the disturbing sensation that maybe there was a djeli or a bard imprisoned within the oak tree, its final burial place.

She walked past me. "Time to return. The magister will be finished." She laughed again, finding her comment amusing.

Although I walked as fast as I could without breaking into a run, which would make me seem as desperate as I actually was for answers or for sympathetic company, I simply could not catch her as she descended the hill. When I strode up, panting, to the roaring comfort of the fire, two brass mugs placed on the stone wall greeted me. I was gripped by such longing for a drink that no nagging thoughts of mist-shrouded vistas and glittering lakes mattered as much as the chance to raise a cup of hot tea to my lips. It was a pungent brew, redolent of distant shores and saturated colors. There was bread and cheese, too, neatly cut and laid out on a brass platter, and I wept a little, eating it, because I was so very hungry. As I drank and ate, the coachman and the footman inspected the carriage and checked the horses' hooves, making ready to depart.

I was just licking crumbs off my fingers when my husband appeared on the track, striding down from the top of the hill to the fire circle and the waiting coach. The rumbling strength of the flames weakened to a lick along the logs, rather as a rambunctious dog cowers under the table when its harsh master enters the room.

"That coat is appalling," he said as he came up. He frowned at the remaining mug and, with evident reluctance, picked it up and sampled the tea.

Food and drink had fortified me. "Appalling it may be, if one considers decently clothed servants appalling, but it is warm. You may have forgotten that my entire stock of traveling clothing and more fashionable warm coats—however lacking in your eyes—had to be abandoned at the inn in Adurnam. Or was I meant to freeze to death before I reached Four Moons House?"

He stopped sipping, his eyes raised to mine with the rim of the cup poised at his lips. He blinked several times, as at light breaking suddenly in a dim room, and lowered the cup. "I am at a loss as to what may have precipitated this outburst."

No one ever said I was wise. I had meant to keep silence, to be meek, to not extend my claws.

"Torn from my family with no explanation. My lineage and clothing insulted. Left hungry because perfectly good food and wine do not meet your ridiculous standards of taste. Almost killed by an act of sabotage that may have done untold damage to buildings and neighborhoods and for all I know to innocent people as well as *precipitating*, as far as I can tell, a riot whose mob might well have torn me limb from limb, and you besides, coincidentally. I had to be given coat and gloves by your *coachman*! Shall I go on?"

As the force of my words sank in, his lips set and his expression stiffened. The fire melted away to embers shuddering among the ashes. "I think that is enough."

I took a step back from such a cold hammer of anger that I felt it like a blow. He set down the cup so hard that it *shattered*.

Like glass. Liquid splattered. He stared at the remains with an odd expression, as if he'd startled himself. Then, without one further word, he walked away, leaving me trembling. What a fool I knew myself to be, recalling Aunt's whispered words: *For now, you must endure this. Give away nothing that might give them a further hold on the family.*

While it was true that the armies of the Second Alliance had battled Camjiata to a standstill outside the city of Havery thirteen years ago, it was Four Moons House and the seventeen mage Houses allied with them that had actually destroyed Camjiata's budding empire. Four Moons House could destroy the Barahals as easily as a nest of mice could be crushed beneath a giant's boot.

I collected my breathing. I wiped my brow and then pulled on the gloves, pretending I was dressing myself in armor, a shell of control behind which I could hide.

"Maestra?" The coachman indicated the bread and cheese. "If you wish, you may finish what is left."

"Don't you and the...ah...the footman need refreshment?"

"We are already fed, maestra."

Fear was a dull ache in my belly, as the stories would put it, but I was a Barahal, descendant of a long line of professional soldiers. You sleep when you can. You eat when you can. I ate it up quickly, for it was excellent bread and even more excellent cheese, sharp enough to make my eyes water. The coachman took away the platter and my cup and left the shattered cup beside the dying fire. The handle lay torqued in the dirt, warped by the power of his anger.

With a heavy heart, I trudged to the carriage, mounted the steps, and sat opposite him, next to a thick fur blanket someone had unearthed and tossed onto my seat. Warmth for the journey! I did not want to speak, but I knew I must.

"It is big enough to cover two," I said, the words sounding thin and forced.

After a hesitation, he said frostily, "My thanks, but I've no need."

He did not look at me as I wrapped the blanket over my lap and tucked it around my shoulders. The journey back to the road seemed even more jolting and jarring than it had coming in, but perhaps that was only the hammer of my heart as I waited for him to say something else.

Which he did not.

The road took a steep slanting descent down the northeastern slope of the chalk escarpment. We rolled into Anderida, the great chace: forest country marked at intervals by villages. In ancient days, the Romans had made charcoal in these uplands for the forges where they smithed their weapons of empire. We passed the rise of Greensand Camp with its old Roman posting station and signposts of a crossroads. The few folk out on the village street halted to watch us pass. Beyond the village, we passed men leading pack mules laden with wood.

We descended to lower ground and waited at the ferry crossing over the River Tarrant, whose name the princes of the Adurni Celts had taken as their title, so my father had written, in honor of the goddess once believed to dwell in the river. A prosperous village—I did not know its name—had sprung up around the ford but at this time of year, folk were busy in the dormant orchards and the withered fields, gathering in the last gleanings, stacking firewood, cleaning the privies, sweeping chimneys, and bringing in mast for the winter ahead. My husband watched this activity as if its rustic simplicity fascinated him, but in truth I could not guess his thoughts.

At the toll station on the north side of the ford, our House seal was all the payment we needed to pass. He did not speak one word for the rest of the day as we rolled along in a silence so tense it seemed I could taste it. Nor did he speak when, near dusk, as frost rimed the trees and the roofs of a tidy village, we rolled into the spacious court of an inn so empty of customers I realized it must serve only the Housed and their agents. He said nothing when the steward of the house came to escort me away to a finely appointed chamber on the second floor, overlooking a garden and, beyond it, the River Tarrant, whose wide loop we would cross again at dawn.

I took off gloves and overcoat and laid them over the back of a chair, against which I rested the black cane, and then washed my hands and face. Three braziers filled with red coals heated the room, and four candles encased in glass lanterns gave light. I ate alone, from a tray set on the elegant small table: The food was excellent, and there was plenty of it, more than I could eat. A washbasin, a nightdress, and an over-robe and fresh undergarments were brought by an exceedingly polite elderly woman, and my own clothing taken away to be tidied. As the door closed behind her, I heard a distinctive click. I went to the window and opened the shutters. It was a long drop to the ground, and outside the glass panes, bars blocked any attempts at a hasty exit. From somewhere below, I heard men laughing as at a shared joke. I closed the window and tried the door, but it was locked from the outside.

I was his prisoner.

I threw myself on the bed and wept.

After the worst spasms had passed and I wiped my eyes and nose with a handkerchief, I forced myself to sit at the dressing table, regarding my wan face in the flecked mirror. I had looked worse, I am sure. Once or twice. I unpinned my hair to let it fall free, and as I brushed it the required one hundred strokes, I listened to the ordinary noises coming from the ground floor, where magisters must bide if they wished to be warm. Maybe he was in the chamber below me, preparing to come up, as was his duty. And mine.

With a grimace, I padded over to the chair to get the cane. As soon as I grasped the handle, the ghost sword flowered into existence. I almost laughed. Magic hides itself! Cane by day, it became a sword by night, when danger most threatens. I paced out an exercise: draw, return, draw, guard, and then into footwork, although I was careful not to stamp too hard. At the end, panting, I spun and clipped off the wick of one of the candles. The flame snapped out as by magic. This was a blade!

The cheery flame of the other candles caught me as with hope. The braziers breathed warmth. What a pleasant, fire-ridden room! Exactly the place no cold mage would care to enter. I blew out two of the candles and carried the fourth back to the bedside table, tucked myself in, and blew out the last candle. With the sword beside me, I fell asleep.

12

Beneath the comfort of warm covers, one's drowsy dawn thoughts wandered pleasantly. Our upcoming birthday celebration was sure to be memorable. Because the family could afford only one birthday feast, I had agreed to wait until solstice to share it with Bee. She had asked for and we had been promised an actual balloon ride. Imagine how it would feel to rise above the rough slumber of Adurnam at dawn! We might hope to see the wide marshy flats of the Sieve spreading beyond the city's skirts, the distant rise of the Downs, and, if we were fortunate, even maybe so far as the mouth of the Rhenus River to the southwest where it spilled into the Bay of Brittany...

"Maestra?"

The truth poured over me like ice water. I sat bolt upright as a girl with tightly curled, short black hair stepped into the room with my clothing draped over an arm.

She startled back. "I'm sorry, maestra. I didn't realize you were still abed. If I may say so, what lovely hair you have, maestra."

Her cheerful smile coaxed an answering smile from me as I brushed black strands out of my face. "That is very kind of you," I said as I climbed out from under the covers. "Is it so very late already? The bed is quite comfortable. It smells of herbs."

"So it does," she agreed cheerfully. "I myself sewed sachets and bound them with amulets to keep out bedbugs and other such irritations."

Not all irritations, though.

My husband strode in as though it were his chamber, but pulled up short like a dog yanked back on its leash. The heat from the glowing coals in the braziers was sucked away in a sharp inhalation. He stared at me as though speech had been ripped from his throat.

I grabbed for my sword, lying on the bed, but all I found in my hand was the cane.

He flinched back as from a blow and rapped his own cane on the floor. "Are you not ready?"

The serving girl goggled at him. He wore an exceptionally fine dash jacket that, fitted through the torso, fell from the hips in loose folds to his knees. This one was paneled in a gold fabric set against a green of such elegance that even I took in a startled breath, because the fabric was so impressive, not because the buttery shine of the beaded gold collar caught high up against his neck looked so very well against the rich brown of his complexion.

I drew my cane across my nightdress like a shield. "Are we in a hurry?"

He blinked. "Ah. We are. Yes. Also, there is a chance the prince's wardens may pursue anyone they believe tied to the incident.... It may not have been so very wise for me to go to the academy to find out what properties of the airship I could best exploit, although I admit I found out exactly what I needed."

"Wouldn't a cold mage deflate any balloon sack just by standing alongside it?" I asked, then bit my tongue.

"That's part of it," he said enthusiastically, then stopped and glanced at the young woman, who quickly bowed her head. "It's best to assume we might be followed."

I remembered the mob, the smoke stinging in my nostrils, the beat of flames against the sky. The howls of anger. Maybe my color changed.

He nodded, as if I had spoken. "Just so. The carriage is waiting." He went out.

The girl smiled in a sisterly way. "He's not a kinsman of yours, is he?"

"No! Not at all. Not in a kinsman blood relation kind of way. We met for the first time two days ago."

She did not take offense at my tone. Evidently, like Bee, she could interpret my mood and draw her own conclusions. "He has beautiful clothes, if you don't mind my saying so."

"The Houses are rich; everyone knows that." I had not meant the words to come out with such sarcasm.

She chuckled. "Surely we do know that, who serve them. But forgive me, maestra. He said the carriage is waiting urgent, and I'm blabbering on. What help can I offer? I'll brush your hair, if you wish."

I smiled. "I'd like that. Just a few strokes, for I must finish quickly."

She was a good companion on an anxious morning, because her words flowed in a soothing spill. "My brother, he's an apprentice at a tailoring shop in Adurnam, where you must have come from. When he visits at festival, he brings us the tailoring books and the fashion books to look over. I know what he would say about *that one*. If you don't mind my saying so."

Leaning closer, I murmured, "What would your brother say?"

"Privately, I'm sure," she said in the voice of a person thrilled to be offered a venue for speaking her mind instead of remaining mute before arrogant cold mages. "Privately, he would say that the finest of clothes must be worn with a coolness that does not draw attention. A man who draws attention is trying too hard."

A brutal hammering rose from downstairs, like someone pounding on a door. Startled, I jerked away from the brush.

"I'm sorry," she murmured, twisting the hair neatly up and pinning it into place. "I hope no one heard me. I meant no offense."

"None was taken in this chamber, I am sure." I was sorry to lose her lively presence, but I knew what I would need to get through another day. "Is it possible for you to go downstairs to the kitchens and pack a basket of bread and cheese and apples, or anything? I would be most grateful to you and to those in the kitchens."

She favored me with a look heavy with sudden pity. "Blessings on you." She looked around the chamber, which in the light of day resembled nothing as much as a luxurious prison house with its barred windows and iron-bound door. "I suppose you'll need them."

It proved an exceedingly long, joltingly uncomfortable, and tediously silent day. After the incident with the shattered cup, I was unwilling to attempt conversation lest I inadvertently anger him, and despite that brief discussion of airships in my chamber, he now displayed no interest in me whatsoever. He even declined my offer to share with him the contents of the basket: an apple, walnuts, two loaves of fresh bread, a wedge of pungent cheese, and two halves of a chicken neatly wrapped in waxed paper. Mostly, I thought about my family. Why this had fallen on me I did not know, but I would do my duty because I loved my family and they loved me. I would do my duty to honor the memory of my father and mother.

We rolled at twilight out of the Great North Wood and past willow hurdles fencing off gardens and then alongside clusters of round cottages grouped in compounds and beyond them substantial rectangular houses set back individually from the road. We had arrived in Southbridge, that part of the old Roman town of Londun south of the ancient bridge.

The carriage slowed as we turned onto the high road. The

road widened to form a square around an old Roman temple. The high road plunged north toward the bridge, unseen in the gloom except for the distant glitter of watch-lights, while we took the rightward passage. We passed an inn whose gateway was lit by twin lanterns, a row of shops closed and shuttered, and a wide, paved court that sheltered a smithy still glowing within, gates flung open to let heat roil out. A burly man covered in a smith's apron strolled into view and lounged at the gate, thick arms crossed as he stared at our carriage. From within the smithy, the syncopated beat of a hammer rang, crossed and elaborated with the lighter rhythms of other pounding: the chatter of a higher-pitched hammer, the sassy countervoice of women pounding grain in a neighboring courtyard. The black-smith simply watched, turning with our passage as if the force of his gaze were driving us out beyond the fiery furnace that was his purview.

Beyond the smithy, the road forked again, a dirt lane ribbon-ing off into fields while the paved turnpike shot east toward Cantiacorum and eventually to Havery, some days' travel away. We passed more whitewashed houses and then a fenced-in area that in summer was certainly a grand garden. Beyond wall and garden lay a burned and blackened ruin, a once-noble structure with a courtyard and more buildings in back, all scorched, roofs fallen in, black soot everywhere. We pulled up in front of the smashed gate.

The eru opened the carriage door and pulled down the step, and my husband climbed out. I hurried after him as he strode past the gateway into the courtyard and halted at the ruined threshold of the main building. He pulled a spark of light out of the air and let it swell into a ball; this he sent spinning over the ruins, like a dog let run on a long leash. By the look of scorched and broken furniture tumbled in heaps or smashed under fallen beams, the place had gone down fast, and recently. In places,

the floor had collapsed to reveal the shattered remains of a net-
work of ceramic pipes by which the Houses warmed their domi-
ciles. It was an adaptation of the Roman hypocaust, providing a
constant flow of heated air beneath the floorboards. Andevai
scraped at the char with the tip of his cane, pulling an object
closer. He crouched to fish it off the ground and, rising, dangled
a cord from one finger, strung with the fragments of cowrie
shells and the crumbling spars of burned vegetal matter.

"Arson," he said.

He crushed the remains of the amulet in his hand, then shook
its dust to the ground with murmured words I did not recognize. He carried a small silver snuffbox in his sleeve, but it contained salt, not snuff, and he pinched a few crystals between
thumb and middle finger and scattered this over the threshold.

A cold wind rose out of the north. A light rain, spiced with
fingers of stinging sleet, misted down out of the sky.

"Follow us after you have scouted the perimeter," he said to
the coachman.

I walked beside him back into town. Every house that we
passed had shutters closed against the lowering night. The hilt
of the ghost sword came alive in my hand, but apparently he
still could not see it.

We reached the edge of the square and walked to the other
inn. The smith waited in his doorway, arms still crossed, speaking no word of welcome. My husband did not acknowledge
him, nor did he stray too close to the smithy, a place of power
opposed to his own cold magic, even if no person who stirred
the embers of fire magic could raise an equivalent level of power
without being physically consumed by an uncontrollable blast
of elemental fire.

No footman or liveried servant waited at the inn's entrance to
greet distinguished customers. As we approached the open gates,
the lanterns sputtered and went out. I could barely distinguish

the griffin talisman painted on the inn's sign. We walked into a courtyard surrounded by the inn buildings and their double tier of balconies. At the door to the common house, he was stymied because no servant waited to open the heavy door, but I was not too proud to fix a hand around the door handle and drag it open.

"Catherine!" He made a gesture of protest.

I ignored him and crossed the threshold into a large, warm, and smoky room fitted with long tables and benches. It was at this hour empty except for the tempting smell of chicken broth and baking squash. Through a second door, which was propped open by a brick, I could see into an adjoining supper room where people were dining and chattering. With a frown, Andevai entered. The blazing fire in the hearth sank like a shy child hiding his face from strangers.

A man carrying a tray piled with dishes emerged from the supper room and stopped stock-still to stare at us, like an actor pretending shock in a Roman comedy. He cleared his throat uneasily. "How can I help you, maester? Maestra?"

"What happened to the House inn?" Andevai demanded. "When I last passed through here ten days ago, I stayed there."

"It burned, maester."

"I can see that it burned. It was destroyed by arson."

"I wouldn't know about that, maester."

"I don't suppose you would. No one ever does. When did it happen?"

"Nine days ago, maester. A rare conflagration."

The fire flickered, struggling to stay alive. "So it seems. It is now too late for us to travel farther upon the turnpike and seek the next House accommodation."

The innkeeper's gaze flashed to the fire, and his breathing quickened. "I ask pardon for not recognizing you, Magister. We never see magisters such as yourself in my inn, begging your pardon. Indeed, Griffin Inn is no place you'll be accustomed to,

Magister. We've no specially heated rooms for cold mages like yourself, like the House inns are fitted with." The man gestured with the tray toward the fire. "We heat with hearths and braziers. Anyway, we've only one room remaining for tonight, an attic room with several cots. Not even a proper bed."

"You can clear a chamber for our use."

The man took in an angry breath. "That I can't, Magister. I can't turn out those guests who've already made their arrangements and paid in advance. I'm not able to collect tithes from my neighbors as the House inn did, with the threat of House retribution backing up their demands should any not pay the tax. Anyway, Magister, even besides the attic room, we've only four sleeping rooms, none of them to your liking, I am sure."

"You are deliberately insulting me."

"I am telling you the cold truth, Magister. Maybe you choose to take it as an insult, if you're not accustomed to hearing the truth spoken to you." The man's knuckles were clenched to a pallor around the tray. It took a courageous man to speak so frankly to a cold mage.

The fire sighed to embers. The hilt of the ghost sword grew cold against my palm.

"We'll take the attic room," I said, too loudly, because I did not intend to see the innkeeper's pewter cups shattered in a fit of rage. "We'll need extra blankets, as many as you have, if you don't mind, maester. But the principles of convection suggest that hot air rises, so up in the attic we should be warm enough even with no brazier to heat the room."

The man had expressive eyebrows; one quirked now, cocking up as he examined me. He looked again at Andevai to identify what possible relation we might have, and nodded. "Supper is served in the supper room, maestra. Or must I also address you as Magister?"

"No. Thank you."

His eyebrows lifted again before he recovered his composure. "I'll send my niece to show you up when we're done serving supper, but you'll have to have your own people carry up your cases or what have you, as we're shorthanded tonight what with the wedding of my wife's cousin's nephew in Londun. I would have shut up the inn and gone over the river myself for the wedding feast if not for—"

A trill of laughter—humanlike but not human—lilted out of the supper room.

The man nodded at me, pointedly not looking at Andevai. "Business is business, maestra. We serve any who pay with hard currency and comport themselves like decent folk. If you're wanting a wash, there's a trough out by the stable where you can fill a pitcher. There'll be a basin up in the room to pour in and wash out of."

"We will receive a tray of food in our private chamber," said Andevai abruptly.

The man's lips thinned. "As I said, Magister, tonight we haven't the means for private service no matter what I might wish one way or another, for besides the lad out in the stables, it's just me and my brother's daughter. She's tending the kitchen, and I'm running food into the supper room, and soon enough I'll have customers here in the common room as well to pull drinks for, the usual locals with their music and talk."

"Even if I were to eat in a public room, you can scarcely wish me to eat in your supper room, since I will extinguish your fire and then all your other customers will be cold."

"Even if you sit at the very farthest table from the hearth, Magister? I just want to make clear I've nothing to be ashamed of in my inn. We're a respectable establishment well known for our savory suppers, our excellent brew, and clean beds. Yet I'll tell you truly, we've never had a cold mage set foot in this establishment, not a Housed mage, not once, just hedge mages and bards and jellies and such."

"This corruption is absurd," Andevai said with a glance at me, contempt trembling like unspoken words on his lips. Yet he would go on speaking. "Jelly is a substance congealed or, in its manner, frozen. A djeli"—he pronounced it more like "jay-lee"—"possesses the ability to channel, to weave, the essence that binds and underlies the universe. Like bards, they are the guardians of the ancient speech. I wish you people would use the word correctly to show proper respect."

A throaty, somewhat monotone voice called from the supper room with a request for more wine.

The innkeeper's mouth had pinched tight. "I'll tell you this," he began in a low, passionate voice, "you in the Houses may stand high, and you may look down on us who crawl beneath you, but there rises a tide of sentiment—"

I saw my supper and my hope for a night's sleep sliding away. "Maester," I cut in, "what if I fetch a tray myself from the kitchens and take it up to the attic?"

Checked, the innkeeper stiffened, maybe not sure whether I was being respectful or derisory.

Andevai broke in. "Catherine, you are not a servant to fetch and carry what others are obligated to bring."

"I want to eat. I'm very hungry. If I fetch the tray, then I know we'll eat."

"Furthermore," my husband went on inexorably, "the Houses are the bringers of plenty, not of want. People should be grateful to us, who have spared them from the tyranny of princes many times over, who have saved them from the wars of monsters like Camjiata who meant to crush all beneath his boot."

"Get out of my house," said the innkeeper so quietly that Andevai did not react, and after a moment I began to think he had not heard because there was no sound at all; even the conversation in the supper room dropped into a lull.

For a moment.

Then the sword hilt burned against my palm like ice.

The fire *whoofed* out with a billow of ash like a cough. I felt as if a glacier loomed, ready to calve and bury me.

"Catherine," Andevai said in a low voice, "go outside. Now."

My skin was chapped from the cold, and my stomach was grumbling, and the soup smelled so good, and it was sleeting outside, and in only three days the end of the year would arrive and with it, on that cusp between the dying of the old year and the birth of the new, would rise my own natal day, my birthday, when I would welcome a full round of twenty years and therefore become an adult. Only now I was severed by magic from my beloved family and standing here cold and exhausted and hungry and far from the home I could never return to and meanwhile about to be kicked out into the night. And the worst of it was, Andevai was probably going to do something stupid and awful, because he was the arrogant child of a powerful House unused to being spoken to by a common innkeeper far below him in birth and wealth and without any cold magic to protect himself, and all I could think of was snuggling into a warm bed and sipping hot soup, because I was the most selfish, miserable person alive.

To my horror, I began to cry hot, silent tears.

"Excuse me, maester," said the throaty voice. A personage loomed behind the innkeeper at the door of the supper room, its bright crest startling in the drab surroundings.

Andevai looked over, no doubt surprised to hear himself again improperly addressed by a stranger, and then doubly surprised to see a troll who was, after all, not speaking to him but to the innkeeper. I sucked back my tears as the prickling anticipation of destruction abruptly eased: He was too startled to be angry.

"You are quite run off your feet, maester—we can see that—but we have run out of wine, I am sorry to say, which comes about only because you offered us such an excellent vintage." From a distance, trolls' smooth, small feathers were easy to mistake for strangely textured skin, but this close, the drab brown feathers of this troll's face stood in contrast to a crested mane of yellow feathers flaring over its head and down its neck. "If we might get more when you are able to fetch it. Our thanks."

"I'll bring it at once." The innkeeper bolted across the common room to an opening hung with a curtain.

"And plates for the new guests," called the troll as the curtain slashed down behind the innkeeper. The creature turned an eye toward me. It wrinkled its muzzle to expose teeth, a gesture perhaps meant to be a grin recognizable by humans as a friendly smile, but overall the effect was of a big, sleek, feathered lizard displaying its incisors as a threat. "We'd be honored to guest you. If you wish to sit with us, of course. My companions are good company, so they assure me. Witty, well read, and willing to put up with me, so that may be a point in their favor. Or it may not be. You will have to determine that for yourselves. I'm Chartji. I won't trouble you with my full name, which you would not understand in any case. I'm a solicitor currently employed by the firm of Godwik and Clutch, which has offices in Havery and Camlun, although I'm originally from Expedition. I've been employed in Havery for the past four years, but we're setting up new offices in Adurnam."

It thrust out a hand, if one could call it a hand, what with its shiny claws curving from the ends of what might be fingers or talons, offering to shake in the style of the radicals and laboring classes. Andevai actually took a step back, and the troll's head tilted, marking the movement.

"So it's true what they say about trolls," he said.

Fiery Shemesh! Could he never stop offending people?

"It is," said the troll as its toothy grin sharpened, "but only we females."

I stuck out my hand a little too jerkily. "Well met, Chartji. I'm called Catherine Hassi Barahal." The name fell easily from my tongue; too late I recalled I was someone else now, although I did not know who.

The featherless skin of its—her!—palms was a little grainy, like touching a sun-warmed rock. For an instant I felt the scent of summer in my nostrils, a whisper like falling water, the breath of cut grass and the juice of crushed berries. Then she let go.

"Interesting," she said as she looked me up and down, as if she saw something surprising in my height, my hair, my eyes, or my features. "Can it be you are a child of the Hassi Barahal house, originally established in Gadir? The old histories call your people 'the messengers,' known to bring messages across long distances in a short time. There's a branch residing in Havery, founded by Anatta Hassi Barahal. The left-handed Barahals, they call them. I see you hold your...ah"—she seemed about to say one word but changed her mind—"your cane in your left hand."

"Why, yes!" I laughed out of sheer surprise. Even in the cold common room, bereft of fire, the air felt abruptly balmier. "Almost no one knows the ancient origin of our House. I'm from Adurnam. The Havery Barahals are cousins. My aunt's great-grandmother's descendants, in fact."

"They are acquaintances of ours. Come sit, come join our clutch."

I followed her into the supper room, eager to stay within the orbit of one who linked me, however tenuously, to my family. She was tall, as trolls were, a hand taller than Andevai, graceful on her feet, although her gait hitched strangely. She seemed unaware of the glances fired her way from the other two tables of diners, well-to-do merchants or artisans by the look of their fashionable clothing, gold and silver necklaces and bracelets, and tiny leather charm cases sewn to their sleeves. Respectable people not happy to be sharing a supper room with a pair of trolls, even if the trolls were dining with people.

"I hope he did not insult you," I murmured, feeling a flush creep up my cheeks.

"It's a common observation made by humans who are born with this property you rats call cold magic. Now, here are my companions. Catherine Hassi Barahal of the Adurnam Hassi Barahals is joining us for supper. And…" She did not turn her torso to look back toward the door but swiveled her head so far around to get a look behind that I gasped. The toothy grin flickered. "My apologies," she said, turning to face forward again as the two human companions hid smiles. "I forget how that startles your kind."

I did not need to turn to know that Andevai had not entered the room, because the fires warming the supper room and the candelabra lighting continued to burn merrily.

"Here is Maester Godwik. Rats, pay attention."

The two humans at the table rose to offer hands to shake in the same radical manner.

"I am Kehinde Nayo Kuti," said the woman in a very pure, mannered accent that betrayed her origins from one of the Mediterranean cities. She was small framed and black skinned, with her hair done in multiple braids and a pair of thick spectacles riding on the bridge of her nose. She wore robes sewn of strips of patterned fabric dyed in deep oranges and yellows and browns quite unknown in these northern climates but ones that made her glow in contrast.

The man was considerably taller, one of the pale Celts with blond hair cut short and a luxuriant mustache in the old style, a local by his easy manner and casual working man's dress of belted tunics and trousers. "Just call me Brennan Touré Du."

"Du? That means 'black-haired.'"

"It's a long story, to be punctuated by a great deal of whiskey and several fistfights," said Brennan with a charming smile, by which I understood I wasn't going to hear it.

Kehinde chuckled, and the two trolls chuffed, almost like wheezing.

"My apologies for not standing." Maester Godwik looked slighter and shorter than Chartji, but instead of drab brown, he was feathered in vivid blue with a handsomely contrasting pattern of black and green along his elaborate crest. He raised a cane as in salute. "Injury, I am sorry to say. Clumsiness comes with age. As the sages say, 'wisdom achieved at long last, but now too damned frail to climb Triumph Spire where the young bucks preen.' I am Godwik. A solicitor with the firm of Godwik and Clutch, with offices in Havery and Camlun and soon in Adurnam. Although if you are generous-hearted, you will not despise me on account of my having taken to the solicitor's trade. Is your companion not coming in?"

"Sit, if you please," said Chartji to me, kindly meant.

I found abruptly that my knees were weak and my chest empty of air, because Andevai had been going to wield his magic to punish the innkeeper for his disrespect, but then after all, he had not done it. I sagged into a chair at the end of the table, with Kehinde and Brennan to my right and Godwik facing me. Chartji kindly brought a pitcher and basin so I could wash. After setting these items beside me, the troll hoisted a bottle, poured the remainder of dark liquid into an empty cup, and shoved it over to me.

"You're trembling," she said. "This should fortify you."

I downed the contents of the half-full cup in one gulp. A sherry burned straight down my throat, so strong the rush blew through my head as Brennan laughed, the trolls grinned, and Kehinde handed me the last hank of bread. It was good bread with a crisp crust and moist insides, still warm.

The innkeeper bustled in with a tray so laden with bottles, cups, plates, and covered dishes I was amazed the entire edifice did not crash to the ground. He deftly unloaded a tureen of soup, a pair of bowls and cups and spoons, and two bottles of wine at our table before hurrying on to the demands of the other tables of diners, now staring askance at us as I set to on the soup rather like, I suppose, an infestation of locusts embodied in a single flesh.

"That reminds me," said Godwik, "of the time when I was a fledgling, and my bucks and I"—he nodded at Kehinde—"my age group, you know, any cohort of young cousins and neighbors hatched near the same time form an association for various enterprises—"

"My people have similar associations," she replied, nodding.

"—decided to paddle the length of Lake Long-Water, as I'll call it in this language, although we call it something rather more complicated in our own. We planned to battle north into the very teeth of the katabatic wind. Our hope and intention was to reach the vast cliff face of the ice, which we, in our part of the world, call what could be simplistically translated to 'the Great Ice Shelf That Weights the North.'"

"Have some more soup," said Chartji, ladling out of the tureen in the most casual way imaginable, very neat-handed despite her claws, "because this will take a while."

"Did I get off track?" asked Godwik, crest rising as his feathers flared.

"Just a bit, Uncle," said Brennan with a grin that made you want to trust him.

"An expedition to measure the extent of the ice would be most valuable," said Kehinde. "If we could confirm that the ice shelf runs unbroken across the pole and could survey the southern face of the ice on the northern continents, we could calculate the surface extent of the ice. By comparing that to such evidence as is available from ancient records, we might thereby speculate whether the ice face is stable or if it is shrinking or growing and by how much."

"A venture is being assembled now, on the shores of Lake Long-Water, by a corporation of clutches," said Godwik, and although it was hard to read emotion in his somewhat monotone and slightly slurry voice, there came about him a change, for I was pretty sure the addled tale-teller concealed a wickedly sharp mind beneath the prattle.

Kehinde leaned forward eagerly. "You trolls may have better luck, then. The lords and princes of Europa have no interest in such an expedition, not since Camjiata's defeat. They do nothing but wrestle for precedence, useless parasites as they are. And, of course, the mage Houses continually place obstacles in the path of scholars. They sue our associations and academies to rob us of funding, and pressure their assemblies and local courts to agree to laws forbidding importation or manufacture of such new apparatuses as would make such ventures feasible. I'm so thrilled we'll be able to see an airship in Adurnam. There's a ship that can cross the ice!"

Heat flushed my face. I worked on at the soup, pretending more interest in my supper than in the conversation, and the soup was indeed very good, flavored with leeks, parsnips, salt, and a smattering of precious pepper.

"No one can cross the ice," said Brennan with a brooding look. "My grandfather was slaughtered by the Wild Hunt. He had been hired to assist a group of scholars attempting a reconnaissance of the Hibernian Ice Sheet in the northwest."

"The Hibernian Ice Expedition was set upon by dire wolves," said Kehinde. "So say the accounts of the men who found the remains of the expeditioners."

"In the village I come from, north of Ebora, where on clear winter days we can see the face of the ice, we know better."

Kehinde was shaking her head. "That there are forces in the world we do not understand is evident to all, but that does not mean that with proper investigation and measurement it cannot be explained by rational means."

"The Hassi Barahals are known as a family who collects information," said Chartji to me. "What have they to say about all this?"

"It's true my father traveled as part of the family business and recorded both his observations and accounts told to him by the people he met," I said, eager to move the subject away from airships. "For instance, many villages, especially in the north, tell tales of the Wild Hunt. Sometimes the Hunt is merely the agent of natural death, marking the souls of those who will die in the coming year. But other tales say that the Wild Hunt hunts down and kills or carries off people who have drawn the notice or the anger of the day court and the night court, which are the unseen courts said to rule in the spirit world."

"Their power is so vast it lies invisible to us," said Brennan. He wore on his left hand a massive and rather ugly bronze ring, which he touched now as if it were an amulet to protect him against the gaze of the unseen courts.

Kehinde crossed her arms, giving him a skeptical look. "What is invisible to us is nothing more than that which we do not comprehend. The tides and threads of magic that can be harnessed and manipulated by mages and bards and others like them do not thereby prove the existence of 'courts,' which no human or troll has ever laid eyes on."

"What of eru?" I said cautiously. "In tales, they're often called the servants of the courts. Although it's usually said they appear as human to our eyes."

Godwik gave me a sudden, knowing look, although how I could read such emotion on his snout of a face I was not sure. Then he winked at me, as if we shared a joke.

"Rats and trolls love to tell stories about rats and trolls," said Chartji, "and tend to see rats and trolls wherever they can. Meanwhile there are dragons in the mountains of Cathay and along the rim of the Pacific Ocean. In the Levant, goblins drowse under the rule of the Turanians. When the salt sickness was unleashed from the deeps of the salt mines of the Saharan Desert, a plague of ghouls overran western Africa."

"It wasn't a 'tale' that forced my people and so many others to flee our homeland," agreed Kehinde. "Greedy men who should have known better forced enslaved miners to dig where anyone could have told them they ought not to dig. When the first hive of ghouls was released, there was nothing anyone could do to stop more from hatching."

"That is my point." Chartji gestured, as in a court of law. "The existence of creatures who are not human or troll does not thereby prove the existence of the courts."

"I saw a sleigh of eru once, each one wearing spirit wings like a shroud about their body." Godwik hoisted his cup and flashed a toothy grin at me as Brennan and Kehinde looked in amazement at his quiet statement. I choked on a spoonful of soup. I wanted to ask if they had all possessed three eyes, but dared not. He took a swig of wine before setting down the cup with a flourish that drew looks from the other tables. "Indeed, it was on that very expedition paddling the length of Lake Long-Water that I was telling you about. My bucks and I, six to a boat and six boats in all, the age group of seven villages—I must call them villages, although they are not precisely villages as you rats build and organize such things. We set out laden with dried fruit and nuts to supplement the fish we expected to catch as we journeyed. You may wonder how it all started! What had transpired in the villages to make us eager to leave."

"I want to hear what observations you made of the ice," said Kehinde, "for I am sure there was a purpose to your investigation, not just the adventurous escapade of thirty-six overly energetic young males."

"I am all ears," said Brennan. "Rat that I am." He winked at Chartji, whose grin sharpened.

Godwik took in a significant breath, as one does before commencing a lecture or a song.

Voices rose in the common room as men entered the inn.

Godwik fixed me in that odd way the trolls had, his head tilted to one side as if he were looking at me with only one eye. "Perhaps, before I begin, the Barahal will wish to check on her companion? I sensed a spot of trouble beforehand, did I not?"

He was an elder. I recognized that now in the lack of glossy sheen to his otherwise brightly colored feathers. Old, and wise, and clever. How in the name of Tanit had he felt the cold tide of Andevai's anger an entire chamber away beyond a closed door? Was Andevai that strong, or did Godwik have senses the rest of us lacked?

"He's being very quiet in there," added Godwik, with one of those toothy grins that somehow translated into the gleam of his intelligent eyes.

I suddenly, overwhelmingly, and inexplicably felt a surge of *liking* for the old troll.

"Thank you," I said, rising. "If I may. Don't tell the story without me, I beg you. For I am eager to see if you ever actually reach the ice or just keep paddling down tributaries."

He chuffed. Brennan laughed. Kehinde made a gesture, like a compatriot on the sidelines signaling to a fellow swordsman that it was a good thrust in a practice bout. Chartji's crest raised, a reaction I could not interpret.

I opened the door letting into the common room in time to see an old fiddler raise his instrument to his chin and pluck the strings, testing its tuning. Another old man set his kora on a pillow, used one hand on a bench and the other on his cane to brace himself as he lowered into a cross-legged position on the pillow, and took the kora into his lap. Two younger old men—not quite so white-haired and creaky of limb—tapped curved hands over the skins of drums, heads bent to listen to the timbre. Around them, another dozen men, mostly old enough to need canes, settled onto benches as the innkeeper pulled ale and carried mugs four to a hand to the tables. They had the typical look of folk in this region: milk-white, freckled, tawny, brown, black, and every variety of mixed blood in between: One man had tightly curled reddish hair and freckles on a dusky face, another had coarse black hair braided, while others kept their thinning hair cut short and swept up in lime-washed spikes. A few had complexions blued with tattoos; some wore mustaches in the traditional style. There were even a few suspiciously Roman noses among them.

At the hearth, a man wearing the gold earrings of a djeli rekindled the fire, as djeliw could do even in the presence of a cold mage. Andevai stood halfway between the door and the nearest table.

"Here, now, Magister, sit beside me." The eldest of the men, a farmer by the look of his simple clothing and weathered hands, spoke directly to Andevai.

Astoundingly, Andevai obeyed. Stiff and silent and proud he might be, but he sat meekly enough beside the white-haired old man and accepted a common mug of ale, and when the old men scattered a few drops of ale at the room's little altar, he did likewise, and when they all drank, he drank. Then he glanced up and saw me standing in the doorway.

The old man followed Andevai's dark gaze with his own. "Eh, maestra. This is no fitting room for a woman. Get you back to the supper room, now. We've men's songs to sing."

I skittered back, chased by their hearty laughter and Andevai's glower, although what it portended I could not guess. Was he angry at me? Irritated at them? Frustrated at being stuck in a common inn for the night? Or was that annoyed arrogance just a quality inherent in his nature?

Hard to say, and, anyway, I was not about to ignore the words of an elder. As the fiddler's bow pulled a tune from the strings and the drums answered in a counter-rhythm, I kicked the brick away and pulled the door to the supper room shut. At the table, I ladled more soup into my bowl.

"So, Maester Godwik," I demanded as a song broke into full flower beyond the closed door. "What transpired in the villages to make you young bucks eager to leave?"

13

Godwik's tale wound down many tributaries. He and his thirty-five compatriots were reduced to twenty-seven after battles with vicious saber-toothed cats, foaming rapids, a marauding troo, gusting winds, and a party of belligerent young bucks from a territory whose boundaries they had violated. But, at last, they reached the great wall of ice that marked the southernmost reach of the glaciers on the troll's continent. Here, alas, Kehinde assaulted him with so many detailed questions about the color, texture, weight, height, volume, and consistency of ice that he never got to the sleigh of eru. Brennan and I by unspoken agreement rose to take a turn around the room. The other diners had quitted their tables some time ago, retiring, presumably, to their upstairs sleeping chambers for the night. We paused beside the door into the common room, where raucous laughter greeted the end of a rousing song.

"Let's go in," said Brennan.

"They said they were singing men's songs."

He had what my father would have called "a hearty laugh." "I know this manner of old men. They were just seeing if they could intimidate you."

"How do you know they're old? You never went into the common room to see them."

"They've been playing the songs old men play."

He was easy to confide in. "Let me ask you, then. One of

those old men—I'm sure he was nothing more than a humble farmer—ordered my...ah...my companion to sit down on the bench and drink with him. And he did!"

"Surely he would obey. They are elders."

"He's a magister."

Brennan shrugged. "He's Mande, as I am. If an elder says to sit, then you sit."

"You're Mande? Not Celtic? The Mande lineages came from West Africa." I eyed his pale skin and reddish blond hair.

His grin flashed. "That's where some of my ancestors came from. I'm also, by breeding, a Brigantes Celt. That's where I get my looks. There's probably the blood of a Roman legionnaire back there as well. Most everyone in these territories is tartan, aren't they? In my village, we call ourselves Mande because we're clients to a mage House whose founders came over from the Mali Empire."

"Four Moons House?"

"For reasons I can't explain, I really can't tell you. My apologies."

"None taken. It seems you left the village, though. The one north of Ebora."

"I don't know how much you hear about it down here, but many of the miners in Brigantia are angry about their working conditions and low pay. What can laborers do when the law courts are controlled by the prince and his jurists?"

"Surely jurists are impartial!"

He smiled sadly, as if sorry to be the one to rip the wool from my eyes. "Of course that is what they say. I've even encountered a few who are. Anyhow, the workingmen and women in my village spent ten years raising funds to sponsor two likely lads to attend the academy in Camlun. I was chosen mostly, I admit, because I was a good fighter and they figured I could protect the other lad."

"Did you?"

He raised his left hand. His knuckles were scarred, and his little finger set crookedly, as though it had been broken more than once. "He learned enough to be taken on at law offices in Ebora. He is now a solicitor, a burr chafing at the robes of the courts."

"I'm surprised the mage House allowed it. Couldn't they have stopped you? The villagers are held in clientage to the mage Houses. Bound by old contracts or by entrenched custom to serve their masters in perpetuity. They're practically slaves." I thought of my own marriage and flushed. "My apologies. That sounds very offensive, doesn't it? It's what I was taught at the academy in Adurnam."

He had a very nice smile, meant to be reassuring, and I felt my face grow warmer even as I reminded myself that an assured man like him could have no possible interest in an inexperienced and ignorant girl like me. "Legally it's not an inaccurate description, just an incomplete one, as Godwik and Chartji and my age-mate who went with me to the Camlun academy would be sure to tell you. What rights you possess as a person who stands in a client status to a lord or a mage House will be different for different people. You remain, however, a dependent, an inferior to their superior rank."

As I was now, bound to Four Moons House.

He went on. "But again, it's never quite that simple. A powerful mage House remains powerful because its elders know how to harvest their fields. One of my great-grandmothers who worked a season up at the magisters' estate house came home with more than her wages. That happens all the time. The child she bore wasn't a cold mage—my grandfather, that was—so he stayed in the village. But the mages keep watch, to see if a cold mage sprouts in one of our stony gardens. Before my age-mate and I were allowed to leave, we had to stand before a mage seeker to make sure no thread of cold magic was wound into our bones and blood. Beyond that, they cared nothing for what we did as long as it caused them no immediate trouble. Honestly, I think it had not yet occurred to them that the law that protects privilege can also be turned around to break it down. We just have to be patient and hardheaded. But had I been a cold mage, even a weak one, I'd never have escaped. They're harsh jailers, especially to their own."

"Are they?"

"I expect their privileged sons and daughters are content. Why would they not be? Those without magic are well trained as clerks, administrators, and soldiers. As for cold mages, the only thing they need fear, so the stories tell us, is becoming *too* powerful and attracting the notice of the Wild Hunt."

"Then you believe the Wild Hunt serves the unseen courts?"

"The Wild Hunt and the courts are facts that do not need my belief to exist. I know what killed my grandfather."

"I'm sorry to hear of his death in such unpleasant circumstances."

"My thanks. You have a kind heart."

Out of the bramble of conversation beyond the door, a new rhythm was struck, followed by a descending line on the kora underlaid by drawn-out notes on the fiddle. The audience whistled in anticipation.

"Come on," said Brennan, touching my arm. "This should be something."

He pushed open the door. I crept in his wake. Women had crowded into the common room, seated on benches over by the innkeeper's serving bar, while younger men stood along the other wall. The oldsters remained at the center, closest to the hearth. Only Andevai sat out of place, stuck at the left hand of the eldest who, gesturing, called the djeli out of his corner by the fire.

Brennan leaned his broad shoulders against the wall beside the supper room door. I closed the door and stood beside him, wondering if Andevai would look my way, see me, and disapprove, but he sat with elbows on the table and head bent, listening to the old man speak into his ear just as the djeli was listening to the play of the instruments. A smile flashed on Andevai's lips at some comment made by the farmer. I hadn't even imagined he could smile! I had a momentary hallucination that, in these surroundings, my proud husband was *comfortable*.

The djeli extended his arms, the full sleeves of his robes belling out like a vulture opening its wings. He called out words in a language I did not know but that I could guess was one of the Mande languages, which like the Celtic languages survived in their purest form among bards and djeliw. The conversations in the room stilled. The old farmer sat back, and Andevai looked up. He saw me just as Brennan bent to speak into my ear.

"The djeli is reminding us that his kind, the masters of speech, hold the traditions of the ancestors. Now he's asking if there is anyone from the Soso lineage here. That's so he won't inadvertently insult anyone when he tells his story, by making the Soso king look bad. He's a Keita djeli and therefore likely to be telling an episode from the Sundiata cycle, in which the Soso king is the enemy and evil besides. So if there is a Soso present, he'll tell a different version, maybe skip over any episode in which the Soso king plays a vindictive role."

Every gaze in the room turned toward Andevai, as if they all knew he would nod and reply with a few words. Which he did, exactly as if their eyes had called gesture and speech from him. A few glanced toward me and as quickly away as the djeli spoke again. The music shifted rhythm so effortlessly that it was like flying along a perfectly smooth road, hooves syncopating and wheels scraping beneath as an anchor pattern, and besides all that, there lit a *tip-top-tip-top* into the gaps. Looking toward me,

Andevai began to stand as if to come over and scold me. The old farmer put a hand on his elbow and *stayed* him.

Andevai sat down like a meek child. The djeli launched into his song, his words punctuated at intervals by responses called from the crowd to questions or cues I did not recognize or hear. Brennan's attention had shifted entirely to the djeli's song, a tale familiar enough to wrap him in its weave. I was forgotten. Even Andevai's gaze drifted to the djeli, whose gold earrings glinted in the firelight as words poured out of him. The singer commanded the attention of every soul in the common room except mine, for I was floundering in the current of an unknown river.

Also, a faint rhythm not in keeping with the song nagged at my hearing. I stepped away from Brennan and pulled the supper room door open just enough to slip through, closing it after me. Kehinde and Godwik were deep in a technical conversation about katabatic winds.

Chartji looked up as I paused beside the table. "Come to save me from these two and their interminable natural history? I can't abide rat music, I must confess, and I'm not tired enough to fall into a stupor."

I raised a hand to ask for a moment's peace. The troll cocked up her muzzle and bent an eye on me as I crossed to the main window, unlatched one of the shutters at the base, and levered it away from the window. Cold exhaled from the bubbled glass, but I did not need the clarity of expensive glass to perceive that the distant scene of blurred blobs of light was in fact a phalanx of torches being borne along the road out of the south.

I leaned into the glass, night's chill a bite on my skin. I bent my concentration and listened past the *tick-tick* of sleety drops sliding off the roof to the ground and the creak of a stable door being shoved open and the burr of a pair of voices that, inside a shuttered house, were oblivious to what was going on outside. There! A party of rumbling feet and stamping hooves slowed with hesitation as a young male voice called to them. At this distance, no person in this inn could have heard his words except for me.

"We're come from Adurnam. Did anyone arrive here before us?"

"A rider came before dusk from Adurnam. Foundered his horse to get here so quick. Is it true what he said? A ship came to Adurnam that sails in the air? And it's been destroyed by those cursed magisters?"

"It's true," replied a different man in a grim voice.

"Are you with the Prince of Tarrant's wardens?"

"No. The prince went to the law court to try to get a legal ruling in his favor. Without a ruling, he's too cowardly to act against a mage House. But some of us aren't cowards. It's time the mages feel the sting of our anger. We've eyewitnesses among us who saw and can identify the cursed cold mage who did it. We almost got him in Adurnam, but he called down a storm and escaped."

"A young magister has taken shelter at the Griffin Inn. It's got no veil of protection to keep you out. But you'll have to act fast to catch him unawares."

My cheek burned against the glass.

A breath of summer's warmth eased in beside me.

"Trouble?" asked Chartji in a low voice.

I jolted back, banging my head against the shutter, then pushed its lower edge farther away so the troll could dip her narrow head in, glimpse the distant torchlight, and duck out again. There flowed from her muzzle a series of clicks and whistles, and Godwik's patter ceased on the instant. Kehinde, too, fell quiet; she shoved her sliding spectacles up her nose. I latched the shutters, feeling chilled to my core.

Chartji cocked her head at me, examining me with one eye, then the other. The movement was itself a question.

"Trouble," I said intelligently.

"Legal trouble?" she asked, tilting her head in that trollish way. "We're experts."

"No. Not precisely."

But I thought, *What if I do nothing? What if I let them reach the inn, and what if they are indeed an illegal crew of radicals sent after Andevai Diarisso Haranwy? He has, after all, done a great deal of damage in Adurnam simply because the mage Houses detest the new technology, and he may be responsible for the deaths of people caught in the airship's destruction.*

What if I do nothing and let them kill him?

Let them *try.* They had ridden all this way in pursuit knowing he was a magister. They'd sent a messenger ahead; they already had allies in town, maybe some already in the common room waiting to strike.

But Andevai would not stand idly by. He would defend himself, and it was not in the capacity of cold mages to distinguish the innocent from the guilty within the circle of their power any more than an ice storm can blister some trees in its path and leave others untouched.

If I did nothing, then it was the innocent people gathered in the common room listening to the djeli's tale who would suffer. Probably me, too. But them most of all.

"Peace upon you and all your undertakings," I said to Chartji in the old Kena'ani way.

In perfect mimicry, she said, "Peace upon you."

I put out my hand and took her claw in farewell. "I thank you for your hospitality. I will not forget it. Now I have to go."

I ran to the door and tugged it open, and thanks be to Tanit that Andevai looked up, and while I could not see my own expression, he could. We did not know each other at all, not really. We were strangers. But I looked at him, and he rose and spoke briefly to the old man as he stepped over the bench.

"Maestressa Barahal?" said Brennan, looking startled as I strode past him, as if he hadn't noticed me go back into the supper room.

"Fare you well," I said to him over my shoulder. I met Andevai with every gaze in the place sidelong on us, no one wanting to be quite so bold as to stare directly on a cold mage.

He said in an undertone, "What?" and I murmured, "Torches, a big party," and he said, "This way."

We walked to the back of the inn as the djeli rolled on with his tale. The innkeeper at his bar set down a pair of mugs as if he'd meant to offer them to us but thought better of it. Andevai pushed open the door into the kitchen, where a lass about my age looked up, red-faced, from the steam of a big kettle of some sickly sweet brew. Her eyebrows flew up as she gaped at us, but we were already through and out the back door into a kitchen yard coated in frost. I grasped my ghost sword, but I had forgotten my coat and gloves, and it was too late to go back because we were already committed. Out here under the cold sky, I could distinctly hear the clatter of hooves, although Andevai did not yet seem aware of the sound. He cast his gaze first toward the wall of the stables and then toward the woven hazel hurdle that fenced off the rest of the kitchen yard.

He spoke under his breath, as to himself. "Where are those plague-ridden wraiths?"

He whistled four low notes.

I twisted the ghost hilt, and to my utter astonishment, the sword drew smoothly free. The naked blade gleamed, its length and weight perfectly balanced in my hand.

Its light cast an odd luster on Andevai's profile, making him look, for an instant, unsure rather than arrogant. As he stared at the blade, his gaze flared and his chin lifted belligerently. "Where did you get that? That's cold steel. Only mage Houses forge and possess cold steel."

There were many things I could and ought to have said, but instead I smirked. I might be dead by midnight's bell. This might be my only chance to gloat. "It's my black cane. You never saw what it really was."

He grabbed my right wrist, and I braced, because I thought he meant to wrest the sword out of my left hand, but instead he tugged me after him to the gate of the kitchen yard.

"Do you know how to use it?" he asked.

"I'm a Barahal."

He unbound the rope and shoved open the plaited gate. We staggered onto a muddy lane crackling with frost where wheels had left their imprints. The lane led away behind a block of row houses. He looked skyward, hearing clearly now the approaching hooves, the ring of harness, a man's call: "There's the Griffin Inn!"

"They might be a party of innocent travelers caught late on the road," he said as we trotted briskly down the lane toward open ground. The sky was overcast except in the north, where stars glittered.

"No. They're looking for you. They mean to kill you for destroying the airship."

"We should never have stopped here. How well can you *actually* use a sword?"

Gracious Melqart, but the man had a knack for being annoying at the most inconvenient times!

"Barahals begin training at the age of seven. It's in the family, if you will, rather like cold magic runs in the House lineages." Yet honesty compelled me, as if the sword's cold steel spelled my tongue. "But I've never fought in anything but the practice hall."

"Here." He cut a hard left onto a narrow lane, blocks of houses on either side.

"Where is the carriage?" I said to his back as I followed. What

I really meant, I dared not say out loud: *Where is the eru, with its wintry gale?* "Where are we going?"

"To the turnpike. Quiet." Bending his head like a man bowed by heavy thoughts, he stared at the ground, lips moving but no sound emerging that I could hear.

And I could hear plenty. Music drifted from the inn falling farther away behind us; the song chased on as the story unfolded, drums a pattern grounding my running feet. A voice called from an upper story, "There! There!" Shouts and cries rose as our pursuers reached the temple square. There was no possible way that we, on foot, could outrun them.

A horn's cry rose shrill and clear, and a great shout as from a host of soldiers shattered the night on the turnpike ahead. Horses whinnied, hooves pounded, and a whistle pierced the air.

"Move," said Andevai in a hoarse whisper. "I can't hold this long."

He lurched on up the rutted lane at an awkward lope, as if his limbs were not truly under the command of his mind. I followed a step behind, and once I had to grab his elbow to stop him from tumbling headlong when he stumbled over a rut. As I steadied him, I saw, on the road ahead where it crossed in front of our dark lane, a company of stern soldiers armed in the House style: The soldiers carried crossbows and spears and wore quilted coats; their horses were caparisoned in the bold designs favored by the Houses, manes braided and stiffened, legs ornamented with bracelets woven of falling threads of fabric that shimmered as the horses paced forward in a stately measure. A House standard hung with amulets stabbed the air within the ranks.

Andevai stumbled again, and I caught him as he winced. "Blacksmith . . . fire's mage . . . powerful. Fighting me."

The soldiers shouted in unison and pushed forward.

"Aren't those House soldiers?" I demanded. "Shouldn't we call to them?"

"Illusion," he hissed. "Must move, get to the inn ruins. Hold them off there until the carriage reaches us."

Two figures darted into the lane behind us. By the way they moved, I knew at once that they carried weapons. Yet it seemed they had not yet seen us within the darkness; they were, perhaps, looking beyond us toward the turnpike where the House soldiers still rode past in a seamless illusion.

"Stay here," I said to Andevai. I broke into a run, grateful for the excellent cut of my riding clothes, which did not impede my strides or my reach.

Too late they registered my approach. I parried a clumsy thrust from the closer one, then shifted sideways to strike a blow upward with the hilt alongside his head that dropped him to his knees. I spun with a backhand sweep that caught low on my blade a staff blow aimed at my head by the other man. Grappling, I kicked him as hard as I could in the knee. He shrieked and collapsed backward. I bolted back the way I had come. Andevai had staggered to a halt; the cursed fool was pulling a useless knife from under his jacket.

"Move!" I barely forced out the word. Sweat broke over my body, and I heaved once but nothing came up.

Andevai moved. He ran down the lane and I pelted after, glancing back once, but I'd laid them down well enough; obviously they were not trained soldiers but rather crude, angry men without much more experience than fistfights outside an inn after an evening's wallow in ale. We reached the junction of lane and wide turnpike. To our left, red fire burned in the square where the doors of the smithy were laid open, white sparks blazing as they showered out of the door and spat onto the vanguard of the House soldiers, but amazingly the illusion held under this rain of sparks. I ran after Andevai toward the ruins.

Men shouted in confusion, their shattered cries of disorder and fear like a counter-rhythm to the patter of drums that fluttered at the edge of my hearing. Was the djeli still singing? Music is its own spell. Who knows what power it wields?

We dashed along the road, the confrontation falling away behind us. Andevai fell onto his knees in the char and ashes of the burned inn, hacking as he bent double. I halted between the stone pillars that had once marked the gate into the inn yard. The lintel slashed a black line above my head. The gates had been smashed and hauled into the courtyard. A harsh light glowed above the temple square; I had an awful premonition that the smithy had caught fire.

Far away, across the river, I heard a bell ringing.

The rain had stopped, but I shivered as the chill seeped into my bones. The sound of footfalls brought me spinning around, my hand so cold it was hard to grasp the hilt. I groaned. There came my assailants, one limping behind and the other jogging ahead. I could not suck in enough air. I didn't think I could kill. And if I couldn't, what would they do to us?

Andevai appeared beside me. "Give me the sword," he said.

The two men closed inexorably on us, big, burly, unstoppable men who held their weapons like they knew how to kill with them. In another six steps they would cut us down.

I recalled words scrawled in one of my father's journals:

My thanks to the gods that fortune has spared me from that most terrible act, that I have never taken another person's life.

"It is yours for this one act." I pressed the sword into Andevai's right hand.

Cold steel in the hand of a cold mage is a wicked thing.

Two strokes, and they fell, dead.

He wiped his brow with his left hand, his expression pure in its anger and not remotely directed at me. Cold steel in the hand of a cold mage severs the soul from the body, so common wisdom has it: They need only draw blood, the merest cut, to kill you.

In the distance, I heard the sounds of a company in disorder, shouting, confusion, a pair of whistles calling for scattered men to form ranks. I stared at the corpses sprawled in the gateway, a step away from me. A wind stirred ash. Andevai looked east down the road.

"Late!" he exclaimed with withering scorn. His brow furrowed as he looked at the sword in his hand. Then he looked at me, and his eyebrows raised, and he offered the sword, hilt first. "If you think I'm going to try to keep it, then you don't understand the properties of cold steel."

"My thanks," I said hoarsely as I snatched it out of his hand.

There came the carriage out of the night, the horses gleaming rather like the sword, as if they, too, were forged of cold steel. Blessed Tanit! Could they be? Or maybe that breathlike mist rising from their nostrils was akin to the exhalations of steam, dangerous and powerful if the pressure grows too high. The coachman hauled the vehicle to a stop in front of us, and the footman leaped down from the back to slam open the steps and wrench back the door.

"Where were you?" demanded Andevai.

"There's more trouble here than what you see," said the coachman. "We discovered a cache of rifles, several hundred in crates—"

"Rifles! Within a two days' journey of Four Moons House? Catherine, get in!"

I clambered in and sagged onto the bench. I sheathed my sword as Andevai climbed up and dropped onto the seat opposite me.

"Rifles!" he said, to the air, to the ancestors, to no one.

The footman closed door and stair; the carriage creaked and shifted as he—she?—leaped onto the back. Andevai slammed back the shutter and stuck out his head.

"What did you do with the rifles?" he called.

"Trouble coming!" called the coachman with a laugh. "Your illusion has melted, Magister."

"It will have vanished when I touched the sword," retorted Andevai. "Not because I lost control of the illusion! Or was too weak to sustain it. Cold steel cuts soul and magic alike. You know that."

"I don't think he was doubting you," I muttered under my breath. "Just reporting a fact."

"The rifles are so much scrap metal now, Magister," said the footman from up behind.

Andevai glanced at me, then closed the shutter so hard the carriage resounded. I twisted the hilt of my ghost sword, and the blade slipped back inside its intangible sheath, although it still appeared doubled in my vision. As the carriage slewed around, he pulled a wisp of illumination like a disembodied flame out of the air and stared at the sword with narrowed eyes.

"It looks like a black cane," he said irritably. "I can think of no possible way the Barahal family could possess cold steel. Where did your people get it?"

I kept my mouth closed tight as a burst of voices shouting in frustrated outrage rose from the town behind us. The carriage gained speed along the road, our ride so smooth I began to wonder if we were actually running along on the surface of the turnpike or if we had risen above it on a tide of magic. My head swam dizzily. My teeth began to chatter.

He swept the thick fur blanket off the seat beside him and thrust it onto my lap. "You look like you need this. You may as well rest, as it's obvious from that mulish expression you're not going to tell me anything." He stared at his hands as if staring at death, his brows drawn down and his expression resolving again into his habitual scornful anger.

I scooted into the corner farthest from him and bundled myself into the blanket, wrapping it tightly around me because I was shuddering. Maybe most of my convulsive shivering was from the bitter cold and maybe it was just exhaustion that had drained all warmth from me. I rested my head against the padded side and closed my eyes.

Perhaps I dozed.

At some indeterminate point, I opened my eyes to see him, wedged in the opposite corner in his smudged and disheveled traveling clothes, with no coat or blanket, staring at his hands as he wove light into helmets and horses, let them dissolve, and pulled new illusions into miniature form.

"The light and shadow must reflect and darken consistent with the conditions of light at the time of the illusion," he muttered to himself as he manipulated the patterns of light lifting and shadow falling.

Tiny soldiers faded, and a face appeared: lips, nose, eyes, and a shadow's skein of long black hair. My face. He was weaving my face in light.

Before he could glance up to study me and see me looking, I shut my eyes.

The carriage rocked, jostling me, then steadied.

With my eyes closed, I could not fight off exhaustion. Thought faded.

When I woke again, he was asleep, propped as uncomfortably upright in his corner as I was in mine. It was the first time I had seen him asleep, his face in repose. Bee would have proclaimed his lineaments handsome: his lean face set off by the beard trimmed very, very short around a well-shaped jawline, his long black eyelashes, his skin the brown of raw umber seen in painters' studios.

But Bee had not been forced to marry him. *It is easy to admire what you must not endure*, as my father had written years ago during the Iberian war.

My husband had killed two men in front of my eyes, and how many more in Adurnam's Rail Yard I would likely never know. I fixed the ghost sword in its sheath between my body and the carriage and shut my eyes, but could not find rest.

14

Yet in the end I did sleep as we traveled east through the night, into dawn, and across the morning and came to a town on whose outskirts rose a House inn. I now understood these inns must be wrapped around with protections able to fend off assaults from whatever enemies the Houses had accumulated over the centuries since their founding. Should be able, although they had failed in Adurnam and in Southbridge Londun behind us.

We pulled into the inn court as hostlers hurried out. I staggered in Andevai's wake into a parlor furnished with a sideboard, two couches, and a polished table with four chairs. While Andevai exchanged formal greetings with the steward in charge of the inn, I collapsed on the blessedly comfortable and unmoving daybed with my cane tucked against me. I fell asleep at once, waking when the door opened and servants carried in food on trays and set the covered dishes on the sideboard with platters and utensils and cups gracefully laid on one of the tables.

"We'll serve ourselves," said Andevai. He was standing at the window, as far away from me as was possible in the chamber. The servants shot nervous glances at him and hurried out, shutting the door behind them.

I staggered up onto unsteady legs and stumbled over to the sideboard, thinking I might expire just from the glorious smell. After washing, I uncovered every dish and heaped up a platter with so much food that my eyes hurt even as my mouth watered. I sat down and started eating.

After a while, having devoured about half the bounty, I paused.

He was still staring out the window into the gauzy light of an overcast day, the light beginning a subtle shift that heralded the arrival of one of the cross-quarter days that divide the year. The festival of Samhain was observed throughout much of the north, marking the end of the light half of the year and the beginning of the dark half. As day follows night, so light follows dark, and thereby Samhain, also called Hallows Night and Hallows Day, was celebrated by some as the end of the old year and the beginning of the new.

"Why don't you ever eat?" I asked.

Without looking toward me, he spoke softly. "Every time I work magic, I am fed."

I set down my knife and spoon, the path of destruction I had cut across the platter looking suddenly ominous. "What do you mean?"

His gaze flashed my way before he turned back to survey the out of doors. "The secret belongs to those who know how to keep silent."

"The mage Houses would have to say so, wouldn't they? Secrecy is the key to power."

He left the window and walked to the table, standing with a hand on the back of a chair. "What do you mean?"

Was that anger that creased his eyes? We were both exhausted, and he looked considerably worse for the troubles we had encountered: His right sleeve was torn, his jacket rumpled, and his trousers stained black at the knees where he had knelt in the ashes.

"It's what my father always said."

"Why would he say that?"

"That should be obvious, if you know the history of my lineage."

He shifted the chair back and sat opposite me. "The Barahals are a clan of hired soldiers, of Kena'ani stock, what others call Phoenicians. Their mother house is based in the city of Gadir on the coast of southern Iberian near the Straits of Hercules. I was informed one evening that I was required to travel to Adurnam to marry the eldest daughter of the Adurnam Hassi Barahal house. Haste was required, so I left the next morning. Beyond that, I was told nothing, and I've had no time to learn anything else."

"You were warned the Barahals would have little conversation and fewer manners."

He crossed his arms and leaned back.

I knew I should not bait him, so I shoveled in more food. Yet, having chewed and swallowed, I was gnawed to bursting by my swelling grievances. I opened my mouth to eat more and instead words poured out. "It's true the Barahals have served as mercenaries for hundreds of years. But we began as messengers. Couriers. We were not always uncouth soldiers, brutes paid to kill."

He did not flinch. No doubt he had forgotten about the two men he had so recently slain.

I backtracked, anyway, lest he think I was criticizing him. "You must know that the Kena'ani built a sea-trading empire three thousand years ago."

"Yes, yes, even I must know that. Everyone educated knows that the Romans and the Phoenicians fought to a standstill in the Mediterranean wars two thousand years ago."

"Well, after that, we maintained our ports and markets and ships against the might of their land empire. In Europa, meanwhile, the Celtic tribes and nations shifted allegiances and quarreled and built their cities and armies with the grain and metals we Kena'ani brought them."

"I'm not sure from this tale how sea traders came to be mercenaries and spies."

"You have to know of the salt plague in western Africa that released the ghouls from the depths of the salt mines."

"Of course. The Koumbi Mande people—my ancestors—were the first ones attacked."

"It happens that about the same time as the diaspora, the nation known as Persia rode out of the eastern Levant and conquered the great Kena'ani city of Qart Hadast, which you may know as Carthage. So my people also had to flee their home. Some went to their kinfolk in Gadir and the Iberian colonies. Many traveled even farther north, to Adurnam, Havery, and Lutetia, for instance. Many were cut off from their old sea-trading routes, so they had to find a new way to make a living. That is how the Hassi Barahal lineage was established. First we became messengers. Couriers often have to fight to protect themselves, so some hired out as soldiers. And that led to scouting, spying, and scholarly work."

"Is spying meant to be less uncouth than soldiering?"

My anger sparked. "Many condemn mercenaries for their trade without considering the culpability of those who pay them. That's what I meant. People with power do not want to share the secrets that allow them to stay in power. Or at least, that's what my father always said."

He kept his gaze steady on me. "So the Barahals decided to make their living stealing secrets from one set of powerful people and selling them to another."

I found wisdom enough to imprison any further statements inside my throat by working halfway through a mound of baked squash drenched in butter. I patted my mouth with a linen napkin and with vast self-control considered three pink slices of roasted beef and a fan of sliced apples precariously tucked against them on the edge of the plate. *Keep silence.*

"I sense there is more you wish to say," he said.

"That's all I feel is safe to say. My father spent his life traveling. He called himself a natural historian. He recorded his observations. Whenever he had reason to sojourn in a city with a branch house of any of the Hassi Barahal cousins, he would leave his full journals with them. In time, the journals were gathered under my uncle and aunt's roof."

"Thus you prove my point." He reached across the table, prized an apple slice from my plate, and ate it. "Those who remain silent cannot have their secrets stolen and then sold in the market, or to their enemies."

I felt anger flush my cheeks. "That's not what my father was doing. Natural historians seek to understand the world. Some scholars hoard what they've learned, as dragons are said to hoard gold and gems. Others choose to share so many may be enlightened."

"To what purpose?"

"To what purpose do the Houses wield cold magic?"

He snagged another apple slice and paused, the apple like a tutor's rod, held to emphasize a point. "Before the Houses rose, farmers and craftsmen labored under the whim of princes and lords, who strove with each other in incessant war."

"That's what the Houses must say, isn't it? I don't see how they are so different from princes. They just use a different weapon to hold on to their power."

"So say the radicals, who desire to overturn the harmonious order of things." He ate the slice of apple, picked up a spoon, and dug into the remains of my baked squash. "But the radicals are disruptive spirits, who sow trouble."

"Like destroying an airship?"

He didn't even blink. "We in the north have lived at peace for many generations because of the stability provided by the mage Houses. What do the trolls who brought over that airship know of our land? They call us rats! They live far away across the western ocean. They're interfering with what they do not understand."

I cut the beef into pieces and slid the plate a handbreadth toward the center of the table. Like my father, I was curious about human behavior. "What is it the trolls do not understand? That the Houses stand in the way of innovation and industry?"

"Do they suppose that the technology of combustion will not come to the attention of the unseen courts as its use spreads? That airships will not be viewed as a threat if any attempt is made to mount an expedition over the ice?" With a two-tined fork, he speared a bit of meat and ate it, and then another piece and a third. I was so engrossed in watching him eat off my plate without apparently realizing he was doing so that his subsequent words floated past like clouds out of my reach. "Are they so naïve and ignorant to believe that the unseen courts will not retaliate as they have in the past, and that when the courts retaliate, many more people will suffer than will ever hope to benefit by these clever toys?"

"You believe in the existence of the unseen courts," I breathed as he stabbed more meat. I sat with all the wind knocked out of me as he ate through most of the meat before I could find breath enough to speak. "How can we know for sure, when no human or troll has ever seen the courts?"

He set down his fork. "I do not 'believe' in the unseen courts, Catherine, any more than I 'believe' in the sun. Like the spirit world, the courts exist despite my belief or lack of belief, whatever that means. Isn't it strange how the new modes of fashion ignore the truth, or claim it is something else? How can you *not* believe in the courts when you are being conveyed in a carriage harnessed to creatures molded in the manner of horses that have not been changed out since Adurnam? If they were ordinary horses, they would have long since foundered and expired. You may naturally perceive the coachman and footman who serve me as men, but they are not."

"Oh," was all I said as I snagged the last piece of meat. I could hoard my own secrets!

"You don't believe me!" he said triumphantly. Condescendingly. He grabbed the last slice of apple. "But it is nevertheless true. Why did your father, the natural historian, refuse to recognize the existence of the unseen courts?"

"He didn't disbelieve. He just had no proof. They are 'unseen,' after all. He recorded a hundred village stories in his journals about the spirit world and the courts. But stories, of themselves, are not proof."

"The Wild Hunt is not a story. Those with too much power, or too much curiosity, are hunted down and eradicated. Much as we hunt down and eradicate pests and mice and crawling things from our houses. Where is your father now, Catherine?"

I set down my utensils and bit my lip. My eyes stung.

He looked at his fork. At my plate. At me. His color seemed heightened. He slapped down the fork, scraped back the chair, and jumped to his feet.

"We've stayed too long." He crossed to the sideboard and rang the bell.

The door opened and an older man stepped into the room. His springy black hair was plaited in rows. His indigo boubou was so crisp and crinkly that the cloth rustled as he moved. "Magister, what is your wish?" His voice was as harmonious as his appearance.

Andevai relaxed and acknowledged him with a polite nod. "A change of clothing both for myself and my wife, maester. Something more appropriate for her, if you please."

"These fit me," I broke in. "Other garb might not be so accommodating for travel."

"Ah. Well, then, fit her with fur-lined boots and cloak and

gloves, a woolen underjacket. She'll need furs for the carriage. Heated bricks."

"I'd like to wash," I said, a little desperately, feeling all my dirt.

"I'll have a basin with warmed water brought, with towels, maestra," said the man. "Then you may at least wash your face and hands."

"That will be all there is time for," said Andevai. "Make it quick."

"And a basket of food to take with us in the carriage," I called as the door swung shut.

I heaped more food on my platter. It was easier to eat than to think of my parents. Or the Wild Hunt. Had the Wild Hunt killed my parents because they'd known something they weren't meant to? But, no, it wasn't possible. They had not died on Hallows Night.

Andevai went to stand at the window, as cold and proud as if we had never spoken or as if he had never eaten off my plate as casually as I might have forked delicacies off Bee's. I had a suspicion that he might not really have been aware he was eating, that he'd done it without thinking.

That he was embarrassed.

Impossible.

I set to the food, aware I had little time to wolf down as much as possible. He spoke not one word further. The older man returned, and Andevai went away with him. After I had used the water closet, a young woman with flame-red hair and creamy skin entered with a brush and cloth to wipe what dirt and stains she could from my clothing as I washed my face, hands, arms, and finally my feet in blissfully hot water.

Boots, a cloak, gloves: all were delivered and of the highest quality and best cut, of a style seen in tailors' windows in shops we Barahals could never afford to enter. At House inns they evidently kept such expensive garments in storage to be changed off like horses, because when Andevai returned, he was magnificent in a striped orange and brown dash jacket, ochre-colored trousers, and a cloth tied at his neck with such a modest knot that I knew I was in the presence of exceptional taste and wealth such as Bee and I and the little girls could only exclaim over in the pages of the Almanac while we sewed our dresses at home from last year's patterns or altered castoffs we'd bought at the petticoat market. The only piece of clothing us girls possessed that was sewn for us by a dressmaker were our riding clothes: fitted with loose trousers beneath an overskirt cut for riding and a shirt and jacket cut for ease of movement in case a riding Barahal woman needed also to use her sword. I smoothed my clothing self-consciously. Andevai frowned—more of a wince, perhaps—and indicated the door.

The carriage waited in the courtyard. Flakes of snow spun in the air; the light had taken on a sheen, as though noncorporeal servants had been busy polishing the underside of the clouds, the better to complement the sartorial splendor of my husband.

"What is it?" he demanded, a flash of self-consciousness in his tightening mouth as he looked at me looking at him. He had very well-shaped lips.

I was seized by a sudden, unpleasant, and almost overwhelming urge to *kiss* him. Just a touch, nothing more than that, just to see what his lips tasted of.

Almost. Then I remembered how we had come to be here.

"Just recalling how good the buttered squash was," I said in a strained voice, feeling heat rise to the roots of my hair as I looked away.

The footman, in outward appearance still male, flipped down the stair and opened the door, then stepped back. Her dark gaze met mine for a heavy moment. At the head of the horses, the coachman caught my eye and raised an eyebrow as in a question but said nothing.

Clutching my cane in a trembling hand, I climbed into the carriage to find it swept and cleaned, a pile of furs heaped on one bench and a covered basket set against the other door, the one we never used. Feeling mutinous, I reached out to jigger the latch. I snatched my hand back just as the carriage rocked with Andevai's weight as he climbed in.

The door was closed. The coachman called his alert. We rumbled out of the courtyard and turned onto the road, heading east. On the town walls flapped banners bearing three horse heads arranged in a star, the sigil of the Cantiaci princes who ruled this region.

I avoided looking at him. It was all I could do.

East we rolled for the rest of the day, halted only by toll gates. We passed by the sprawling city of Cantiacorum and much later the stolid walls of Rutupiae. We descended into the great valley carved by the Rhenus River, crossing streams via bridges or ferries. As night engulfed us, we continued on, passing by villages lit by sentry lamps and guarded by shivering night watchmen. Andevai did not speak; neither did I. Not too late, although it was hard to tell with the sky overcast, we arrived at another House inn, greeted as always by a remarkably alert staff given the hour. I was shown to a room with a bed, and, after pulling off my boots, I threw myself across it with my ghost sword beside me and slept until dawn.

Indeed, I was surprised to find it light when an elderly woman roused me, showing me a basin where I could wash. She explained that there was not time for a bath as she helped me straighten and brush my clothing in the kindliest manner imaginable; she then admired my hair as she brushed it out and helped me pin it up again. A shy girl brought a tray laden with poached eggs, a rasher of bacon, bread warm from the oven, and a luscious pear.

After eating, I went out to the courtyard where Andevai

paced by the carriage and, seeing me, unclenched his hands. The footman nodded. The coachman touched the rim of his hat, eyes crinkling in the smile that did not touch his lips. In the mirror in the Barahal house, he had appeared as a man, no different than he looked now. Perhaps he was simply a man. Or perhaps he was so powerful a creature disguised in human seeming that even a mirror could not unshadow his glamor. Andevai had referred to them as servants of the courts. Which meant Andevai, or the magisters who ruled his House, were so powerful that they could bind and rule creatures whose magic was surely as powerful as their own.

Feeling every jab of the bitter cold, I climbed into the carriage, my limbs like sodden logs except where they were lancing with a myriad of pains as comforting as stabbing knives.

Andevai settled in his usual place, at the opposite corner.

"Why did you let me sleep?" I asked as the footman closed the door.

He looked as surprised as if I *had* leaned over to kiss him. "Weren't you tired? Anyhow, I had certain—necessary offerings—that I had to attend to."

The steps were raised; the carriage shifted as the footman leaped onto the back. I braced myself as the wheels ground over gravel and bumped up a ramp; then we made the road, the constant road, running east into a brightening day.

"We are almost home," he added, although it was difficult to tell whether the words were spoken with joy or perturbation.

In the misty dawn light, he kept the window open. I huddled in the warm furs and stared at the land outside, dense with spruce or pine and the occasional stand of birch and here and there warmwood like oak and beech on south-facing slopes protected by the configuration of the land. Forest opened to pasturage, and in the distance rose a village of round houses set in a precise ring. Here and there, flocks of goats and sheep probed for the remnants of summer's grass. The mist burned off; the sky was cloudless, a wintry blue the color of Brennan's eyes. What had become of Chartji and Godwik and Brennan and Kehinde? When they reached Adurnam, would they guess the truth about who had destroyed the airship?

We passed other villages. Every field was plowed under against winter's freeze. Orchards, tree trunks packed in straw, raised skeletal arms.

He watched the landscape, and I watched him sidelong. He had trimmed his beard and mustache. It was a masterpiece of subtle sculpting, highlighting the strong line of his jaw. Had he no body servant to tend to his clothing and toilette? I tried to imagine the coachman wielding razor and scissors but could not, and decided that among those employed at the inns, there must be men specializing in this service for preening young bucks like Andevai. Yet then why would he not travel with his own body servant? To the Houses, it would be an insignificant expense; they had entire families and clans and villages bound to them, what Brennan and the law called clientage, which might extend unbroken for generation after generation with lit-tle hope for change. I was fortunate, really. When my father and mother had died, the Hassi Barahal clan might have done any-thing with me they wished, according to the law, but the Kena'ani valued their children too much to sell them away.

Aunt and Uncle's hand had been forced. Their anguish had been real. So I had to ask myself, Why? What did they owe Four Moons House, and why would a mage House possibly want a daughter of the Hassi Barahal clan in its keeping? Did the Hassi Barahals hold some secret that might damage the mages, and by taking me, had the mages therefore bound my family to silence, with me as an unwilling hostage?

It simply made no sense.

Andevai grabbed the edge of the window, his body tense as

he gazed over the landscape. What did he see that was hidden to my eyes? Harvested fields making an expanse of white stubble. A double ring of stockade, an outer palisade surrounding gardens and byres and sheds and an inner man-high fence surrounding a village of blocky, mazelike compounds. A slope fenced for pasture with a stream glittering along one side. A pond skinned with early season ice, as fragile as if it were spun of sugar. A grove of black pine with one towering giant in its midst.

A man, stiff and slow with age, was leading an ox toward the village.

Andevai watched for a long time, leaning out to keep the houses in view as we trundled east. When at last he sank back onto the seat, he covered his eyes with a hand.

Had I seen a tear? Or was that only a trick of the light?

15

After a while, he lowered his hand and slid shut the window, leaving us in the dim confines, ripe with the smell of our sweat after so many days.

I had begun to shiver, despite the smothering furs. "I...I wanted to ask if there is anything I should know. Proper greetings? Words or gestures I should not use?"

"Do what I tell you, and don't speak. There's far too much for you to learn to start now. Afterward there will be time."

"After what?"

"We must be purified to pass onto the estate. Then you'll be brought before the head of Four Moons House and accepted into the house."

"Isn't he a very powerful magister?"

His tone sharpened. "Naturally he is. And for another thing, don't sound foolish, Catherine. Just say nothing. Don't embarrass me—" He broke off. After a pause, he finished. "Don't embarrass your people."

The carriage slowed as we turned off the main road onto a gravel road that crackled beneath hooves and wheels. My pulse outraced the leisurely pace of the horses. I wondered if it was actually possible to faint from fear as the sensational tales we read in the almanacs and saw on the stage would have it. I must endure this, just as my father had endured the wars and had written of his hatred for all that made life a misery for ordinary people. I must endure, because I must. That was all. It had to be done. It was already done.

The carriage stopped. Andevai drew in a breath. The door was opened, the stair lowered. He got out.

As I made ready to follow him, he gestured like an ax striking. "It's forbidden to bring cold steel into the gatehouse. Leave it in the carriage."

The sword already felt like a part of me. I hated to leave it, and yet when he frowned, I knew I had no choice. Swordless, I followed him onto a wide fan of raked gravel fronting a massive white stone gate with four arches. Each archway was fitted with massive iron-clad wood gates, and above each arch was carved one phase of the moon. Walls stretched out to either side as far as I could see, high enough that I could discern nothing on the other side except the crowns of trees. To our right, built out from the wall, stood a spacious lodge, the gatehouse. Its walls were decorated with bright geometric lines and patterns. It was set off from the road by a low garden wall, behind which lay a desiccated garden, oval in shape and notable for pruned evergreen hedges, a single unremarkable stone pillar as tall as a man, and an elaborate tiered fountain. Water ran down this excrescence of stone to splash into twin basins formed like the halves of melons. On the rim of the fountain rested several bowls.

Andevai halted at the gate with hands extended, palms up. I copied the gesture, so afraid I would do something wrong that tears blurred my vision.

A pair of men in servants' livery came running from the lane beside the house to take up stations within the garden. The door of the lodge was opened. Four women, wearing indoor slippers, hurried down the steps to stand on either side of a brick path that led by a circuitous route, not a straight line, to the square vestibule. Two young men dressed in fashionable clothing came out, smirking and nudging each other. I could not see Andevai's face, but his posture became more rigid and he seemed to be breathing faster. As people took up positions on either side of the steps, they started calling to one another in a rhythmic way. Others took up this chant and began to clap and sing. My ears burned.

As if summoned by the song, a woman emerged from the interior and stood on the threshold. She was tall and robust, older than my aunt but not elderly, and dressed in a long robe made of a black cloth marked with white patterns. Her complexion was lighter than Andevai's, her brown skin dusted with freckles, and her hair was tied up in a scarf that had pulled back just enough to reveal tightly kinked dark red hair. She raised both hands, as if giving permission.

I followed him meekly through the gate. We halted at the fountain, where he picked up a bowl, dipped it in the water, and advanced to a stunted leafless tree festooned with amulets, ribbons, and charms. He poured the water at the base of the trunk. I groped for a bowl, and someone laughed. He turned, saw me, and his eyes widened as he made a sudden panicked gesture with one hand. I stared stupidly at him as a whisper passed through the gathering, causing the song's cadences to falter. He pointed.

Oh! With a foot, I indicated the other basin to see if I was meant to use it instead, and several voices choked down gasps. Andevai changed color. Clearly I had committed some horrible, inadvertent offense. I shut my eyes, wishing I could vanish just like the heroes and heroines in the tales.

But couldn't I? Not vanish precisely, but hide myself, even in the sight of cold mages? The realization hit me so hard that my mouth opened and I sucked in courage enough to open my eyes and demand with my gaze that he find some way to let me know what to do. With his chin, he indicated the other basin, so I knelt at its rim, all the while watching him and his efforts to direct my ignorance without speaking and without gesturing in a way that would make him look as ridiculous as he must by now feel. Everyone was staring, but I knew better than to look at them. By sheer will, I took up a bowl from the other basin, filled it, and with an iron resolve paced to the tree and emptied the bowl rather more clumsily than I had hoped over the earth. Atop the cold dirt, water stiffened into a lacework of frost.

He gestured that I should follow as he walked to the lodge's entrance. He knelt on the lowest of the stone steps. The song ceased. Folk watched with the patience of vultures. There were more of them now, having come in from the fields or the house or the servants' wing.

"Magister," Andevai said. "I return to you."

"Be greeted on your return to your home." The woman with red hair gestured, and an attendant offered him a bowl of water. He drank and handed back the bowl.

Awkwardly, I knelt beside him. When I opened my mouth to speak the greeting, nothing came out, not even a croak. She examined me without moving or speaking, her gaze as unfathomable as ice. My hands went cold and my face flamed hot. Let this agony pass quickly!

Behind me, someone tittered.

Anger creased her expression, and the sound cut off. An attendant offered me a bowl of water, but I was shaking so hard that drops slopped over the side. I barely managed to slurp down a mouthful and hand the bowl back before spilling the entire thing. Although no one spoke, I felt both curiosity and contempt like spoken words. Andevai did not look at me. I thought he was flushed, no doubt humiliated by my awkwardness.

She turned her back on us. Andevai rose. I rose, half tripping on the step. We walked at her heels into a wide entry hall, where Andevai took off his boots. I followed suit. We stepped up into a long room whose walls were painted with scenes of an unfamiliar landscape with a wide river, many exotic birds, and strange-looking trees. Benches lined the walls. A stool carved out of a single block of wood sat on a raised floor at the other end of the chamber. Servants took my cloak, coat, and gloves. She sat on the stool, facing us. Andevai sat on a quilted square of cloth, and I folded down gracelessly beside him on a separate square of cloth. He offered me no encouraging smiles, no glances of camaraderie. He kept his head bowed and his gaze fixed on folded hands. As soon as the chamber was empty and the doors closed, the woman spoke.

"I did not want her to feel shamed in front of strangers, so I said nothing. For her sake, if not your own pride, you might have prepared her better, Vai."

"We faced unexpected trouble on the road," he said to his hands, his expression quite rigid. "But that means nothing, Magister. You are correct. I did not think."

"Now she must come before the mansa, likewise. So be it."

"I saw how Suma and Cuirthi were hovering like wasps, waiting to sting me."

"The poor manners of a hyena do not excuse the man."

"You are right. Their behavior does not excuse mine."

"Get through this day, and I will send some of my own women to serve and assist her."

"For this I thank you, Magister."

She grunted. "Do not forget, Vai, that you do not answer to me, but to the mansa. He expected you to return two days ago. We must talk no longer." She clapped her hands.

The doors opened, and attendants entered carrying trays. One was a basin and pitcher for washing. The other held a tureen of white porridge streaked with honey and several small bowls and spoons. My mouth watered. I heard a murmur and turned; folk crowded in the door, peering in: A pair of fashionable young men nudged each other as if in expectation of a good laugh. A pretty young woman in exceptionally rich clothing stared at Andevai, but I couldn't judge whether she admired him or despised him: Love's gaze could look like the intensity of contempt, as the poets said. Anyhow, he did not once look toward her.

After we washed our hands, the woman spooned out porridge with her right hand and offered him a bowl; she then offered the second to me. Of course I reached with my sword hand. A man's laugh rang out. Andevai's lips thinned. Emotion sparked in the flare of his eyes. I pulled my left arm back as though I'd been slapped.

Lips thinned with annoyance, the woman nodded toward the doors. At once they were shut, leaving us again alone. With a speaking look, she offered me the bowl with her right hand, and this time I accepted it with my right hand, although I wondered if I dared eat under her scrutiny. Yet when she took a bowl for herself, I knew I dared not refuse to eat—not if she were eating, too.

The magister balanced the bowl on her right thigh and ate, as did Andevai. Naturally I wanted to eat with my left hand, but instead I set the bowl on the curve of my inside right knee and, praying to every god known in the ancient days of Kena'an, I scooped and ate with my right without the bowl falling off my leg. I was so relieved to be finished that I felt tears in my eyes and blinked to smother them.

When we had finished, her attendants cleared everything away. The doors were again opened to allow in what seemed a crowd of elaborately dressed men and women. The young men whispered to each other as they glanced at Andevai with smiles as sharp as cold steel.

"Now," said the magister, "you must bathe more quickly than I would like for the proper doing of it."

"No surprise there with Vai," said one of the young men. "Him accustomed to the dirt as he is." Others sniggered.

The magister raised her voice, declaiming, "The new year rides down upon us. We must make fast our shutters for the hallowing tide." This comment quieted the sniggering.

As Andevai rose, I rose and was taken into hand by a pair of healthily robust women as alike as cousins. They led me down a bewildering maze of corridors—no straight lines in this house!—into a chamber half filled with a tiled pool steaming warmth. A curtain hung from the ceiling. The pool extended beneath it. I heard men talking on the other side.

"She's always favored him, rather like she favors those hounds of hers. Faithful pets, eh?"

They laughed, but fell silent as others entered the chamber, maybe Andevai.

"Maestra," said the elder of my attendants in a low voice. "Your clothes?"

"I…I…Am I meant to bathe? I don't know—"

"Did the young magister not tell you?" she replied with a grimace.

The other spoke over her. "He wouldn't likely know it needed telling, would he? He hardly knows himself. The spirit works in peculiar ways, does it not? Such a potent brew poured into so inappropriate a vessel."

"He's just ignorant, Brigida. Here, now, maestra. To enter past the warded gates, you must be purified. For you, immersion is enough. When the mansa accepts you formally, there will be other rites, and lessons in the proper rituals."

My ancestors had a similar ritual. Stripping off my clothing and dunking myself in heated baths I could manage. I unbuttoned my riding jacket as they worked on the fastenings of my riding skirt.

"We can bring you new clothing, something more…suitable, maestra."

"I'd rather keep—"

"Yes," they agreed, as if expecting nothing else from an outsider like me. When I was naked, they looked me over much as they might examine a broodmare, studying its conformation. "Your hair, maestra."

I unpinned it.

"Ah! Ah!" they exclaimed as my tresses fell free, and on the other side of the curtain fell a silence, voices stilled, ears listening. "What lovely hair, maestra! A true glory!" Their voices rang within the stone, and I wondered if they were speaking so loudly to make sure the men across the way could hear their praise.

Only a curtain separated that side from this. I was vulnerable. How easy it would be for someone to brush past that curtain and thrust themselves onto this side. I ventured a toe in the water, thinking I could hide in the pool. It was blessedly warm.

"No, maestra. Here is a brush and soap. Clean yourself first."

I dipped the brush into a bucket of hot water and scrubbed until they were satisfied.

"Maestra! The bracelet! The locket, too. You must enter with nothing."

I removed both.

"Is the bracelet a gift from your mother?"

"No." I would not tell them that I had only two things left of my mother: first, the warning she had spoken that had taken root in my head; second, a single memory not of her face but of a strong arm carrying me, of her body smelling of sweat and steel. I descended steps into the water, to my knees, to my hips, to my breasts. The water lapped around me, stirred by a similar descent on the far side of the curtain, and I thought, *that is him entering the pool naked like me*, and I ducked under to let the water swallow me because it was easier than thinking of his body.

Like all the pure elements and like mirrors, water offers a conduit into the spirit world that lies intertwined with our own.

What lies in the spirit world we cannot see; we haven't the vision to perceive it. Some can reach into the spirit world and draw out filaments of its essence. In this wise, blacksmiths handle fire, potters earth, bards and djeliw the air that gives breath for songs and tales. As for the cold mages, no one outside the Houses understands the source of their power. It exists, as the great ice sheets exist, covering the northern reaches of Hibernia, covering the lands north of the Baltic Ice Sea, covering the Helvitic Alps. Reaching, so Kehinde at the inn had speculated, across the northern pole of the world to join with another vast shelf of ice that smothered the north of the continent we called Amerike which lay beyond the western ocean, the continent that had given birth to trolls instead of humans. How my father would have wished to converse with Godwik, who had also seen the face of the ice!

A shining face, masked and unkindly. The cold sun, glinting on the ice, blinds. A sharp deadly voice says, *We need a new weapon for the war. A courier who can walk between the lands.*

I came up gasping for air, my heart thundering as if I had woken from a nightmare twisted out of my memories and fears.

"Again," called the women.

From behind the curtain, I heard a splash as Andevai came up, his attendants calling to him as mine had called to me: "Again."

With a gasp, I dropped beneath the surface, eyes open.

Diviners pour water on a flat surface and see true visions within.

I saw Bee, striding down an unknown street on her short legs in a haste of anger and weeping, her mouth moving in full furious spate. She was yelling at someone, but it wasn't a street after all; it was a canal of rushing light, and she was walking all unaware into the mouth of a golden dragon whose fire flowed like water to obliterate her.

I flailed to the surface, except that the air seemed still and sticky, as though it were not air at all. As through a long tunnel resonant with echoes, I heard female voices speaking far away.

"Poor Esi was very disappointed. It's all she's talked of this year, a betrothal for her with Andevai. She would never accept being second wife to an outsider like this one, so I wonder why the mansa did not have his nephew take this one as his third wife and let Esi marry the young man? That would have solved the problem."

"Prohibited in the contract, so I heard. That the girl could not be brought in as a secondary wife. It is Kena'anic custom, I believe, that states a man may marry one woman only."

"That can't be true!"

"It's said a Kena'ani woman may marry more than one man, if she chooses. What would you think of that, eh?"

Their laughter swept like waves.

"When I was young, maybe! It's just as well, for Esi's sake, that she was not allowed to marry Andevai. Youth is handsome, but youth fades. His upbringing, his people, will always drag him down. Sss! Why do you think he was sent to the duty of this contract? If harm comes of the binding, better it fall on him than on one of the precious lads."

"Maybe. Maybe not. The high magisters say little, but you know it's whispered Andevai has as cold a reach as they've seen in three generations. Maybe they thought he was the only one strong enough. Is she still under?"

I was still under, arms flailing and groping upward, and yet my hands never broke the flashing surface. My lungs were empty. There was no floor to push off of, nothing under my feet, only an abyss of black water like my future into which I was sinking.

Drowning.

I am six years old and the water closes over my head and my mother's strong hand slips out from mine as she is wrenched away by the furious current. No amount of clawing at the rushing liquid aids me. I have to open my mouth for a breath of air, but all that rushes in is water, filling my lungs and dragging me down into the depths.

The spirits that guarded the House did not want me. They were dragging me down into my worst memory, the one I had tried so hard to block out.

We are drowning in the Rhenus River, and I have lost both Papa and Mama.

"Daughter," a male voice says urgently. His powerful arms push me up.

I breached, heaving and coughing, and there I stood in the tiled pool, the water up to only my shoulders as I shook in the grip of memory, blinded by tears.

"Once more," they said.

I was afraid.

After that I was always afraid of deep water, which is shameful for the Kena'ani.

But I had no choice.

I pretended that a mother's bracelet ringed my wrist, giving me my mother's courage. I pretended that my papa was waiting with his stories and his cheerful smile. He would never let anyone harm me. I took in a huge shuddering breath and dropped down under the water.

And came up again, water streaming down my face. I glanced around, fearing it had been too easy, that I had drowned in truth and emerged as one of the rephaim into my stone tomb.

The sleep of the dead was not likely enlivened by men singing crude songs about male anatomy and sexual prowess or its particular lack, which I heard from beyond the curtain separating life and death or, at least right now, woman and man. I was warmed through from the heated water but shivering in my heart as I dripped up onto the stone. Yet, after all, memories cannot kill you. My companions roughly toweled me dry, although my thick hair remained damp. It had to be combed out wet, no easy task, although they seemed happy to fuss over my hair as they plied me with questions.

"He'll not have approached the marriage bed until the mansa has accepted you into the house."

A pause, pregnant with intention. I cleared my throat. When they saw I didn't mean to answer this impertinent comment, they went on.

"Is it true you Kena'anic women can take two husbands?"

I was thankful to find something to feel annoyed about, because now I could talk. "It's not common but not unknown. If a woman of stature is head of a trading house in a foreign city, she would, of course, marry a Kena'ani man who would spend much of the year traveling for trade. Then she might choose to take a secondary husband from among the local families, someone whose connections would bring benefit to the house."

"How can it be that men would put up with such an arrangement?"

"Why do some people demand it of women but not of men? It is just another way of doing things. As my father would have said, folk will have their customs according to their nature and their surroundings."

"You're a bold speaker, young one. I would advise you keep your lips pressed firmly closed when you meet with the mansa."

But they were not unfriendly as they pinned up my hair and wrapped it in a scarf according to the fashion of the House. I heard no hostile edge to their voice, unlike what it seemed Andevai was enduring over on the other side under a litany of songs, laughter, and taunting jokes. Of his voice, I heard no whisper.

"Is it your custom that his attendants should speak so cruelly to him?" I asked.

"Young men will taunt," said the tawny-haired woman. "It's their way."

The other continued. "It isn't that surprising, Fama. He is not in his rightful place."

"Honestly, Brigida, you and I both know they resent him because he received abundance where they received scant. Still, they should not hold these grudges. It brings conflict and trouble upon all of us."

"Sss! Best speak of such things later." They exchanged glances that spoke of shared knowledge. The House was like a sea of hidden currents and shifting whirlpools ready to suck me down.

They examined my travel-worn riding clothes with frowns. "You'll need fitting clothing. In time. In time. Go softly. Be respectful. And *don't speak*."

Out I was hustled down a corridor whose walls were woven patterns. I caught a glimpse of a room with a vast hearth and many seats, but my chest was too tight for me to be able to see. It was all I could do to place one foot before the other, to be given coat and cloak and gloves, to be shown a door and step into the overcast day where I walked as stiffly as a sun-struck ghoul along the twisting garden path and over the gravel to a waiting landau.

I halted, staring at the unfamiliar equipage.

The harnessed team consisted of four good-looking horses chosen for build rather than matched by color, a detail of practicality that gave me the courage to accept an attendant's arm as I climbed the steps into the carriage. The magister, warden of the gate, already sat in the seat facing the four-arched gate.

What had happened to our carriage? My sword? The eru and coachman who had accompanied us all this way, whom I had come to feel were my only allies? Like me, they were bound to Four Moons House. Servants might pity me, but they had no power to change what was now happening.

I climbed into the carriage and sat facing the magister with my back to the gate, trying to breathe normally and not in gasps and bursts. Andevai strode out of the house looking like he was eager to leave or eager to arrive or eager to be shed of all this, and I supposed he had come later because he was dressed yet again in a flattering jacket, tailored to his form and ornamented by a thin gold necklace. I looked away.

"Magister," he said from the base of the carriage.

She gestured to give him permission to enter.

I had not asked to enter! One humiliating mistake after the next! I had to behave as my father would have, observing, recording in my mind, and remembering so I could write it down and try to make sense of this bewildering rhythm of rules quite unlike the pragmatic customs of my own people. That's what I would ask for, first of all, when I dared ask: notebooks, ink, pens. If I kept my father's spirit in my heart and imagined his hand guiding mine, then I could behave as he had behaved, a steady walk down turbulent, storm-ridden roads.

Three footmen perched on the back, faces without expression.

A command spoken. A song for our passage. As we crossed under one of the arches, invisible threads caught on me, strings binding my lips and fingers and knees. Then we came clear of the shadow and the pressure released. We rolled to a halt. The warden of the gate descended, Andevai moved to the seat opposite me, and we two alone continued on our way. The horses shifted into an easy trot down a wide avenue that curved first around one slope and then around a copse of black pine and then around a wide pond dense with reeds. We drew up at a ring where the avenue circled a crude stone pillar and split into five paths. Andevai descended and poured water from a flask at the base of the pillar. He turned and looked at me, and for a moment I felt as uncomfortable as I had when Fama and Brigida had examined me when I was naked, as though he were inspecting me and deciding whether what he saw was adequate to the purpose. I did not understand his expressions at all; he was remote from me, and yet must a man not hold back a part of himself if he is to learn how to kill?

He made an impatient gesture. Aei! Of course, I was to make an offering as well. I must copy what he did. Had I already forgotten?

The servants' expressions did not flicker by even one twitch as I clambered down, crunched across the gravel, took the flask from him, and poured water at the base of the pillar. What a fool I must look!

We took the second turning and for some while drove through a vast expanse of orchard. I caught sight of field-workers walking in groups, carrying huge sheaves of straw that they heaped at the base of sapling trees planted among their elders. He leaned forward, scanning the laborers in their humble shawls and simple woolen tunics.

"Stop!" he said. A smile obliterated his habitual mask of annoyed hauteur.

He flipped open the landau's low door and leaped out before the carriage came to a complete halt. By now, the field-workers had seen the carriage. He strode beneath the trees, and a young woman hurried over to greet him. She was tall and, I suppose, handsome, although that was difficult to tell from this distance. Her complexion was much like his, her hair wrapped in a scarf the color of clay. They embraced, then parted, but stood close together, speaking in the flood of words that betokens close knowledge, much to relate and much to hear. The other field-workers trudged away under the trees.

I shut my eyes.

Obviously, this was not Esi, whoever she was, for Esi had been spoken of as a woman born into the highest ranks within the House, descendant of those who had founded Four Moons House long ago, or of those who had married in accompanied by wealth or other valuable connections, or of those who had bred magisters and thus gained prominence.

A mere field-worker, given attention by a House mage, can hope only to become a concubine, if a woman whose status is little more than slave can even be given so high and mighty a title.

What did I expect? Handsome men are likely to find lovers, and how much more easily they may find them when they are also powerful and rich! It was best to face the truth.

I opened my eyes.

She stepped away from him and took three paces toward me before he caught her wrist and pulled her to a halt. They exchanged heated words. She scolded him; he retorted. Even so, they parted with another embrace. He strode back to the carriage as she ran after the other field hands.

He swung up in one huge stride and sat down hard on the seat opposite.

I could not help myself. "Who is she?"

His gaze struck with such fury that I flinched.

But I wasn't to be cowed. I had already drowned, hadn't I? I was already dead to my old life. "If there's some arrangement I need to know about, best you tell me now."

He stared into the orchard as the field-workers walked away into the trees, a song rising as they walked. He spoke so low I thought he was hoping that the footmen, seated behind him, would not hear what he must now confess.

"That is my sister. Seven years ago, walking among those field-workers, that would have been me."

16

It is an odd thing, truly, to feel a twinge of compassion for a person you have no reason to wish to feel sympathy for. An odd thing. We halted at another stone pillar and made another offering. Then we drove up a gentle slope in a straight line as the orchard fell away behind us. The great house, with its central round tower and main edifice with a two-storied wing flown out to the right, loomed before me like a beast waiting to devour me. Whatever words I might have been thinking of saying expired on my tongue.

Or so I thought. For then they abruptly flew out of my mouth. "You were a common laborer? A slave to the land? To Four Moons House?"

"Just keep silence, Catherine," he said in a flat voice. "Can you manage that much?"

I closed my lips on silence, its taste like ashes.

The main estate of Four Moons House was a palace, in its own way, with round rooms at either end and its bulk stretching behind. The carriage pulled up before the grand escalade. Out of the interior swarmed a host of people who formed two lines for a formal greeting.

An elderly man wearing white robes and the gold earrings of a djeli limped out, leaning on a cane, speaking in a kind of sing-song chant. "He returns! He returns! With his power, he was sent out. With his power, he returns. It is sure he has accomplished what was demanded of him." Here he looked at me, and naturally he took a step back, as if surprised by what he saw. The scarf that looked so handsome on the House women made me feel ridiculous.

Up the stairs I walked, looking neither to my left nor right, keeping my head high; that was the sum of what I could manage. I could not look people in the eye; it might not be the custom here. I was also afraid of what I might see in their expressions.

A hand to be shaken, in the radical way, or a kiss between equals as was the custom of my people; there was none of that here. There must be giving way, the lesser before the greater and I in Andevai's wake, or at least within the ripples made by his passing. We mounted the steps, made an offering of water at the threshold, crossed under the door, and passed beneath a roof so high that birds flew in the rafters. To the right and then the left, through corridors wide enough to be chambers and all with heat rising from the floor. Left again, and right, and I found myself standing in a large room beside a high bank of arched windows over windowpaned doors. The glass looked over an expansive and prettily landscaped garden enclosed by the wings of the house, and a high stone wall.

"Catherine," Andevai said, grasping my left elbow with his right hand.

I wished I had my sword as he guided me toward closed double doors reinforced with strips of sullen iron. My father had written: *The strength of the most powerful cold mages can be measured by the magister's ability to extinguish fires and shatter iron.*

A servant opened the right side door. Andevai stepped back to allow the elderly djeli to go in first. Then I had to walk beside him. My throat was choked with tears. My pulse was a hammer of sound in my ears, like runaway horses.

The mansa was standing at a table beneath a rank of

windows, surveying papers strewn across some kind of architectural drawing unrolled and fixed at its edges to lie flat. He could be no one else. He was tall and heavily built. He looked neither old nor young. His face was black and his eyes blacker, although his hair, close-cut, was a coarse, tightly curled red. Maybe he resembled the warden of the gate. Maybe they were cousins, or maybe they weren't related at all but simply both descendants of blacksmiths and sorcerers, their ancestors the mixed children of the Afric south and the Celtic north who had made common cause long ago. They had countered the power of chieftains and princes but had not become lords themselves, at least not in name. For after all, the only son of a prince may rule after his father whether he is a good prince or an incompetent one, but if the only son of a magister is not a mage, then nothing can raise him to that position.

The mansa looked at Andevai, and the mansa looked at me, and I stopped dead because my heart could not beat and my feet could not move. Maybe they spoke formal greetings, the three of them between themselves. I could not be sure because I was empty.

Then the mansa spoke directly to me. His voice was a voice, nothing special and nothing strange in it, except that it commanded me.

"Are you the eldest Hassi Barahal daughter?"

"I am the eldest," I whispered, eyes cast down, remembering Aunt's words.

"You are the eldest Adurnam Hassi Barahal daughter?" he repeated.

"I am the eldest."

"You are the eldest Hassi Barahal daughter?"

"I'm the eldest."

"If I may, Mansa," said the djeli. "What she says is no lie, but I am troubled. If you will allow me, may I ask?"

The mansa nodded.

"Repeat these words as I speak them," said the djeli in his resonant voice. "'I am the eldest daughter born into the Adurnam Hassi Barahal house.'"

"I am the eldest—" *daughter*. I meant to speak the word, but no sound came out of my mouth. "I am the eldest—" *Hassi Barahal*. Still no voice emerged. "But I *am* older than Bee is," I said hoarsely.

"There was another one?" asked the djeli. "Another daughter of the Hassi Barahal family, in the house, when you were taken?"

My face burned hot and my hands burned cold. *Lips sealed*, my father had said. *Tell no one*, my mother had said. *Give away nothing that might give them a further hold on us.*

"There was another girl of the right age in the house?" demanded the mansa.

Andevai blinked, and blinked again. "Yes, Mansa."

"You asked three times?"

Stammering, Andevai forced out words. "Th-three times. They said to me exactly what she said to you. She is the eldest. So I married her, by the binding marriage, sealed by a bard, just as you commanded me to do, Mansa."

"And did you first ask, specifically, is this one the right girl or is that one the right girl? The girl we wrote the contract for?"

After a silence, he said in a chastened voice, "No, Mansa. I did not ask specifically about the other girl."

In the depths of the earth, wreathed in fire, lies coiled in slumber the Mother of All Dragons. Dreaming, she stirs, and the earth shakes, and volcanoes spit ash and fire, and the world changes.

In the depths of the ocean, deep in the black abyss, there drifts in a watery stupor the Taninim, called also leviathan. Yet they may be roused, and if they are so, then the lashing of their tails smashes ships into splinters and drives their sundered hulks under the waves while the shores are swept clean in a tidal fury.

In the depths of the ice, wreathed in ice, sleeps the Wild Hunt, and when it is woken, all tremble in fear.

So we are told.

But when a magister powerful enough to rule as the head of a mage House is struck rigid with fury and he is standing not ten paces from you, then you will wish you had to face one of the others instead.

The house was built of stone, and yet it shuddered. Glass in the paned windows cracked. The iron bands on the door groaned, as though shrinking in fear. Beneath the floor, ceramic shattered.

"What a fool you are!" said the mansa.

"Mansa," said the djeli, "you can send out a young person on your errand to rest your feet, but it won't rest your heart. Let me discover what has happened." He turned to face me, extended a hand palm up in a gesture that might have seemed reassuring if it were not a spell to call my voice to speak truth. "Is yours the blood of the Hassi Barahal clan?"

I opened my mouth to speak, and then I closed it, because the word I wanted to say would not come out. All I could say was, "So I have always been told."

A sick dread crawled in my belly. I swayed, sure I was about to faint. Andevai stared at me as if I were a serpent that had reared up to confront him. To contest him.

To cheat him.

"They said—!" he exclaimed. "They said *she* was the eldest Barahal daughter."

"Is that what they said?" asked the djeli. "They must have chosen their words carefully, knowing the contract was sealed by magic."

"What are you saying?" Andevai whispered, face ashen, his triumph in ruins.

"It seems there is no Barahal blood in her at all," said the mansa in a voice so soft it should not have made me shudder like a leaf tossed in a tremendous gale, and yet it might as well have been a roar. "And you, Andevai, you are too much a fool to have seen the trap even as they sprang it. How they must be laughing now. I wonder, how have we transgressed that a child born into a village of simpleminded field hands, the children of the children of slaves, should be a vessel of such abundant cold magic? And yet, in the end, one may as well have tried to train a dog to dance."

"But I destroyed the airship—"

"That was the lesser of your assignments. The marriage was the crucial one. So much at stake! And you brought us this useless female!"

"Mansa," Andevai said desperately.

"Get rid of her."

Andevai grabbed my arm and dragged me to the door, pushed it open, and shoved me out. I staggered a few steps before I caught myself short and turned, knowing I must go back inside and ask a question or demand an explanation.

Andevai shut the door in my face. I sank to my knees, sagged against the door, and winced back from the touch of iron bands so cold they burned.

There is no Barahal blood in her at all. All strength sapped from me, I collapsed forward along the floor. No Barahal blood at all.

I lay this charge on you as well, Aunt had said to me when I was only six years old, when I had come to live with them, *that you must protect Bee, for there will come a time when she will need your protection.*

Four Moons House had wanted Bee all along.

That being so, what did it make me?

The sacrifice.

17

Lying against the door, too weak to rise, I could hear them perfectly.

"How can it even be possible that you—even you—after all the struggle we've undertaken to educate you properly—could have made such a fundamental and devastating error?"

"Mansa," interposed the djeli. "There is no canoe so big that it may not sink. Also, he is young."

The magister snorted. "You have always favored him. Did you breed the filly who birthed him?"

Air can change consistency when the temperature drops suddenly, as it might once a year when the rare ice blizzards swept down off the glacial shelf. My lips stiffened and I thought for an instant I could lick ice out of the air.

"Andevai!" The djeli spoke firmly. "Control yourself!"

"My mother did not—"

"Do not wield your anger against the mansa. It is forbidden."

"My mother did not—"

"Your mother," agreed the djeli, "is by all reports a woman as strong as iron, industrious, forgiving, even-tempered, and loyal. Mansa, it serves no purpose to insult a woman who does not stand here to defend herself. The young man knows who his parents are. That is all I have to say on the matter. Now I am finished with it."

"I hear what you have said, Bakary," said the mansa. "Yet can it be that in his arrogance he has forgotten his mother is alive only due to our generosity? It is we who obtain at much difficulty and cost the medicine that staves off her illness. Has he forgotten what his village owes Four Moons House? Remind him!"

The djeli sighed, then spoke in a cadence something like song and something like poetry.

"It is the Diarisso lineage that possessed the handle of power, the essence of spirit, which in the old country we called nyama.

"It is the Diarisso who warded off the terror that came out of the bush, that which attacked the great empire, the cities and towns and villages, the fields and houses.

"It is the Diarisso who with their chains of magic guided the people, guided them safely across the hidden paths of the waterless desert, and so to the sea, to escape the flesh-eating ghouls, the salt plague that overtook the kingdom.

"Twenty thousand marched out of the city; mothers carried their children; sons carried their elders.

"Ten thousand only reached the shores of the middle sea.

"They found the Kena'ani ships, they handed over the gold, and the ships carried our people north to this shore, so far it was, as far as we could journey away from the plague.

"Three hundred and twenty-nine years ago, this happened.

"Then at that time, when they reached the north, the Diarisso lineage founded the first mage House. Later, some among the children of their children founded Four Moons House."

The mansa spoke. "Do you remember, boy, what your people owe to Four Moons House?"

"I do," Andevai mumbled.

"Your ancestors had no sorcery, no weapons, no provisions, no water, no strength. You would have perished in the desert had we not fed you and carried you. In exchange, we accepted your labor and the labor of your descendants as guarantors for the debt incurred."

"I have failed you, Mansa."

"Of course! How I expected you, such as you are, to succeed I cannot imagine. And yet the task was so simple."

"Mansa," interposed the djeli, "if the young man was not aware the Barahals hoped to cheat him, he would not have been alert to answers devised to fool him. Outright lies on their part would have burned. It is obvious they schemed for many years in order to cheat us. They even had a girl ready to substitute in their daughter's place. I must say, it was exceedingly clever of them."

"Yes, Phoenicians are known for their cleverness, are they not? They are stoats in our poultry yard." His tone, which remained angry but respectful when replying to the djeli, darkened to scorn. "What is it? You may talk."

Andevai spoke in a tone so humble it was like scraping the floor. "I make no excuses for my failure, Mansa. It is my responsibility alone."

"Yes, yes, I suppose it was inevitable." Evidently groveling appeased the mansa, because he went back to hammering on my people. "Especially when faced with cunning and self-serving mercenaries like the Barahals. They fostered the rise of Camjiata through their secret networks. They pretended they had no part in the monster's early successes and his later wars. They proved themselves adroit, indeed, in holding out empty hands to plead their innocence after his capture. It is pure accident we found evidence of their complicity, which we could use to control them. Yet the Hassi Barahals still scuttle across the continent like so many cockroaches."

Indignation, once stirred in a cat's heart, is like nourishment.

My fainting heart began to swell and strengthen. Still listening, I carefully turned my head to survey the hall.

Two attendants stood on either side of the double doors leading to the corridor. They were, I thought, making an effort not to stare at me lying stretched like a slaughtered heifer before the mansa's closed door. Otherwise, this large, elegant chamber was furnished with four low, wide benches padded with pillows and a mirror set against the wall at the end of the chamber opposite from where I lay. A mural painted along the walls depicted a desert crossing: powerful, handsome men and strong-as-iron women clothed in gold and orange striding over the tumultuous sands with their chains of power wreathing them like vines, using divination to forge a path and using a chain of sorcery to keep the salt plague and its ghouls at bay. They were followed by a train of much smaller sized people, their children and dependents and retainers, and the even smaller figures of their slaves.

"There is much you do not understand," the mansa was saying beyond the door, evidently to Andevai. "You are young, and inexperienced, and ignorant." He clearly expected no answer to this self-evident description, because he kept talking. "Now listen carefully. The diviners warned us in their maze of sand and shells that a general would rise to trouble Europa with his schemes. But we did not realize until too late the threat the Iberian Monster truly posed. We did not realize that he had gained a mage House as his willing ally. We did not know until too late that he was using the vision of a woman who could walk the dreams of dragons to plot his campaign of conquest. Too late, we understood that the dreamer had attracted the notice of the masters of the Wild Hunt. Too late. Do you understand?"

"Yes, Mansa," Andevai murmured.

"The Wild Hunt obliterated Crescent House, but not to aid us. They care nothing for us. We are less than vermin in their eyes. Yet, ironically, the Hunt's intervention saved us. For it was only after the death of Crescent House and the woman who walked the dreams of dragons—the woman Camjiata had married—that the Second Alliance could capture Camjiata and defeat his army. But I tell you now: Peace will not last, for princes will quarrel and laborers will remain ungrateful for that which benefits them. War and suffering wait at the door, eager to enter. So we listened closely when the diviners told us their shells and sands revealed that the eldest daughter of the Adurnam Hassi Barahal lineage will walk the dreams of dragons."

Walk the dreams of dragons?

What did that mean?

In the tone of a man goaded by curiosity into imprudence, Andevai spoke. "Can such people truly exist?"

The mansa said, as if Andevai had not spoken, "Am I doing the right thing, Bakary? To bring a woman who walks the dreams of dragons into a mage House puts us all at a terrible risk. We know what the Wild Hunt did to Crescent House. We saw the ruins."

"It is true, Mansa. So my father taught me and his father before him. This is known to us, but we never speak of it. To bring one who has learned to walk the path of dreams into a mage House is like bringing fire into a field of dry straw. One spark and all is consumed."

"Yet she is too valuable to lose. I thought it would be enough to bind her to us through the contract and let her remain, untouched and untrained, in her family's arms. If we bound her and kept her hidden in plain sight with her family, then no one else could take her, and we placed no risk on our House. That way, we held her in reserve. In case the storm came."

"Plans are dust thrown into the wind," said the djeli.

"So the storm comes, as we feared. We must take the risk." The mansa's words fell as heavy as iron.

I shifted to get a better look at the glass-paned wall that

looked out over the garden: high arched windows, paned doors, velvet curtains swagging from the walls and tied back with ropes of red braid. Warmth breathed up from the raised floor, embracing my belly. Here in the protected halls of Four Moons House, it was difficult to imagine what risk they faced.

"I n-never knew...," stammered Andevai, and an older, simpler accent surfaced in his voice, quickly stifled. "I had nay idea—no idea. Only a story I heard as a boy about a woman born with the gift that is a curse. She learned to walk the dreams of dragons, and so the Wild Hunt killed her. If that's so, Mansa, and if an entire mage House was destroyed by the Wild Hunt because of one dreamer, then what would be so terrible that you would risk bringing such a person into Four Moons House?"

His question was met with a drawn-out silence.

When the djeli spoke, it seemed his voice penetrated the foundations of the house. "Camjiata has escaped his island prison."

If the roof had fallen in on me, I could not have been more stunned. Perhaps I made a noise. The attendants glanced toward me and as quickly away. Bad enough to be humiliated like this without them smirking at me in my mortification. I dug deep for the concealing glamor, letting it embrace me like a cawl.

The mansa's anger stung like sleet. "The Houses will keep the secret of Camjiata's escape for as long as they can, but all too soon the news will get out. And when it does, the Barahals may try to seek him out and gain his protection. They do not know what the girl is, but we can be sure Camjiata will recognize her importance immediately. He will claim her, if he finds her before we do."

"The other girl," murmured Andevai. "When I saw Catherine, I was sure Catherine must be the one waiting for me... and then they told me she was the eldest.... She said she was two months older than the other girl."

"So there is still time before the eldest Hassi Barahal

daughter reaches her majority and the contract expires," said the mansa.

A new uneasiness stirred in my heart. I pushed up my head to see if my arms worked and lowered myself down again. The attendants paid no attention to my movement.

"What must I do, Mansa, to regain your favor?" Andevai asked in a low voice.

"Return at once to Adurnam and marry the Barahal girl, as you were commanded to do."

The djeli said, "The marriage already made was bound by an irrevocable chain, Mansa."

"Then it must be undone."

"It can't be undone, Mansa," replied the djeli patiently. "You know this as well as I do. And furthermore, the contract stipulates that the girl must be the sole wife of the magister who marries her."

"So she will be," said the mansa, each word ice, purposefully, deliberately. "The one you married in error is useless to us, Andevai. Indeed, she was party to the fraud. The marriage will be undone and the other girl recovered and brought under our control before the winter solstice. Andevai will carry out his duty to show his obedience and prove his worth."

From the chamber on the other side of the door, silence fell. The attendants at the other double doors yawned, oblivious to the tension pouring out over me. In the garden, a breeze set the treetops swaying. I heard, rising from elsewhere in the building, the voices of children in full spate, laughter and teasing and stories and dares.

"Aiei!" The djeli's sigh penetrated the air like storm winds, making me shudder.

"But, Mansa," said Andevai, "I don't understand. A binding marriage…a chained contract…"

"Can you not see the solution even so?" demanded the mansa. "Is even this beyond you?"

"But, Mansa," said my husband, "the only way out of such a contract is through the death of one of the parties involved."

"Yes. Kill her."

18

The words were simple, the silence that followed complex, ugly, smothering. It was so quiet I was sure I heard my husband blink.

"I beg your pardon, Mansa. I have not understood you."

"You heard what I said."

I pushed up gently to hands and knees, careful to make sure my head did not spin, but I was not at all dizzy. My heart was cold steel. I shifted to my feet and walked to the corner, a hand tracing the wall because I was part of the wall and nothing more than the wall, and after that I was window, nothing more, and then I was the door that did not open, curse it, but the next door did. I slipped through and closed it behind me and was out in the garden, all this really before I realized I had developed the thought, *I. Have. To. Run. Now.*

The garden was a rectangle, with its length extending to a wall beyond which rose evergreen trees. Several paths wound between tall yew hedges, perfect for skulking, so I ducked behind the screen of densely packed leaves and worked my way like a scuttling rat from hedge to hedge toward the far wall.

A bell rang, and I jerked as if a rope had caught me up short. But it was only a calling bell, because in response I heard the shouts and laughter of children racing down interior corridors of the wing that lay to my right. I reached the high wall that bounded the garden. It had no gate whatsoever and was far too high for me to climb over.

I had to go through the house.

I saw a sturdy double door set next to the corner where the wing to my right met the garden wall. Here I paused, panting, my hand on the latch.

"Catherine!" Andevai's voice carried into my prison.

Kill her.

I had no sword, only my wits and determination. My hand tightened on the latch, and it clicked blessedly free. Mouthing a prayer to Tanit, I slipped into a gloomy corridor. Halfway down the long corridor, children pushed through an open door in a mob of chattering and giggling that subsided as they vanished into whatever rooms lay beyond. None had seen me in the shadows. At the opposite end, where light spilled through windows, doors stood ajar into the main building. I could not go back into the garden or ahead into the main house.

I followed where the children had led and found myself in a narrow corridor lined with heavy coats hanging from posts on one side and a series of doors on the other. From behind the closed doors I heard the noise of children—ranging from the boisterous, cheerful young to the gossipy intense olders—settling down to lessons. I had fled into the school wing.

A new bell rang with an alarming clangor. Men shouted in the distance with deep voices full of malevolent purpose. A breath of shiveringly cold air stirred, like an invisible icy hand searching behind the furniture and down unseen halls for what it had lost.

Kill her.

A matron's voice called sharply, "In your seats! That's the warning bell. In your seats! Silence!"

A foot scraped softly on the plank floor. Too late I shoved

back behind a layer of hanging coats. A hand pulled aside a fur-lined sleeve and a small face peered at me.

"Who are you?" the child whispered with a puzzled frown. A boy with a brown face and close-cropped black hair, he was neither scared nor angry. He looked like he might be very sweet, as long as he liked you.

"I'm Cat," I said with an attempt at a friendly smile, nothing too pathetic or false, I hoped.

"To hide," he added, "you have to move four coats down and stand where the thread is. That's the concealing spot they made."

"That who made?"

"It's a holding illusion," he said with a bright grin. "The matrons say they're too young to weave magic, but they're not, and they promised to teach me if I keep their secret. Go there. It'll hide you. No one knows but me and Sissy and Cousin."

Footsteps drummed elsewhere, the flooring trembling with an echo of their movement. Soon they would come this way.

"Maester Kendall!" a woman's voice called, and he skipped off, opened the door of the last schoolroom, and plunged inside to a fall of excited laughter from his cohort.

Men were stomping this way. I sidled four coats down and stopped when a thread tickled my nose. There I stood, no more than a coat myself, with a cozy fur lining and a heavy wool outer shell, just right for wearing out in the winter air.... So why, then, were coats hanging so conveniently in this corridor if not to be used by children at their break? Which meant that either they played in the garden, where their shouts and laughter might entertain—or annoy—the mansa, or there was another exit to the outside from this wing.

"Search the schoolrooms!" barked a male voice.

Like the other coats, I did not move.

Down they swept, footfalls shuddering on the flooring, doors flung open, childish voices raised with questions, matrons tersely demanding apologies. Two young men in soldiers' livery paced down the coats, rippling them with strong hands, and yet... they walked right past me. At length the searchers satisfied themselves that no fugitive lurked in the schoolrooms. With no explanation to the matrons—who asked for none—they slammed shut the double entry doors and locked them from the other side.

There I stood, shrouded by coats. Through the now-open doors, I listened to the day's lesson, which was apparently the same in every age cohort's classroom, made simple for the little ones and extensive for the eldest.

A history lesson.

Listen, my father had written. *Listen to hear if they are telling the truth or only part of the truth, for that is the lesson of history: that the victors tell the tale of their triumph in a manner to grant accolades to themselves and heap blame upon their rivals. Ask yourself if part of the story is being withheld by design or ignorance.*

Only he was not my father. It was all a lie.

Tears wove runnels down my cheeks as one matron's voice above all the others droned on.

"We in the Houses are a tree grown from two roots. We are twin, one born in the north and one born in the south. Our ancestors in the south fled the salt plague and at the end of their journey met our ancestors in the north. We are Celt and Mande, rich in spirit. Those among us who can handle the nyama of the spirit world joined together to form the Houses. Thus, we are grown into what we have now become, we who can grip the handle of power. This all of you know, for it is the story of your ancestors. But there are other peoples in the world who are known to us, each with their own qualities and strengths...."

I cautiously stuck out my head and peered down the corridor to my left. The outline of a door was discernible, a gateway leading out.

A schoolroom door snicked quietly open, bringing with it a swell of matronly voice listing the various well-known peoples of the world and their well-known characteristics: The noble Kushites are gifted rulers, wise and tolerant; the Greeks are philosophers and lovers of art; the Romans are masters of war and engineering; the cunning Phoenicians have plied the seas of commerce for untold generations. The door shut, but the recital went on in muted tones as two girls padded down the corridor and halted in front of me. One had long hair braided tightly and an intelligent gaze in a face whose lineaments and complexion resembled those of the younger boy I'd spoken to earlier, while the other had a white face and blond hair. Nevertheless, there was something similar about their eyes.

They considered me and then looked at each other, their gazes speaking without words. They were young, perhaps twelve winters, fresh faced and healthy and blooming. Then the little beasts each stuck out a hand, palm up, asking for payment.

"You must be what they're looking for," said the dark one, with the innocent smile of a child who understands the blackmailer's art.

"Pay us," said the fair one, "and we'll pretend we never saw you."

"Where does that door lead?" I murmured.

"Are you bargaining with us?" asked the dark one, her eyes wide in surprise.

"Knowing how loud we can scream?" added the fair one reasonably.

I knew how to handle girls like this. Never let them think they held the whip of life and breath over you, or you'd be cursed.

"Of course I'm bargaining," I retorted in a low but suitably intense voice. "I'm Phoenician. We have to bargain. It's in our blood."

They grinned, as bright as a burst of lantern light on a murky night. I braced myself, expecting them to giggle, but they had exceptional self-control. Clearly, they were used to sneaking around where they weren't supposed to be.

"I know how to unlock the door," said the dark one.

"You can get outside and go through the park," added the fair one. "But once you're outside, we can't help you."

"Why are you willing to help at all?"

The fair one sighed and rolled her eyes with the dramatic glamor that wears itself like a burden. "I'm a diviner," she said with the weariness of one who has already had to explain this too many times. "Or I will be, when I grow up. Of course I know these things."

"We discussed what we should do," added the dark one. "You're no danger to us, so we're willing to let you go. But we need something in exchange."

I could not give them the bracelet Bee had given me. Beyond the clothes I was wearing, I possessed only one other object: the locket in whose heart nestled a tiny portrait of my father. But Daniel Hassi Barahal was not my father. So what would I be giving up by giving it to her? Only my hopes and dreams.

I slipped the chain over my head and handed the silver locket to the fair one. She popped the clasp and squinted at the portrait in the dim light, her fingers tracing the fine silverwork and the chased filigree that decorated the back.

Her frown was soft in the shadows, and for an instant she looked far older than her tender years. "Not what I expected."

Her words made me shiver, like a memory of the eru's greeting, but instead of explaining herself, she handed the locket to the dark one, who examined it with a jeweler's precise measure.

"Done," she said with a nod. She dropped the chain over her neck and pressed the locket down beneath the loose wool jacket that was buttoned up to her neck.

With no further speech, they skated along the polished wood floor in their soft indoor slippers. I took in a breath for courage and hurried after them. The dark girl with her long legs outpaced her fair cousin and slid to a halt before the heavy door. She bent down by the elaborate lock with a smile that reminded me of Bee's most mischievous expression. She seemed to be whispering to the bat's head that adorned the upper part of the lock. The fair one stationed herself at the wall to keep watch.

Was that a glamor shivering in the air, briefly seen as a net of shadow and light? Then it was gone. She slid the crossbar free and tugged open the door, and I slipped outside onto a vestibule and thence out through another door—this one unlatched—into a cold so sere that my lips went numb. I peered cautiously over a stately manicured wood composed of pine and spruce shouldering skyward beneath gray clouds. Bundled in quilted coats ornamented with brightly colored belts, soldiers ran through the trees; their heads were wrapped in cloth against the cold, only their eyes visible beneath red-brimmed hats like so many red-capped finches.

The woods were closed to me. I could not go back into the house. I hugged the wall, became the wall in its dressed smoothness, and ran in the other direction. I had to do what they would not expect me to do: I raced for the grand escalade. If I were bold, I might conceal myself by walking out on the same carriage road I had come in. I could become the pale graveled stone that paved the road. Either no one would see me, or the mansa and his djeli would see right through my pathetic veil and then I would be dead.

At the corner where the wing met the facade, my feet crunched in a spray of gravel. I halted to steady my breath and dig deep for the glamor. All now depended on my ability to veil myself with a glamor.

A flare of complicated emotion burned through me. Who

was I, if not the eldest daughter of the Adurnam Hassi Barahal house? Why could I hide myself, listen, and see down chains of magic? Why had my mother told me to keep it a secret? Why had an eru called me "cousin"? Had Aunt and Uncle devised the scheme to sacrifice me in place of Bee? Had Daniel Hassi Barahal and Tara Bell been in on the cheat all along? Was the story that they were my loving mother and father an invented fiction that I had swallowed whole? Was I really an unwanted, useless, and expendable orphan plucked from the streets?

Wouldn't it be easier to be dead than alone? Yet my heart beat too strongly to give up. What I felt was not precisely anger, nor was it blinding grief. It was something deeper, and more ancient, as determined as rock and as rooted as the great trees whose spirits animate the forest.

I would not die for their convenience.

White spun in the air. It had begun to snow. I could be snow. I drifted with the flakes onto the graveled court spreading like a pool beyond the granite escalade. No one would expect such a bold ploy. In front of the eyes of watching soldiers, I paced the measure of lazy snow, and they did not see me.

But someone else did.

Hooves made a crackling din as a carriage rolled around the curve of the drive. The coachman dragged the horses to a stop a stone's throw from me. The footman leaped down from the back and flung open the carriage door without lowering the steps.

From away behind the kitchen wing, dogs yipped and set up barking, released to the hunt. What was concealed to their sight they might track with their keen noses. Against dogs, I had no chance.

The eru looked at me, captured my gaze. "The bonds of kinship demand I aid you, if I can."

The coachman did not look at me—his gaze gathered in the

soldiers and servants crowding expectantly on the escalade, some of whom were staring curiously at the carriage and others lifting their gazes in search of the approaching dogs—but the invitation was clear.

"You must obey them if they command you to hand me over to them," I said hoarsely, "for you are servants of Four Moons House."

The coachman snorted.

"Are you so sure our situation is what it has seemed to you to be?" asked the eru.

The soldiers stirred, parting to make way for the djeli. No glamor I possessed would shield me from the djeli's sight, his handle of power whose chains reached into the spirit world.

I leaped up into the carriage. The eru shut the door behind me as shouts rang from the stairs and the carriage began to move. My cane was laid across one of the padded seats. I grasped the hilt, feeling the sword's power through my palm.

"Halt!" cracked a command, and the carriage jolted to a stop as if it had run into an iron wall.

Was that the mansa's power?

The carriage rocked beneath me as a moving body jostled it, and a whispery sound tickled my ears with unseen feathers. There were two doors in the carriage: the one Andevai and I had always entered and exited by, and the other one, the one whose shutters he had told me I could not open. Could not, or must not?

The unopened door latch shifted now, clicking down, just as a hand jostled the latch of the door behind me that I had entered through.

"I saw a shadow enter the coach," cried a male voice, not one I recognized, "right after the footman opened the door."

"Open!" commanded the djeli.

Fear hurts behind your eyes, like bright sun shining. I licked my lips as the other door, the door Andevai had forbidden me, cracked to let in a skirl of wind that cut with knives. I felt my skin opening, blades slicing shallow cuts as blood oozed like tears, but when I touched my cheeks, they were dry.

"Hurry," said a voice on that wind, the eru's voice, deep and strong. "Until the mansa's hand is forced by stronger chains to release this carriage, we cannot move."

As one door opened behind me, I plunged out onto the other side. A blast of wind slammed shut the carriage door behind me.

The carriage and I rested on a rise within an ancient forest of spruce, the wheels of the carriage fitted perfectly within a rutted track that cut away through the trees. Far away, down the direction Andevai and I had come earlier in the day, I saw a single stone pillar, surely the same one where we had poured an offering. The managed orchards and deciduous trees of the estate were missing. In my hand, in daylight, I held a sword whose blade had the hard sheen of steel. In this place, it looked perfectly ordinary, although in the world I knew it appeared as a sword only at night.

Impossible as it seemed, I had crossed over.

In tales and song, the spirit world exists in perpetual summer. Not here.

Here I stood in a landscape etched so hard by winter that the trees seem scratched on a copper plate against a sky whose grayish white pallor made me wonder if the blue had been drained from it as one might drain water from a tub. No sun's disk was visible in what I took for a cloudless sky. As my eyes adjusted to the glare, I realized the track had a shimmer as fine as if silver thread were woven into the earth, a trembling current of magic coursing along its length.

"Cousin, run down to the pillar. There, speak these words: 'As I am bound, let those bound to me as kin come to my aid.'

Quickly. We'll pick you up there. Whatever you do, do not leave the path."

The eru blazed, a nimbus of bright orange and flaring blue roaring off her skin. Her face still wore a human shape, but her aspect was so bright she was difficult to look upon. Her third eye was the most ordinary thing about her.

"Run," said the coachman. He looked no different than he had before, solid and imperturbable. The horses steamed exactly as a china kettle steams when water is boiling inside.

Grasping my sword more tightly, I cautiously emerged from behind the reassuring bulk of the carriage. Of the massive building itself, I saw no sign at all. According to the tales my father had recorded, it is life—spirit—that interpenetrates both worlds. Transparent wisps as fragile as the wings of ghostly moths flickered in the air, the souls of human beings alive in the physical world, soldiers and servants running to the escalade that existed only in the world I had just left. Farther back, within the space that would in the physical world mark his audience chamber, the mansa's spirit blazed as brightly as that of the eru. He had not pursued me. Why should he, when he had others to hunt for him?

The spirit flames of other cold mages moved toward the front of the house at the call of horn and hounds. I could not recognize my husband's spirit among the gathering cold mages. All I could tell was that threads of power laced them, knotting and tangling through the unseen barrier that separated the two worlds.

The threads pulsed as power was drawn out of the spirit world into their bodies: *The spirit world fed them.*

No wonder they were so powerful.

Yet they were still blind. Cold mages cannot see through the veil between worlds.

But djeliw can.

The djeli stood at the other door, holding it open as he looked into the empty interior of the carriage. Like the coachman, he looked perfectly ordinary to my vision, just as he had in the mansa's chamber, no glamor, just an elderly man wearing pale robes and gold earrings. He looked through. Somehow he looked past the closed door, and he saw me. He spoke to an unseen person behind him, but I heard nothing although his lips moved. No doubt he was alerting the soldiers and lesser mages, telling them to fetch the mansa.

They will not have me.

I ran.

My feet crunched on what I had mistaken for the glitter of magic but was actually a skin of frost atop the soil. Yet with each step away from the house, the brighter the frost shone, the harder the light became that illuminated the spirit world. A hawk's high call pierced from the heavens like a spear in my heart. A body flashed within the trees, then another. Cold is not just a temperature; it is also fear. A pack of wolves coursed alongside me, loping parallel to the path, tongues lolling, their breath the only warm thing I felt. They were huge, shaggy creatures fit for the bitter winters, fashioned to drag down the great beasts who roamed the barren land. My father had written in his journals of watching dire wolves cut out and run to death a woolly rhinoceros.

Were the wolves pacing me in aid of the mansa? Running me to death? Or were they merely denizens of the spirit world, eager to eat a weak creature like myself who had strayed across? To feed on her, as the cold mages fed on the spirit world?

One lunged for me, and I yelped and stumbled sideways. The weight of my flight pressed against a curtain of air, almost enough to halt me. But my left foot came down off the track and at once, impossibly, a wolf appeared there to snap at my exposed boot. I have good reflexes, and good training. I jerked that foot back onto the path and at the same time unsheathed the sword and slashed at the wolf's muzzle, the tip of my sword grazing its jowls.

With a yelp, it twisted away from my stab. Blood welled in its fur. It tensed, ready to lunge in for the kill. My breath came in bursts, a mist like the tremor of my spirit with each panting exhalation. I raised my sword between us. The wolf did not leap after me onto the track. They waited, crowding close, every cruel gaze fixed on me. They could not cross onto the path.

A shrill whistle jolted me. I threw a glance over my shoulder to see a vast shadow roiling down the track like the approach of a storm. I could see no sign of the place I had started running from, the ground where the mansa and his retainers had crowded very like the wolves waiting to rip out my heart and eat my entrails. I saw only the surge of a storm bearing down on me.

I ran. I was so frightened I felt almost as if I had sprouted wings, I ran so fast.

The storm raced at my back, a thundering gale made cacophonous with the howl of wind, but there was also a shrieking wail like a tortured spirit being whipped forward. The ground beneath my feet began to sprout flakes of ice as sharp as obsidian, cutting into my boots. The stone pillar rose before me, an obelisk like a nail of stone spearing up into the heavens and so tall I could not discern its point.

I leaped up onto the squared base and sheathed my sword, tucking it firmly through the waistband of my riding skirt. I wrapped my arms around the pillar, turned my face into the carved face of the stone, and clung there with all my strength as the gale hit.

If I had fallen naked into a lightless pit and had barrels filled with crushed ice and red-hot razor blades poured over me, it would have been easier to endure. Was this the mansa's power seeking to tear me free? To rip me from the path so his creatures could eat me and thereby consume my spirit and cause my death in the mortal world?

The cold was so profound, like the winter wind out of the barren lands that could freeze a man where he stood, that I could hold on only by falling in my mind into the stone, becoming stone, joining with the reliefs carved into the granite face. Impervious to cold.

Pillars mark crossroads, a branching of a track, a choice of direction.

Death lay behind me. What lay ahead or to either side I could not know. But I refused to die, and furthermore, I would not let Four Moons House get hold of Bee. Whatever else I knew—and that wasn't much—I was absolutely sure Bee had never been involved in this scheme in any way, except as its victim, like me.

I would never let Four Moons House get her.

Never. Not as long as I had breath.

I flattened myself into the carvings, one grain among many seething within the spire like so many trapped sparks. Birthed in fire and crushed beneath the implacable weight of the earth, I was stone, immovable, untouchable. But I had a voice.

"As I am bound," I said into the stone, "let those bound to me as kin come to my aid."

Between one breath and the next, the carriage rolled up beside me.

"Cousin." Within the scream of the storm, I heard the eru's voice as clearly as I had often heard the bells ringing out over Adurnam in their nightly conversation. "We are here, beside you."

I had trusted all my young life in the memory of my father, the bold adventurer. I had trusted the care and concern of my aunt and uncle, the generosity of the clan toward one of its daughters.

What allows us to trust? Kinship ought to, but it does not always.

What, then, causes trust to flower? A smile, perhaps. An offering of tea and bread to a hungry, chilled, and confused young woman, made without expectation of return.

Pillars mark crossroads, a branching of a track, a choice of direction.

I leaped down, groping. A strong hand met mine and closed over it, pulling. I slammed into the side of the carriage, found a latch, opened a door, and as the hand released mine, I crawled in, my skirt tangling in my sword. I fell hard onto one of the benches.

Opposite me, still and silent and calm, sat the djeli.

I wrestled the sword from my skirt, set my hand on the hilt.

The djeli raised a hand. "Listen," he said, and there was that in his voice that expected one to stop and to hear. "I am no threat to you."

I drew the sword but because I respected a man as old as he was, I let the blade rest lightly across my thighs and kept a wary gaze on him without staring him straight in the eyes. "You were coming through to get me."

"No. I entered the carriage to speak to you. Unlike you, with your spirit mantle, I cannot cross into the bush. Just as the mansa cannot cross."

"What do you mean, a spirit mantle?"

"You wear a curious mantle in the spirit world. I don't know what to make of it, I admit. Do you?"

"How could you see me through the door of the carriage? You saw into the spirit world!"

"I can see because I would be no djeli could I not see. But I cannot walk there."

"Did the mansa send those wolves to eat me? That storm to freeze me?"

"What magic the magisters wield, or their limitations, is not mine to know. My destiny is joined to that of Four Moons House because I speak the history of their lineage, the Diarisso lineage, and of an old war. Later, it becomes the tale of flight across the desert away from the salt plague. After this it becomes the story of those who joined hands and secrets and became the first cold mages."

"But you also see into the spirit world. You are tracking me. What do you expect me to do? Give myself up to be slaughtered? Allow my dear cousin to be handed over as I was? I think not."

On we rolled as a wind howled around the carriage but could not disturb the two of us sheltered within its confines.

He smiled, as the elderly can do, a complicated mix of amusement, sadness, wisdom, and calculation, and he had a crinkling at the eyes and a sympathy in the lips that made me want to like him. But I had not the luxury to like him. I shifted the sword on my skirts.

"You are no Barahal. So what are you, who can cross into the spirit world, and why are these servants aiding you and disobeying the master of Four Moons House?"

"Answer your own questions. I owe you nothing."

He sighed. "You are correct that we sit at an impasse. I will get out at the gate, because I must. But you are still marked for death."

"Is that a threat, or a promise, or a warning?"

"It is a phrase. To the Ancestors we will come, one way or the other. We are part of them, as they are part of us. So is it sung."

He lifted his staff and I tensed, raising my sword, but he did not attack me. He rapped the roof of the carriage, a rhythm as much speech as beat. The carriage, bowling along like a well-thrown ball, slowed, steadied, and pulled to a halt.

I braced as the djeli opened the door that led into the mortal world. I set a hand on the latch of the door into the spirit world, ready to bolt, but he only stepped outside into the cold afternoon and said to me, in the words of the language we spoke within the Kena'ani clans where I had grown up, "Peace be with you and in all your undertakings."

The words rang strangely; I had never expected to hear them here, and for once I was genuinely too surprised to speak. Beyond him I saw the wall that ringed the estate stretching away out of sight. Might I actually escape?

He shut the door, and we rolled on. I felt, as a string on a fiddle must feel when the bow commands it, a vibration pass through me as we crossed under the House gate. I heard a shout of surprise and cracked open the shutter. The gatehouse fell away behind, and young men in soldiers' red came running after as if, like the wolves in the spirit world, they meant to pace us as far as their legs, or their magic, could carry them.

Were the spirit wolves still following us? The mansa would not give up the hunt so easily. He wanted Bee, and a man like that did not just relinquish the things he wanted.

Andevai was not sitting here to command me not to open the other shutter. Now that I had escaped from the house and the wall of magic that enclosed their estate, I felt a surge of satisfaction in realizing that I need not listen to Andevai's arrogant, condescending words ever again. That was a triumph worth celebrating!

I laughed once, and then I wiped away tears. After that, I closed the shutter and, with sword raised protectively, cracked the shutter of the window that looked out onto the spirit world, bracing for a blast of wintry wind. The breath of wind that brushed my face seemed balmy by comparison to what had come before. I peeled back the shutter.

We drove through an autumnal countryside. Amid the dark spruce, especially in lower sinks, rose downy birch, alder, rowan, and a few doughty ash trees, their leaves burnished gold. Wind spun falling leaves. Deep in the trees, a herd of hairy beasts ambled on their way, hard to discern in the shadows. Had we traveled this way a month ago, this is the landscape I would have expected to see. A herd of red deer grazing in a clearing opening out beside the track lifted their heads. At first I thought they were looking at the carriage, but their interest was caught by something behind us. First one and then four and then the rest bolted away. I leaned out to see the pack of wolves loping in the distance. It seemed they were slowing down, veering off.

A beast stalked out from the trees, a huge saber-toothed cat, its coat the gray-black of the underside of a storm cloud. A second and third emerged behind it, colored in the manner of tundra cats that must blend with snow and rock. Rippling with power, they bounded out of my sight. I sat back hard, barely breathing. My heart galloped out of rhythm to the steady drumbeats of the horses' hooves.

"Where will we go? Can we outpace wolves and cats?" I shouted out the window, into the spirit world. "Who are you? Who am I?"

I heard only the eru's laughter in answer.

Yet it seemed not mocking laughter but the laughter of those sympathetic to you, who see amusement in the prospect of you working out on your own that which has bewildered you. No doubt I had laughed that way myself, waiting for Bee to make a connection that appeared entirely obvious to me. So she often laughed at me, a laugh full of kinship, not scorn.

I sat for a while, watching the spirit world, with its gray-white sky and absent sun, everything so sharply drawn that my eyes stung to look on it. I shut them for a time. Maybe I dozed as the urgency of the chase drained away.

Then I started awake, recalling everything that had happened. When I leaned out the window to look behind, I saw no sign of wolves or cats. The terrible fear and tension eased. I sheathed the sword and sat back against the upholstered seat with a sigh.

The sound rose out of the earth like mist and filtered down from the sky like rain. A horn's call, one might call it, if one had no other word to use, as much a long chuckling laugh as the *tarantata* of a trumpet's rallying shrill, as much the eerie moan of a conch shell as a drawn-out cry of despair. I had never heard anything remotely similar, not in all my too-brief life.

The call licked the air like fire and breathed all the way down into my bones. I knew I had to run. Run. *Run.*

The carriage slowed, scraped, and jolted to a halt. The eru leaped down, face creased in a solemn frown. Her third eye did not frighten me, for she only looked at me with two eyes. The third looked elsewhere, sidelong, as at a sight I could never see and would not wish to glimpse.

"My apologies, Cousin. We cannot convey you as far as we would wish."

"Is that the mansa's command, calling you home?"

The eru's laugh made me shudder. "Is that what you think it is?"

I tried again. "You are a servant of Four Moons House, being called home."

"We are not servants of Four Moons House. Although you will find a pair of us in each of the mage Houses. They believe or choose to believe we are their servants, but we are not their servants. Rather we are watchers in the service of a greater power that at all times keeps a tiny whisper of its attention for those among the human lineage who may become too powerful."

The horn call blared a second time, gaining strength.

I clutched the lip of the window until my knuckles whitened. "You'll abandon me here!"

"Alas, our masters call. We must obey the summons." Her

expression was difficult for me to read, composed with some portion of humanly compassion and yet a greater measure of something like disdain that was perhaps merely a degree of aloofness to the petty travails of a mortal creature like myself. Or else she was angry. Impossible to say. "As for you, you must depart into the mortal world, for it is not safe for you in the spirit world without a guide. Especially not this night, when the hunt rides. You must find the cunning and the strength to make your way on your own in the world you know. One thing: The cold mages cannot pursue you on Hallows Night and Hallows Day. They dare not walk abroad when the hunt rides. Yet this night of all nights is an ill time for every mortal creature. Find shelter when the sun goes down, and depart at dawn to gain what head start you can."

"The djeli said I wear a spirit mantle. Tell me what that means."

"It means we are cousins. Go now."

She reached inside and firmly slid closed the shutters. An instant later, too quickly for her to have walked around the carriage, the latch of the other door clicked down and the door opened. I climbed out not into the autumnal beauty of the spirit world but into the shivering cold of winter's twilight in my own. The clouds lay heavy and dark above; the last light drained like hope from the empty landscape of frost and field. There was no wind.

Sitting above, the coachman lifted his riding whip in salute.

The horn rang a third time around us, the sound rolling like thunder away over the hills.

The whip came down across the backs of the horses, whose hooves no longer touched the earth. The eru leaped up onto the running board, and from her back roiled a disturbance in the air. She was spreading wings.

A wind out of the north howled over us, almost bowling me

over. The carriage and the eru and the coachman and the horses dissolved into a thousand shards of ice, and I was battered as by a vortex of bladed leaves so hard I shut my eyes.

And when the wind died and I opened my eyes, the eru and the coachman and the coach and four were gone. I stood alone, in the middle of nowhere, with nothing but my sword and my bracelet and the clothes I wore, as snow began to fall and the gloaming of Hallows Night swallowed a now-silent world.

19

Broken woodland surrounded me. In the clearing in which I stood, snow dusted the grass. I had thought we were on the toll road, so smoothly had we traveled, but no road revealed itself to my searching and desperate gaze. Perhaps in the spirit world this was a line of power unseen to the mortal eye in the physical world, for I could see nothing but the last shadows of the trees beneath the darkening sky.

The hunt rides.

There! A taper wavered in the gloom to the north of me, then vanished. Voices lifted and faded, then lifted again in song underlaid by hands clapping and a drum's accompanying patter.

East lay the House. Out of the north came the singers. Between south and west lay little enough choice except for a barest glimmer as faint as a thread of spider's silk caught between two trees. It might be a path. Even if it wasn't I could hide in the trees. Keeping my sword sheathed, I paced as swiftly as I could without breaking into a run whose haste might trip me up. A rustle like the pelting race of animals through brittle grass chased around me and quieted, but I dared not pause, knowing that spirit wolves—or a family of hunting saber-toothed cats—might have followed my scent out of the spirit world. Could the animals of the spirit world cross into ours, as I had crossed into theirs?

The enveloping canopy and loamy scent of spruce loomed

before me. Beneath the trees, the path continued on as straight as if surveyed by Roman engineers, laid with a glamor so slight it was as if the track exhaled. It was easy enough to follow for a person with my vision.

Branches swayed above me. A weight dropped so fast down out of the trees that I flailed as netting tangled over my head and in my hands. I gave myself a single breath to strangle my panic, then crouched and pulled the sheathed sword free right on the earth between rope and soil. Pushing the sword's hilt before me to lift the net, I wormed forward. When I found the edge of the netting, I peeled it back from my head just as two men stepped onto the path before me. I grasped the netting, dragged it up and sideways, and flung it with all my strength at them as I sprang in the other direction.

I slammed against another body. A hand's powerful grasp chained my sword arm. The man who had captured me was tall and bundled in winter's clothing. That was all I could tell, except that he smelled of sweat and wool. I dropped to my knees to get a new angle, my sword's blade glittering as I torqued it toward his face.

He made a noise between gritted teeth, something between a grunt and a laugh. He got a knee up between us and kicked me back so hard I stumbled into the netting and slashed at empty air. But I had a cat's grace. I did not fall, as they expected me to. My chest hurt, but I could still breathe.

The taper had reached me. In its flaring light, I found myself surrounded by seven men wearing quilted wool coats hung with charms and armed with the bows and spears of hunters. The eldest had a seamed face; the ends of many gray-streaked braids, each bound with an amulet at its tip, stuck out from beneath a wool cap drawn down over his ears. The youngest was a stripling, younger than me and wide-eyed with amazement at finding a creature such as myself alone in the forest with a sword on such a night.

"Ah!" said the man I'd slammed into, licking blood off his thumb. "I am cut by your blade. Does the cat scratch on purpose, or is it only startled?"

"I know how to use my sword," I said, addressing him. "You dropped the net on me."

"You are a knowledgeable person," he agreed. "Still, we are seven, and you are one."

The elder spoke up, his common speech thick enough that I had trouble understanding him. "No wise hunter makes a killing after sunset on Hallows Night," he observed. "Especially not with cold steel."

How did he recognize cold steel?

Two men folded the netting into a neat bundle that the stripling settled over his shoulders. They set out with the stripling, who coddled a hand drum hanging by a leather loop from his neck. Behind came another pair of men single file with a stout stick braced on their shoulders and a dead animal dangling down, tied by its legs. At first I took it for a tundra antelope, for the edge of the Barren Lands lay perhaps ten days' walk north of here, and animals might stray. Then I saw that it possessed three horns; two sprang up from just above its pale ears, and the third, in the center of its quiescent brow, was knit with a silver glamor.

The tall man and the elder waited.

"Are you a woman of this world, or a spirit creature that followed us out of the bush in the form of a woman?" the tall man asked, not kindly but not angrily, either. He was just asking.

When had my breathing become so unsteady? I hadn't been running, but so many shocks tossed into my path one after the next made me dizzy. Ahead, the stripling began tapping out a pattern on the drum as if it were a protective shield.

"Peace to you," I said, in the greeting of the countryside, which I'd read about in Daniel Hassi Barahal's journals. "Do you have peace, friend?"

The old man chuckled. "I have peace, thanks to my mother who raised me. And you?"

"And me, I am fine, thanks to—ah—my power as a woman." Although at the moment it was difficult to know what power that could be. "And the people of your household, they also?"

"There is no trouble. And your people?"

This could go on for a while, and the night was advancing, and I was standing in one place rather than putting miles between me and those who wanted to kill me. Despite knowing there were certain forms, I could not bring myself to lie about "my people" even for the sake of courtesy, so I chanced rudeness. "Forgive my hasty words, but we are out late on an ill-omened night. I am called Catherine. Have you a name to share?"

"In my house, I am called Father," replied the old man with a grin that made me smile. "As for a stranger met on the road, you may call me Mamadi."

The tall man spoke with more impatience. "In my house, I am called Duvai. We are hunters, going home much later than we meant to. Hallows Night is no night to wander the forest."

At least they weren't answering questions with questions!

A howl rose, but neither reacted; I wasn't sure they heard. Maybe the sound had reached me on a wind blowing between the worlds, although the branches here did not stir.

"Best to keep moving," said the old man, setting off after the taper, now almost out of sight among the trees, and the faint patter of the drummer. The tall man nodded at me politely and followed his elder.

As they walked away, I wondered what horn had summoned the eru and the coachman. Who were their masters? The cold sank deeper and the night grew darker. There was a taste on the air that truly frightened me; the breath of wolves warmed my neck. I sheathed my sword and followed, wishing my fur cloak was a spirit mantle in truth, if it would keep me warmer. They did not slow their pace or offer any comment as we trekked at a brisk stride through the forest, catching up with the others. The charms and amulets woven onto their clothing clattered quietly.

Once again there rose on the wind a howl, and this time the hunters reacted; they spoke bantering words between their party, joking, it seemed, at the expense of the nervous stripling. They spoke a manner of half-breed language that took some part from the common bastard Latin known throughout the north but that was otherwise a tartan of Celtic and Mande. I could not specifically understand them, and certainly could not speak in their way, but I could follow parts of it, because I heard similar dialects spoken between pupils at the academy. It seemed this was the lad's first expedition into the bush, shepherded by experienced men, and because he had survived it under their supervision, naturally they were teasing him.

I said to the tall man's back, "When you say you hunted in the bush, do you mean you actually crossed into the spirit world, went hunting, and came back? I thought no mortal men could do that."

"Flowers plucked carelessly soon wither," he said in the common speech.

"I beg pardon if my words seem carelessly chosen, like thoughtlessly plucked flowers," I replied, "but on a night like this, and in such circumstances as we have met, you can surely understand why I would ask."

"I take you for city bred, by your clothing and your manner. Hunters walked into the bush long before others did. Even before djeliw or blacksmiths. Long before there were cold mages. What was never known to those who have not learned history can be excused."

At the mention of cold mages, I thought his tone shaded toward ice. "If you're from nearby," I continued, still probing, "then your people are surely bound to a mage House, for there is such a House close by here, is there not?"

My not-so-innocuous query evidently offended him, because he lengthened his stride, and although I am tall, I had to hasten to keep up. On any other night, I would have forged forward on my own, but no one raised in the north leaves their home after dark on Hallows Night. No one. Not even the scholars who tut-tutted as with their intellectual scalpels they dissected the unsophisticated folk beliefs of ignorant villagers.

Woodland gave way to stretches of pasture and columns of orchard to the stubble of hayfields and strips of plowed fields that had been harvested weeks ago. We plunged into a grove of black pine and halted at the base of a tree whose girth proclaimed it a venerable giant. Its trunk was hung all over with animal horns. The tall man waved at me to step back as, by the light of the wavering taper, they made a half circle and sang more than spoke words while the old man took his knife and nicked the shoulder of the dead beast they carried. Blood trickled sluggishly to dribble at the base of one of the trees. A pressure as of an invisible hand or a flavor as of quivering life or a smell and sound made my head ache. Then it was gone, and wind breathed through the trees. I shuddered and was glad to see them start forward again, for there was power here I did not understand, and I did not want to be too close to it.

A howl rose again, and for the first time I understood it was not the voice of wolves but of some other hunter entirely, something far more dangerous. I quickened my steps until I walked practically on the heels of the tall man, but he deigned not to notice me.

We crossed out of the pine grove. As we walked along the

shore of a pond skinned with ice, the stripling fell back to walk alongside me.

"Duvai thinks you're a spirit woman who followed us out of the bush," he confided, "but if that's so, then you would be beautiful and you wouldn't be shivering and look so tired."

"My thanks," I said with as much sarcasm as I could muster in my tired and unbeautiful state, but then I laughed, because I was accustomed to lads of just this age at the academy. While it was only the bold ones who talked this way with the older pupils, I was pretty sure they all thought the same dreadfully tiresome things.

"My apologies," he muttered, chin dipping; most likely he was blushing. "But Mamadi says you have human blood, like us."

I knew how to fence. I took a chance at a counterstrike. "So this is your first trip into the bush? Do the hunters of your village often cross into the spirit world?"

"Oh, no!" The young who are male can never resist showing off their knowledge, no doubt because they possess so little. "The veil between the worlds thins in the days leading up to Hallows Night. A very powerful and clever hunter will know where to find the crossroads that lie between the worlds. Even for him it will be a very dangerous crossing—"

He realized he had said too much. With a grunt meant, perhaps, to be some manner of excuse for breaking off the conversation so abruptly, he loped forward to the front of the procession to put as much distance between him and me as he could. The old man chuckled, although I'd thought him too far away to hear.

The lake ended in reed-choked shallows netted with ice. As we made our way down a fenced slope next to a stream, I realized I had seen this place before. A village spread across the hollow below. The walls and houses of its compounds looked much like the interior of a beehive, many-celled and complex. Two stockades ringed the village. The outer separated the village from the fields, and the inner separated the residential houses from the ring of gardens, work sheds, and other shelters. Torches marked the gates of each stockade. I had seen this village from the carriage when we passed; it was the only place in all that long journey Andevai had shown any sort of interest in. We were close to the toll road, although I could discern no trace of it in the darkness. Maybe I should have run, but it was night and it was breathtakingly cold, and besides all that, the air breathed its own warning of danger. Alone on Hallows Night, with no fire and nothing more than the clothes I wore and my sword, how could I hope to survive? *The hunt rides.*

Outside the stockade, our party was greeted by a group of young men and women putting the finishing touches on a heap of debris—wood, dry dead leaves, desiccated undergrowth— piled just beyond the entry gate. We passed through the open gate to the outer stockade. Inside, on a path leading between gardens, the men conferred in low voices and then the party split up. The old man and the other four adult men with the beast headed off to a shelter where coals glowed in a damped- down hearth fire. Duvai gestured to me, and with the stripling almost bouncing in his excitement, we headed for the inner gate. Two young men armed with spears and longbows—no muskets, of course, in territory beholden to a House—stood at the inner gate.

"Peace to you. How are you all?" I asked the guards as we came up.

"Well. We are well thanks to the mother who raised us," they mumbled, glancing at the tall man as if for direction, but he only lifted an eyebrow.

"And everyone in the compound?"

"Well. They are well." They refused to look me in the eye—naturally, as I might be a spirit who had walked out of the spirit world specifically to do them mischief. But I could not ask after members of their families, because I did not know them, and they glanced aside and beckoned to the tall man and said, in what they clearly hoped would be an undertone, fearing to insult me in case I was what they feared, "Duvai, what is this? Did you bring it with you or did it follow you?"

I knew the custom of the countryside. Daniel Hassi Barahal had written of it in his journals.

"I ask for guest rights." If I surprised the gate guards, which I did, I surprised the tall man even more. Perhaps he had genuinely thought me a spirit and was now realizing he had been mistaken. By the lights of the torches at the gate, I could see he was older than me, well grown and good-looking, old enough to be called fully a man but not yet middle aged. There was something about him that seemed familiar, and it was only because I had just been thinking about Andevai—as unfortunate as it was that I should ever feel obliged again to think of him—that I wondered if I saw a resemblance between the two, although Duvai's hair and complexion were lighter.

The men at the gate said what they must. "Enter and be fed. Enter and sleep without evil dreams."

With an exhalation of relief, I crossed between the torches and into the enclosure within which compounds and houses clustered. Dogs barked but quieted quickly, recognizing the tall man and accepting me as one of his companions.

In the dusk it was difficult to count the structures, but the enclosure ringed a fair amount of ground. I estimated there were at least two dozen tapers, which meant at least a dozen compounds burned tapers at their entrances. Even in sophisticated Adurnam, every household burned a taper or a lamp at the door on Hallows Night. At the far end of the village opposite the gate rose a larger round structure, its conical thatched roof like a hat blocking the heavens. From that direction came the sound of a drum talking an easy rhythm, at which the stripling laughed and essayed several steps until the tall man curtly cut him down with a few words. The drum died, as if the man had silenced it, but its demise was followed by laughter, a short rapid phrase of song, and a second, lower-voiced drum beating out an exploratory bass. Out of this desultory introduction, a woman's deep alto rose in a long stream of melody whose power halted me in my tracks.

"Feet hasten where there is news to be delivered," said the tall man to the stripling, and the lad hurried off into the dark. "A warm hearth on a cold night is welcome," he said to me, and I took that as an invitation.

We entered a compound whose doors, opening onto a common courtyard, stood close together like friendly relatives. Every door was ornamented with a burning taper, and women were working and talking and making jokes. A child ran along the narrow alley between the buildings, and a pair of women laughed as they crossed the broad, open space with baskets atop their heads. I smelled some manner of glorious cooking; surely that was meat sizzling!

As we approached a door almost opposite the compound's gate, a woman about Duvai's age came to the door to greet him. When she saw me, she frowned. She was a short, lovely woman, wearing a striped wool robe. Inside, a cast-iron stove, surely a sign of prosperity in a humble village like this one, gave off heat.

"Peace to you, on this evening," I began as a pair of toddlers, a half-grown lad, and a middle-aged woman gathered on the other side of the threshold to stare at me.

The woman did not invite me in; instead, she came out and drew the tall man apart and spoke in an undertone while folk emerged from the compound doors to see what was going on. I felt like an exhibition at one of the academy's lectures. Young and old, female and male, dressed in rustic clothing, these were country folk, not poor precisely because none had the starving look of the beggars I saw on the streets of Adurnam, but the compound was certainly without any of the niceties city people expected. A freestanding brick fire pit cradled a blaze that beat back the night's gloom. Several log benches and stone mortars rested beneath a big, leafless tree.

Out of the crowd pushed a young woman who looked a few years younger than I was. She hurried over to the tall man and his companion. After being invited by gesture to approach, she spoke in a voice so quiet even I could distinguish nothing above the murmur of conversation among the people watching me. But she threw glances in my direction as she addressed the hunter and the woman I guessed was likely Duvai's wife. I began to think this newcomer also looked familiar, because this was the kind of night in which I was bound to see everything in a suspicious light.

"I won't!" said the wife with an audible anger that startled her companions.

Duvai said, "She has already asked for and been offered guest rights. To cast her out would offend the ancestors...." Again the words flew beyond my comprehension.

The girl beckoned, and I went to her. She led me to a low door set back from the main ground by a tiny, private court-yard. This was the only house with two tapers on each side of its entrance. Before we reached the threshold, the door was opened from the inside and an elderly woman looked me up and down. Before I could start with a new round of greetings, she opened the door wider and made it clear I should enter.

The earthen walls were so massively thick that the chamber within was smaller than it seemed from outside. Its single room lay mostly in shadow, and it smelled of fresh pine wreaths over-laying a tincture of soured milk and the bite of recently peeled onion. Four benches were stacked beside the door. A bed stood opposite the door. An old chest was set at the foot of the bed, and five bundles of herbs hung from the rafters. Besides the hearth set into the wall and a spinning wheel, that was all.

The elderly woman offered a bowl filled with water. I was so thirsty that I drank it all, but before I could speak to thank her, a quavering voice spoke from the bed.

Her dialect fell too thick for me to penetrate. Instead, the girl spoke for her. "Let Andevai's bride approach the mother of this compound, if she wishes to speak."

I would have—should have—bolted, but the words chained my heart and my feet. Maybe it was only curiosity that would kill the cat, or perhaps she who lay invalid on the bed had power enough to hold me here, even if she seemed to give me a choice in the matter. The girl I recognized too late: She was the girl I had glimpsed striding through the orchard with the other work-ers. Duvai, then, must be Andevai's older brother. Impossi-bly—or perhaps not—I had run to exactly the wrong place. Could it be the eru and coachman had betrayed me? Yet why bother to stage an elaborate escape? More likely the mansa, or the djeli, had power enough to direct my steps this way.

The shape in the bed spoke again, and the girl repeated so I could understand.

"Just because you think you see a wolf does not mean one is there." She added, "Mother possesses sight."

I was breathing hard and fast. "That's your mother? Andevai's mother?"

"Our father's mother, so our mother. Go to her. She won't bite, Catherine. Your name is Catherine, isn't it? I asked already, in the orchard—my brother's wife will surely become a sister to me!—but he refused to let me meet you."

The old woman spoke as in answer, and the girl grimaced and shrugged. "He's ashamed of us. That's what they've taught him there, to feel ashamed of his people." She glanced at me sidelong and the next words were not unfriendly precisely but with a bite I had not heard in the grandmother's tone. "Do you look down upon us also, Catherine?"

"No, no, not at all." Now I had to approach the old grandmother lest my behavior be deemed haughty. What had I to lose by being friendly when I now knew he had rejected them? I knelt beside the bed on a pillow set there for visitors. "Grandmother, my greetings to you on this evening. Is it peaceful with you?"

We went on in this way for a while, and the longer we spoke the stock phrases that were easiest for me to understand, the better I could tease out meaning from her country way of speaking and the gaps made by words that I simply did not know. Andevai's sister filled in what I missed. I was not even aware when the long ritual of greeting shifted into another type of conversation entirely, for ancient grandmothers generally feel they can interrogate those who enter into their circle, and I *was* her grandson's wife and therefore now her daughter.

"Duvai's wife naturally believes her husband brought a spirit woman home from the bush to take in as his second wife," she told me, with help from her granddaughter. "That is why she took so badly against you. She is not a mean or ungenerous woman, but she is jealous of his attentions, for she believes he is a man whom all women—especially spirit women who see him walking in the bush—must desire as a husband. Also, he will become head of the family one day soon."

"Why would she think me a spirit woman out of the…ah… bush?"

"You have the smell of the spirit world in your bones. But I have seen spirit women, and spirit men, and changeling children, and I know you are not one of them but something else."

"Do you know what I am?" I demanded.

The girl hissed warningly at my impassioned tone, but the old mother smiled. "I sense you are confused. Why are you come to our village? I admit, a wedding night celebrated on Hallows Night would be ill-omened, so better that you wait on the bedding. Still, I would think you better served in a big house with plenty of rich food and fine clothing to wait out the hallowing."

I held my tongue, thinking furiously. What could I say that would not condemn me?

"Yet here you are," she continued. I did not think her sight extended actually into my thoughts. It surely took no great skill to look at my weary, rumpled form and figure that something drastic must have precipitated my departure from a powerful mage House on the deadliest night of the year, especially since Andevai's sister knew perfectly well that I had only hours before arrived at Four Moons House in her brother's company. "And now you are our guest, whatever else you may be. I expect you are hungry. Kayleigh, bring meat and porridge. How tired the feet become after much walking!" She lifted her hand a hand-breadth off the blankets.

This, I realized, was an invitation for me to sit rather than kneel. The attendant brought a stool, and I thanked her nicely and examined Grandmother's face for Andevai's lineaments. Like all of the villagers in these parts, she was what Brennan had called "tartan," of mixed descent, lighter than Andevai and Kayleigh but without Duvai's brown-gold hair. She was very weak, but her gaze was alert. A frail hand stirred on the blankets. Moved by what impulse I did not know, I took gentle hold of her hand and we sat for a time in silence, my hand warm against her cooler skin. I felt oddly comfortable, almost at peace, with drums talking nearby and her breathing as steady as a heart's beat.

"What is the name of this village?" I asked at last.

"Haranwy. We are a well-fed village, through our hard work. Growers of grain."

"And hunters," I added, more tartly than I meant, "who tell me they can walk in the spirit world."

"What would a city girl like you know of hunters? Or the spirit world? To attract the interest of Four Moons House, you must have been born into a rich or a princely family, or to one that has harvested many cold mages out of its fields."

What expression showed on my face I don't know, but she chuckled again. "It is the fate of the young to believe the old know everything or the old know nothing. I am merely curious about my grandson's destiny. We are rarely allowed to see him."

Kayleigh came in carrying a tray with water and a cloth for washing and a bowl of gruel topped with a strip of meat whose savor made my mouth water. She set the tray on my lap with a pleasing smile that made my own lips stir. Yet all at once I knew—as a goat must know in the instant before its throat is slit—what Andevai's sister was about to say.

"Vai is at the gate, on a very fine horse! They always say they'll let him visit on the festival days, but then he never does. You never said, Catherine, that he was right behind you. Did you get separated on the road? I suppose he was looking for you! I don't think he has the least idea you are here, though. Isn't that strange?"

"Kayleigh."

"Yes, Mother."

"How does the wind speak in the compound?"

"Duvai let it be known at once that no one speaks until you give the word, Mother."

"Let the cold mage come to my bedside. As for the other, a closed flower waits until daylight to bloom. Even the beasts prefer a quiet byre in which to feast."

The girl shared a glance with me and rolled her eyes almost exactly as Bee would have done. Then she took herself out, sparing a grin—of happy complicity, assuming me to be as glad to hear news of Andevai's arrival as she was—before she closed the door.

My hands were shaking. I looked around the small house, seeking windows, but there were none, only a hearth set into one wall with a chimney funneling the smoke out and the attendant standing by the door. I was trapped.

20

"What did I ever do," I muttered, "to deserve this destiny?"

She sighed sharply. "I have let it be known that none will mention your presence here until I say to do so. Knowing the hunters ranged deep into the bush and seeing you arrive with your hair and those looks on a cross-quarter eve, people naturally wonder if you are a spirit woman or a real woman. That is why you were brought to me. My son is too ill to receive such visitors."

"Andevai's father is ill?"

"Vai calls him Father, but you would say his uncle. He is my elder son, who sired no sons of his own, alas. My younger son, who sired my two grandsons, has crossed over. Duvai waits too impatiently for the household to pass into his hands. That is the destiny of some men, to see in the passing of one they love an opportunity to better themselves."

Despite everything, despite all my efforts to stay strong, I began to snivel, trying to choke down my sobs.

"If you sit in the corner, he will not see you. Not if I do not wish him to see you, and I do not wish it, for I know what is in your heart."

I wiped my nose with the back of my free hand. "W-what is in my heart?"

"You fear Vai because you fear the mansa. What does the mansa want from you that he brought you into his house?"

She had power as great as that of the mansa but so different it could not be named.

"My death," I said before I knew I meant to say it.

Not even this surprised her. "Ah. A sacrifice. This corner"—she indicated the foot of her bed—"is darkest."

I carried the tray to the corner and sat in the darkness with my sword at my left hand and my cloak pulled around me, the hood over my head. I was still shaking but suddenly ravenous. At least if I was going to die, I would die with a full stomach! I quickly washed and then, cradling the bowl in my left hand, swept the meat to my lips with my right.

The door opened.

Duvai came in first and Andevai after him in a wave of cold that made the hearth fire shudder. They did not stand close. Andevai in his fine, expensive clothing made the humble room appear shabby and sad in comparison, and he held himself aloof, as if he feared he would ruin his clothing by touching anything in the room. Certainly he would have looked down his nose at his older brother, except that Duvai was half a head taller. The contrast was strong: Duvai was taller and bigger, and perhaps as many as ten years older than Andevai, and the hunter was an impressive-looking man with the confidence and pride that comes from being respected by those he lives among.

"Here he is, Mother," said Duvai in a clipped tone that so shocked me with its displeasure that I swallowed the last hank of meat before it was fully chewed. My gulp was, fortunately, covered by his scornful words. "My brother has come home at festival, by the generosity of the mansa who lifted him to a higher station and therefore protects us out of thanks for what a noble son we have given to a House full of sorcerers."

"I am here, Mother." Andevai did not look at Duvai, and it was difficult to know whether it was pride, dislike, vanity, or envy that had cut the chasm between them. "I regret that I have not been here as often as I might have wished, but I am here now. I was following the toll road, and night came on just as I reached Haranwy."

Duvai gestured too broadly. His voice was deep, and his words unexceptional, but his tone was cutting. "We welcome him on a festival night, as we are required to do, now that he is a powerful man in the world. Perhaps his presence here will keep the Wild Hunt at bay on such a night. Or perhaps it will attract them, as honey attracts bears and carrion attracts wolves, they whose arrow and whose spear cannot be turned aside, not by any human power or cunning or strength. Not even by his."

I braced, my left hand at the sword's hilt, but Andevai had more self-control than I had realized. His jaw tightened. The hearth fire dimmed, but it did not go out.

His grandmother certainly did not fear him. "On Hallows Night, the masters cut out the souls of those who will cross over to the other side in the coming year. My son is infested with fever. His body will not outlast this winter. This I have seen. I also have few enough days left in this flesh, so I will see you, sons of different mothers, embrace this night. Even if you cannot like each other, then promise me for the sake of the village never to fight one another. I will always be watching."

Duvai grunted, almost inaudibly. "It will be as you wish, Mother," he said.

I had not thought it possible for Andevai's haughty posture to grow more stiff, but it did. "It will be as you wish," he echoed softly.

The two men embraced, but I had seen snarling dogs more companionable. They parted awkwardly.

Andevai went over and knelt on the pillow. He took his grandmother's thin hands in his own and bent to kiss her hollow cheek. "I missed you, Mother."

Duvai snorted.

This time the fire did go out, and a spurt of ash rose. Strangely, the tapers that lit the room kept burning undisturbed.

"Let the festival be danced," she said to Duvai. "I will hear and dance with you. On such a night, trouble may come to the gate if things are not done properly."

"Of course, Mother," he said with more warmth than before. He said nothing to Andevai but left. The attendant emerged from the shadows opposite and knelt at the fire to set new kindling.

"Don't bother," said Andevai. "It won't light until I'm gone."

She continued with her task as if she had not heard him.

"You are come late, Vai. You who study the magic of winter are most at risk. You dare not walk abroad on the day when the veil is thinnest and the hunt rides. For I am sure the tales tell us that the ancient ones who rule in the other world distrust magisters most of all."

"They hunt down those who become too powerful and draw their notice, so we are told, but you can be sure I am not taught enough to become truly powerful. Not I, the son of slaves."

"Is that a bitter apple, son?"

He grimaced. "I asked for nothing. I wanted to be a hunter, not a cold mage."

"Yet you are what you are."

"So I am. Now I am responsible for all of you, as I am reminded every day at the House. Trouble runs at my heels like a pack of wolves. The mansa has ordered me to kill a person."

"That is a heavy task. What manner of person?"

"I have to do it. I have no choice. That is not why I came, Mother. This night and day I cannot travel abroad—no magister can, although our servants can ride where they wish, evidently." How annoyed he sounded! How glad I was that the eru and the coachman had the power to tweak the noses of the proud House mages! "So I stopped to see you," he continued, as humbly as an affectionate child. "The visits I make here are what sustain me through the rest of the year. It will be a colder winter than most...." He faltered, voice choked, and after a moment continued. "Best I go see Fa now, to greet him, and then to see my own mama. What news of my mama, Mother?" His voice trembled on the words. Beyond the walls of the house, the drums rolled loudly and in unison as youthful voices whooped and cried out, breaking into song.

"The Hallows fire is being lit," remarked the old woman.

"There is no place for me at a fire's lighting," he answered curtly.

The drums fell into a shared rhythm, one that made my shoulders twitch. I recognized the measure of the drum, calling "koukou," which we'd learned from friends in the city. The sound came closer, as at a procession winding through the compounds of the village.

"Best you wait until dawn to greet your mama. No good for her will come if she is woken now that the medicine has taken effect, for they dosed her before dusk. You may as well go on to the celebration. Let the old and ill take their needed rest while the young dance." The procession's clamor lessened as it moved away through the village. "If you go to Kayleigh now, she'll fit you with proper clothes."

He lifted a hand to touch his fine, elegant jacket with a self-conscious lift of his chin. "Is Kayleigh well, Mother? Is there any trouble for her?"

"No soldiers have trampled through our village's fields since you went up to the House seven years ago."

He ducked his head as if the words pinched him. "But they will. There's worse, Mother. The mansa himself told me today that he intends to take Kayleigh to his bed, to see if more magisters can be bred out of our bloodline. What am I to do?"

"What can you do, Vai? The magister who sired your father

on me did not ask my permission. The magister's gift—if indeed it came from him—lay quiet in your father, but it has woken in you."

"More curse than gift."

"Truly, Andevai, if you could be shed of it, would you?"

"No." He cupped a hand over his eyes to shield his face. "Even to what I endure at the House, I will suffer it in order to learn." When he lowered the hand, his expression was knit of iron. "It would not matter even if I wished. I belong to Four Moons House, as does this village. I must obey them, or it will be the worse for all of you."

"Has the mansa threatened you?"

"That he chooses today to inform me of his plans for my sister? That he reminds me that without the medicine provided by the House, my mother will die? That he mentions this village's obligations to the House? Are these not all threats? Because I failed to properly do what he asked me to do? Maybe there is nothing I can do to make it right no matter what happens. But my only leverage—as the Greeks would say—is to gain enough favor in their eyes by doing what I am required to do. Then, perhaps, the mansa will, one time, allow me to spare Kayleigh being dragged off to suffer his attentions."

"I doubt it."

He hissed in a breath. "I am trapped. What is one life set against all that?"

"A question you will have to answer."

"They despise me, Mother. Whatever stories I may tell my mama so that she does not worry, you know the truth of it. I am nothing to them, only they cannot waste me because I am too powerful."

"Is there no other House where you can go?"

"They dare not cast me out, because they know another House will take me. They will not trade me away because I am too valuable. Even if I ran away, no other House will shelter me. They wouldn't dare risk the mansa's enmity should he discover where I was hiding. Anyhow, if I were to leave my teacher on bad terms, what other teacher would take me in?"

"Is there no life for you outside a mage House?"

"Why do you even ask?" he cried bitterly. "Do you think I would be better off an outlaw starving in the hills? No princely house can take me in, because the mage Houses would turn on it and destroy it. No guild will take me, for the same reason. And, anyway, what guild would admit a poor village man with no guild connections, no property, and no craft? I suppose I might walk to a city and seek work as a laborer. No cold mage survives for long outside the protection of a House. People fear and resent us. My own father's other son fears and resents me! Even a magister cannot stay awake always. You know the saying: Saber-cats, wolves, and mages can be killed when they sleep. But, anyway, let's say I could. I might be able to escape them. Let's say I could travel to Qart Hadast or into the Barren Lands or across the ocean to Expedition. I have skills, and I have power—then what? I could hunt, maybe. I remember what hunting magic I learned from Fa before the cold magic bloomed and the House took me away. But do you think I would abandon you and my mother and sisters and my kin and the village to the mansa's anger? Because he will punish you to get back at me. So even if I could walk free, you cannot."

Even wrapped in my fur-lined cloak, I was by now shivering where I crouched. Crystals of ice skinned the surface of my uneaten porridge as the sorcery of winter radiated from him, released by his emotions. The fire was laid but not alight, and the elderly woman had vanished.

"These are harsh chains," said his grandmother in the same gentle tone she had been using all along, "although even you cannot say for certain what the mansa will do."

"Please say nothing to Kayleigh of what I learned! Let her have peace for as long as she can."

"Go on, Vai. You have friends who have missed your company."

He left.

After the door closed behind him and the fire spurted up with a flicker and licked along the wood with gathering strength, I leaped out from my corner. I gulped down the last of the cold porridge before I set the bowl down on the chest at the foot of her bed and let her see the sword; although out of courtesy, I kept it in its sheath.

"I thank you for the food, Grandmother, and your kind words, but I have to leave. I'm sorry for his troubles and for yours. I am quite sure that it is wrong for an entire village of people to be held hostage and in such an indenture for so long with no recourse, but I will not offer up myself just because—"

"Why does the mansa want you dead?"

Her question compelled me. It was as if she had ensorcelled my tongue. "Andevai married the wrong woman. He was sent to the Barahals to marry Bee, but he was tricked by Bee's parents into marrying me to save Bee."

"You were party to this deception?"

"I knew nothing of it! The Barahals deceived me, too. They lied to me, just as they lied to him! I am expendable, to the Barahals and to the mansa."

"So you mean to run for the rest of your life, never able to rest?"

The weary, horrible prospect unrolled before me like a path overgrown with vicious brambles. I would run and run and be torn until at last I collapsed with the wolves at my throat breathing death into my face. And yet even so, I could not accept defeat.

"If I can survive until the winter solstice, then they might still wish to kill me, just for the revenge of it. But as soon as Bee reaches her majority, the contract expires. So she has a chance if I can find her before they do. I'll never let them take her. Never."

The door opened. I whirled while pulling the sword half out of its sheath. Three elderly women entered, and by the time I accepted that these were not the mansa's soldiers, several older men had entered as well, including Mamadi. I retreated to the foot of the bed with my back to the wall as the men set out the benches. Eight men and seven women of advanced years took a place, men on one side, women on the other. Last, Duvai entered, supporting a bent and frail man who could barely walk. He looked as old as the tiny woman in the bed, yet I guessed he was her son. He wore about his neck and had pinned to his clothing many amulets, and in his rheumy eyes I saw blindness.

Duvai brought him to me. He traced the air around me without touching me, and a shiver of power crawled along my skin. Duvai helped him sit on the first bench. Still holding on to his nephew, the old man spoke to the assembly in a voice as hoarse as a frog's spring croak. "The spirit world is knit into her bones. But she is not a spirit woman. Hers is true human flesh. Therefore, she did not deceive us in asking for guest rights. It is a serious matter to consider handing over one we have promised to shelter."

"The mansa will punish us," said one of the women, "if we do not turn her over."

"Give her to Andevai," said a man, "and let him do what he must."

"To kill in the village on Hallows Night," said Mamadi, "is a very dangerous thing. Spirits will flock to her blood. That they would enter this village would be a very ill thing for the village."

"Then hold her prisoner," said that first man, "until Hallows Day has passed. Let her be taken back to the House, or have her throat slit beyond the stockade. We'll be rewarded."

"Rewarded as we were before," asked another woman, "to see our noble son snatched away by the mansa?"

"Will we be rewarded for offering guest rights to a traveler who asked properly and then breaking our word?" demanded another woman. "What troubles will rain over us in the years to come, because we have done a wrong thing? She must be released to go on her way. If the mansa's hunters track her down later, then it will not be on us that she is dead."

"If we do not tell Andevai," said another man, "then how will he know she was here? If he does not know, the mansa does not know."

They discussed the matter while I stood there pressed against the wall, amazed so many spoke in my favor. Or not in my favor, precisely—I never felt they cared much for me one way or the other—but in favor of a code that safeguarded guests. This was not about me, but about the integrity of the village.

When all had made their arguments, the old hunter spoke again in his frog's whisper. "If she has been offered guest rights, then we risk a worse thing if we turn her over to the mansa. If other villages should hear—and they will hear, you can be sure—then how can we expect them to greet our hunters and our women out gathering if they are caught betimes needing shelter? The mansa may fine us, add to our burden, even kill some among us, but his power is limited to this world. If we go against what the ancestors and the gods have told us is right behavior, then we offend a deeper power. And trouble will come down much harder on us, and on our children and on their children."

Last of all, Andevai's grandmother spoke. "If we prosper only through the suffering or death of another, then that is not prosperity."

It was agreed by a nodding of heads, some resigned, some reluctant, but in the end no one objected.

Duvai said, as briskly as if he had been waiting eagerly just for this opportunity, "Vai cannot leave the village until dusk tomorrow. If I set her on her way at dawn, we can fairly be said to have given her shelter and not left her vulnerable or tried to trick her into being trapped by him later. After that, it is out of our hands."

Silence followed his words.

Torn equally by shame, gratitude, and suspicion, I whispered, "My thanks to you."

I did not know what reaction I would receive for these paltry words, but to my surprise, after Duvai left to make his preparations, they invited me to sit among them. They were curious about who I was and where I came from. They asked nothing about Andevai or how I had fallen into the trouble that currently engulfed me. Being an inland village, they had not heard of the Kena'ani, not even to call them Phoenicians, but they were interested to hear I was city born and raised, and they asked questions about where I came from and what life was like in a city. Duvai's uncle, the best traveled among them, had been once to the city of Havery, when he was a young man, and he had never desired to repeat the experience. They might have kept me in the smoky little house all night had Andevai's grandmother not intervened.

"Let the guest be fed and invited to the celebration," she said.

The elders took their leave.

She said to me, "Trust can only be offered where it is also received."

"I ask for your pardon, maestra. But I was raised by people I thought were kin, who I thought cared for me. They threw me to the wolves the moment they feared for their own daughter. Why should I trust anyone?"

Yet I had trusted the eru and the coachman. Why?

She gave a soft noise, more of a grunt than a laugh. "As you heard, no one argued to spare you for your own sake. Rather for the village's honor."

"You might have said all that in my hearing to make me believe I can trust you."

"My hearing is weak. I could not hear what you just said." The tenor of her voice made her point clear. I had insulted her and, indeed, the village. "You may walk where you wish, leave if you feel you must. No one will stop you. Duvai will await you at the gate at dawn."

Thus was I dismissed, and I opened my mouth to speak, regretting what I had said, and then pressed my lips closed before I spoke words I was not sure I meant. To babble out meaningless assurances of my respect would only condescend. Maybe I ought to have been more trusting, but I dared not. The one thing I was sure of was that Duvai would be pleased to make his younger brother's life more difficult. How far he was willing to go against the mansa I could not know. The villagers had no recourse if the mansa acted against them. The village belonged to the House.

Just as I did. But I did not have to live here, or stay here.

The elderly attendant gestured to show I had overstayed my welcome, so I took myself and my sword and my weary heart into the cold as she shut the door firmly behind me. Outside, the compound appeared deserted. Snow spun lazily. I ventured out the compound gate and stood against a wall, staring toward the structure at the center of the village, with its thatched roof and a railing built around under the eaves. Smoke eked from stone chimneys and heat radiated from the open doorways. Inside flashed movement; drums beat, accompanied by the stamp of feet and calls of encouragement. Drums have their own magic. My toes twitched, and my feet shifted as my shoulders hitched a little back and forth.

"Catherine?" Kayleigh stood at the compound gate, looking around without seeing me where I stood not ten paces from her.

I said nothing, and when she walked away, I hurried the other way. It was easy enough to remain unseen when it seemed the entire village had crammed into the festival house. Night is a friend to cats on the prowl. At the inner gate, I became air and walked right past the two young guardsmen; not so difficult in any case because they were diverted by the sounds of the celebration they were missing.

"Did you hear Vai? Says he'll still outlast us tonight."

"You'd think if them at the House treat him so poorly he'd have been humbled, but he's the same as he ever was."

They laughed as I passed out of range. Three older men stood vigil at the gate of the outer stockade. Outside the stockade, a bonfire blew heat into the cold night. In the farthest aura of its light, just beyond visual range, pairs of eyes glimmered and four-legged shapes moved, prowling the perimeter. Waiting.

I stopped short. I took in a few breaths to steady my pulse as the sound of drums rolled like a shield around the village. Then I turned around and crept back past the inner gate, against the wall. A burst of laughter surprised me. Andevai strode among his age-mates up to the inner gate to fetch their friends; several older men had come to take their place at guard. The young men jostled and talked in a rapid release of insults and jokes as they coursed away back toward the celebration. Andevai walked as easily among them as he had, I now realized, moved uneasily within the House. He looked much less affected in the homespun clothing worn by country folk. He and his friends looked like the kind of young men a young woman might happily flirt with. Laughing, they pushed into the festival house while I remained alone in the dark.

Everyone had either gone into the festival house or bided behind closed doors in their compounds. They had a place to be, while I . . .

I became aware of a shadowy figure spinning and hopping into the open ground, its movements woven in with the rhythm of the drums. I held still, willing myself to become the stockade behind me, nothing more than poles of wood tied tightly together. Nothing to see. Nothing to take notice of. I could see in the dark that it was no man who approached me. It was a tall creature with horns and feathers and a mantle shimmering over its massive form. It spun and spun, the mantle flaring around it like sparks spinning in a vortex of wind. But there was no wind. And the mantle was not woven of cloth; it was woven out of threads of magic. The air had become deadened, and my ears grew as full as if stuffed with cotton until I could not hear the drums except as vibrations trembling up through the soles of my feet.

Although I had drawn a cawl of concealment over me, the creature spun closer and closer until it became clear it knew I was there. That it saw me. That it meant to investigate me as a guard investigates a suspicious noise and a movement where there ought to be stillness.

Like a cornered rat, I tensed with a hand on the hilt of my sword, ready to draw and fight my way free.

Yet I saw as with fractured vision: The creature was not a single entity but three. It was a mask, a big puppet built over a simple framework of wood. I could see right through the feathers and fabric and frame to the inside. A man, an ordinary man, carried this armature across his shoulders. His skin was painted with clay, thick strokes forming symbols I did not recognize. The clay glimmered as if smoldering with heat. As he spun, his gaze slid right over me once, a second time, and yet again, but he did not see me.

But the third entity saw me. Horned and feathered, it loomed above me like a twirling giant limned with silken threads of white fire, its trailing cloak like luminescent mist. It had eyes darker than the night and infinitely deep, and with these eyes it stared into my heart, and I knew it could devour me and that it would devour me if it decided I was a danger to the village on a night when perilous spirits might try to invade.

Some throat-catching instinct made me release the hilt of my sword.

Do spirits blink?

It spun away into the night, vanishing down one of the narrow streets and leaving me untouched.

My breath came in painful gulps. Shuddering, I chafed my gloved hands, but that did not warm them. I clawed at my frantic, muddled, matted thoughts as I fought to find a calm thread of reason: It had turned away. It had chosen not to harm me. It had recognized I held no animus toward Haranwy Village.

"There you are, Catherine!"

Perhaps I shrieked.

Kayleigh laughed as if I had made a joke, and rested a hand on my arm in a companionable, sisterly way. "Grandmother sent me. Did you get lost?"

Maybe the village's guardian spirit had let me go, but forgetting that Andevai had been commanded to kill me would be fatal.

"I need to . . . relieve myself. There is perhaps a . . . uh . . . dunghouse?"

Kayleigh snickered. "Your pardon. That's not the word we use. We have a place, but it will be cold this time of year. If you don't mind, my mother has a pot in her house you can use."

She led me again into the compound of Andevai's family and

to a door no larger than the others. Inside, past a small, square entryway, stood a different room entirely. Hung with lace curtains and furnished with a circulating stove built into the hearth, a fine four-poster bed, a small elegant table supporting a wicker sewing basket, and a beautifully carved wardrobe that shone with the luster of rosewood, it might have passed for a city merchant's bedroom. The main room boasted a plank floor instead of the packed dirt of the entryway. These accoutrements looked so out of place that I forgot my manners and stared until Kayleigh reminded me to take off my boots and step inside.

Two girls slept curled up on a cot. In the bed lay a woman whose face was so wasted and sunken, her complexion such an ashy, unhealthy gray, that it was impossible to discern any relationship. Heat soaked me. I took off my cloak and draped it over my arm, then wiped my brow.

"Here," whispered Kayleigh, drawing me aside and behind a screen.

She offered me a covered chamber pot and left me alone behind the screen with the pot, a bench, and a smaller wardrobe with one of its sliding doors open. A man's expensive and fashionable dash jacket had been folded on a shelf; it was the jacket Andevai had been wearing earlier. A glimmer teased my eye, and I pushed aside a pair of polished boots to see a sheathed sword, tall and slim like my own, propped in the wardrobe's corner. I tasted the metal's sharp flavor in the stifling air. Andevai carried cold steel, the better to kill me with.

But not tonight. Tonight he would laugh and dance with his companions. Fury scalded me. But I did actually badly have to use the chamber pot. I did my business, and afterward Kayleigh offered me warm water to wash and a comb to tidy my hair.

"I've never seen hair like yours," she said, untwisting a black strand from the comb and pulling a finger down its length. She touched her head, her hair confined beneath a tightly wrapped scarf. "It's so thick and straight, and as black as night. Your eyes, too, they're such a beautiful color, like amber."

I did not know what to say, so I busied myself braiding my hair. "You have so many fine things. Were these wardrobes made in the village?"

She regarded the larger one with pride. "The rosewood came all the way from Havery. Andevai had it brought in for Mama. He stints on nothing for her." She bit her lip as her gaze flashed to the sword I held close.

"Is there something else you want to say?" I asked, more brusquely than I intended.

"There's nothing else."

I wasn't sure I could enter a conversation with a girl whose brother had been ordered to kill me and whose grandmother and uncle had convinced the village elders to spare my life, at least until I left their village.

"Do you want to sleep?" she asked. "No one will come in here until dawn."

"No," I murmured, thinking of the guardian's depthless eyes, and yet as the word emerged, a yawn cracked my jaw. "But maybe I could just sit down one moment."

Weariness chose for me. I slept.

I woke with the taste of smoke on my tongue and the whisper of flames dying within the closed stove. Kayleigh was gone. The girls slumbered peacefully, while the ill woman's sleep was clearly drugged; a bead of drool caught at the corner of her lips and her eyes rolled beneath closed eyelids as if in her dreams she was seeing horrific sights hidden from the rest of us. I sat up, pulse thundering in my ears as panic stormed through me. But my sword lay on the cot alongside me, my boots sat neatly beside the door, and my cloak had covered me. I was rumpled from sleeping in my clothes but otherwise untouched. I checked behind the screen; the smaller wardrobe remained as I had left it. I touched the other sword, but a hissing spray of sparks burned my fingertips. I licked the smarting skin. Stealing the sword was clearly out of the question.

None of the sleepers stirred. I crept to the door, pulled on my boots, and swung my cloak over my shoulders. For good fortune I kissed the bracelet Bee had given me.

I slipped outside into the shocking cold night. The celebration drummed on, its beat stronger and faster. Clouds covered the sky. I had no idea how late it was or how long I had slept.

Duvai's house lay silent and dark, exhaling heat from the fine stove within. Surveying the houses with their thatched hats, I recognized that many of them breathed threads of smoke from brick chimneys. Were so many furnished with the comfort of stoves? For a humble rustic village, there was more here than I had realized.

I crept to the festival house, encountering no guardians, and sidled up to one of the doors. When none of the villagers crowded inside paid me any mind, I squeezed in to the very back with a shoulder shoved against a pillar of wood. I raised up on my toes to peer over the assembly, who were clapping and swaying with the drums. Older folk sat on benches at the front. The drummers sat or stood, some straight-faced with concentration or grinning like madmen as they watched and answered the dancers. If a rhythm were like a chain of magic, and maybe it was, then I would have been able to see the threads that linked them to the others, for although they were separate individuals, together they were one conversation in constant movement. The folk dancing in the cleared space were young men, stripped down to their trousers and to light linen undershirts so drenched with sweat that the fabric clung to their torsos.

Naturalists claim that however much the female may be said to love the accoutrements of fashion and furnishings, it is the male who is driven to display himself. Blessed Tanit, it was very hot in here! There are always two or three young men in any group who compete for the highest degree of attention, who want to be the best. Or who are the best, with a subtle flare that touches the essence, until the interaction between what they are doing and what the drummers are doing becomes the thing.

Andevai was a very good dancer, and furthermore he was shamelessly flirting with the attention of the gathering while competing for that attention with several other extremely spectacular young men who were also easy to look at. Who would imagine him as a contrite young man who had buried his head in his hands before his grandmother with so much humility? The dancers egged each other on as the women clapped and whistled and shouted encouragement, and the older men smiled as they shook their heads as if remembering past glories and regretting lost youth.

What woman does not enjoy such a display of male athleticism and grace?

A dead one.

With a flourish, the drums sent the young men to the sidelines, to a chorus of whooping and praise, and beat a new rhythm to call young women into the circle. The young men crowded over to a long table. Andevai broke off a piece of dark country bread he would have scorned, I am sure, if it was offered to him in the dining room of a perfectly respectable inn. He ate with the others with every indication of relish, all of them chattering and jostling as they worked their way down the table of common platters laden with festival food.

A hand brushed my elbow, then took hold firmly as a male voice spoke in my ear. "He who tries to wear two hats will discover he does not have two heads." Duvai indicated the door. "Dawn rises, and with it the open gate."

21

I slipped out in his wake, as we sailing folk like to say. He walked with the rangy stride of a man accustomed to treks through trackless countryside. He handed me a wool cloak, its weave coarse and scratchy.

"Put this on over the other. Such fine cloth marks you from a distance."

With the homespun cloak concealing my form, I passed through the inner gate beside Duvai without incident. The stripling was waiting in the shadow of a long thatched shelter where slabs of frozen meat hung from the rafters. He handed a pack and gear to Duvai and a smaller pack to me.

"I can come—" he began brightly.

"An obedient son brings wood to his mother's hearth," remarked Duvai. The lad took the hint and with a sigh of resignation watched us go.

Duvai knew the land and the season. The barest hint of gray lightened the snowy landscape as we crossed the outer gate. If there were wolves in the shadows, they faded as day crept out from the thicket of night. Snow crunched under our feet.

"Anyone can follow our trail," I said, glancing behind at the footprints leading away.

He said nothing, just kept walking southeast in a direction that led us away from both the House and the toll road. He set a strong pace, but I had long legs and the strength to keep up.

Maybe he was testing me, for by the time we reached the edge of the land cleared and husbanded by the village, I was warm despite the cold. We halted beneath the snow-kissed branches of spruce. He knelt, scooped up a palmful of crisp snow, and blew it back the way we had come, a scatter of misted breath and a sparkle. A wind skirled over the ground, whipping the grass and rustling in the skeletal arms of the orchard. It rolled back over our footprints and, like the sweep of a brush, erased them.

"Are you a cold mage, too?" I demanded, stunned by this display.

He rose. "I am no cold mage. A good hunter must understand what lies around him. That is all. Best we go quickly and make distance."

We walked, Duvai in the lead and me three steps behind.

"Why do you have two hats?" I asked his back. "I mean, what did you mean by that?"

"I was speaking of Andevai. He tries to wear two hats, but no man can. He must be a magister of the House or a son of this village. He cannot be both."

"Why not? Can a person be only one thing?"

"A person must know what he is."

"Be what you are," I murmured, echoing the eru's words.

"To be what you are is the kernel at the core of every person," he agreed. He strode at a pace that would tire me in time, but I was determined to show no weakness. In a way, Kayleigh had done me a favor by giving me that sleep in the warmth of her mother's house.

"What illness eats at your mother?" I asked.

"She is not my mother," said Duvai. "My mother was not willing to play second kora when her husband took another, younger bride, so she returned to her own village, taking her bride price with her."

"But not her son."

"The son remains with his father. My sisters grew up with her, under the hand of a Trinobantic lord instead of a mage House."

"Who is the better master, prince or magister?"

"Why should I prefer one master over another? Do you?"

His bluntness surprised me. "I do not, I admit." I hesitated, but I could never keep a prudent tongue. "What happened to Andevai and Kayleigh's mother?"

"The city medicine keeps her alive. Suffering is what comes from love."

"That's a hard way to look at it. How did the House come to take Andevai?"

"Cold magic knows its own. Their seekers found him when his power bloomed the year he turned sixteen, and they took him away. That is what masters do—they take what they want."

"Yet you still live in the village."

"Do you believe it so easy to walk away? Maybe that is what they teach you in the city. But I wonder if people in the city are any freer than we are here. As long as we pay our third in crops and labor, we are left mostly alone. Others have far less than we do."

"The village will be punished when the mansa knows you helped me escape."

He laughed.

"How is that funny?" I demanded.

On the hard skin of snow, each footfall's snap reverberated through the trees. There was no wind at all, and the deathly stillness was beginning to make me uneasy.

"Do you worry for us? Even if you do, you did not walk up to my brother and give yourself into his hands. So your concern for my village is kind to my ears, but I am not sure how much it really means."

"I don't intend to die for the mansa's benefit. I'm just sorry I stumbled onto your village and brought you into this, ah, difficulty."

"Yet you would not have lived out the night had we not given you guest shelter."

I shrugged as I kept walking. "You're right. Yet I would not change what I've done. And I'm still sorry for any trouble it may cause you."

He grunted in answer and picked up the pace. We had begun to climb into hill country.

"You caught something in the spirit world," I said to his back as I quickened my own stride to catch him. "That was no antelope seen on the tundra of this world, with that third horn."

He glanced at me sidelong as I came up beside him. "Few see the third horn. I would think you a spirit woman in truth for having the sight to see it. But Fa knows more than I do, and if he says you are human flesh, then you are human flesh just as I am human flesh."

"I am not a spirit woman," I said, because something in the way he spoke made heat flush on my cheeks and down my neck. It wasn't that he was flirting with me; this wasn't flirting—it was more like hunting. "It must be dangerous to hunt in the spirit world," I added, sure the words sounded curt. Maybe it was best they did.

"So it is. But such a catch brings good fortune to the village. Its meat will feed the hungry, and the splinters of its bones will strengthen amulets, and its hooves will be melted down to a glue that will strengthen our bows. The powder of its horns will heal the sick. All these things, coming from an animal carried out of the bush, will give us protection against the evils of the coming year."

"Unless the mansa punishes your village for aiding me."

"None will tell him, and my brother does not know."

"Do you like your brother, Duvai?"

"That is a question."

"My apologies. I was rude."

"You speak your mind but are willing to admit your faults."

I glanced at him just as he looked at me and smiled. With his assured stride and broad shoulders, he made an attractive figure, especially when he smiled. He carried a spear, a longbow, and a knife, and I had to trust that he meant no harm to me out here in the forest where no one could hear my cries. I touched the hilt of my sword, expecting to find it had again become a cane with the daylight, but for some reason today of all days—a cross-quarter day—I swung a deadly sword at my hip. It was no ghost today. That gave me some comfort.

"Where are we going?" I asked, to distract his smile.

"Southwest. Toward the sea and Adurnam."

"Won't they assume I'm fleeing to Adurnam?"

"It seems likely, but the magisters think as city people do. They never walk long distances. They will think you mean to flee along one of the toll roads or take a boat on the Rhenus River."

I shuddered. "I'd rather not take a boat on the Rhenus River. I'd rather walk."

He smiled again. Perhaps he meant only to be reassuring, but the smile brought a flash of charm that made me wonder why his wife was so suspicious of a chance-met woman brought to her door. He was a man who knew who he was, and that made him powerful and, I supposed, enticing. "Tell me about the city. Which mage House rules there?"

"The Prince of Tarrant rules Adurnam. He doesn't like the mage Houses. There's a city council as well, like an assembly of elders. It passes ordinances and regulates the watch and the customshouse, such things. But because all members of the council are all appointed by the prince, many feel it is not truly an assembly that governs for everyone but only for the prince's relatives, cronies, and supporters."

"Would they be wrong?"

"It's always been that way. But now people are beginning to speak out against the council, the prince, even the mage Houses." This political turn made me uncomfortable. "Perhaps you would tell me more about the countryside hereabouts. What landmarks I should look out for. If there are shelters along this ridgeway, for I doubt I can survive a night camping in the open."

We passed the morning in this wise, him talking about the land and me listening. I was good at asking questions. Anyway, there was always something I needed to know. The man who was not my father had taught me that, by leaving his journals as my only inheritance, even if those journals no longer belonged to me.

We moved higher up into the hills, following eroded ridge lines from whose height we saw occasional vistas open over the broad lowland valley, where the sacred and queenly Rhenus River flowed. A mist floated above the water, giving it the look of an unraveling satin ribbon. Where had my parents died? Or were they even my parents? Two people, among many, had drowned, and I had come into the keeping of the Hassi Barahal family. Had Aunt and Uncle known I was no Barahal, and had they deliberately raised me to sacrifice in Bee's place? Or had they believed I was the eldest Hassi Barahal daughter? I recalled the scene of my hasty wedding, restaging it again and again in my mind. But all I could truly remember was Bee's stunned expression and Uncle demanding "the documents" in exchange for me.

Wind shredded the clouds, and the lazy breath of snow subsided, but with the sun's emergence from behind cloud, the air grew colder. About midday, the sun sweeping in its low curve above the horizon, we paused at a crossroads to pour water at an offering stone. The libation coated the stone with a frail skin of ice where it pooled. He offered me bread and salty cheese, which we ate standing up because it was too cold to sit.

After we had gulped down the food, he indicated a path that speared away up across rolling countryside, easy to see from the crossroads.

"That way," he said.

My heart clenched as if a hand had squeezed it. "Are you leaving me here?"

"To reach Haranwy by dusk, I must return now. That is your path. If you follow the main way, it will take you across the chalk hills to Lemanis, if you know where that is."

"It's in the Romney Levels." My uncle had plenty of maps. From there the drained levels opened in the south into the marshy Sieve and the river, difficult country to pass. But a decent series of roads ran from Lemanis west across the higher ground of Anderida to Adurnam. It was slower than the toll road, but it cost nothing except the time it took to walk it.

"How far to Lemanis?" I asked.

"Two days for a strong walker."

I gestured toward the open countryside. "Anyone standing where we are might see me walking out there. Is this the safest way?"

"There is no safe way. Did you think there was?" He studied me with a bold gaze that made me frown, and my glare brought a curve to his lips that made me flush. "Vai is not the only man in the world—"

"I never thought he was!"

"—who might wish to do you harm. You are young, and female, and alone."

The spark of challenge in his expression burned me. "Why did you help me?"

"We must do what is right."

My breath steamed in the wintry air, but I found I had no answer to that. "My thanks to you and your people."

I nodded and turned away from him, and I set my feet on the path, walking into the lonely afternoon. I heard his footfalls behind me as he moved back the way we had come, and soon enough I could no longer hear him and soon after that I could no longer see him.

I walked, and I walked, and I walked. I was accustomed to walking. Bee and I walked all over Adurnam. The path was easy to follow, its branching spurs never to be confused with the main route toward Lemanis. The sun shone without warmth. The trees spread in wild tangles below the highest ridges, but up here I was utterly exposed. Anyone from miles around, standing at the right vantage point, could see me. Yet what else could I do except walk? There was no safe way.

I made good time. I spotted no life beyond a hawk, a pair of grouse, and a hare springing away across a stony clearing. Even such villages and farmsteads as I glimpsed in the distance looked abandoned. The world might as well have been driven into hiding by the Wild Hunt.

Of that dreadful passage no breath stirred that I could discern.

It is easy to think while walking.

The history of the world begins in ice, and it will end in ice. Here in the north, we live under the shadow of the ice, its ice sheets and massive glaciers, and no human can walk there without being killed or driven out. Daniel Hassi Barahal wrote that the Han people who rule in distant Cathay in the far east do not fear the ice, and the people who live near the belt of the world, known as the equator, rarely feel the ice's breath because of the ever-present heat. But he also wrote that of these lands, he could only report what he had been told or read since he had not traveled there himself to vouch for its truth: *Who is to say that our teachers know of what they speak or speak of what they know?*

This is what I thought I knew: Two thousand years ago, the Romans and Phoenicians had battled to a standstill, and in the end the Romans kept their land empire and the Phoenicians kept their ports and traded across the seas without impediment. Over time, as the empire of the Romans weakened, the Celtic chiefs broke away one by one and restored their ancient principalities and lordships, at times warring or feuding with their neighbors and at others allying against some more hated prince. But although the various Celtic peoples cast out their Roman overlords, they retained many things Roman: roads, bridges, aqueducts, a calendar, laws, literacy, and the city ways and city speech of Romans.

When, about four hundred years ago, the Persians swept across the north of Africa and conquered the trading city of Qart Hadast, many Kena'ani merchant families were forced to flee to other ports and cities. Across Europa, Celtic princes were eager to welcome them in exchange for a tax on their profits.

About one hundred years after the Persian conquests, the salt plague broke out south of the Saharan Desert, when ghouls crawled up from the depths of the salt mines and in their invading hordes tore apart the empire of Mali. The great diaspora, breaking in waves over a hundred or more years, flooded into the north, bringing West African refugees with their gold, their horses, and their magic. Refugees born to noble houses in the south married their wealth and honor into the princely lineages of the north. Others, feared and respected but never loved because of their sorcery, discovered brethren among the Celtic drua, and their secret societies flourished close to the ice; out of this partnership grew the powerful mage Houses.

But the refugees did not only flee north. A fleet from the crumbling Mali Empire sailed across the Atlantic Ocean, guided by Phoenician navigators. They reached the distant western continent, which was later named Amerike in honor of the Celtic explorer Rhisiart ap Meurig, and there they met, in South Amerike, previously unknown human nations and, in the north, the venturesome trolls. Their interest piqued by the new arrivals, trolls sailed east in their own exploratory ships and made landfall on the coast of Iberia, and thus began commerce across the stormy and unpredictable Atlantic Ocean.

Like-minded trolls and humans founded the city of Expedition on the Sea of Antilles, an inland sea separating the northern nesting grounds of the trolls and the southern continent with its human chiefdoms and kingdoms. But the inhabitants of Expedition proved to be a busy people with radical notions and an insatiable desire for new technologies that the mage Houses in Europa deplored and the princely houses might take or leave, depending on how it benefited them. In such tumultuous times, the old order will grow rigid and brittle as it strives to maintain the old ways.

Twenty-five years ago, a young Iberian captain who called himself Camjiata rose from obscurity during one of the periodic wars between Iberia and Rome and decided that Europa would be better off if he ruled all of it. Some princes aided him; some, allied with Rome, fought him. In the end, the mage Houses combined with the Second Alliance to overthrow him. But even they feared to kill him outright, so they imprisoned him on an island and left him to rot. Yet peace did not come. The common people became increasingly restless, muttering radical words like rights and demanding radical steps like an elected assembly, but what power did ordinary people have? No more than did the daughter of an impoverished family, however far back we could trace our illustrious Kena'ani lineage. Which was to say, no power at all. Not even the power to know who you truly are.

For who was I? Striding along, I felt no different in my physical form even though the djeli had told me I "wore" a spirit mantle. My hair, my hands, my strong legs, my height—none of this had changed. I still recalled the journals I had reread so many times I had passages memorized. I knew every wall and corner of the house where I had grown up and was acquainted with many a hidden alley in Adurnam. I had friends and rivals, if not so many as Bee. I sewed my own clothing, because we were too poor to hire it done. I loved yam pudding. These things made me Catherine.

But there were things about Catherine I no longer knew.

Sometimes you think so hard it's as if you are talking out loud. Or perhaps I was talking out loud to myself, for I was sure I heard my name.

"Catherine! Please! Wait!"

I drew my sword as I turned. A cloaked figure hurried toward me along the path with a bulky pack bumping against her shoulders. When I looked beyond my pursuer, I saw no sign of any others approaching in her wake nor could I find on the horizon the landmark stone of the crossroads where Duvai had left me. I had walked a long way. Afternoon settled its wings over my shoulders.

"Catherine!" She swept back her hood to reveal herself as Kayleigh, her hair and ears covered by a wool scarf. "I beg you, Catherine. Take me with you!" Panting, she came to a halt before me. "Andevai told me . . . the mansa means to take me to his bed to breed . . . children. Please." She wiped her brow as if to wipe away her sorrows and fears. "Don't make me go to him. Let me escape with you."

22

I lowered the sword but did not sheath it. "How are you come here?"

"I followed Duvai. Last night I heard him mention to Fa which way he meant to take you. Please allow me to accompany you."

"I don't—"

"I have provisions, two blankets, a spade, and a length of canvas and rope."

"I have no home and no money," I said, but I already knew how this conversation would end. I could not send her back to suffer what I had myself fled. "I don't even know how I am going to manage."

"You know a place to go, away from here. I know no place except the village and the estate. I'm a hard worker. I will not burden you, if you will just allow me to walk with you and show me how to go about finding work and a bed wherever it is you mean to go. Even if it means crossing the water, like the stories say you merchant people do on your ships. And two are better than one, aren't they?" She smiled hopefully.

I sheathed my sword and began walking. "Do you know anything about my people?"

She was as tall as I was, and her stride matched mine. "Yours are the tribe who wore purple, isn't that right? You fought a war with the Romans. You have queens instead of princes. A girl cannot be married until she spends a night in the temple sleeping with whatever man comes calling—"

"That's not true!"

"I've bitten you," she said contritely. "I did not know."

"No, I understand you did not know. You have nothing you need apologize for. It's one of the lies the Romans told."

"What are your stories, then?"

What stories belonged to a person whose entire upbringing was a lie?

"There are tears in your eyes," said Kayleigh. "Is it a sad tale, how you came to be married to my brother? It can't be because he's been unkind to you, for he'd never mistreat a woman. Why did your people make such a contract with the mage Houses? Have they mage bloodlines also, hidden away?"

"It's just the cold wind," I lied, for she obviously did not know that Andevai had been ordered to kill me. "There is nothing to tell." Yet to walk in silence seemed awkward. I did not want to ask her to tell the stories of her people, because she might then discuss her brother, and that subject I wished desperately to avoid. "Let me tell you the story of the great general, Hanniba'al. He crossed the mountains with his army and his elephants and took the Romans by surprise."

Kayleigh knew the art of listening, and I enjoyed telling the tale. From one tale into another, as the old saying goes. The path unrolled beneath our strides and the afternoon passed into dusk earlier than I wished. Hallows Night and Hallows Day were ending, and with the setting sun, the Wild Hunt must fade back into the spirit world. Leaving magisters free to safely ride abroad and begin their own hunt for me.

We reached a standing stone that marked a crossroads where a well-worn path headed east through the hills. Several distant smears marked villages amid clearings. The countryside hid the river.

Kayleigh approached the stone and let precious drops of ale from her leather bottle moisten the stone's base. She scanned the landscape. "It's almost night. There will be a shelter on the leeside of the hill. There always is, at a crossroads stone. Should we rest while it is dark?"

"No. We'll stop and take something to eat. The moon will rise soon. We'll have light enough for walking. Best we go as far as we can while the weather holds." I glanced back the way we had come, and she did, too, but we saw no sign of pursuit.

We climbed a side path down to a wattle-and-daub hut. After relieving ourselves in a solidly built latrine off to one side, we retired to the hut to eat a scant meal of bread and cheese, grateful for roof and walls. We did not light a fire although it grew dark. As soon as the moon rose, we set off again.

Kayleigh's nerves were not, it seemed, as steady as mine. She glanced back frequently. The chalk of the path ran before and behind like a beam of moonlight, part of the scaffolding of the sky drawn here on earth.

"Did you not pass Duvai, coming after us? Did he not see you?" I asked.

She turned her head away and spat on the path. Our footsteps thudded on the path in a steady rhythm, hers falling in the gaps between mine.

"While Fa yet lives, Duvai is not head of the house, but he will be. His mother is not my mother, even if we share a father. So he does not—yet—have the right to command me to do as he wishes. No more than he has the right to command Vai now that Vai is gone to the magisters."

"So Duvai did see you and let you pass?"

Her face was hard to read in the moonlight, but her lips

pressed tight. "He did not let me pass. I did what I must. He never saw me."

"What will happen when he returns to find you have fled?" I pressed. "Will he be blamed?"

"Why should I care if he is blamed? I won't go back for Duvai's sake!"

"I don't expect you to return. But if men from your village come after and find you, they'll find me. And if Andevai comes after and finds me, then he will find you."

"They won't come after me. But don't you expect Vai to search along the toll road? Isn't that why Duvai set you on this path instead?"

"So I hope. So Duvai told me, that the magisters would expect me to flee along the toll road or the river. It seems," I added cautiously, "that Duvai and Andevai do not get along."

I was not sure she would answer me. We walked some distance in silence with the wind shushing through the trees below and bending the grass and bushes that grew along slopes still visible under the moon's light. The air tasted of winter and made my eyes hurt. My fingers, even in gloves, ached with cold.

"They did not share a mother's womb, as Vai and I did. So there is no peace between them. That's often how it is with people, haven't you found?"

"I would trust my cousin with anything."

"Would you?"

I touched the bracelet Bee had given me. "Yes. Anything."

"Would she do the same for you?"

"Yes, she would."

"Then you understand me. Also, you know what is said: Two bulls don't bide quietly in the same pasture. Both Duvai and Andevai are ambitious. That makes trouble for everyone."

"You are not ambitious? What did you hope for? I mean,

before you heard about what the mansa wanted. Is there someone your elders expect you to marry?"

"There is always talk. No one in our village, but maybe some
men in villages not so far away if it pleases my family and theirs.
If we get permission from the mansa."

"Do you need the mansa's permission to marry?"

"Of course we do. The mansa's deputies oversee the villages.
There must be work for those sons and daughters of the magisters whose sorcery is too weak to harness. The seneschal and her
deputies measure our third in labor and crops. Every year the
newborns are brought up to be sealed into the House. Certain
lads are taken away to work as grooms for the soldiers of the
House. And girls..." She glanced over her shoulder, as if fearing
the mansa's soldiers might be coming up behind us on the path
to take her away.

"Tell me if you get tired," I said quietly.

"Never!"

We both laughed. This country girl was not so strange after
all. We traded stories of lads and young men we had fancied.
She had spoken to a soldier from the House cavalry one time, a
handsome fellow with blue-black skin and a charming accent,
the magicless son of a mage House based in Massilia.

"Where is that, Catherine? You seem to know such things."

I told her it was a port city on the northern coast of the Mediterranean Sea, the sea that separated Europa and Africa. I told
her how the Kena'ani had plied those coasts for centuries despite
the interference of the Romans.

"But the Romans built the roads and brought civilization to
the north," said Kayleigh.

"To the barbaric Celts. The refugees from the empire of Mali
were already a civilized people, of course. What happened to
the soldier?"

She shrugged. A village girl had to be cautious in speaking to soldiers. Bad things could happen. There was also a young man from the same village as Duvai's mother, a day's walk east, who was a charming fellow, one of the tawny Trinobantic Celts, a very fine fiddler with a hunter's lineage. "He is someone I could marry," she said, "for a young soldier in the House is usually not allowed to keep a wife, only a concubine. But Duvai's mother resents our village because of what happened, so she will speak against any marriage between me and him."

"What happened?"

"She left because of my father marrying my mother, as he had every right to do!"

"I might suppose a woman would be uncomfortable seeing a second wife brought in—"

"She was herself the second wife! Everyone says she was proud of her youth and beauty, and treated her elder wife with no respect at all until the poor woman lost her wits from crying so much and died. Even sweetest butter will sour when stirred by a bitter hand. When my father grew tired of her boasting and complaints, he found a more amiable wife. She took her bride price and went home. He could have stopped her, but no one wished him to, for the entire village was happy to be rid of her."

"She left Duvai behind."

"Boys belong with their fathers. Now she has poisoned her village against ours with her gossip and whispering."

"Surely your hopeful suitor no longer matters, anyway, if you have left all that behind."

She looked startled, almost missing a step; the enormity of the choice she had made was staggering. "I am rid of such troubles."

She spat again on the path before plucking an errant strand of hair that had escaped her scarf and releasing it to the wind as if it were her past, blowing away behind us. I licked my cold-chapped lips and felt the strain of a long walk weighing down my legs. The moon had reached zenith. We had been walking at least four night hours. All told, I supposed I had been walking fourteen or more hours since dawn, although of course the day-time hours in winter were of shorter duration and the nighttime hours longer. Tiredness was making me clumsy and dull.

"Do you think we might rest?" asked Kayleigh.

"Not yet."

With the wind rising steadily like a beast slowly curling out of slumber, we walked for at least another hour. Rounding a corner and stumping to the top of a gentle rise, we reached a crossroads stone, a squat pillar more chipped at than shaped and no taller than my head.

The wind had changed timbre and smell. It blew into our faces from the south—one might almost say out of the stone—and it might even have been said to possess the memory of warmth, something once known and mostly forgotten. This change kindled in me a strange emotion, in the way one imagines the breath of a mother on a cold, frightening night calms her restless babe. I waited until Kayleigh had poured a few offering drops at the base of the stone, and then I went forward myself and let fall the last drops from the first of the two leather bottles Duvai had given me. It was a vinegary drink, tart and bitter, but in the instant of offering, I smelled as through the stone itself a sweeter, summery scent like flowers in bloom. I blinked, wondering if the shadows of the landscape beyond the stone had altered, but after all they had not. In moonlight, I saw the path ahead of me, and the empty hills, and very, very far away and below us in elevation a tiny burr of light marking a town's watch fire. Was it possible we might reach Lemanis, the first leg of our journey, tomorrow? Sooner than I had dared hope?

The stars lay half hidden beneath a gauze of moonlight. My

eyes warmed with tears, although I did not understand why I should wish to weep.

"Ah!" said Kayleigh.

I turned at her gasp.

Riders approached us on the path, hooves and harness muffled. She grabbed my arm, wrenching me sideways, and at first I thought she was trying to pull us out of sight, so I went with the drag of her weight. Then she kicked out my legs from under me, and not expecting this assault, I crumpled as the riders closed. She threw herself on top of me as I thrashed and shoved and got my left hand free. I punched her hard enough that she grunted, and with a burst of furious terror, I heaved her off me and scrambled to my feet as the rider in front pounded up and resolved into Andevai.

His mouth set in a grim line, he drew a sword. Its cold-steel blade gleamed where moonlight kissed it. His mouth was set in a grim line. The wind died, and the air grew so cold so fast I shuddered convulsively. I fumbled at the twisted mess of my garments and belt, knocking my bundle of provisions aside as I groped for my sword's hilt.

"Are you all right, Kayleigh?" he demanded.

She struggled up and limped over to him. "Of course. Did you have any trouble following me?"

"None at all." He clasped one of her hands, then let her go, still looking at me as if he expected me to vanish. "You laid a bright trail."

His companion, wearing the livery of a House servant, pulled up a length behind him, mounted and leading another horse. He was no villager.

"You betrayed me," I said hoarsely as I grasped the hilt.

Kayleigh looked at me across the gap between us. "I bear you no ill will. It's only that he is my brother, son of the same mother, and I would do anything for him."

"You would go willingly to the mansa's bed?" I cried with all the scorn I could muster. "To bear the mansa's bastard children who may be taken away at any moment to be raised in the House and not by you?"

"If I must, and if it will aid Vai, then I will do that," she said with no tremor in her voice.

I could not fault her loyalty.

All I could do was draw my sword.

Because I expected him to come at me on the horse, using weight and height against me, I glanced to either side, trying to gauge where the land was most rugged, where I had the most chance to bolt while the horse would have trouble following in the half-light. As if he guessed my intent, he dismounted and strode forward so quickly I scarcely managed to wrestle the bundle from my back and fling it at him. He danced aside as the bundle sailed past him to smack on the dirt. I skipped back to place the stone between me and him.

He attacked.

He thrust. I parried. He cut; I caught his blade on mine, the steel singing where it met. Twisting away, I slashed back; he ducked left out from under the blade, which sliced across his right shoulder deep enough to catch in fabric, penetrate flesh, and cut free.

With a harsh curse, he stepped back to catch his balance. I grinned, too wildly, I am sure, for in a battle for one's life, one learns to treasure each reprieve and indeed each breath. The standing stone covered my back, but being at my back, it also limited my movement. I leaped sideways, onto the path, and he charged after me.

I was lighter and quicker and my technique was cleaner, heritage of a childhood spent training with the sword, but he was bigger and stronger, and he had reach. All he needed was reach. Cold steel in the hands of a cold mage needs only to draw blood in mortal flesh to cut spirit from body. How easily he could kill me!

Because I was left-handed, I backed around, keeping the stone to my right shoulder. While he had the grace of a man who knows how to dance, he did not have my fine-tuned control or, evidently, my ability to read in his body his next move. I made sure the stone got in his way more than it got in mine. I thrust, prodded, and slashed; he parried too easily, for I was already tired, and he had ridden while I had walked and was therefore fresher. If I ran, he would catch me. All I could do was fight for my life.

I shifted preparatory to a more desperate attack, but he fell back to test his right shoulder where my blade had cut. A thread of blood seeped through. I'd taken first blood, much good it would do me: Cold steel in my hand did not sever spirit from flesh with first blood. Yet because he was right-handed, the injury might give me an opening. I measured his stance for an opening.

"Look out!" shouted Kayleigh.

Blessed Tanit, I was wearying fast. The old trick caught me: I glanced toward her. His blade flashed forward. Instinct carried me; I slammed right, my shoulder meeting stone, trapping me. My blade shivered against his, my strength not enough to hold him off as he pressed forward. He halted as our hilts caught, so close I could have kissed his lips, which were slightly parted with intense concentration as he stared into my face. My trembling arms and exhausted body were about to fail me.

"Blessed Tanit," I murmured, "accept your daughter's spirit with love."

His expression changed, flooding with an emotion I could not name.

"No," he said, not to me. He jerked back, pulling his sword out from the tangle between us. Giving way. Giving up.

Somehow in the breath of his retreat, the edge of his cold steel caught under my chin and parted my skin as gently as a summer's breeze parts the petals of a blooming rose with the merest flutter as it passes.

Such a weakness of limb and heart assailed me that I sagged against the stone.

He gasped, eyes widening with an expression I could not possibly interpret or comprehend as he leaped out of range.

Languid, I raised my right hand and with its back brushed my glove against the curve of my jaw. When I lowered the glove, a moist line glittered on the smooth leather.

"Catherine," he cried. "Your *blood*!"

"Am I not falling dead quickly enough?" I cried. A spark of such fury roused me that I was determined to drive him back until I stuck him through and pierced his selfish, vain heart.

Blood dripped from my jawline to spatter on my glove. Without meaning to, I flinched, and so the next drops falling split the air with the heat and life that abides in the blood of all living things. They fell like raindrops onto the base of the stone against which I still leaned, and when the drops splashed, too faint to be seen and yet thundering like a storm across the heights, the stone turned to mist against my shoulder and I fell through.

23

Into summer.

I broke into a sweat. Birds warbled and chirped and shrilled around me in a melodic uproar, and a huge crow fluttered down to earth a sword's length from me. It tilted its head to peruse me first out of one eye and then the other in a way that reminded me oddly of the troll and solicitor Chartji, from the Griffin Inn. As I climbed to my feet, it cawed loudly and flapped away. I paced a circle around the standing stone to take in my surroundings.

That I had landed in the spirit world I did not doubt. Hillside rolled away on all sides into a green summer forest dense with trees I could not identify, although I recognized beech and ash. Was that a river glimmering far off to my left? I supposed that direction to be the east, but I could not be certain, because although the sky was not precisely cloudy, the heavens were veiled by a strange haze that concealed the sun. Yet the air held as much heat as if the sun were shining. Birds flitted over banks of flowering shrubs and waving grass that carpeted the open ground between the crest, where I stood, and the beginning of forest fifty or more paces below. Butterflies bright with blues and yellows and reds made the air seem alive with color, and the place *smelled* so overwhelmingly of life that I wondered if I might choke on it.

I stood on a path paved with grains as white and fine as salt ground by mortar into sand. It gritted under my boots as I shifted my weight. My chin stung. I stripped off my gloves and cautiously touched a pair of fingers to the wound, a petty, inconsequential cut still oozing blood. I ought to be dead. Maybe I was dead. Didn't dead souls pass over into the spirit world? I pinched myself, and the bite of my fingers hurt, so either I lived or the dead felt pain.

Movement at the corner of my eye alerted me. An indistinct shape stalked the forest's edge, shadows rippling. My hand tightened on my sword's hilt, but when a pair of saber-toothed cats emerged from the trees, I felt as cold as if a winter's wind had blasted down from the north. Cold steel offered no defense against such massive beasts. I looked both ways down the path. In the direction in which I was reasonably sure I had been walking, a change in the color of air marked where the hills fell away, and hazy, deep greens and muddy blues marked a lowland marsh. The Sieve was nothing more than a vast marshy wilderness, some of which had been drained and penned off into levels where crops could be grown. Last night—indeed, how had it become day?—I had glimpsed a burr of fire that surely identified the old Roman-founded market town of Lemanis.

Beyond the standing stone in the mortal world waited Andevai and his sword and loyal sister and attendant servant. The two cats ambling gracefully along the tree line below did not approach. A third, the one whose shadow I had first spotted, trailed behind them.

Stay on the path, the eru had told me.

I still had to warn Bee.

After tucking my gloves into my belt and loosening the tight chain of the heavy winter cloak so air could circulate around my back, I started to walk. I settled into a pace neither so fast it might appear as if I was running, a temptation even to lazy predators, nor so slow that I might seem weakened or injured, for every natural historian knows that hunting beasts are most attracted to those in the herd who lag behind. The hunt culls the sick, so it was always best to look strong no matter how exhausted one's legs were and how the burden of running was beginning to weigh on one's heart.

Blessed Tanit might protect me if she willed, but natural historians suggested that the gods were merely a story devised by humankind to explain the mysteries of heaven and earth. Even if that were not true, Fiery Shemesh, whose glorious, blazing disk I could not see within the silvery haze that made the sky, was likely no god of *this* world. The cats were this world's creatures, beautiful, deadly, and aloof. They did not glance my way, but I knew they knew I walked the path. I had no food, no water, nothing but winter clothing, beneath which my flesh became slick with perspiration. Nothing but my determination, Bee's bracelet, and a sword that had been given to me by an eru.

The biggest cat suddenly raised its head, and with the most astonishing grace imaginable, bounded up the slope toward me, head level and gaze intent. My throat tightened until I could scarcely breathe, and my heart stuttered, *galump galump galump*—only those heavy beats were not my pulse pounding in my ears but an actual drumbeat.

I glanced behind.

I did scream, then, or perhaps it was a shout of fury. Tears spill not only from sorrow. Sheer bloody outrage can make you cry.

The djeli Bakary had told me that he could see into but not walk in the spirit world, while cold mages neither see into nor walk there. Yet here came thrice-cursed Andevai on his horse, riding after me as if he crossed into the thrice-cursed spirit world as easily as snapping his fingers.

What choice had I? I turned, planted my feet, and made

ready. I would have one chance to kill him before he cut me down.

The cat's roar shattered birdsong. The horse skittered sideways; Andevai hauled it back onto the path, but two more cats—were there five now?—came running up on the opposite side, keening and roaring as they raced, muscles bunching and stretching. Their beauty was so startling that a person might smile at the terror of beauty before death closed in a pounce.

They did not touch the path, and it was clear Andevai knew they could not, but the horse could not know. He battled it as it shied and reared and, finally, dumped him sidelong off the path onto a stretch of grass. Relieved of his weight, the horse ran at me.

"Blessed Tanit, do no harm!" I croaked as the great cat rippled across the grass and with a leap came down on Andevai's chest just as he was trying to get up. He was slammed back by the force of its weight.

I flung up the arm holding my sword to hide the awful kill. The horse broke sideways at the flash of steel and clattered to a halt, reins dangling and eyes flaring, not three paces from me. The cats had not pursued it. They were circling the cold mage.

He was not dead. He was not even bitten or clawed. The saber-toothed cat simply stood on him, pinning his sword arm and chest. It slewed its lovely head around to stare at me. Was it deciding which morsel looked more delectable? Or asking my permission to eat him?

"Oh, no," I said, voice quavering and heart trembling. "Don't look at *me*! I don't want to be eaten. And I can't…I can't…" Even after everything, I could not say, *Kill him*.

I lowered my sword and whistled softly and wished I had an apple as I slowly, very slowly, reached for and took hold of the reins. The horse came gladly to a steady hand.

Aunt and Uncle could not keep horses, as they were too great an expense, but the scions of a mercenary house must learn to ride in case they are called away to travel in the service of the family. I knew how to set my foot in a stirrup and swing onto a saddle, how to gather reins in hand and brace myself awkwardly because the stirrups were set for a longer leg than mine. I used thighs and the pressure of my seat and a clucking sound made twixt tongue and palate to suggest to the equine that it ought to walk. A well-trained horse will move without much urging, especially if it is near to large predators and believes that moving will take it away from them.

We started down the path, but I turned in the saddle to see what was going on behind me.

He raised his head. His voice had a strength I admired, considering the position in which he currently found himself. "You can't steal my horse!"

A second cat ambled over and kneaded its sheathed paws gently on his torso, while the first lowered its huge head and licked his face. He swore in a string of curses.

I laughed as I rode away. Maybe I wept, too, or perhaps that was only sweat seeping down my cheeks. A shrill cry cut the air, and I felt my heart contract as with a fever, but after all I spotted a hawk gliding that had surely made the call. Surely it had been no human agony.

I put the horse through her gaits and settled on a shog that jolted me to my bones but seemed not too tiring to the horse, breaking it at intervals with a walk. After some time had passed and when I spotted a stream not too far afield from the path, I reined my doughty steed aside and let her water and graze while I made inventory.

One excellent horse. Two saddlebags, the first containing a very fine suit of fashionable clothing rolled up within heavy canvas, as well as various and sundry necessaries such as an exceedingly sharp razor, a spoon and knife of excellent polished

silver since no doubt nothing available in rustic inns encountered on such a country path could ever touch the lips of a proud
magister, and a hoard of coins. The second bag held provisions:
dried meat, a half round of cheese, a leather bag filled with nuts,
and apples, perhaps to sweeten the horse.

I took off both cloaks and tied them like a bedroll, making
sure my gloves were secure. I did not think of my husband, not
at all. It was not that I cared for him in any manner, because I
did not and could not, but the thought of any person being
mauled and devoured made me feel sick. Ought I wish I owned
a crueler heart, one that exalted in death and savage vengeance?
I could not, even though he had been commanded to kill me.

Blood drawn by cold steel in the hand of a cold mage ought
to have cut my spirit from my flesh and dropped me as dead as
dead. Instead, my blood on the stone had opened a pathway
into the spirit world. *My blood*. An eru called me cousin. A djeli
said I wore a spirit mantle. An aged, dying hunter had said that
the spirit world was knit into my bones.

Maybe I was dead. I brushed impatiently at tears and
squinched up my face. Was this Sheol, that he should pursue me
into it? That made less sense than anything else.

I sucked in balmy air, moist and flavorful in my lungs, ripe
with green and growing things, and forced myself to think things
through, to pretend I wrote in a journal as a means to form order
out of chaos. Wasn't that what Daniel Hassi Barahal had done?
He had recorded his observations for the family, as was his duty.
But behind the words the Barahals might sell for profit lay
another layer of his thinking: He was trying to make sense of the
world he observed by setting it down in sentences—not to capture it, for the world can't be captured and caged, but to see if he
could discern a pattern beneath the bewildering variety, the con-
fusions and contradictions and the beauty and the ugliness.

I was flesh and blood; I never doubted that. While I had no

evidence that the Amazon Daniel Hassi Barahal had married was actually my mother, I had equally no evidence she was not. So if Tara Bell was my mother, then who was my father?

What if my father was a denizen of the spirit world?

The woman I believed to be my mother had said *Don't tell anyone what you can do or see, Cat. Tell no one. Not ever.* If the spirit world was knit into my bones, didn't it make sense she would want me to keep it a secret?

There. That wasn't so hard, no matter how absurd and impossible it seemed, or how numb the thought made me feel, or how my hands began to tremble.

Had Daniel Hassi Barahal truly believed he was my father? Had Aunt and Uncle not known? Had they thought they were giving Four Moons House the right girl, against their will? Had Tara Bell lied to all of them? Could I never stop questions from chasing around my head? To distract myself, I offered an apple to the horse, who snuffled it appreciatively out of my hand.

"I suppose you have a name already," I remarked.

She flicked an ear and raised her head. She was a big mare, and I suspected she had an even temper and a bold heart to take in stride crossing with her master into the spirit world. Her master, who was either being eaten or had fled back into the mortal world to consider his next course of action. I had to find a place to cross back. I considered the stirrups and had shortened one when the horse shied. I grabbed the reins and she stilled, eyes flaring and ears flattening.

I turned.

One of the cats had followed us. The big cats wore summer coats more shadow than sun, and this one had a pelt as dark as sable. It walked long and lithe, more of a lazy stroll, but halted at a reasonable distance just as if it could gauge the horse's degree of panic. The cursed thing sat on its haunches and set about licking a paw, but I knew it was eyeing me.

"You've already had your dinner!" I shouted, and then clamped shut my mouth as I wondered if it were licking *Andevai's blood* from its claws.

A cold shudder ran right down through my body.

"Horse," I said in a level voice to my new best companion, "it is time to go, slowly and quietly, without fuss." I led her to the path, and once on the path, I shortened the other stirrup and then mounted. All the while, the saber-toothed cat washed its paw and watched me as if I were a large and plump and exceedingly tasty deer it was gathering up the effort to chase. My steed and I commenced a steady walking gait, not too fast and not too slow, and cursed if the cat did not rise gracefully and pad after, keeping its distance but always keeping us in sight.

To be slaughtered in the spirit world. What did that mean for Andevai's spirit? How awful one's last moments must be. If he were dead, then I was free, but I could not precisely rejoice. *It is easy to admire what you must not endure*, so Daniel Hassi Barahal had written. If it was done, then it was done. I had only defended myself, and Bee.

But how on earth, then, had he managed, or even thought, to shout after me about his cursed horse?

I rode the rest of the day, husbanding my strength and that of the horse. Once we passed a boundary stone, but I avoided it and kept moving. The summer day seemed peaceful, and to think of crossing back into the teeth of winter made me wince. The cat still followed us, and twice when I had glanced back, I glimpsed a second cat, but later it vanished, leaving only the one. How easily you become accustomed to a fear that merely buzzes your shoulder but never alights. It was curious, that was all—a curious cat.

So it was that in the lingering summer twilight, half asleep in the saddle as I rocked in rhythm to the horse's smooth gait, I came down into low country as flat as if it had been ironed. The chalk path gave out in a tangle of scrub vegetation, with thick forest beyond. The loss of a vantage point made me feel small. As I tried to decide what to do next, a hoarse cry like that of an anguished monster bellowed from deep within the forest. Twilight certainly had begun to draw a cloak over the world, and a chorus of frogs, of all things, rose from an unseen pool. The sable cat circled us and flowed over in its lazy way to stand before a wild blooming thicket with flowers strung like tiny bells from drooping branches. As the wind brushed through them, did they *tinkle*?

The cat yawned in a catlike way that happened also to display to great advantage its impressive saberlike canines, which measured the length of my forearms. I began to think the creature—it was male and probably young—was showing off. It vanished into the shrubbery with a flick of its tail. I pressed my mount forward enough to identify an overgrown track leading into the undergrowth and thence beneath the trees.

I could follow it. But a moment later, I spotted a thread of smoke away to the right, barely visible against the hazy sky. Smoke meant fire. Fire, I deduced, suggested a being not related to a cold mage. I turned away from the thicket and rode parallel along the flats beneath a line of ragged cliffs held together by clumps and tufts of grass.

I soon realized I had misjudged the fire: Whatever hearth expelled the fire came from the cliffs north of me, not from the flats. The twilight hung as though suspended, and it was not yet dark when I spotted a round stone tower, very like an ancient dun although as stout as if it had been built yesterday. I dismounted and led the horse up a track scraped into the earth to reveal chalk. As I came closer, panting at the steep climb, I heard fiddling. At the height, I paused under the canopy of a vast oak.

A bent old woman sat on a flat stone bench with a fiddle set to her chin. She sawed a mournful tune while a fire burned merrily within the confines of a circular hearth constructed of the same flat stone used to build the dun. The dun had a door, closed, and three high windows, shuttered, and an air of being entirely deserted, like a corpse whose spirit has fled. Beyond the fire and almost lost in the darkness stood a stone trough and next to it a well ringed by a waist-high wall of white stone and capped with a hat of thatch from whose supporting pillars hung a rope and a brass bucket. The horse whickered, smelling water, and the fiddler ceased in midsong and lowered the instrument.

Without looking around and in a voice that sounded much younger than her stooped form appeared, she said, "Peace to you on this fine evening, traveler."

Hearing the village speech here in the spirit world surprised me, but I managed a reply to her back. "Peace to you. I hope there is no trouble."

"No trouble indeed, thanks to my power as a woman. A fine afternoon and a fine day it has been." She still did not turn around. "How does it find you?"

We ran down through an exchange of greetings until I finally asked, "My pardon, but is there some reason you keep your back to me, maestra?"

"Is there some reason you are unaware it is foolish to look any creature in the face in the spirit world before you are sure what manner of creature it is?"

"It is?" I blurted.

She laughed. "Na! *Come*. Into the light," she said, by which I recalled my surroundings enough to realize that night had fallen and the spirit world breathed in darkness while her cheery fire alone lit the world. There was no moon, and there were no stars, yet neither did the haze that blinded the heavens feel like clouds. Here beyond the aura of light, I began to think the forest below the cliffs had begun to breathe and actually *move*. A twig snapped.

I led the mare out from under the oak and, staying well back, circled the hearth until I came around to stand behind another stone bench. I faced the woman across the fire.

She was old, with a crooked back, and as thin as if she had not had enough to eat for many months. But she held my eyes with the confident gaze of a person who is sure of her authority in the world. Her loose, comfortable boubou, the robe sewn out of strips of gold, red, and black cloth, appeared practical for journeying and easy to wear. Her skin was quite black, unusual in these parts, and a scarf wrapped her head, although it had slipped back to reveal twists of silver hair. She wore gold earrings.

"You're a djeli," I said. "A djelimuso." A female djeli.

She opened a case and placed the fiddle and bow within, then closed it and looked at me. "What are you?"

"I'm Catherine," I replied. The horse shied and snorted. I yanked down on the reins just as a pair of saber-toothed cats ambled out of the night and flopped down beside the well.

"Are these also your companions?" asked the djeli with remarkable calm. When she shifted her head to look directly at the big cats, her earrings caught strands of firelight and sent it shooting like arrows into the night, and then I blinked; after all, the earrings were only gleaming slightly, as any polished surface must do.

"Not my companions, but they seem to have followed me." I did not see the sable male cat; these might be two of the ones I thought had stayed behind to guard ... or to eat ...

"Andevai!"

How any man could manage to look so haughty and offended while limping I could not say. And yet, infuriatingly, it was indeed Andevai who emerged out of the night, appearing very much the worse for the wear with his clothing rumpled and stained. Besides that, he looked immensely annoyed. Behind him strolled another three of the big cats, whose demeanors bore the smug satisfaction of a petted house cat that has just deposited a mouse before its surprised human. And I was very surprised.

With not even a polite by-your-leave, and ignoring the huge saber-tooths, he approached the roaring fire.

The djeli rose. "Peace, traveler. I hope the night finds you at peace."

He pulled up so sharply that I laughed, for it was as if he'd been reined in.

"I have no trouble thanks to the mother who raised me," he said politely. "May this night find you at peace."

Honestly, they went on in this vein for far longer than I could ever have dragged out a greeting with my inadequate command of village customs. I thought they might wind down through the health of unnamed fathers and uncles and mothers and cousins into the well-being of the cattle, dogs, chickens, wheat, and barley and what troubles the vegetable garden might have seen since the two had last met, which, since these two had evidently never before met, would no doubt take a century to complete.

"Are you finished?" I demanded when there came a pause, rather embarrassed at my rudeness but really beginning to shake now. I could use fear if I turned it to anger. "Begging your pardon, maestra." I drew my sword, and the cats rose as if in answer, yawning to display their ferocious teeth, although they stayed by the well. "I thought you were *dead*."

He swung around to look at the cats, then back to face me. His own sword remained sheathed. "A more correct statement would be that you *wished* I was dead."

"I *wished* no such thing. I am sure I hold no animosity toward you at all except for the small detail that *you* tried to kill *me*. Indeed, for all I know, you did kill me, and I am wandering here as in Sheol, with saber-toothed cats stalking my trail and you plaguing me. I suppose you intend to attack me again, perhaps by the light of this lovely—" I broke off.

The fire was burning without stint.

His presence was having no effect on the fire.

"I want my horse back," he said wearily, paying no attention to this marvel.

"Why are you not extinguishing the fire?" I demanded.

"Because," said the djeli, "while magisters draw their power *through* the spirit world, they have no power *in* it."

The look he shot at her should have been a spear of killing ice, but the fire burned regardless and nothing happened to her for violating such precious secrets.

Fiery Shemesh! He wielded no cold magic here!

I snorted, and his gaze flashed to me as his lips curved into the supercilious frown I was becoming familiar with. But I also noticed how stiffly he held his right shoulder; dried blood marred the sliced edges of his coat.

"You're strong and fast, but your technique is sloppy," I said as I sheathed my sword with a flourish meant to challenge him. I was beginning to see that the angrier he got, the more he climbed the pinnacle of arrogance, but without cold magic to throw around, and unless he decided to physically attack me with his sword arm injured and within the aura of firelight under the gaze of the djeli, he could do nothing but listen. And I had a lot to say, words I had swallowed for too many days. "My question, though, is why you did not use the weight and height of the horse to your advantage but instead dismounted to attack me. No Barahal would ever make such a mistake."

"I wasn't aware," he said cuttingly, "that you were a Barahal."

"A weak rejoinder! Not up to your usual standard. Next thing, you'll accuse me of being in on the fraud."

"You aren't actress enough to have managed that. It was obvious you knew nothing of the scheme."

I lost my rhythm at this unexpected parry. No cutting retort sprang to my lips.

"Anyway," he added, speech clipped as if the words were difficult to get out, "I thought if I was required to kill you, as I had been commanded to do, that I ought to show enough respect to you to do so face-to-face."

"How decent of you, truly! What courtesy you've shown me! First, you drag me from my home against my will, refuse to let me eat perfectly decent food, are rude to perfectly respectable innkeepers, and then when you're told to kill me because of a mistake you made and through nothing I have ever done, you try to kill me."

"I didn't try very hard!"

"You tried hard enough! You drew blood!" I touched my fingers to the cut on my chin.

He flinched, then drew himself taut. "You should be dead," he agreed coldly, his color very high and his posture very rigid.

"But I'm not!" I cried. "No thanks to you!"

He shook his head. "If the Barahals had given me the other girl, then none of this would have happened, would it? She would be married according to the contract, and treated well and living better than you could possibly have been in that rundown and ill-furnished house, while you would remain safe and unmolested in the bosom of your so-called family. It seems to me they're at least as much at fault for handing you over while knowing the mansa would discover the cheat and take out his anger on you. So why aren't you railing at their part in this?"

Tears pricked at my eyes. "What makes you think I'm not?"

He had the decency to look startled. A foggy notion crept into my head that he might be ashamed, and that his shame might be fueling his anger. No, that way lay insanity. He was whipping himself because he had not yet fulfilled the mansa's command. He might even conceivably be worried about his village, or his loyal sister, and I was bitterly reminded that he had brought an escort and a spare horse for Kayleigh, which was far more than Aunt and Uncle had arranged for me. They, who had thrown me to the wolves. I hated them all over again. Hated them. Loved them. Choked on despair and anger and sheer exhaustion.

The djeli watched us with a slight smile.

"I ask your pardon for my poor manners," I said hoarsely to her. "I've had some trouble on the road."

"So it appears," she said.

"Might I rest at your fire?"

She extended a hand, not quite in invitation for me to sit but more like a request for payment.

"That's how it is with djeliw and bards," muttered Andevai. "You have to pay them lest they ridicule you."

"An unexpected complaint coming from a cold mage," she replied without heat, "for you magisters might be said to be cousins in some manner to us djeliw and bards."

"Magisters may be, bred from a long line of sorcerers and intermarried with the druas of the north," he retorted, "but I am not cousin to any of you. I was born into a village of farmers and hunters."

"Your village serves the mansa and the House," I exclaimed. "You are servants and slaves."

He lifted his chin. "Not in the old country we weren't. My people have always been farmers and hunters. We are proud of that, as we should be."

The djeli swept her extended arm in a gesture she might have made if she were singing, to emphasize a phrase. Our company agreed with her; her smile made her face rounder and lent a glow to her cheeks. "Yet a farmer's son has been taken into a black-smith's house and taught his secrets. There's a story."

"Not one I can tell." He dragged his left hand over his closely cropped hair, encountered chaff, and flicked the dry grass off before surveying his village garments with a fastidious grimace. How it must annoy him to stand so disheveled, and in such humble attire! He glanced sidelong at me. For some reason, the way he was looking at me made me abruptly wonder what it would be like to draw my fingers along the pleasing line of his jaw.

Blessed Tanit, the man had tried to kill me!

"*I* could tell you the sordid tale of how we met, journeyed together, and parted at odds," I said in a tone I hoped might scathe him and purge myself, although I addressed my words to the djeli. "But alas, its immediacy, and lack of a tidy end, pains me far too much to reflect on."

"Then tell me the stories," she said, licking her lips, "that your father told you."

"He wasn't my father!"

"Wasn't he?"

"He wasn't my father! They lied to me. He did not sire me."

"He gave you his stories."

"He wrote them down for the family, and I was allowed to read his journals and to believe he was my father."

"What is a father?" asked the djeli. "Do you have an answer?"

Curiosity and the cat: You know the story.

I led the horse around and away from the hearth and tethered her from a low-hanging branch of the oak. Then I walked to the well, but not so quickly as to startle the big cats. The biggest female thrust her shoulder against my hip. I staggered, steadying myself with a hand on her huge head. Her coat was coarse but also oddly comforting. A noise rumbled through her body, like a purr. Tentatively, I scratched at her head, and she rumbled yet more.

"Catherine," said Andevai hoarsely, hand on his sword's hilt, "if you move off slowly—"

"If they wanted to eat me, they could have done so already. I'm the one they're guarding." Flung with bravado, the words fell like truth as soon as they left my lips. I spoke to the cat as I kneaded it behind the ears. "Let me get to the water and I'll fill the trough for you."

The beast withdrew her weight. I eased past her and slung the bucket over the hook, winched it down, and hauled it up. First, I filled the stone trough with water for the cats. Then I carried a full bucket to the horse, who was eager to drink. I unsaddled her, freed her mouth from the bit, gave her an apple, and paid out enough line so she could graze. I returned with bucket and saddlebags and set the bags on one of the stone benches and myself beside them. Andevai frowned as I pulled out a leather bottle and held it out to the djeli.

"My thanks," she said, with a gesture meant to decline the offer, "but just as stones cannot ease hunger, your mead cannot ease me. Only stories can feed me."

I tossed it to Andevai, who caught it one-handed. Then I took out the second bottle for myself, draining the last of the sweet mead. The djeli released her fiddle from its case and set the instrument across her thighs.

I said to the djeli, "I never mentioned a father to you or that he had stories."

"Everyone has stories," she replied, "and every creature has a sire."

"The truth is, I don't know who sired me. Do you know?"

She narrowed her eyes and examined me, and I returned her gaze boldly. "The spirit world is knit into your bones, and you wear a spirit mantle close against your mortal flesh," she said.

"That much I can see. Your blood is what allowed you to cross from the mortal world into this one."

With a grunt, Andevai sat down heavily on the third stone bench. Lips pinched tight, he peeled off his heavy coat to reveal a wool tunic slashed at the shoulder and, folded within the lips of cut fabric, the bloodstained linen of a shirt. "Blood opens the path between worlds," he said, wincing as he tested the movement of his arm. "As every hunter knows."

I flushed. "I was only defending myself! Is the wound... bad?"

"Not so bad as to stop me riding."

"How comes it you can so easily cross into this world and back?"

He rolled his eyes, the expression making him look much younger and considerably less sophisticated. "You spent the night in my village—sheltered and fed by my family—and you cannot answer that question?"

Of course. My cheeks burned. I did not like to look stupid. "You're like that stripling I met with your brother's hunting band. You were being trained as a hunter. And then your magic bloomed and you were taken away to Four Moons House to become a magister."

"If I know how to find the gates that open around the cross-quarter days, if I know how to walk and guard myself in the spirit world and return to the mortal world, that is because of my people, not because of the magisters."

"Why not stay in the village, then? Remain a hunter?"

He took a long draught of mead and, lowering the bottle, tucked his legs up on the wide stone bench to sit cross-legged. "The question is not worthy of you, Catherine. I am a magister of rare and unexpected potency."

His cool vanity annoyed me. "In our world, but evidently not here." I gestured toward the djeli, whose fingers ran up and down the length of the strings of her fiddle as if seeking the weakened point where the string was most likely to snap. "Is it true? That you magisters draw power through the spirit world but have none in it?"

"The secret is not mine to share. Likewise, what of you, Catherine? When my blade cut you, you ought to have…" He faltered and looked past the djeli toward the oak tree whose vast canopy blotted out a portion of the sky. His expression was as shuttered as the deserted dun. "But you did not."

"I ought to have died." I touched my tender chin.

He uncrossed his legs, set them soles to earth, and looked at me with a gaze that seared me with its icy anger. But he had no power to freeze my words on my tongue. I knew I shouldn't taunt him, because I had weeks left to survive before winter solstice freed Bee from the contract, but all that pent-up fury had to explode.

"How frustrating it didn't work out so well for you! I suppose you're accustomed to everything falling just as you like it, you with your magister's rare and unexpected potency and the might of Four Moons House behind you. You with"—*your handsome face*—"your sister willing to throw herself into the mansa's bed on your behalf and—"

He rose sharply. I had gone too far, even considering that I was the one who had been sacrificed. He walked away to stand under the oak's branches. Even with my cat's eyes, I could barely see him in its heavy shadow. I looked at the djeli to see what she made of this, but her expression retained that smilingly amused interest, not as if she were laughing at us but as if she were well pleased. I had thought her a bent old woman at first, but maybe that had only been the way she played her fiddle. She sat with the erect posture of a woman sure of her place, and the firelight—was it brighter than it had been before, or exactly the same?—had smoothed away the deep wrinkles I had thought I noticed before.

"I ask your pardon," I murmured, abruptly embarrassed at my outburst. "I'm tired and hungry and I've been running for my life."

"Tell me," she said.

Andevai shouted a wordless cry of warning. The mare whinnied in panic. A dark shape flowed past them, and I leaped to my feet as the black-pelted saber-toothed cat that had followed me ran in under the tree with a second smaller cat at its side. The two beasts raced to the pride lounging by the well, ignoring the horse, but the mare jerked hard at her slipping tether, which I hadn't tightened firmly enough. I didn't mean to aid Andevai, but the horse was blameless, and if she pulled free and bolted, I was sure the cats would pursue her and pull her down, unable to resist the chase. I ran to the tree and held the line while he tied a better slipknot.

A hot wind rose out of the east; its gust made me sneeze.

"Beware," called the djeli. "A dragon is turning in her sleep."

Light splintered in the east. Was the sun rising at last? Yet so soon after night had fallen? He'd secured the horse, so I ducked out from under the outer branches and walked through waist-high summer grass to the cliff's ragged crumbling edge, where the land fell steeply down to the flats and tangled forest. A rim of fire limned the horizon with a burst of fiery gold. In the mortal world, according to the maps I knew and what I thought I understood of where I was standing, that fire rose in the southeast. But it was not fire and it was not sun. The wind that shook the tops of trees did not move like wind but like an unseen hand wiping clean the slate on which all is written. And what came behind it was hot and sharp and painful and obliterating—

His hand gripped my wrist with an iron strength. I was so

blindsided that I knew this time I had idiotically let down my guard, and this time nothing would stop him from plunging his sword into my heart and ridding himself of me.

Forgive me, Bee.

Steel hadn't yet pierced me. I tried to pull my wrist out of his grasp but only slid partway before he fixed his fingers through mine and held on like a madman clinging to his delusions. He hauled me backward. I stumbled clumsily with the grass hissing around us, and we tumbled in under the overhanging branches of the oak and fell to the dirt onto our hindquarters. A shivering bell, barely audible, rang. The air seemed to vibrate as a string might vibrate, plucked by a bard's hand.

My heart, my flesh, my bones, my spirit—all these thrummed as though caught within the vibrating string, within the almost inaudible thunder of a distant drumbeat that rolled on and on.

And then the air quieted and the world fell still. I was sitting on my backside, panting, with my left hand in a fist against the earth and Andevai holding my right hand, our fingers twined intimately together.

He released me at once, shaking free as if the touch of my skin hurt his, and scrambled to his feet. To check on the horse. Who was fine, perfectly fine, grazing at a fine stubble of grass over on the hearth side of the fine old oak. I could not catch my breath.

"Are you still there?" called the djeli. "Or were you caught in the tide of the dragon's dream?"

A rising clamor drifted from beyond the canopy: *Birds.*

Like a woman who carried four times my years in her bones, I creaked to my feet and took one slow step and a second. I grasped hold of a low-hanging branch to steady myself as I looked over what had once been the levels with a summer forest whose foliage was mostly familiar to my eyes. As in a trance, I pushed through the leaves and beyond them to get an unobstructed view.

The world had changed. A wide, flat, open landscape spread away to the horizon. This was no place I had ever seen. A lazy river spread so wide it might as well have been a shallow sea, its many channels weaving a net through solitary islets and green carpets of reed. Scattered across higher ground rose slim-trunked trees crowned with swords as leaves and trees alight with flame-red flowers. Everywhere flocked birds in such number and painted with such bright colors that the sound and sight rendered me mute with wonder.

"Come back to warded ground," said Andevai. I had not even noticed him walk up beside me. When I glanced back, the tree I had thought was an oak looked entirely different, with a huge trunk and stubby branches more like roots, covered with clusters of white flowers.

"It's the same tree," he said, noticing my startled gaze. "If you stay out here, you may be caught in another tide. Now perhaps you do not wonder why it is dangerous to hunt in the spirit world. Besides the beasts and monsters, I mean."

"What happens to those who are caught in the tide?" I asked as I stared at the fluttering, rippling landscape of birds and river and dawn sky drenched with rosy gold but without a sun.

"They never come back."

"Why didn't you leave me out there, then?"

An icy, contemptuous look was the only answer he gave me. He turned and walked away, under the shadow of the tree.

24

Dazed, I followed him under the canopy. I kept walking, out to the open brick hearth, and I sat down on the stone bench as heavily as if I'd been kicked. The tree, the dun, and the well—not to mention the seven big cats—looked exactly as they had before, untouched by the tide that had altered the world beyond. The fire burned steadily, and as I stared at it, aware of Andevai moving about under the oak tree engaged in what activity I could not guess and did not want to know, the observation belatedly occurred to me that the fire was not consuming the wood along whose lengths the flames licked.

I understood nothing: not this place, not my companions, not my life.

I hate tears.

Tears had not brought back my parents, not the tears I had wept when I was six nor the ones shed occasionally as I grew up an orphan reading my father's journals and so desperately missing him and what he could have given me had he only been there in person, he and my voiceless mother, the Amazon warrior who no one ever spoke of.

Tears flowed unbidden now. I pressed a fist into my belly just below the curve of my ribs to stop myself from sobbing out loud. The djeli put her fiddle to her chin and tuned the strings. Was she indifferent to my crying or simply polite enough to give me what privacy she could by pretending not to notice me?

"Catherine? Are you weeping?" He strode out from under the tree.

The sable cat leaped up on the rock beside me and sat on sleek haunches as it yawned widely. This display of fearsome teeth and muscular bulk brought Andevai up short. He muttered a crisp, ferocious curse.

Gracious Melqart! The man had bothered to *change his clothes* out of the practical but rustic country garb he had previously been wearing and back into the fashionable clothing worn by men born to wealth and style. Wrinkles marred the perfection of dash jacket and sleek trousers, and his boots were wiped clean but still smudged. Seeing him revert to the form in which I had first beheld him dried my tears better than any sympathetic words could have. How on earth had he managed to change clothes with that injured arm? The man was clearly insanely devoted to looking fashionable.

The cat leaned against me. Much the same size and height as me, it possessed the warmth of a living soul. Its presence gave me comfort, not least because I knew perfectly well, as did Andevai, that it could rip him open. I scratched the back of its neck, and it rumbled a purr.

"That beast is wild, not domesticated," he said in a choked voice. "It could turn on you at any moment, however much it seems sympathetic to your situation just now."

"It rather reminds me of you, then," I retorted without wiping my tear-streaked face. "It was kind of you to forebear to murder me just now, when I was unprepared to defend myself. I appreciate it. But I can't know when you will change your mind. When you will hear the mansa's command echoing in your thoughts. When you will think of your village, for which I am sure I do not blame you for wanting to spare them whatever punishment you can. I would do so myself, had I kinfolk who care for me as yours clearly do for you."

"You are mocking me."

"Am I? Why do you think so?" The tears were drying. I withdrew my hand from the big cat's nape. "Or is it only that you expect mockery, having become accustomed to it in Four Moons House, where, I am given to understand, they despise you for being the son of slaves and yet envy you for the rare and unexpected potency you carry in your person. I think that when small-minded people envy and despise, then they will mock, thinking it their only weapon. I am not, I hope, a small-minded person. I will not mock you. I'll tell you straight to your face that I don't trust you and can't trust you, and that despite my concern for the generous and upright people in the village who decided it was better to aid me and keep their faces clean before the ancestors than to betray me and truckle favor with the mansa, I intend to stay alive. I intend you shall never have"— wasn't it better never to use her name, especially in the spirit world?—"the other one. After the winter solstice passes, the other one makes her majority and can no longer be coerced into marriage. Perhaps then I might be allowed to live, since there will be no particular reason to benefit from my death. Do you think that is remotely possible?"

His gaze seemed likely to freeze me where I sat, only he had no mage power here. He had only a sword that, in the spirit world, seemed just an ordinary sword. But I also had a sword, and I had a friendly pride of saber-toothed cats to guard me. Also, I had wounded his right shoulder.

"I think it not likely," he said as slowly as if each word were being scraped from him by gnawing teeth, "that you can escape the mansa's anger once he has set it on you."

By rising, I silenced him. "I'll do what I must to survive. Can you possibly expect me to do otherwise?"

He crossed to the third stone bench and awkwardly drew on

his greatcoat. "The mansa will spread his net wide in looking for you. He will call in favors owed him by the local princes and dukes. His net will be difficult to evade."

"I am used to evading those who seek me."

A man with such cursed remarkable eyes ought not to be allowed to stare so provocatively at women. He seemed about to speak, then did not.

"What does it mean," I asked, "to walk the dreams of dragons?"

He smiled with an edge of triumph, as young men would do when they know they're about to win a victory over a rival. "Ask the scholars of Adurnam. I can't tell you."

"Can't, or won't?"

"In this matter, there is no difference."

"You're leaving."

"I must be seen to be hunting."

"*Seem* to be? Is this some new scheme to trap me?"

"I could tell you that I've changed my mind. That I won't kill you. But you'd be foolish to believe anything I told you."

I laughed, and his cheeks darkened. "Why this fine speech, Andevai?"

A bored and superior expression transformed his face, reminding me forcibly of our first meeting when he had appeared scornful and distant. But other emotions besides arrogance and disdain might trigger such a mask as he tried to conceal what surged in his heart.

He spoke in a throttled voice I could barely hear. "By their actions, by hiding you and aiding you when they know perfectly well what my situation is, the elders of my village have shamed me into considering what constitutes right behavior. They made a decision to risk themselves rather than offend the ancestors. To hand over a guest is to spit in the face of the elders.

To murder someone who is innocent just because she stands in the way of grasping at a treasure is wrong. I must act in the manner my people have shown me is right."

"He who tries to wear two hats will discover he does not have two heads. Are you a magister or a village man?"

"That's what Duvai has always taunted me with. Maybe it's true, but even Duvai can't see a bird in the air and know whether it harbors an egg in its nest."

"Whatever that means! Strange of you to speak so highly of your village elders, only after your sword drew my blood and I did not collapse dead at your feet. Had I died, then your touching and heartfelt protestations would not sound so sweet to my ears, would they? For, indeed, in that case, I would not be around to hear them at all!"

If a man could look more imperious and contemptuous than he did at this moment, I would have been surprised to hear it. "Maybe I did not realize what I was capable of. Maybe, afterward, I was sorry to have found out!"

I was trembling, my hands in fists and my eyes stinging. "Are you saying you regret trying to kill me?"

He looked away. "I make no excuses. It's done."

The male cat nudged my back with his head, the smooth, hard curve of one of his incisors sliding against my shoulder. I leaned back, feeling peculiarly safe.

Andevai looked back at me, at the big cat, at the rest of the saber-tooths over by the well. He coughed slightly, clearing his throat as before a speech. "If I can draw the chase to the toll roads and rivers, I'll do so. If I can draw the net away from Anderida, I'll do so. In that case, a person fleeing in the direction of Adurnam might do well to travel one of Anderida's quiet old roads. Once the eldest Barahal daughter reaches her majority, we have no hold over her, by the terms of the contract."

The djeli drew a long, pure melody out of her fiddle, but

paused before it came to a cadence, holding the bow from the strings as if not sure what came next.

Visibly startled, Andevai turned to her. "What is that?" he demanded.

"It's the payment you have made to me," she said with a considering look first at the fiddle, as if it were hiding something from her, and then at him. "By telling me your story. It's not quite ready yet, but this song will be yours when it is earned." A tone lingered on the breeze, more felt than heard.

He hesitated, as might a hound suddenly realizing it faces a wolf. "Then you have received a fair payment, for the shelter I've received here?"

"I have received what is fair," she agreed. "Where are you going?"

"Back to the mortal world. And you?"

"I stay where I am bound, as I must. Later, perhaps, we will meet."

"Perhaps we will meet another day. Until then, let your day be well."

"And your day, likewise."

Leave-takings could take as long as greetings, but in the end he walked to the oak, ducked under its canopy, and returned leading the mare. I realized at that moment that I was not going to set the cats on him.

Walking past me, he spoke. "I left what is yours under the oak. Do what you must, Catherine. I will do as I must."

"Wait," I said. "I don't know how to get back—"

But without looking back, he trudged up a dusty track that wound away into the higher country. The sable male padded after him and halted on the track, tail lashing, to watch until he vanished beyond stands of wide-canopied trees bearing colorless thorns and white flowers.

What an idiot I was, standing here while he walked away! I

had absolutely no idea how to return to the mortal world. I dashed over to the oak and found my bundle on the ground. As I grabbed it, the cloth flapped open and a heavy leather pouch thudded to earth beside my gloves. Inside lay silver denarii and five gold aurei. Yet the coins weighed heavy in my hands. What message had he meant to send me by leaving them with my things? That he was sorry? That he wanted me to live? Was the coin meant in payment for the cut? Had he, in that last moment when we grappled, actually changed his mind and only cut me purely by accident as he broke away? For so it seemed to me now, looking back on it.

Or perhaps he was far more clever than he looked. Perhaps he had deliberately trapped me here; perhaps I was actually dead and could never return.

I strode to the fire and faced the djeli, who lowered her fiddle. How had I first mistaken her for an aged, frail, starving woman? She was not young, certainly old enough to be my mother if I had a mother, but with a healthy shine in her face and a robust, healthy build.

"How do I return to the mortal world? Must I run after him and hope to catch him so he will show me the way?"

"The cat and the horse do not eat the same dish." She raised the fiddle. "A dry mouth cannot sing."

I laughed. "It is the way of djeliw to speak in riddles, is it not?"

"You mistake me for a Celt. It is I, Lucia Kante, who cups knowledge in my heart. I await the ones who will learn from me, but you are not that one."

The big male sashayed up and thrust his head against my hip to be petted. After I had rubbed his ears and nape, I drew up a bucket of water, carried it over, and set it down beside the djeli, and then retreated to sit beside my cloaks and coin. Maybe I wasn't a Barahal, but I had been raised among a people for whom bargaining was the same as breathing.

"Is this water your offering?" she asked.

"A dry mouth cannot sing," I answered, "but perhaps water will not quench your thirst. Are you a mortal woman or a creature of the spirit world?"

"I am the person I am, a multitude held in one flesh."

"Most tales say that time runs differently in the spirit world than in the mortal world. I would not want to stay here too long. I need to go back. Will you show me the way back?"

She held out a hand, palm up. "For a payment. The same as he made."

"Let me tell you a story," I said. "Since it seems that's the coin you seek. In the beginning, the people who call themselves Kena'ani founded the city of Tyre. There presided the gods and goddesses, the kings and the high men of the temple, the queens and the priestesses. Their ships explored the great sea. In time, the children of Tyre founded trading towns and ports like Gadir all along the coasts of the Mediterranean Sea and farther afield south along the coast of Africa and north along the coast of Europa. In time, there was born to the king of Tyre a daughter named Elissa. When she grew to be a woman, she understood that the king, her own father, hated her and wished to sacrifice her. So she fled Tyre with her people. The blessed Tanit raised winds, and on these wings brought her to a distant shore. Elissa bargained with the tribe that lived in that region. She said, 'Let me have for my people only as much land as one ox hide will encompass, and we will settle there and be content.' Thinking her simple-minded, the tribe agreed, but she trimmed the ox hide into a leather cord and extended that cord to encompass a mighty swathe of land. Her people called the city founded there Qart Hadast, the new city, and she became its dido, its queen."

Perhaps the air of the spirit world breathes a fragrance that intoxicates. How else could I possibly have looked upon Andevai and not despised him, merely because of the way he had looked sidelong at me and the way his hand had felt, holding mine? Intoxication leaps from mind to tongue. A dizzy compulsion overtook me as I kept talking, and talking, and talking. I was the vessel full of wine and she the one drinking. As long as she listened, I could not stop. I told the tales the Kena'ani tell their children, of the trials and struggles of the gods in ancient days, of the long war against the Romans, of the Persian invasion and the arrival of refugees from the empire of Mali. Of mercenaries and merchants, spies and historians. How Daniel Hassi Barahal had ridden into the world at the same age I was now and traveled across Europa and the north of Africa in the service of his family, seeking secrets to sell for profit, and in the service of his own desire to comprehend the way of the world.

No cat, he, but curious just the same. He had midwifed babies into the world, escaped brigands, climbed mountains, and sat through the interminable sessions during which Camjiata's law code was argued into fruition. He had traveled south to Rome and Qart Hadast, east to Galatia and the very border of the Pale. He had ventured north into the ice with a party of determined explorers, and west to Land's End beyond which the ocean crashed against a desolate shoreline.

The man I had believed to be my father.

As I talked, the djeli assayed a bowed melody here and a plucked tune there. Her feet rapped a rhythm on the earth. Now and then she spoke in response, or sang a phrase to punctuate my story: *It's true. I hear you.*

How or why or when sleep overtook me I did not know. I only knew I slept because I woke between one breath and the next, as if a melody had called me out of an entrancing dream that had something of Andevai in it, curse him. A fiddle played a graceful tune as sinuous and proud as the stroll of a cat. I touched tongue to lips and wiggled my fingers and toes; yes, I was awake. Warmth drenched my back.

I looked over my shoulder. The young male cat sprawled along the other half of the length of my stone bench, ears twitching with cat dreams. All the cats were drowsing except for the big female, who watched with interest as I stirred. The sky had grown dark, as with night; the fire burned as it ever had; the djeli played her music.

I sat up cautiously, not wanting to startle a saber-toothed cat. The music ceased as the djeli pulled a flourish out of her bow and lowered the fiddle. Fire and shadow flatter women, so it is said, but her rosy youth was not the fire's flattery. I recognized her as the same djeli who had been here from the very first, only now she looked a mere decade older than I was.

The cat stirred, rolled, and with its weight pushed me right off the stone. I shrieked and, without thinking, shoved it back, and it batted at me, claws sheathed. It did not know its own strength. The paw, connecting with my shoulder, sent me spinning, but I laughed and steadied myself against the brick wall surrounding the fire. This hearth was a center point set equidistant from the three exterior points of oak tree, dun, and well. A triangle, in fact. Bee, with her mathematical mind, would have seen it from the first. Andevai had clearly understood it when he'd dragged me back into the shelter of the oak to escape the tide. This place was warded. Beyond the wards of oak, tower, and well lay the spirit world in all its danger and beauty; here, one might rest without fear.

"Why did the cats not kill him?" I asked. "When we first crossed over, they leaped on him. I see now they were protecting me. But why did they not kill and eat him?"

She frowned. "Marriage does not stop at two. A woman and a man may marry, but they are not alone, her and him only. His family and her family also are bound by obligations and rights. To have devoured him just like that would have shown very little respect for the relationship, don't you think?"

"You're saying these cats are my kin."

The young male yawned, showing his teeth, but the gesture offered no threat. He was just slow to wake up. He leaped—more like a flow of muscle and flesh—down off the stone.

"And how," I continued, as questions like rain fell into my head, making a great deal of noisy splash, "did you even know Andevai and I are—were—married?"

"How could I not know? It breathes in the air between you."

I bit my lip. Maybe she had not meant desire. Andevai and I had been chained into a contract by magic, a chain anchored in the spirit world. It was likely the denizens of this place could recognize such bindings even if they seemed invisible to me.

"What does it mean to walk the dreams of dragons?" I asked.

"Like you I am curious."

I laughed. "Spoken truly. How are you come here?"

"I bide where my chains bind me."

"What do you mean?"

"Everyone has troubles."

I nodded, respecting her limits. It was time to go. "How do I cross back into the mortal world, maestra?"

"There is a door, is there not?"

A door! I looked at the dun, with its closed door and shuttered window. A forbidding place because of its air of emptiness. But it might not be empty. It might be full. An entire world might lie inside the dun.

I laughed bitterly as I made ready to depart, layering on my cloaks, the humble covering the fine. Hidden in plain sight, like a sword that appears to be a cane in daylight. I tied bottle and coin pouch to my belt, fixed my sword so I could draw it easily, and drew on my gloves.

"May your day pass well, maestra," I said to the djeli.

"And yours. May your journey go well."

"And your fire burn strongly."

One could go on in this way for a while, both coming and going, but she released me.

"May we meet again when it is proper to do so," she said, and put the fiddle to her chin and played such a sprightly tune that my feet wished to walk. I hurried across to the dun. I eased the blade from its sheath just enough to make a tiny cut on my little finger. Sweat prickled on my back and neck as a drop of blood welled from the skin. I touched it to the latch, then pushed. It clicked down with a resonance as deep as that of a struck bell, ringing long and low through the stone. The door swung easily open.

I sucked in a breath of suddenly raw, cold air and braced myself for the temperature change. Just as I stepped through, a shadow leaped from behind and knocked me forward and down to my hands and knees. I felt the hot tremor of a monster's breath on my neck, and with my heart thundering in a panic, I scrambled forward through rubble until I slammed my knee against a jumble of stone blocks and the pain brought me up short. A dusting of snow covered the ruins of an ancient dun, its walls standing only head height with the crumbling courses resembling teeth with gaps between. The sun shone in splendor, but no heat touched the frozen earth. My nose turned to ice. The air I sucked in was so cold it stabbed in my chest. My fingers had already begun to stiffen. After a dazed moment of paralysis, I floundered out of the ruins through cold-whitened grass.

Ahead stood a venerable oak tree so ancient that its trunk was as vast as a house, and it was actually bulging, almost as if two trees had grown together to become one. A faint buzzing tingled on my tongue; I could almost taste the sound.

"My pardon, maestra! Where did you come from?"

I turned.

A young woman stood beside a humble well ringed with stones and covered with a thatched roof. Bundled in heavy winter clothes and a man's long wool coat, she looked used to hard work and to laughter between times. Two empty buckets sat at her feet; she held a pole in her right hand, ready to whack me.

"Ah," I said wisely. I staggered a step sideways and caught myself on the tip of my cane. In daylight, in the mortal world, my sword appeared again as a simple black cane. "I was just . . . in the ruins. I'm traveling, and I had to stop and . . . ah . . . relieve myself."

"You don't want to be stopping here." She did not lower the pole. "There was a jelly buried in that oak a hundred years ago. She haunts this place still. They say she was a powerful and wicked woman, Lucia Kante, and that she eats children. That's what my mam told me when I was wee and inclined to go wandering off. I'm sure it's not true, because only the savages who live in the Barren Lands eat babies, and they're not civilized enough to have jellies. But it's still better to keep your distance. You know how jellies and bards will mock you if you don't give them what they want."

"Oh," I said, displaying my gift for fluent and clever speech. The buzzing of bees spiked until it rattled in my head, then ceased as abruptly as if a door had shut.

Suddenly, it seemed I had got my bearings and could see beyond dun and oak and well. Some paces past the well ran a road. A pair of wagons, one coming and one going, rolled along, their occupants paying no attention to us. The road led to a town sprawled from the height down a gentle slope that led to the flat Levels below. A very old stone wall contained the town, and even from here I marked its arched gate with the name LEMANIS carved across the lintel.

"I'm Emilia," she added, lowering the pole. "It's cold weather to be traveling."

"Well met," I said, "and the gods' blessings on you. I'm called—"

She shrieked.

A striking young man sauntered out of the ruins. He had a reddish brown cast of skin; his coal-black hair, straight and lovely, fell unbound halfway down his back. That he was lithe and long, well muscled and well proportioned, was easy to see since he was stark naked.

She stared for one long breath, then grabbed the buckets and ran away toward the gate.

"Who are you?" I demanded.

"Cat," he said, looking quite put out. "How can you say such a thing? You know me."

"I've never seen you before in my life. How do you know my name?"

"Have not seen me before in your life? None of that mattered, that we came when you called? Tracked you down far out of our normal range so we could protect you from that high-strung pretty boy prancing around in all his flash and conceit? That means nothing to you?"

I groped for and found solid stone. I sat. Hard. "You're looking pretty flash right now yourself," I choked out. "You're naked."

He did not even have the decency to look down at his exposed body. "I'm not naked. I'm in my skin."

I untied my outer cloak and threw it at him, and he caught it and flung it around his shoulders with a grin, as if he enjoyed the fabric's rippling flare.

"Who are you?" I demanded again, as my heart sank like a stone cast into the sea. The cursed creature had followed me over from the spirit world. This could not be a good thing.

He had a pout that would make your hair stand on end, a look that accused you of not doing exactly as you ought to know was right in regard to his comfort.

"Cat," he said, with a sigh that shuddered through the length of him and contained the entirety of his disappointment in my stubborn blindness, "I am your brother."

25

"I have no brother."

The young man man drew a hand over his glossy hair exactly as a cat might preen. I thought he would lick his own hand, but he did not. "It's true we weren't birthed from the same womb, but the same male sired us. How am I not, then, your brother?"

"You are either mad or deluded."

"It is so tiring to watch you being stubborn. And I admit, I feel a bit of a chill. Is it always this cold in the Deathlands? How does one cope?"

"By wearing clothes, for one thing. In your current state of undress, you'll be hauled in by the local wardens."

"How complicated this all is!" he said with a grin that, despite my shock, made my lips twitch. "How very exciting! Will I wear something like you have on? I thought maybe that was your skin, rather wrinkled and smelly, but you never know with creatures over here, do you?"

"I am wearing women's clothing. You will wear men's clothing."

"Is there a difference?"

"Yes. Now be quiet and let me think. Come over here by the oak so we can stand out of sight of restless eyes." He followed me obediently enough and trailed a hand along the bark. I rested both hands against the trunk, palms flat, and shut my eyes, but all I heard was a buzzing sound, as if thousands of bees were confined within. The sound made my flesh tingle and my mind fill with insane thoughts.

We came when you called. What had the eru had me do? Call for my kin at the stone pillar. I'd thought my call had somehow broken the mansa's hold on the carriage, and maybe it had, but what if my voice had reached farther yet into the unknown expanse of the spirit world? What did I know of the chains that bind kin in the spirit world or how far they might reach?

His face resembled mine, although his eyes had more of a yellowish orange tinge while mine were commonly described as amber. His hair was so thick and silky, as black as if swallowed by night, that it alone would capture people's notice, as mine often did. His skin was darker than mine, but that was not uncommon here in the north where the progenitors and grandparents of siblings and cousins could range from the palest of Celts to the darkest of Mande and might include forebears of Roman, Kena'ani, or other ancestry as well.

Yet looks are not everything. At this moment I felt rather massively annoyed by him in a way that reminded me of being annoyed at Bee. If I were a cat, I might have said he had the right scent, if by scent one embraces a larger concept having to do with smell, taste, heart, bond, well-being, and a sense of belonging.

I stepped back from the oak. "For the sake of argument, let's say I believe that you believe you are my brother. What am I to call you?"

" 'Brother'?"

"Haven't you a name?"

He pulled his long hair through his fingers as if surprised and delighted by a new toy. "I know who I am, but I can put no name to that. Others know me, but that relationship is not reducible to a word." He dipped his head toward my ear and inhaled deeply, audibly, as if inhaling *me* and who I was. He winced and drew back. "Whew! You need cleaning."

"Why did you call me Cat? You cannot have known that is the pet name I've been called by my"—*family*—"by others."

"But you are Cat." He clearly seemed to expect I would treat him in the manner of a long-lost relative, when in fact he was just another chance-met stranger on the road. "You don't believe me," he added. "Why else would we come to aid you, and be able to find you, if you did not call for us?"

"We?"

"My mother and aunt and sister and cousins and niece."

"I met your mother already?"

"Of course you did."

"She was the djeli?"

He laughed. "Cat, you are not stupid. So I wish you would not pretend to be."

I cast my gaze at the sky. Clouds softened the horizon; the sun sank, and soon it would be night and deathly cold even for a denizen of the spirit world masquerading in human form in the mortal world. The cold air congealed my words, or maybe I did not want to say them, because saying them would make it true. Or make me believe it could be true.

"Are you saying you are one of the saber-toothed cats who came to my rescue?"

He sighed as if, having told me all along there was a view to the outside, he was forced to confirm it by opening the shutters himself.

"Are you saying my father is a saber-toothed cat?"

He waved a hand dismissively. He had the most absorbing way of moving, like beauty made flesh. "Oh...him. What does anyone know about him? My mother once called him a...How would you say it?" He tapped his chin. "A tomcat?"

"If you mean to say he roams around to satisfy his base desires, fighting with other males and impregnating females, then, yes, he would be called a tomcat."

"Yes. That's it."

"That's not a flattering portrait of the man—the creature— who sired me!"

"No," he agreed without heat. No doubts or unmet dreams about his sire tormented him! "Didn't your mother tell you anything about him?"

"She's dead."

"Oh,"he said. "That happens here in the Deathlands, doesn't it?" He broke off to eye the heavens with a squint, frowning briefly. "The day is not much longer meant to brighten us here, is it? Will it be warmer at night?"

I glanced toward the road. The fields wore a cloak of snow, the kind whose surface has grown hard from days exposed to sun and wind and bitter cold. Traffic passed at intervals; on such a day, not many folk cared to be out and about. A man leading a laden donkey glanced our way, and a party of armed men dressed in tabards to mark their service to a nobleman's household clattered past.

"No, it will be colder, and we will freeze to death. So the first thing is, we've got to travel without drawing notice to ourselves." How quickly I proceeded from "I" to "we." I made the calculations in my head. I had to reach Adurnam and warn Bee. I was alone, and young, and female. He was male, definitely that, and it appeared he felt obligated to protect me. Also, I was beginning to really shiver. "We will walk into Lemanis. You will keep your mouth shut. I will find us a modest room in a modest inn. There, you will remain while I hunt clothing for you."

"Mama will approve of you. Out hunting for me already!"

"Be serious! You must say nothing until I have devised a suitable story that people may not believe but will accept."

I started to walk, and I was relieved that, as he strode beside me, he had the prudence to keep the cloak pulled shut with one hand so as not to display any more of himself than he had to.

His bare feet flashing below the hem looked frightful enough, padding across the snow. We reached the road and clambered up onto its pavement, an artifact of the old empire.

"First of all, you must have a name." I frowned at him. He did look like me; no one would think it exceptional if I claimed him as my brother. The most singular difference was in our complexions, mine lighter and somewhat golden, not uncommon among the Kena'ani, while he had that reddish brown coloring. "Roderic," I said, "for your complexion. I'll call you Rory for your pet name."

"I like to be petted." His smile startled a pair of women beating rugs outside the gates. They simpered as he slowed to eye them very much in the manner of a tomcat thinking of going on the prowl.

I elbowed him hard in the ribs. "Move on, you imbecile. Beyond anything, we must not attract notice." With him sauntering beside me, it was too late for that.

The surrounding gardens and fields and copses lay bare under winter's hands. The view opened westward across the Levels to where the sun sank into the high country of Anderida.

We passed under the unguarded gate. What was there to guard against? The princes and mage Houses kept the roads and towns at peace under their rule, and while a few cohorts of restless youth might ride in small bands in the countryside pretending to raid cattle, or hiring themselves out to a lord or a mage House for a season or two, most such bands had long since been absorbed into the great households of the noble and the wealthy.

Lemanis bore the stamp of better days. Its streets did not bustle. Some of the stone buildings had fallen into disrepair, and gardens lay fallow in generous yards where, by the evidence of mounds of dirt and decayed piles of debris, other structures had once stood. A pair of competing inns always stand close by any town gate. Both appeared modest and reasonably clean. Trained by merchants, I felt no compunction in asking to see the available rooms in each establishment and then afterward playing the one off the other given that few travelers could be expected in this cold season to warm half-empty coffers. Young and shivering as we were, we might even have awoken sympathy in the breasts of these robust innkeepers. As odd as a barefooted and clothing-less man in winter would appear, the tale that he had been robbed and stripped of all his belongings, including baggage, carriage, and horses, while his beloved sister cowered in protective hiding behind a hedge of yew offered a fine incentive for luring in locals for a drink in the days after we had gone on our way.

By the time I had settled on a night's stay at the County Members, with its gracious hearth and a small but respectable upstairs room for which I bespoke all four beds, I realized Rory was also his father's son in one regard at least. In a quiet town where no excitement beckons in the depths of the winter season, he had attracted an audience of appreciative females. Cursed man! He was still smiling at the women who had trailed into the common room in his wake. Clearly he was going to be a terrible nuisance. They tittered and whispered among themselves but fortunately did not follow us up the narrow stairs. I pushed Rory into our room, untied my cloak, removed my gloves, and shoved them into his arms. Then I shut the door in his face before turning to face the innkeeper.

She chuckled, her rosy face crinkling with laugh lines. "A rare handful, that one. I know the type. Who's the elder between you?"

The question startled me, but I am nothing if not quick to find my feet. "He is, of course, but I have always had to act the role, ever since our parents—" Here I broke off, not sure if we had decided our parents were alive or quite dead. Best to keep it as close to the truth as possible. "We have the same father but different mothers. There has been trouble."

"Ah. Folk do say it is better to be quarreling than lonesome, but two women in the same house are like pepper and honey in the same pot."

"Yes, indeed. I was wondering if you know where we could find clothing for him."

"My cousin lost her eldest son just a year back. She kept his things. It's respectable clothing that might fit him. Although it'll be nothing as elegant as what you must be accustomed to," she added as she looked over my fine cloak.

"We would be grateful for anything, and will pay what it is worth," I assured her.

"Will you come downstairs so I can enter you in my ledger?"

I cast a glance at the door, a serviceable slab of wood showing the wear of years; it had been patched around the latch, as if rough handling some time in the past had broken the latch and needed repair. Like everything else, it was scrupulously clean. As the innkeeper descended the stairs, I paused to listen, but all I heard was Rory prowling in the confines of his cage.

When I reached the common room, the innkeeper was just sending one of her daughters out to the cousin for the clothes.

"I'm sure we can find something for you, too, dear," she said as she sat at a table and opened her ledger. "A clean shift, perhaps. It will be easy enough to clean your outer clothes with a brush so you can be ready to travel in the morning, although I am not sure how you can do so having lost your conveyance. The warden is out on a complaint in the countryside. Sheep stealing, of all things! That hasn't happened for years! He'll be back in a day or two and you can make your report then."

I flushed as it belatedly, and too late, occurred to me that our tale of woe would bring keener attention to our persons. All because of Roderic and his cursed nakedness!

"We can't wait so long. We've got to be on our way in the morning. But a clean shift and a bath"—I sighed, not playacting at all—"would be glorious."

"Poor thing," she said in a kindly way that would have made my heart cringe if I had not in fact been a poor thing, running for my life even if the robbery was itself a lie. Yet was it? Hadn't Aunt and Uncle, and Four Moons House, stolen my life from me? "It would be little enough trouble to heat up some water for you, maestra. And for the young man, too, although I must warn you I intend to keep my daughters away from him."

"Well you should! I make no defense for his flirting ways!"

We laughed companionably as she paged through the ledger. The large bound volume had been in use for some time, as the earlier pages were yellowing and filled with names. She reached a half-finished page; the most recent date recorded, 4 November 1838, had a single line written beneath: *Captain of Diarisso, with four men at arms.* The Diarisso lineage had founded Four Moons House. It was not a common name.

"Are soldiers staying here?" I asked as casually as I could, looking around so as to spot them before they spotted me.

She shot me a startled glance, and she also looked toward the door, then back at me. "My dear, no. They are since gone, of course. Lord Owen doesn't like to have House cavalry riding about roads he oversees, does he? But even a lord cannot say no to the magisters for fear they will call in a cold spell just when the fruit trees are budding and the wheat sprouting. As long as the cold mages can hold the threat of famine over the rest of us, the princes have to do what they say, do they not? Now, maestra, if you'll just give me your names so I can record it here."

My heart stuttered, but I calmed myself. Cautious and watchful I must become.

"Catriona," I said, choosing the local version of my name, "and Roderic Bara—" I bit my tongue.

"Barr?" she asked, nib poised above the ledger.

"Barr," I agreed as she carefully wrote the name two lines below, and then went back and filled in a new date: 10 December 1838.

"Not that I can complain about the custom, even from House soldiers," she went on, "for you see how little traffic we get in this season. The mines are closed down for winter, although the forges are now lit, but none of them will travel until spring. Crops and cattle are long since taken to market. Folk do not travel this time of year. You were fortunate to escape traveling in that terrible blizzard. Those soldiers came galloping in on its wings and were forced to bide here four entire days, although they were so very well behaved I'd like to meet their mothers. You'd think a cold mage had raised such a storm, wouldn't you?"

December tenth.

Five weeks had passed while I argued with Andevai, told stories to the djeli, and slept in the spirit world. Four Moons House could easily have reached Adurnam and taken Bee. But could they have forced her to marry Andevai without a legal ruling that I was dead? Might they try to force her to marry a different magister with a legal ruling that my marriage was fraudulent? Uncle would fight in court, although it was most likely he and the family had fled the city the night I'd been taken.

Two girls bustled past with heads ducked low, making for the stairs. One held a bundle of clothing in her arms; the other was biting her lower lip and trying not to giggle.

"*Where* are you going with those?" demanded the innkeeper without rising.

The girls halted, blushing. "These are for—"

"I know who they are for. And *you*, missy, are not taking them upstairs."

"I'll take them up," I said, for anything would be better than trying to carry on a conversation with the innkeeper while that date pounded in my head. "If a bath—"

"It will have to be in the kitchen out back," said the innkeeper, "which is where we keep our tub, but we've a screen to give you privacy. Nothing fancy."

I smiled at the girls as well as I could manage and scooped up the clothes. "My thanks, maestra. Just let me know when all is ready."

"And what don't fit," the innkeeper called after me, "I can tailor to measure."

The girls giggled.

I took the steps two at a time, rapped once to give him warning before flinging open the door and charging in. The room was exceedingly narrow, more of a long corridor from door to window, with two beds lined along one wall, a side table between them, and two along the other. Decently swaddled in the cloaks, he lounged on the bed to the right of the door. Warmth drifted up from the hearths and stoves below. I dumped the clothing on the bed opposite and began shaking it out. It was quite serviceable, nothing in the height of fashion: loose trousers in the Celtic style, a town jacket with a hint of dash but well made enough to weather many years' wearing. This was not garb for heavy labor but for town work; perhaps the deceased had helped serve drinks at the inn.

I walked to the window. "We have eleven days to reach Adurnam before the solstice," I said, walking back to him. "If I recall Uncle's maps correctly, it must be about one hundred miles from Lemanis to Adurnam as the crow flies." I returned to the window to look out over the inn yard. "We can't afford to hire horses. I'm not sure we can walk so far in ten days."

"You're pacing," he said with another yawn.

"What are we to do?"

"I say we eat, for I'm powerfully hungry." He snagged cloth, hoisted it, and swung out his bare legs to pull on—

"You can't wear those! Those are women's drawers."

"They're soft. They feel good." Without the least idea of modesty, he wiggled out buck naked from under the cloaks and pulled on the drawers over slim hips. "I like them."

"You don't wear women's clothing."

"Why not?"

"You're impossible!" I separated men's garments: drawers, stockings, trousers, shirt, waistcoat, and the jacket in a dreary brown fabric that was nothing a fine blade like Andevai would ever be caught dead in. "It seems impossible that five entire weeks have passed while I told a few stories!"

He fingered the man's drawers. "I don't like these. They're not as soft."

"The ones you have on are meant for *me* to wear, you disgusting beast. I'm going to turn my back, and you're going to take off *my* drawers and dress properly. Five weeks! How can it happen?" I walked back to the window. Through the open gates of the inn yard, I could see a slice of the main street and the gate, empty of traffic as dusk strangled the winter day.

How should he know why time flowed differently there from here? He was a saber-toothed cat, by all that was holy! A spirit man, the villagers would have said, walking out of his beast's body and into this one as a man. His mother was a cat, and his father was, evidently, a cat.

I tried to imagine having a saber-toothed cat as a sire, a spirit animal who had walked into this world as a man and had congress with my mother. Did I really believe it, with no evidence except Rory's word and the cats coming to protect me?

Trembling, I leaned my head against the dense whorls of glass, feeling the cold seep through. The eru had called me "cousin." She had seen the spirit world knit into my bones when even the mansa, despite his immense power, had not guessed. But the djeliw had known.

What had Daniel Hassi Barahal known? Was my bastard parentage why he had handed me over to the Barahals to sacrifice in Bee's place? I considered the story Bee and I had been told. He had fallen in love with an Amazon from Camjiata's army. They'd fled together to make a new life but had tragically drowned in the Rhenus River, leaving behind an orphaned daughter.

Was *any* of it true?

"Why are you crying?" Roderic's gentle tone, with a slight scratch like the lick of a cat's tongue, opened the vein of my grief. I began to sob. He came up behind me, suitably dressed at last, rested hands on my shoulders, and stood quietly until the river ran dry.

"You still stink," he said as I wiped my eyes.

"Let's go down," I said as I turned to face him. "And . . . thank you."

He touched his nose to my cheek, not quite a kiss, but the gesture heartened me. I had kin. I wasn't alone. And furthermore, the mansa's soldiers and seekers would be looking for a solitary woman, not one traveling with a man.

Good hot soup and thick ale followed by a hot bath, however humble the tub, and the pleasure of clean drawers and shift did much to strengthen my resolve. When I returned to the common room, I discovered Roderic seated on a bench with his long legs outstretched and a mug of ale in one hand as he embellished the tale of our altercation with brigands with the delight of a born liar. No longer was it a half dozen brigands but thirteen or twenty, hard to count in the muddy light of a cloudy dawn. Certainly his audience had swelled from the innkeeper's infatuated daughters to an appreciative crowd, including the very Emilia we had met by the well, a ruddy-faced girl with red-gold hair.

As the tale unfolded, I realized he was retelling in altered form one of the episodes from Daniel Hassi Barahal's journal I'd related to Lucia Kante.

"There's been trouble with roaming bands of young men these last two years," interposed the cousin of the innkeeper. She wore a scarf in muted tones wrapped over her gray hair. I wondered if she had come over to see how Roderic filled out her dead son's clothes. Was she, too, grieving for what she had lost? "Leman-is's council and Lord Owen have sent pleas in plenty to the Cantiacorum prince, but in his proclamation he blames radicals for stirring them up. He says he can do nothing until we police our own. Last year, Falling Stars House sent soldiers to sweep through the Levels, rounding up outlaws and villains. Some of our lads joined up just for the summer. We thought our boy would be home after Hallows, but he never did come back."

"My condolences on your loss, maestra," I said politely.

Someone in the back muttered an imprecation, and people shook their heads with a frown.

"Ach, nay, lass," she replied, touching an amulet that hung from a cord around her neck. "He's not passed. The House captain liked his measure and how he sat a horse, so they took him into the company. We hope for some good to come of the connection. He's not been allowed to visit home yet, but he sent money and a steer for his sister's wedding."

"He said he'd send for me," said Emilia tartly, "but I've not heard one word since he rode off all high and proud. I suppose he's too good for the likes of us now."

"The lad will do what's right," said the innkeeper sternly.

"Until the House soldiers run afoul of radicals and he finds himself staring down a musket held by one of his own kinsmen!"

"That's enough, Emilia!" said an older man standing in the back. With an expression that betrayed how ill used she felt, she stepped back as he went on. "Lads will make promises to lasses. You know how it is. Drink, duel, and dally. And a bit of livestock raiding when they're bored. I don't suppose you lost any cattle, did you, Maester Barr?"

This lame joke forced a few chuckles.

"Only the horse," replied Roderic. As his grin widened, I was sure he was about to say something that would annoy and embarrass me. "And a very fine and handsome horse it was, to be sure. A glossy creature, more brown than bay, and exceedingly well groomed and ornamented."

He was laughing at me with his cursed eyes as my cheeks went up in flames, although I was sure I did not know why.

"That reminds me of a song," said Emilia.

The women laughed; the men groaned. But the fire was blazing and the night was long, and folk will want entertainment after the tedium of a day's work. Emilia's song detailed the amorous adventures of a water horse who fell in love—if *love* was the right word—with a series of young women who passed beside the lake in which the creature dwelled and from which he emerged in the form of a good-looking young man of exactly the right sort to catch a young woman's fancy. She had a clear voice and a pleasing timbre, and every local knew the chorus, whose euphemisms about mounting and galloping embarrassed me. We did not sing these sorts of songs in the Barahal house. Rory caught right on and sang the chorus as if born to it.

In the laughter and pounding of tables that followed, I said, to no one in particular, "I thought kelpies drowned and then devoured their victims!" The words, innocently spoken, only caused the gathered folk to laugh even harder until I am sure my face was as red as if burned.

I retreated to the bartender's domain as Emilia—like Bee, she enjoyed being the center of attention—began another song, this one mournful and dreary and containing numerous references to summer rain, sodden flowers, and dead lovers. The bartender was a young man who smiled sympathetically as I rested against the bar. He slid a mug of ale down to me, and I sipped, savoring the brew. Two men with distinctly foreign features approached the bar and asked for a drink. They spoke, haltingly, the formal Latin of the schoolbook, hard for locals to understand here in the north where three languages had been thrown into the same pot and stirred. They were obviously not southerners like the woman Kehinde whom I had met with Chartji; she'd been from Massilia, and whatever other languages she might speak, she'd spoken Latin with the flawless casualness of the native speaker. So had the trolls, now that I thought about it. Only Brennan had used the local cant.

"*Salvete*," I said to the men as I set down my mug. *Greetings*.

"*Salve*," replied the elder. The younger made a gesture of greeting, cupped hand touched to chest, but said nothing and kept his gaze lowered.

"You are come a long way," I said politely, for they both had long straight black hair not unlike my own and complexions something like Rory's, but with features so distinctive that I wondered where on Earth they had come from. They were not from around here.

"A long way," agreed the elder. He seemed about to say more but stopped. From his expression, I thought it likely he was stymied by the language.

"You are from Africa," I said to encourage him.

He shook his head. "From Africa, no. From Africa, we are not."

"From beyond the Pale? In the east?"

"This I know not, this pale. My apologies, maestra."

The younger addressed words to the elder in a language I did not recognize. Some of the words rang familiarly, but its cadence had a music of its own, entirely new to my ears.

The elder shook his head again, then turned to receive two mugs of ale from the barkeep. With a smiling nod to seal the end of our conversation, he took himself and his young companion away. I shifted to watch their progress and caught a glimpse through the crowd of a table half hidden by the big brick hearth in the corner of the room closest to the blazing fire. A clean-shaven and rather light-skinned young man sat there, hands on the table and a cap held in slim fingers; he had Avarian eyes, slant-folded, and an oval face with broad cheekbones. After a moment I realized, with a start, that he was a woman, older than I had first thought, with black hair cropped short and an old scar on her left cheek, and in all ways dressed exactly as a man.

The bartender leaned across the bar to follow my gaze with his own. "Foreigners," he said. "Five of 'em. They're staying at the Lamb, across the way. Got here yesterday with ten mules and twenty bundles of wool cloth from Camlun. But the warden's sure they were smuggling rifles. He meant to take them before Lord Owen, but then a lad come in this morning with the cry of sheep stealing and off the warden must go. He told this lot to stay put until he come back or he'd ask Lord Owen to set the militia after them."

"Rifles!" I thought of the rifles the eru and coachman had claimed to have destroyed in Southbridge. The men pursuing Andevai: *It's time the mages feel the sting of our anger.*

"You heard of them? It's a new kind of musket, like."

Emilia finished her song to a burst of acclaim and cries for a new song. Someone said he'd go for his fiddle, and another pair left to get drum and lute. Emilia leaned over Roderic, flirting as he sipped ale and imbibed her attentions.

The bartender glanced once around the room as if fearing eavesdroppers, then bent closer. I bent closer as well, his mouth close to my ear and his breath strong with ale as he whispered, "Mages hate rifles, anything like that. And foreigners are usually radicals, aren't they? Still." His hand brushed mine. "If there's no illegal merchandise, there's no proof, is there?"

"Where would rifles be coming from?" I asked, wondering what he would answer.

"I wouldn't know about that," he said with a grin. "Still, she's a fierce-looking woman, isn't she? Seems a shame to me for a woman to go cutting her hair all short like a man's, though. Yours, for instance. You have hair as black and lovely as a raven's wing."

Fiery Shemesh! The man was flirting with me. "Uh, my thanks." I shifted my hand away as surreptitiously as I could and ponderously veered back to the subject. "That woman looks Avar, or something like Avars would look, I would think. I've only ever seen one. In Adurnam." And him an albino, but I was not about to mention the headmaster's assistant here or my ties to the academy college.

"City girl, eh? Thought I heard it in your speech. They do look strange, I'll say that. Though they haven't made trouble since the warden told them to stay put. Very quiet folk. And one's sick with a flux or some such. Says he's too sick to travel, anyway, like to die. They've set him alone in a room and change off tending him."

"Who wants to run from the law in the middle of winter? Even radicals can freeze to death. Or get sick and die."

He offered to top off my mug of ale. "You fancy radicals, there in the city?"

"I don't fancy anyone," I said in my most quelling tone. "I am"—hard to imagine I would ever be glad to have an opportunity to say this!—"married. But an emergency called me home, and my brother came to fetch me. Then we had that trouble with brigands, so while I'm sure you're a fine young man, I'm not in a mood to flirt even if I were unmarried."

He shrugged, humor flashing in his good-natured face. "A man has to try, when he is smitten. Your gold eyes are a treasure as grand as they are precious. And twice as hard, for the cruel words with which you reject me."

I laughed.

"Yannic! Get those drinks pulled!" shouted the innkeeper from the other side of the room above the hubbub of the crowd.

One of her daughters sashayed over and shoved a tray onto the bar before the man. "You can flirt when there's no customers."

"How can I do that if no customers means no flirts? You can't be expecting me to take up with Em again, can you? After she threw me over for Daithi, thinking him likely to gain a fine proud position as cavalry man for Falling Star House? Which he did, and more fortune to him, for he'll need it. Whilst I drown my sorrow as I may. What am I to do when a fine proud gel fetches up at my bar and talks to me with her pretty ways and golden eyes?"

"Get on with you," she said to him. Then she winked at me.

It got quite busy, with folk calling for drink. I moved to the end of the bar and found a stool on which to perch. The innkeeper had left her ledger forgotten at one end while she bustled out among the tables as the crowd settled and more folk pressed inside having heard, I supposed, that there was music to be had for the evening. The fiddler began tuning his instrument, although how he could hear in the din I could not fathom. Idly, I flipped through the ledger's pages, for I cannot resist a book set before me no matter its kind. Writing draws my eye; I am impelled as by sorcery to read even if it is an accountant's list or a solicitor's instructions or, as here, nothing more than a record of travelers who have passed through this inn. The first entry was dated to the year of May 1824 in a hand more slanted and spiky—exceedingly old-fashioned, like that of an elder taught to write in the previous century—than the penmanship of the current landlady.

Eighteen twenty-four had been the year of Camjiata's downfall. The beginning of the end had come on Hallows Night, at the very start of the new year, with the destruction of the only mage House that supported him; his wife, Helene, had perished in a mysterious conflagration that had also consumed the estate buildings of the House. Months of battles, each more desperate than the last, had followed until his final surrender on Lughnasad, in the month of Augustus. I noted how few travelers had stopped at the inn in the months of Maius, Junius, and Julius. No doubt folk feared moving on the roads when they could not know what trouble they might stumble upon. But in mid-Augustus, after the news of his capture spread, the dam burst. The flow of travelers picked up, hastening to do their business before the cold set in. Peddlers, coal and iron merchants, people who could not afford the toll roads, local traffic: all passed through Lemanis. Where were they going? What were they coming from? I could see the birds fly, but at this remove of years and with no more information on the page than name and date, I could have no idea what eggs if any they had in their nest.

The drummers hastened in to cheers and jibes; a swirl of frigid air kissed my nose and faded as the door was shut against the winter night. Good cheer, ale, and music will keep away unwanted spirits and untimely wraiths. Rory still sat on his bench, a giggling young woman on either side. He caught my gaze on him, lifted the mug, sipped, and made a comical face. I grinned. He did not like the ale, although I thought it a perfectly good country brew.

My gaze dropped back to the ledger, the column of dates and names.

Where I saw one entry among many, written no differently than any of the others except in my heart: *3 September 1824. Daniel Hassi Barahal, Tara Bell, and child.*

26

Although the music was still playing, I went upstairs to my empty chamber and stripped down to my shift. I tossed and turned on a narrow bed but could not sleep. On midmorning of 9 September 1824, a ferry carrying upward of one hundred passengers had nosed out onto the Rhenus River on a routine crossing in fair autumn weather. It had not reached the far shore. Every soul aboard the ferry had drowned except for one child, who had been plucked by a fisherman from the deadly current.

Daniel Hassi Barahal and Tara Bell had stayed in this inn on their final, fateful journey, with a child in their care. Me. In this inn. Perhaps in this bed. I sought in my memory but found only blank pages. No, there was the man's laugh and the way my mother had held me tightly against her in a rocking coach. If she had been my mother.

Blessed Tanit! What if the real Catherine had actually drowned and Aunt and Uncle had simply found an orphan to pretend to be her? Wouldn't that make more sense?

Burrowing under the wool blankets as though safety or answers could be found beneath, I dozed fitfully and within the weaving of sleep and dreams, I found myself sailing across a blinding expanse of ice in a schooner that skated the surface of a massive ice sheet. Behind, a pack of saber-toothed cats as black as if dusted in coal pursued the ship. A personage stood beside me. Light glinted on his brow, as if a shard of ice had gotten embedded in his forehead. I knew he was my father, and of course he looked nothing like the man named Daniel Hassi Barahal whose portrait I had once worn in a locket at my neck. I'd given away that locket to a pair of girls in Four Moons House in exchange for an open door.

An open door meant something, surely, but in my dream I could not work out the connection.

A light scratching, a rustle as the door opened, a giggle: these woke me. I buried my head under blankets, feeling the presence of too many people in the room and them engaged in rumpling the bedding.

"Rory," I said into the blankets, "I'm trying to sleep."

Voices murmured, his and hers, breathy with desire; the door clicked shut, followed by footsteps slipping away to some other private place. I was, again, alone. A dreamy languor swallowed me. What would it be like to kiss Andevai? Surely he affected that trim line of beard because he knew it emphasized the aesthetically pleasing line of his jaw. A few people, like Bee, were beautiful because they were so vibrant that the gaze is drawn to them whenever they are nearby; a few have become accustomed to being praised for beauty and expect those around them to be grateful to dwell in beauty's shadow. Andevai was, apparently, vain enough to care how he looked, but what I had taken at first for arrogant vainglory I now suspected had more to do with insecurity. He did not undervalue his cold magic, but he hauled other burdens. He, too, seemed not entirely sure of what he was, caught between his village and his House.

He had pulled me back within the wards, when he might have left me out to be swept away by the tide. The ghost of the memory of his fingers entwined with mine had left its imprint on my skin.

He hadn't meant to cut me. He'd stopped himself. He'd said,

"No." It had been an accident. He was ashamed. That's what made him act that way, gates closed and guard up.

What an idiot I was! Falling into sleep making up stories about a man I did not know and who had been commanded first to marry me, a woman he had never met, and then who, having botched the task, had been ordered to kill me. He had destroyed the airship, and perhaps lives with it. I had seen him kill two men; I knew what he was capable of. His blade's cut would have dispatched me if—for this was the only conclusion I could reach—my true father's blood, knit into my bones, had not protected me from the cut of cold steel.

His face meant nothing. It was just a face. He was a cold mage, even if he was not the actual son of Four Moons House, even if the magisters scorned him for his birth in a village they considered bound to them as unfree people little better than slaves. He was bound to the House by old laws; he was theirs to claim, to raise and train, and to unleash on the world when they needed his magic to enforce their will. Or, to be fair, to curb the excesses of the princes and lords as the magisters were said to have done in the early days of the mage Houses. As the old saying went, "Fear the magister, but if you pay him what he demands, he'll give you what you need. If only the prince's hunger could be satisfied as easily." Yet in these days, many hated the cold mages as much as they hated the princes and the old hereditary councils. The radicals said that those who had little because they were denied more than a pittance would, in time, rise up to demand a larger share.

I had been content once with what I had. Now it seemed I was caught in the flooding current of a river, torn away from all I had once thought was mine. The Barahals had sacrificed me. Four Moons House wished to kill me. At least the cats hadn't eaten me.

The latch clicked. Humming softly and a bit off-key, Rory

slipped into the room. A bed creaked as its ropes shifted under his weight.

"Rory?" I whispered.

"I was trying not to wake you." He sounded cheerful and not at all tired.

"What have you been doing?" He started to speak, but I cut him off. "No, never mind, don't answer." I knew perfectly well what he'd been doing. I could smell. "Are you moon-dazzled? By which I mean *insane*? Folk don't take kindly to men dancing into their towns, however so humble and isolated that town may be, and...ah...rollicking with their young women."

"Wasn't that included with the food and the bed?"

Perhaps I was only tired. But something about his tone of genuine surprise, and my mood, made me snicker. "You're awful. You know, I have only your word that you and I share a sire."

I sensed the change even before he spoke, a cat gone spiky with feline contempt. "Are you implying I am lying to you about such a matter?"

I stuck my head out of the blankets. The waning quarter moon was rising, visible as a hazy fragment of pearl through the thick glass. I saw him sitting upright with a rigid set to his shoulders as if he were trying to decide whether to claw me for the insult.

"No. But I woke up one morning assuming I knew everything about my world and my life, and now I know nothing." His posture softened infinitesimally, but I could tell he was still offended. "If I've insulted you, then please forgive me. I've had a terrible time. I don't know what to think about anything." My voice choked.

He said, more softly yet, "Go to sleep, little sister. I've arranged for us to leave at dawn."

And so we did. Who knew he had it in him to arrange for transport! I laughed when Emilia appeared at dawn with a sack of wayfarer's food, and she delivered us to a pair of older men in charge of a wagon filled with barrels of salted fish.

"Giving him two meals, eh?" said the driver with a laugh as she handed the sack to Rory in exchange for a quick kiss.

She said, "No man governs me, Uncle. I'm of age and can do what I like."

"So you say and so you will, until it gets you and the town into trouble." The driver was a stout man, his brown hair half gone to gray. He nodded amiably at me. "Come on up, gel. I'm called Leon. You sit beside me. My cousin—he's also called Leon, but you can call him Big Leon—and your brother can take turns walking alongside."

I got up beside the driver. Big Leon was a broad-shouldered, dark-complexioned man a good head taller than his paler cousin, and he gave me a searching and suspicious look so dark and penetrating that I began to get a little angry. Then he shook his shoulders with a twitch of his mouth, almost an apology, before he clambered up beside me on the bench. He braced a musket against his outer leg and slung a crossbow and bolts across his back. We moved out, the wagon rolling at a stately pace behind a pair of well-kept oxen.

"Expecting trouble?" I asked, noting the cousin's easy way with his weapons.

"Always good to travel in company," said Little Leon. "Folk like their salted fish. There's always some who will take what they want without payment. Sheep, for instance. Or you and your brother losing your goods and carriage and horse to brigands."

"Twins?" asked Big Leon abruptly, looking first at me and then at Roderic, like maybe he had a country superstition that twins would bring bad luck to a journey.

I stuck with the story I'd told the innkeeper. "No, he's older. And a cursed lot of trouble, if you ask me."

Little Leon laughed appreciatively. "That we saw, eh? Him and Em are well matched." Unlike his taciturn cousin, he was a talkative fellow who told us far more than I had ever wanted to know about Emilia and her notorious ways. His gossip did make the miles pass, though. He then regaled us with the gripping drama of his escape from the Great Hallows Blizzard, as folk were calling it now. The storm had howled out of the north on the second day of November and not let up for five relentless days. He'd been on the road to deliver a wagonload of pig iron from a furnace called Crane Marsh Works in Anderida to the blacksmith in Lemanis, and had barely made the village of Rhydcerdin as the whiteout descended to blind him.

"I heard the dogs barking and the temple bell ringing. That's what guided me in."

I gestured toward a land barely dusted with white. "I see little trace of snow now. How can it have thawed off at this season?"

"It weren't a natural storm, lass. Some thought it was the Wild Hunt's last gallop, but I am of the opinion it was one of them mansas taken by a rare fury. The snow came so deep that for weeks no one moved except from house to privy and privy to byre, maybe to the inn for a pint once a few paths were shoveled out. Then not seven days ago came such winds as were not natural winds. All the night they blew. I thought they would scrape the soil right off the bones of the earth. When we woke the next day, we came to find that the snow had been blown away, and to what place I am sure we will never know. I can't say what spirit raised that wind, or if it were a withering of cold mages acting in concert what managed it. Were you caught out in the storm?"

"We weathered it in a safe place." But a sick feeling dug at the pit of my stomach, because I wondered if the mages of Four Moons House had called down the blizzard to kill *me*. "Did anyone die?"

He glanced at Big Leon, who was scanning the countryside

with the gaze of a man who sees brigands everywhere. As the sun rose, the clouds began to shear off to reveal a blue sky. We fell in beside a river, flowing west. "Not so I heard. How far does your brother mean to walk?"

Rory wore a fur hat and a wide grin, striding with the easy grace of a man enjoying the novelty of the landscape. He did not look tired, as if staying up half the night carousing and engaged in other activities was as refreshing as sleeping.

"As far as he wants," I said. "How far are you taking this fish?"

"To the Crane Marsh Works. This is what's owed them for the pig iron. It's part of the winter feed for those who work the furnace. I was meant to bring it weeks ago, but I've only been able to move out now."

In my thoughts, I paged through Uncle's library of maps. West across the flats on a decent road, and thence up into eastern Anderida, home of mines and ironworks since the days before the Roman invasion. The Romans had left roads and paths aplenty to move the precious metal. The mansa had sent soldiers along this route first thing, looking for me. After six weeks, I hoped my trail was cold. Evidently Tara Bell and Daniel Hassi Barahal had chosen this route as well, going in the other direction, and their trail was not just cold but thirteen years dead.

"Your brother booked passage for you all the way to Crane Marsh Works," the carter added, with a curious glance at me, as if wondering why I hadn't known. "Last night."

"I went to my bed early," I said, "for I was exhausted after our harrowing encounter with the brigands."

"How many were there?" asked Big Leon.

"I was hiding my eyes," I said, perhaps too glibly, for the comment earned me a sharp, assessing look. Big Leon then hopped down from the moving wagon and fell back to walk at the rear beside Rory, musket under his right arm while he tamped tobacco into a pipe.

"Never mind him," said Little Leon. "You know how some folk are."

"He walks like a soldier."

"Him? Why, I soldiered in my youth, and you'd not guessed it, had you?"

"What, in the Iberian wars? Him, too?"

"Him, too, but we don't talk about that. We don't dwell on old grievances here, lass, for you know how kin might have got mixed up on opposite sides of that war. Why, I'm the son of a Atrebates mother and a Trinobantic father, a mixed marriage if there ever was one, for you know the Atrebates Celts sided with the Roman invaders while the Trinobantes Celts fought against them."

"The Roman invasion?" I laughed. "That ended two thousand years ago, not thirteen years ago like the Iberian war."

"Yet folk recall them just the same, whether it were Caesar or Camjiata. Hard to say who might have fought on which side, eh? So tell me about Adurnam. I hear there's a temple there dedicated to Ma Bellona, the Mother of War, She of the bloody hand, that's so big a thousand men can stand in the forecourt without touching one shoulder to another. Is that true?"

Behind, someone began coughing convulsively, and I whipped around to see Rory with the lit pipe in hand, doubled over, hacking. Big Leon calmly removed the pipe from Rory's fingers and began smoking as he walked; after a bit, wiping his eyes and starting to laugh, Rory loped after.

"Yes, it's true," I said, turning back. "I've seen such an assembly with my own eyes."

Traveling by wagon was not fast but it was steady, and both Little Leon and I liked to tell, and to hear, tales. By the afternoon of the second day, we read the signs that meant we were approaching a blast furnace and mine. The land began to fold and rise; the woods—mostly elm, oak, lime, and alder—were heavily coppiced. Charcoal stacks or their blackened remains dotted the surroundings. Smoke smeared the blue sky, and gradually a sound could be discerned, faint at first and then rising into a din matched by a miasma of fumes that made my eyes water and my nostrils prickle. A pond made by damming streams spread silvery-blue waters alongside pits and mounds of dirt and heaps of slag. The huge stone edifice of the furnace spewed smoke that covered half the sky as we approached. I covered my mouth and nose with a kerchief, eyes streaming. Rory started to cough. Both Leons tied kerchiefs over their faces.

Two young men came running.

"Here you are come, Leon! After that storm blew off the snow, we put bets on what day you'd arrive. Old Jo won! Who are these folks?"

No snow or ice remained where the furnace baked earth and air. Men pushed wheelbarrows of raw ore over a bridge of planks and dumped it into the furnace's fiery maw. What else transpired I could not discern, because the area below was roofed with timber. A bellows wheezed. Water splashed from a wheel and rolled along a wooden sluice.

We drove past and found ourselves in a tiny hamlet consisting of a barracks, a byre, and a temple to Komo Vulcanus, He whose knowledge is hidden, whose portals were wreathed with evergreen and myrtle necklaces from the year's end celebration. Big Leon left us without a word, entering the temple precincts as several men came to the threshold to usher him in.

Set apart from the other buildings, a pretty cottage stood backed up against an uncut copse of yew. Raised on bricks and rimmed with a porch on the side facing the furnace, the main building had no chimney at all, but it was attached via a covered paved walkway to a brick building in back whose chimney produced a healthy trail of white smoke. A man stood on the porch watching over the valley.

"Who is that up there?" I asked, not sure why my pulse began to race.

"Eh, the cold mage," said the carter, surprised I had to ask. "Falling Star House sends a young magister out each winter when the furnace is fired up. To keep a watch."

"To keep a watch? That sounds ominous."

He grunted. "Och, I did not mean it so. The Houses need iron, too."

"Don't they forge cold steel?"

He glanced sidelong at me. "What would a lass like you know of such stories? Anyhow, the mansa of Falling Star House is a responsible man. That young fellow there will keep a watch over the valley, and if there is a fire—for you can be sure fire is the worst danger to them who work the furnace—he can put it out. Might be you could sleep in the magister's kitchens. I can have a lad sent up to ask."

"My thanks," I said, scanning the sky. My eyes felt gritty, and I blinked away tears. "We've an hour's light left in the day. We'll keep walking."

He wished us well and did not argue. Even here in wild Anderida, there were few places you might walk for an hour without coming upon a hamlet or a village where a bed might be begged and a supper paid for with copper coins. The lads insisted we take a swallow of ale before we left. Rory charmed them into opening one of the barrels right away, and I plied my most polite brusque smile, and sooner rather than later we ended up walking south on a spur of the Roman road, toward Hawkwood Furnace. Rory carried a tiny gourd filled with salted fish along with the bundle of travelers' food Emilia had given him. In exchange for his services, I presumed.

"We might as well eat the fish now," he said, "for I'm hungry and we've not eaten anything more than that stinking cheese and dry bread this morning."

They were very strong, and the tiny bones satisfyingly crunchy. I saw him lick his fingers, each one, after savoring the salty morsels, and so I did the same.

"We'll smell of fish forever," I said.

"That would be nice."

We strode along companionably into the dregs of the afternoon. At times we chattered about inconsequential things; at times we remained in charitable silence, not needing to talk.

In the way of those whom Lady Fortune favors—not that I would dream of asking for favors from a Roman goddess—we came upon a farmstead just as dusk lowered its mantle. The folk who lived there were of old Atrebates stock, black of hair, pale of skin, and short of stature. They greeted us kindly and did not remark on our height more than five or six times over the course of a country meal of millet porridge and boiled mutton. They refused to accept any coin, it going against the custom of hospitality, so I gave them stories instead. The great tales whose warp and weft weave history fell no more strangely into their ears than the ordinary goings-on in Adurnam, which lay only a few days' walk away but which they had never heard of. We sat up late by a smoky fire in a hearth backed with an iron plate, and they listened, in their way, as intently as the djeli Lucia Kante—whatever she had been, ghost or spirit—had in hers.

In the chill mist of winter dawn, they set us on our way with a quarter of precious cheese and the last loaf of yesterday's bread.

Some hours later, at the big furnace beside the village of Hawkwood, we turned west into the southern reaches of Anderida. The tracks were easy to follow. Often, we could mark our goal by the columns of a temple standing atop a distant hill. Every prominent hilltop had its temple enclosure or stone pillar, however humble. I did not mind walking. Stagecoaches and toll

roads were too easy to watch. The weather held as we made our
way from one furnace to the next, past the scars left by abandoned mines and alongside empty pastures that in spring would
greet starving cattle with fresh shoots. Out here, no blizzard had
struck; no snow had come down at all in the last six weeks, we
were informed. The weather had held mild.

On the next night we were met with pitchforks and hostility
and only grudgingly allowed to sleep above a farmstead byre,
with the snuffling and snorts of the livestock as our lullaby. But
on the night after, we—guests! utter strangers! how exciting!—
entertained a hamlet so full of fellowship that drums and fiddles
were brought out for a sweaty evening of dancing. I had to warn
Rory off a smitten lass, no more than fifteen, whose ardor was
innocent and therefore dangerous to her and especially to us if
he mistook her glowing infatuation for worldly experience.
Many ales later, when one man put a hand on me in a place it
was not wanted, Rory turned on the fellow with a look so like a
snarl it was as if I could see behind the appearance of a man to
the animal he was in the spirit world. And though my unwanted
suitor had served ten years in the warband of one of the cousins
of the Prince of Tarrant, who lived hereabouts, the former soldier backed up so fast that he stumbled over a bench and fell flat
on his ass to the general delight of the assembly.

"I could have handled him easily enough," I objected the next
morning when we had set off again. Although the weather
remained fair, my stomach felt sour and the skin around my
eyes tight as a headache settled in.

"I do not doubt it." He squinted his eyes against the rising
sun and rubbed his face with the back of a hand. "But he made
me angry. It was like he'd clawed me."

"Yes, that's just how our generous hosts would have felt
toward you if you'd gone one step further with that sweet-faced
lass."

He frowned. We'd started out sluggishly, still muzzy from last night's celebration, but I picked up the pace, and we walked for a long while in silence. The weather remained fair, if cold, but as long as we were not drenched by sleet or drowned in snow, the cold actually made it easier to walk because the ground remained firm. If my nose shone perpetually red from cold, that was a small price to pay for solid footing.

Early on, we glimpsed men in the distance, felling trees; otherwise we might have been alone in the wide world but for the quiet hamlets and farmsteads with their chimneys breathing smoke. Folk did tend to bide inside at this time of year, when the days ran short. Even dogs did not bark for long at us; as soon as we came close enough for them to clearly smell Rory, they tended to slink away with tails tucked.

We paused to take a bite to eat when the sun reached its highest point.

"We should make Mutuatonis by nightfall." I sat on a stone field wall, feet dangling.

He leaned beside me. He wore his long dark hair in a single braid, like a woman, for these days men cropped their hair short. Perhaps it had been otherwise in other times and other places, but I had never seen a man wear his hair as long as my own was. Yet none of his admirers seemed to count it against him.

"Can you see that prominence there?" I pointed to the southwest, to a hill bulging higher than the rolling land around it. "That should be Cold Fort, if my memory of maps is correct. When we get a bit closer, we'll know for sure. There's a temple atop it, within the old earth ramparts. In ancient days it was a fort, maybe a barbarian prince's royal seat."

He wasn't looking toward the distant hill.

"What place is that?" He indicated a manor house far to the south of us, half screened by a row of poplars. "I smell meat cooking."

"A lord's estate. Not a mage House, as you can see by the arrangement of chimneys."

"Every building must have fires against the winter cold, mustn't they?"

"Cold mages kill fire. They heat their homes in the Roman way. Furnaces on the outside heat air that flows inside below a raised floor."

"What lord lives in that fine manor?" He wrinkled his nose. "Can we go there to beg for our supper?"

We were too far away for me to smell anything. "One of the cousins of the Prince of Tarrant, I suppose. He'd have no reason to show hospitality to the likes of us. I'm getting cold."

I hopped down and we set out again.

"From Mutuatonis we have a choice whether to follow the old Roman road west to where it meets the toll road. Then we would turn south and pass through Newfield before reaching Adurnam. But if Four Moons House still has seekers and soldiers out looking, it will be easier to find us on the toll road. Otherwise, we can cut across the chalk hills and stay in the countryside."

"They will expect you to return to Adurnam?"

"They must assume I will try to reach the Barahals. Although why I would want to see them ever again after they betrayed me..." It seemed my life had turned into an unending parade of betrayals, and while I could comprehend what had led someone like Kayleigh to play the part she had, it was awfully hard to find forgiveness in my heart for all those so willing to sacrifice me.

"Why go to Adurnam? We could leave the Deathlands. Go home."

"It is your home, maybe. It isn't mine. I don't understand the first thing about it. What would have happened to me if Andevai had not pulled me back within the wards when that...tide... swept through? Would I have died?"

"You would have changed. Maybe that is like what you call death here. You would have become something other than what you are now."

"What am I?" I murmured. The words made me dizzy. "Rory, do you know our father?"

"I never met him. He is not a personage you meet."

"He must have met your mother, and my mother. In order to sire children. If it's true we were both sired by him, he would have had to have been a cat in one form . . . a man in another. . . . You must know something more about him."

"No. Except that one thing my mother said."

"That he was a tomcat."

"That he was a tomcat. And not the sort of personage you go hunting for. If he wants you, he'll call you to him."

"That's really all you know? Aren't you curious to know more?"

"No. Should I be?"

"Do I wear a spirit mantle?"

He narrowed his eyes to look at me, then closed one eye to peer at me, opened it and closed the other, and looked, then opened it and, with both eyes on my face, made a gesture of defeat. "I can smell it, but I see only your human flesh."

Before I could reply, he lifted his chin, tilted his head, blinked, and brought me to a halt with a hand on my arm. "Listen." One moment he had been a relaxed and genial companion; now he was a predator alert to danger. "Horses and men behind us. I smell iron and cold steel."

I did not for one instant doubt him, although I could not sense anything amiss. The sky was flawless, its blue made brilliant by the clarity of the winter air. A breeze had been blowing out of the south all morning, just enough to set the tops of bushes swaying and to send fluttering kisses of movement across fields of uncut grass. Beyond the open ground rose yew woods, screened at their edge with bare-branched sapling beech and straggling bushes. Not more than a mile away rose the ridge where the ancient Celts had built Cold Fort and the Romans later raised a temple to claim the stronghold for their own gods.

"It's best if we leave the path," I said hoarsely.

The wind died as the words left my lips. *Died* was not the right word. It was as if a vast bellows had been turned inside out and sucked the wind back into the lofty caverns where the tempest is born. The temperature dropped from cold to frigid; my lips tasted the fall as though I pressed ice to my mouth.

"There's a cold mage with them," I said, barely able to voice the words because I could not find enough heat in my lungs. "They're tracking us."

I saw no sign of pursuit. They might not yet have come into view. But strangely, although the wind had utterly failed, an odd motion drew ripples across the clearing behind us.

Something was wrong with the light on the grass.

In Southbridge, Andevai had woven an illusion.

"They're in the field," I gasped, heart racing so hard I heard its hammering as hooves thudding on the ground. "Magic conceals them."

I started to bolt, blindly, down the path, but Rory tugged me to a halt. "Is there a crossroads?"

"I don't know." I was becoming frantic. They would kill me if they caught me. To force its prey into a panic is exactly what the predator desires. I had to think. "The ancient forts are built where lines of power intersect. Cold Fort lies on the highest point at the southwesternmost sweep of the ridge."

Perhaps our stillness made our pursuers bold. Or perhaps the magister riding with them wasn't very strong or simply became tired of holding the illusion, now that we were so close. From the field behind us, a bolt came sailing over our heads. Suddenly

I saw seven horsemen pounding toward us, six in soldier's livery carrying crossbows, with sheathed cavalry swords dangling along their flanks.

Rory said, "Into the trees. *Now.*" He pushed me.

Terror grew wings on my back, and I ran, wishing I was an eru with wings that might fly me into the safety of the spirit world, if you could call that place safe.

I heard a man shout, "I knew that jo-ba was lying. He's in league with her."

I heard the hammer release, the sing of a bolt.

A sharp sudden scream of warning.

As I reached the edge of the underbrush, I cast a look over my shoulder to see a saber-toothed cat hurtling in among the horsemen, muscles bunching as it sprang to topple the lead horseman from the saddle. Confusion reigned as the horses bucked and sidestepped, trying to get their heads out from under the reins so they could flee the deadly beast's massive claws. Two horsemen had pulled out of the fray and were racing toward *me*. Branches scraped my arms as I shoved through the tangle of bushes. The fabric of my cloaks caught, dragging me to a halt, and I twisted, yanking at the cloth to free myself. Branches snapped as a rider drove his mount into the undergrowth. I plunged farther in, but once beyond the leafless fringe of deciduous trees, I entered the yew forest whose dense canopy sheltered no concealing undergrowth.

I spun as the soldier broke out of the bushes, crossbow raised as he sighted in the gloom. A bolt hissed past me; he dropped the crossbow on its leash as I untied my outer cloak. Closing, he drew his sword. I swept the cloak open and flung it over the head of his mount. Ducking to my right, I threw myself behind a tree trunk. He grappled with the cloak, cursing as the horse shook itself into a halt under a low-lying tree limb. His head slammed hard into the branch, but I was already running. My riding habit was cut for practicality, not fashion; the Barahals took their riding seriously. The fabric did not hinder me as I dashed deeper into the woods. The trees had a brooding majesty, but all I could truly discern were the possibilities these gnarled boles offered for dodging armed riders. Another was gaining on me. This young man had a fashionable coat rather than a soldier's kit. He had a sword, and he rode well, and by the way he shouted a command over his shoulder to a soldier spurring his horse to follow, I guessed he must be the magister who had woven the illusion.

I clambered over the moss-covered ruins of a fallen tree, raced along the trunk to the exposed roots, and jumped down, using the cane for balance as I caught myself in a crouch. Then I kept running, having gained two more breaths of distance between me and them, because they had to go around and furthermore were hampered by young trees and shrubs that had taken advantage of the opening in the canopy to steal light for growth. I saw and heard no sign of the others. Of what had happened to my brother I dared not contemplate.

Abruptly out of the forest appeared three soldiers, bearing down on me with swords raised. Bright tabards wrapped them, marked with the four moons of their house: full, half, crescent, and new. Yet light glinted on their iron helmets; sun would not glint so beneath a canopy too dense to allow undergrowth.

The light and shadow must reflect and darken consistent with the conditions of light at the time of the illusion. So Andevai had murmured in the carriage when he'd thought I was asleep.

I ran straight into them, brandishing my cane, and where it slashed through the illusion, the hard glare of its cold steel blade shone. Cold steel cuts cold magic.

A shout of anger chased me as I ran on. I scrambled into a gully and splashed across a stream whose eddying shallows were rimed with fingers of ice. I broke onto a path crowded with uncut bushes and winter-sleeping beech and ash, and lashed my way through to emerge into a long, narrow clearing. The ruins of an old rectangular building whose entrance was crowned by a Roman arch greeted me. Holes had been dug about the tumbled walls as though thieves were seeking buried treasure. I was for a moment alone. The holes made the approach to the arch and the ruins behind it a maze deadly to running creatures. Blessed Tanit watched over me, for there was a big hole somewhat triangular in shape, like her sigil, directly in front of the archway. I spread my other cloak over the hole and weighted the ends with bricks and kicked and flung leaves and debris to cover it. I heard the cursed magister's mount snorting as he pushed past the thicket and rode into the clearing. I backed under the arch.

He had the haughty pride magisters were famous for, the curl of lip, the spark of cold fire in the eye. He wore the fine clothes whose weave and tailoring were apparent even at thirty paces and carried a sword hammered out of cold steel in his right hand. Seeing me, he glanced over his shoulder, looking for his companions.

"That's right," I shouted at him. "We've played you for a fool. You think your cold magic is so powerful, but you're blind. A lowborn slave wields more power than you will ever handle or know. How it must burn!"

Young men can be very predictable. If Andevai had endured such a difficult time in Four Moons House despite his ability and the benefit the mage House gained from it, then his age mates within the House, the aspiring magisters born to that status, must truly envy and despise him for what he possessed that they lacked.

With a grimace on his dark face, he spurred the horse straight at me.

I actually started to laugh, and that only made him more angry, and more blind.

The beast plunged where my cloak gave way, stumbling to its knees into the hole. He lost his seat and slid over the side, grasping desperately at the saddle. I loosed a prayer heavenward: Blessed Tanit, do not harm the innocent beast. Then I lunged forward. I whacked the magister on the head, and as his body went limp, I dragged him free, wrenching his leg out of the stirrup. Grasping the reins, I hauled the horse out of the hole and led it a few paces, but its gait was smooth. It was spooked but uninjured. I mounted just as an actual soldier burst onto the scene. The magister moaned, crying out, and I urged my fine steed forward, past the ruins and into the woods on an overgrown track. This was a cursed good horse, strong and willing.

"Go after her! There's a reward if you bring back her thrice-cursed corpse."

A whistle shrilled, and answering whistles rose from the wood.

I had a choice between two paths. I sent my steed down the leftward track, which soon opened into a decent trail. We went flying along past a farmstead and, not long after, a compound of a half dozen round houses fenced by a round palisade. A pair of children, standing outside, shrieked and called after me; they had brown faces, heads wrapped against the cold. A man, much lighter, appeared in the low doorway of one of the houses. He raised a hand as though to hail me; then I saw his gaze fix behind me. As I passed, he ran to grab the children.

A wagon track offered a wider route. I turned right, heading for Cold Fort. The woods fell away into cleared fields, and another lordly house rose away to the right like a dollhouse. Beyond the cultivated lands rose the ridge, with at least two lighter scratches on the slope marking paths chewed through the turf to reveal chalk soil below. Away to the right, a road intersected this track. On it, heading my way, galloped four riders. The sight struck my breath right out of me as brutally as a sword cut to my chest. I crooned to the horse, asking for more speed, more heart. He opened up stride like a warrior, and we reached the intersection before them and hit the path up the slope.

Naturally we slowed, and someone loosed a bolt at my back, but either his heart wasn't in it or his aim was bad, for the bolt stuck, shivering, in the hillside. Three breaths later, a sting like an insect's bite burned my right leg, and I looked down to see a bolt caught in the folds of my skirt. With a curse, I grabbed it and flung it away, but warmth trickled down my leg.

"Up! Up!" I said, willing the gelding to climb. I looked down to see the quartet meet up with the single soldier. They conferred; then a trio started up the path behind me while the other two headed onward. Did they mean to climb to Cold Fort on another track and cut me off?

But I had made my decision and chosen my path. I had lost Rory, maybe forever. I had to reach the temple and hope I could cross into the spirit world, where they could not follow. My leg was beginning to throb. At least, I thought bitterly, I had blood already drawn to open a gate onto the other side.

My horse, as befitted the mount given to a son of the House, was superior to theirs in courage and conformation. He was magnificent, a princely horse eager to show me his mettle. We reached the ridgeline having gained on our pursuers. Wind cracked over us. The land spread away below: the yew wood; a lordly house with gardens and corrals and a stockade within which a surprising number of cattle, as small as carved playthings, crowded despite the late season when normally most would have been slaughtered.

I turned my mount toward the massive earth ramparts of the old hill fort. Pillars and a roof marked a temple within the ancient walls. As I rode along the undulating ridge slope, I spotted figures atop the ramparts, signaling. Did priests live in the temple year-round?

Behind me, the trio was closing, and on the road below, the pair had dismounted and, leaving their horses, climbed on foot.

Farther away, I saw a dozen riders converging in the area from which I'd come, maybe in the hamlet where the man had gathered in his children. As if called by sorcery, six horsemen appeared in the earthwork's narrow front gap.

Fiery Shemesh! They had reached Cold Fort before me. I saw no sign of Rory.

Only one direction was left to me, a rash run down to the west where the town of Mutuatonis sprawled by the River Ouse with a hazy cap of smoke rising from its busy hearths.

"Catherine Hassi Barahal!" A man's voice called from the soldiers waiting at the gap.

So they would lure me in with hearty cheer and false promises before they cut my throat!

"Catherine!" the man repeated, gesturing to get my attention.

Before I plunged down the slope on my final doomed run, I hesitated. I knew that voice.

"Brigid's luck!" interposed a stentorian tenor. "I did not believe you, brother. Yet here she is, just as her cousin said she would be!"

The men at the ramparts were not wearing the livery of Four Moons House. They wore the green-jacketed uniforms of the Tarrant militia. The officer in charge was a tall, lean Celt with a thick mustache, a clean-shaven chin, and short hair stiffened into lime-whitened spikes. Four troopers flanked him, two with hair stiffened and lightened in the same manner while two kept black hair clipped tight against their heads. The sixth man seemed slighter than the others, although equally martial in his tailored military garb. He beckoned with a wave of his hand.

"Maestressa Barahal! It *is* you! Come on! Come in! Beatrice told us to meet you here, to bring you in to safety."

Blessed Tanit.

For the soldier who called me in was none other than Amadou Barry, the academy student Bee was so currently infatuated with.

27

The officer was the cousin of the Prince of Tarrant. After offering me a soldier's cloak to drape over my shoulders, he sat me down on a bench beside a brick hearth sheltered by a slate roof. There, warming his hands at the fire, he introduced himself as Marius.

" 'Marius' because," he explained with a chuckle, "I was destined to be an officer in the Tarrant militia from the day I was born. That's what we younger sons do: train for war, go to war, die in war, or limp home to our hearths to await our next raid. Not that we do any raiding these days. Although my neighbors have some cursed plump cattle that could do with a little exercise."

Plump cattle made me think of Rory. Was he dead, or had he gotten away? Despite the crackling fire and a mug of mulled wine brought by one of the temple priests, I could not get warm. Negotiations had begun at the ramparts, where Amadou Barry stood in heated conversation with the furious cold mage whose face, I was glad to see, was stained with dried blood. Twelve crossbowmen stood on the earthworks above, weapons trained on the mage. The angle of the gap and the outer ridge of ramparts hid the House soldiers from my view.

"Amadou will set him right," said Lord Marius, following my gaze. "There is not much a magister dares do to us in such circumstances, although I dare say he might try. But we outnumber his forces. My lads are certainly better trained and more experienced."

"He's carrying cold steel. He could kill Maester Amadou or any of you by only drawing blood." As he might already have dispatched Rory.

"I suppose he could. But would he? There's your question. A runaway bride—if that is indeed what you are—is scarcely worth angering the Prince of Tarrant, much less... Well, never mind that. The princes and the Houses have learned to cooperate when they must and leave each other alone the rest of the time. Is that the husband you're running away from?"

"No!" Heat scalded my cheeks; yet for what possible reason need I blush?

"Good fortune for you, then. He looks a singularly unattractive fellow."

The parlay broke off as the cold mage gestured angrily with a gesture so obscene I covered my mouth with a hand as I gasped. Lord Marius chuckled. Maester Amadou shrugged with a careless ease I admired and turned his back on the magister and his cold-steel blade.

As he walked back toward us, I said in a low voice, "I thought Maester Amadou was a student at the academy."

Lord Marius was a laugher. Everything seemed a joke to him. "Amadou Barry is older than he looks. I very much doubt he is what you may have thought him to be."

"Then what is he?"

"Och, lass, that's not my tale to tell, is it?"

He rose, and I did likewise, shaking out my rumpled and dirtied skirts. A priest brought another mug of warmed wine, and Amadou poured a few drops on the altar before coming over to join us. He sat. We sat. I stared sidelong at him, seeking signs of age in his face. I had thought him a year or two older than Bee and I, a polite, naive, spoiled, and privileged son of bankers recently arrived from resettled Eko on the coast of West Africa; I had thought he and his younger twin sisters were attending the academy because it was fashionable for wealthy, well-connected families to send their young people there for an education.

"Was it even true, that story?" I blurted out before I knew I meant to speak. "About your family fleeing ghouls in Eko, and how you and your sisters were put into the water on a boat while your parents and cousins—"

Shame blooded me as his expression changed.

Of course it was true. No one could mistake that look of fractured grief.

Then he smoothed it over with the ease of practice. "Yes, it's true, but it was thirteen years ago. I was barely fourteen. My three sisters and I, and our mother's sister, were the only ones to escape that terrible day. We endured a long voyage, with a Phoenician shipmaster and crew, I should note, fine sailors all, and came to family in the north. Poor shy Fadia was shipped off to marry this beast here"—Marius laughed as at an old family joke—"leaving me and the little girls with our father's people."

"My apologies. I spoke as the alligator bites." I spoke because of my own grief and fear, I thought, but I did not say that aloud.

He smiled in a conciliating way that irritated me.

"But if you were not a student at the academy, then why were you there?" I snapped.

"If I had some other motive for being there, you will excuse me, maestressa, for not divulging that motive to you now, as it has nothing to do with our present situation. Let me just tell you that your cousin Beatrice told me you were in danger and that you would come riding up to the temple of Taranis Jupiter, Maa Ngala"—Lord of All—"on the fifteenth of December."

"How could she possibly know? I've not been in communication with her!"

"Have you not? She seemed so very sure that I assumed you had sent her a message. When she described the temple, I recognized it as Cold Fort. Thus we are here." He drank his wine, and one of the priests hurried over to fill his cup. "Do you mean to say you sent her no message?"

He had the look of a man trained to coax out secrets by the expert application of casual questions.

"Where is she?" I asked to deflect him. This might be another trap. I could not believe Aunt and Uncle had been so foolish as to remain in Adurnam, knowing Four Moons House would discover the deception. They had even tried to convince Andevai to come back the next day; Andevai had himself recognized that they hoped to run away *with me*. And if they wanted to run away with me, then surely they regretted what they had been forced to do.

The sun sank toward the horizon, smearing a rosy glamor across the western sky. The troopers were setting up tents. Nearby, in a kitchen building whose shutters were all open to admit light, priests prepared a meal with the help of a few of the soldiers. Meat sizzled. How Rory would have loved that smell! I wiped a tear from my eye.

"You are aware," Amadou Barry said in the gentlest tone imaginable, "that your uncle—your entire clan—has been engaged for years as spies."

"Where are my aunt and uncle?" I asked, hearing how choked my voice sounded. Yet I was not about to reveal the whole of what I now knew. I had to hold something in reserve, should I need to bargain.

"They left Adurnam on the day after you were sent off with Four Moons House."

"Then how came Bee to speak to you?"

Lord Marius laughed again. I was beginning to find his laughter annoying, because it was obvious he was a man who had never suffered defeat or penury or even disappointment in love. The cousin of the Prince of Tarrant must be accustomed to having the world at his feet and Fortuna as his lover. If he had married Amadou's older sister, he was also wealthy even beyond what portion he had received within his own clan.

"She did not leave Adurnam with her parents and sisters and household. She stayed behind." Maester Amadou was a very handsome young man when he lowered his eyes to give the impression of innocent embarrassment, but really, he was too pretty. It was that prettiness that disguised his years, that made impressionable young women—and others, too, I am sure— underestimate him, assume him to be something other than what he was. And I did not even know what he was; all my expectations were exploded.

For then he added, his color changing, "When I discovered her situation, I offered her my protection."

My gaze sharpened. Maybe my claws came out. "What does *that* mean? Surely not—"

He would not look at me. "I would not trifle with her. As for the other, it is impossible."

"He means," interposed Marius, "that his aunt offered the girl shelter. So that's where you will find her, biding securely and unmolested in his aunt's house in Adurnam. As for the other, a man may be smitten, darling, but may otherwise be obliged to marry according to his family's needs and wishes."

"You need not tell *me* that! I have become intimately acquainted with the chains of obligation."

"Yet you fled your husband and the mage House."

"The mansa ordered me *killed*!"

Marius whistled appreciatively. "I couldn't have made augu- ries on *that*!"

Even Amadou looked surprised.

I felt I owed them an explanation in exchange for saving my

life. It's never wise to leave debts unpaid. "Four Moons House wanted Beatrice, not me. My aunt and uncle gave me to the magisters instead, and afterward when the mansa discovered he had been..."

"Cheated?" asked Marius with a hopeful chuckle. "Defrauded?"

"Given the wrong female," I finished with such a cutting glare that even the bluff military man barked out a surprised laugh and made a conciliatory gesture. "He was angry."

"Killing you seems an unexpectedly harsh response," murmured Marius, smoothing the red-gold splendor of his mustache with finger and thumb.

"He was very angry," I said dully.

"Where do you go now?"

"To find and warn my cousin. Four Moons House still wants her."

Amadou sipped thoughtfully at his cup and set it on the bench. "Why would Four Moons House so desperately want the daughter of an impoverished Phoenician clan, no matter what secrets the Barahals might have to sell and what business they might have done for Camjiata back in the old days?"

I felt a pinch of curiosity, wondering at the true extent of Barahal double-dealing. But I knew better than to reveal more than I already had. "I can say nothing more until I talk to Beatrice. Surely you understand."

"She's got you there," said Marius with an amused snort.

"We'll escort you to Adurnam and your cousin," said Maester Amadou.

"My thanks." Tears welled, and I blinked them back. I said, in a low voice, "Saw you any prisoner among the House soldiers?"

"No. Do you expect there to be?"

"No," I whispered. "No."

He waited a moment, to see if I would say more. When I did

not, he gestured decisively. "We leave at dawn. We can make it in two days."

Marius nodded in answer, and the discussion was over, just like that.

At a signal from one of the priests, Marius rose to make the offering of the first cut of roasted meat at the altar, pouring an entire cup of wine over it. Afterward, we retreated to the largest tent, sparely furnished with a pair of campaign cots in the back half, each one neatly made up with blankets. An attendant took our cloaks and hung them from iron hooks. We sat in the front half on unfolded camp chairs, at a small table. Two braziers heated the interior, and three lamps lit our campaign meal of roasted beef, turnip, and apples. I was ravenous, despite everything, and it was easy to eat with their conversation flowing briskly around me. The two men knew each other well and bantered like brothers. Marius was about five years older, the same age, it transpired, as Amadou's older sister.

"How did a young woman newly arrived in Massilia come to marry a Tarrant nobleman far to the north?" I asked Marius.

He cast a look at Amadou, who shook his head. The lord shrugged as he smiled at me. "Do you Phoenicians like music? I'd be a sad son of the Tarrants if I could not entertain my guest with a few songs."

"After all I have been through these last weeks," I said, very rudely I am sure, "you will excuse me if I seem burdened by a lack of trust. What if you are in league with Four Moons House, and mean to use me to lure Bee into your clutches?"

"Then we are at an impasse, Maestressa Barahal," said Maester Amadou in the same polite voice he had used to cow our academy proctor, Maestra Madrahat, by being better mannered and milder than you could ever be. "I have divulged as much as

I can. You have revealed as much as you are willing. Either we trust each other, or part ways."

"That I have little choice but to accept your help must be apparent to all of us." I did not mean my tone to grate so grudgingly, but it did. "If I seem unappreciative, it is just that I have been running for my life under difficult circumstances, as I am sure you can deduce by my state of disorder and dirt. If you can get me alive to Adurnam, you will have my thanks and my cousin Beatrice's as well."

Amadou's mouth tightened on unspoken thoughts and emotions.

Lord Marius laughed. "What's this, brother? Have you actually fallen for a woman's fine eyes and pleasing form?"

"Excuse me, Lord Marius, but I cannot like to hear my cousin spoken of in such a trifling way."

"Oh, it would not be trifling in Amadou's case, I shouldn't think." Marius rose and fetched a case from beneath the cot on the left. He brought out a small harp, set it on his knee, and began to tune it. His features relaxed into a serious expression as he listened to the vibrations of each string. He seemed suddenly removed from us, following the overtones, and for a moment I thought a door might open into the spirit world and we might fall through.

A burst of male laughter from outside slammed closed the shutters of reality over my dreaming. At a nod from Amadou, the trooper attending the door stepped out. One breath later, he returned with another soldier in tow.

"What news?" Lord Marius asked without looking up from his harp.

The soldier started to laugh, thumped his own chest twice, and coughed to contain himself before addressing the two men. "Lord Marius. Legate."

Legate? I stared at Amadou Barry, but he was not looking at me. Only the Romans in their much shrunken imperial republic used the term *legate* for highly placed commanders and ambassadors.

"There's a...naked...man at the ramparts. He *baldly* requests permission to—"

I stood so fast I banged a knee against the table and had to catch its edge to prevent it from toppling over. My heart had galloped ahead. I could barely string coherent words together. "Let him in. Quickly! Can clothing be found?"

Lord Marius set to laughing in earnest. When he had controlled himself, and wiped his eyes, he managed to speak. "A naked man, come to my camp? Is it your abandoned husband, Catherine Hassi Barahal? Come to display himself for your benefit?"

My flush must have reached my ears as his words forced me to consider the prospect of facing Andevai Diarisso Haranwy in very different circumstances than any we'd previously shared. The two troopers and Lord Marius kept laughing while Legate Amadou Barry, whatever else he might be, had compassion enough to take pity on me.

"If you vouch for him, then certainly we can allow him to join our company. Sergeant, let him enter the camp."

The second trooper hurried out.

"By all means!" cried Lord Marius, placing the harp carefully back in its case and securing it. "Let me go view this prodigy for myself. Dare I hope—" He broke off and looked at me. Amadou put a hand on his forearm, in the way a man might quell a dog's yap. Marius chuckled and strode from the tent, leaving Amadou to give the order to fetch clothing.

I grabbed a cloak off the hook and hurried out in Lord Marius's wake, with Amadou following. The news had spread through camp. The soldiers were calling out jokes, although in no way did they relax their vigilance.

"Best you stay back, maestressa," called Lord Marius over his shoulder. "The House company has camped beyond the ramparts. They have crossbows."

So I stood, shifting my weight from one foot to the other, as the officer and five men strode ahead. Amadou remained beside me.

"Who is it?" he asked.

"I think it likely it is my brother."

He raised an eyebrow. "I did not know you had a brother, maestressa."

"No. I expect you did not."

A trooper ran past, carrying a bundle of clothes. He, too, vanished past the angle where the ramparts opened.

"He saved my life just today," I added. "I wasn't sure he was still alive—"

I pressed a fist to my mouth, unable to speak. My companion wisely held his tongue. Had he said one cursed sympathetic thing right then, I think I would have clawed out his eyes.

I heard men talking and talking, laughing and joking. It took forever and a day exactly as if they were conducting a party and had forgotten me entirely. I would have run to find out what was taking so long, but I thought of crossbow bolts and did not. At long last strode a half dozen men into view with Rory among them, limping a little—his feet were still bare but he was otherwise decently clothed—and his head thrown back as he laughed at some soldierly quip.

I might have moaned first, as despair fled my heart, entirely routed. Then I shrieked. "Rory!" I ran, and I flung myself at him so hard he staggered back at the impact and got an arm around me as I pressed my face into the coat he was wearing.

"You're safe," I cried like a player in the theater. "I thought you were dead."

"They were too startled to manage an effective counterattack. And the remaining horses went wild. All but one bolted."

I glanced up just as he licked his lips, looking suspiciously pleased with himself.

"I didn't know you could do that," I said with a glance at the soldiers now watching us with the sentimental expressions of men who pretend to be big and tough but in truth dandle babies on their knee with the greatest tenderness and affection.

"Neither did I!" he replied with a grin. "It just…came over me."

We both started laughing, and I broke away and wiped my eyes. "Are you hurt?"

"A shard of bone cut one paw. Nothing important. Now who are these fine fellows who have given me these fine clothes? And is that *beef* I smell?"

I introduced him as my brother Roderic without offering a single detail more, and our hosts graciously had another platter of food brought as well as a fourth camp stool. Rory chatted and laughed with Marius and Amadou, ever so charming, pausing at intervals to try on boots that soldiers brought in, none of which fit.

I stared at him, scarcely able to believe he had survived. His features, his gestures, his long black braid: All these had become as familiar to me as if I had known them my entire life long, yet I had first encountered him only a few days ago. I did not understand it. Was this what kinship meant? A sense, deep in your bones, that the person next to you is part of you? Inextricable from what you are? That you could not be who you are without their existence as part of the architecture of your very self?

We are none of us one thing alone and unchanging. We are not static, or at rest. Just as a city or a prince's court or a lineage is many people in one, so is a person many people within one, always unfinished and always like a river's current flowing onward ever changing toward the ocean that is greater than all things combined. You cannot step into the same river twice.

"Philosophizing over there?" asked Rory, as if he could hear my thoughts. "You don't usually stay silent for this long, Cat. Unless you're deliberately ignoring me, I mean."

I shook off my reverie. "Just worrying," I said.

Lord Marius rose. "It will be a long night. I suppose the company pursuing you may take it into their heads to attempt a night raid, so I'll keep half my men awake and half asleep in their boots."

"I'll take the second watch," said Amadou.

"My thanks, *Legate*," I said with what I hoped was a biting smile.

He had the grace to look shamefaced. He and Lord Marius left the tent to us.

"What is a legate?" Rory asked.

"A very important man in Rome. I cannot figure it. It seems true that he and his sisters and aunt fled from Eko—"

"Eko?"

"You don't know anything, do you?"

"No," he agreed cheerfully. "Not a thing! That horse meat was tasty, though."

I laughed, and then grimaced, realizing he was not speaking of our supper. "You stopped to eat not knowing if I was alive or dead?"

"I discovered, dearest sister, that I am not entirely myself when I am in my natural shape here in the Deathlands. It took me a while to come to myself. Once I had, I followed your trail immediately. And am very glad to have discovered you alive and unharmed. What is Eko?"

"It's a place very far away from here on the coast of a land where once rose a rich empire. A terrible plague devastated the country. Those who could, fled and made homes elsewhere, but of course their descendants never forgot where they had come from. In recent years, some intrepid settlers rebuilt the old port of Eko, thinking to return to their lost homeland. But they were attacked and overrun. The survivors returned here to Europa to the families and clans from which they had come. I thought Amadou Barry was just a young man from a well-to-do Fula banking family, who happened to be among those who attempted the resettlement and ended up making a new life in Adurnam after the disaster. Now I hear him addressed as a legate, which means he is connected to Rome! In what capacity he could possibly carry the title of legate I cannot be sure, nor why he was masquerading as a student..."

Rory yawned. "He smells clean. He and the other one mean us no harm, not like those hyenas waiting out beyond the old earth walls."

"Hyenas? What is that?"

"Never mind. Foul creatures. I hate them. Hyenas, I mean, not our rescuers. I'm tired. I need a nap."

He took possession of one of the cots and pulled the blankets up over his head. His breathing slowed immediately. Could anyone fall asleep that fast?

A cough startled me; a soldier poked his head in and gestured. "If you would like me to turn down the lamps, maestressa? Stoke the braziers?"

"I thank you."

He did what needed to get done, chores I would have performed in my own house. In the house I had thought was mine. The confusion that boiled in my heart made me restless. Aunt and Uncle had betrayed me, and yet they *had* made an attempt to save me before giving up and letting Andevai take me. What had they thought would happen when the deception was discovered?

For no matter how hard I stared at the outcome, I had to believe they had not known they were sending me into mortal danger. Merely into lifelong servitude. The Barahals knew how to serve; that's how they made their living. Had Daniel known of the contract? Why had he and my mother left Adurnam right after the capture and imprisonment of Camjiata? Thirteen years ago. The same year, it seemed, that the Barry refugees had fled the disaster at Eko—1824 had been a very eventful year, hadn't it?

I rose, thinking to walk outside to calm my tangled thoughts, but as soon as I stood, my legs quivered and I almost collapsed. I staggered over to the empty cot and sat hard, trembling. I barely had the strength to lie down and pull the blankets up over myself as I shivered with exhaustion. I shut my eyes and plunged into sleep.

A man sang in my dreams, and the plucking of harp strings opened a path between this world and the other side, a shimmering ribbon of pure sound that ran as a river of silver fire. Rory was chuckling, or purring, and then a scattering of shouts and a clattering of weapons pulled me from the depths and into the night-bound tent. It was dreadfully cold but for a ghost of warmth drifting up from the last banked coals. The red gleam gave me just enough light to see that the other cot had no one in it.

Had I only dreamed Rory's return?

As if my thought were a call, he came into the tent. He was chuckling softly in that purring way he had, and he was sneaking, clearly unaware I was awake and perfectly attentive to his prowling. Where had that cursed fool gone this late at night? I meant to rise and speak, but try as I might, I could not rouse my limbs or move my lips to ask what was going on.

"Sleep, little sister," he said as he stretched out on the other cot, back among the blankets. "The magister and his troops made an attempt to attack over the ramparts, but they were sent scuttling with tails between their legs."

I woke suddenly into dawn's gloom, eyes open and legs twitching, and inhaled a lungful of exceedingly cold air. Rory slumbered on the other cot. Shuddering with cold, I slid out from under the blankets, pulled on my boots and gloves, and hurried outside as under my breath I cursed soldiers who had no need to carry chamber pots for their morning relief. In a company of men, they could just pee wherever they wanted. Last night's wine pressed against my bladder.

Outside, I paused to get my bearings. Sentries ringed the ramparts. Lamps ringed the tent behind mine, and I heard men talking in low, intense voices. I scanned the scatter of buildings huddled within the ramparts. The temple stood at the height, where its pillars could catch the first rays of sun, not that there would be any sun today, given the glowering drape of clouds. The outdoor hearth under its roof, a fire still burning; the kitchen shed shuttered tight; the priests' cottage with a thread of smoke rising from its chimney; the military tents. Feeling awkward in a camp where I was the only female, I dug down for the glamor and slunk unnoticed to the privy. After I had done my business, I emerged into the lingering gloom of an overcast winter dawn.

"Cursed cold mage! Him and his thrice-cursed cold steel!" Lord Marius strode into view in an exceedingly Celtic fury, like a storm cloud in full spate. "I'll have them in court. I'll be sending a solicitor to Four Moons House, I tell you, to demand blood price. One cut. One cursed cut. His spirit cut from him. How I hate them!"

He passed by without seeing me. A trooper led up two horses, one burdened with a figure wrapped in a blanket and tied onto the saddle: a dead man.

"Marius, is this wise?" called Amadou, jogging up. A stain

marred his jacket sleeve and his back was covered with flecks of grass, as if he had been pushed onto the ground. "You'll be riding alone. An easy target."

"They'll not attack the cousin of the Prince of Tarrant in broad daylight, knowing that if I turn up as a corpse, Four Moons House must accept full blame. That ass-biting turd of a cold mage took a fool's reckless chance. I can't imagine what possessed him to think he could crawl into *my* camp with his soldiers and kidnap a person to which I—*I!*—had given my protection. I'll ride to the manor and send reinforcements. They'll see what they've woken by offending one of the Tarrant kinsmen!"

Without any indication he had seen me, he mounted and, with the other horse on a lead behind his own, rode off alone through the ramparts.

"Break down the camp," said Amadou in a voice accustomed to command.

The men obeyed with alacrity. At the academy, I had thought him charmingly modest. If I had called him the vainest youth I had ever met, I had only done so to twit Bee for her infatuation. Certainly compared to a man like, say, Andevai, he had no vanity to speak of.

He walked over to the tent I had slept in just as Rory emerged. They spoke briefly. Amadou swung around and surveyed the camp, his gaze passing over me before he turned back to my brother with a puzzled shrug. Rory did not point me out, although he obviously knew right where I was even if no one else could see me. I had forgotten my glamor.

I sat by the hearth and brushed off my skirts, shaking off my concealment.

"There she is," said Roderic.

Legate Amadou Barry walked over. "I hope your rest was a peaceful one, maestressa."

"What happened to that soldier?"

"Blooded by cold steel. We had a few minor injuries, but he alas is dead. We'll leave immediately after the camp comes down. You'll ride at the center of the formation lest their cross-bowmen decided to take a shot at you. However, it seems we've driven them off, for they are nowhere to be seen this morning."

A man had died on account of me.

Blessed Tanit, make his passing gentle and his journey an easy one. Give peace to his family.

The low-hanging clouds made gray of the world. Our mood as we set out had the harsh tone of untuned, jangling strings. Later, it began to rain.

The next day in the late afternoon, without further incident, we reached Adurnam.

28

No one had warned Bee. A servant opened a door, and I entered the sitting room behind Amadou. At first, his body shielded me from her view. I beheld a spacious chamber lit by many lamps against the encroaching dusk. The walls were painted with chevrons and angled stripes in red, black, and yellow. An oak mantel carved with lizards capped a brick fireplace inset with a circulating stove; the fire within radiated so much heat that I began to sweat, and to think about how filthy I was. I could not catch my breath.

On one of the Roman-style couches sat a proud-looking woman no older than Aunt Tilly, wearing embroidered damask robes whose vivid orange and green shone. Her elaborate coiffure of braids was complemented by gold earrings shaped like hoops that dangled to her shoulder. She was an elegant, graceful, beautiful woman of Afric ancestry; Amadou resembled her. The twin sisters were seated on stools on opposite sides of a table, stringing beads and coins and other small objects onto a chain. Both set down their work and glanced up with bright smiles.

"Amadou!" they cried, and then they glimpsed Roderic, behind me, and looked away.

As Amadou walked forward to greet his aunt, I saw Bee seated on the other couch holding a sketchbook on her lap and a pencil in her left hand. Her thunderous frown, directed at the open page, made me giggle, in some part with delight but also because after all this time I was so desperately relieved to see her alive and well. Yet what was she so angry about?

She heard my chortle. She looked up. With a deafening shriek, she flung sketchbook and pencil halfway across the room as she leaped up. Her expression entirely transformed, she charged across the space between us and threw herself into my arms. I would have wept, but Bee's embrace was so crushing I could barely get air into my lungs much less find breath for sobs.

We stood this way for a while, smashed together, holding tight, my cane pressed between us. I could not think. We were reunited. That was all that mattered.

Eventually, I opened my eyes. Over her head, I watched Roderic making his courtesies to the aunt, who clearly found him as charming as he found himself. Amadou pulled up two wooden stools with legs carved to become antelopes, and the men sat down in front of his aunt. Rory smiled at the twins as Amadou bent forward to confer with his aunt, who held his right hand between hers.

Bee must have felt my attention shift. She released me from the vise. I took in a long gasping breath, then staggered forward, aware I had snubbed the woman who had sheltered Bee. But she was gracious, and her nieces seemed genuinely if shyly pleased to see me again, although I am sure I had not ever been kind enough to them at the academy to deserve their generous greeting.

"You remember my half brother Roderic, Beatrice," I said, hoping I would not have to kick her. "It's been ever so many years since we last saw him."

She fixed her full-bore stare on me, drilling for secrets. Then she swept over to him.

"How could I *possibly* forget dear Rory!" With a flourish, she kissed him smartly on either cheek and rather more warmly than he had clearly expected.

He glanced at me as if for aid in dealing with a flower whose beauty might hide poisonous thorns.

Bee stepped back from him and eyed Rory an instant more, then cast a look toward Amadou so brimming with fulmination that I would have laughed if she had not appeared ready to stick a knife in him...or to kiss him. It was difficult to tell. He pressed a palm to his forehead, realized he was doing so, and looked to his aunt with a plea.

"Please sit," his aunt said. "This is unexpected."

Water was brought, then coffee and candied ginger, boska, and cherries. Amadou described, succinctly, our meeting at Cold Fort. He was clearly concerned that Lord Marius had not yet rejoined us, and his aunt took the opportunity to suggest she and he go to the factotum's office and see about sending a messenger to the prince's court in Adurnam. The twins likewise were dragged along on this expedition. It was done so smoothly that I had scarcely realized she had deliberately engineered matters to leave us alone, when Bee stung.

"Who are you, really?" She rose with fists on hips, arms akimbo, to glare at Roderic. "Come along to charm my innocent cousin into calling you her *brother*."

He blithely transferred himself to the nearest couch, stretched out his long legs, and leaned back with arms crossed. "I do not need to defend what is true."

The battle of wills commenced as they stared each other down. Obviously, neither was going to blink first.

"He really is my brother," I said, running a hand up and down the smooth length of the cane that had been given to me by an eru who had called me "cousin." "Or at least he could be. If we share a sire."

"The hair is like," she admitted grudgingly. "You've some

resemblance about the face. Perhaps. Why do you have a cane, Cat?"

"To protect myself at night. You won't believe what has happened to me."

"I might," she said ominously, like a storm about to break. She flung herself down beside Rory, ignoring him in exactly the way she ignored her little sisters when she wasn't interested in what they were doing. Her gaze followed me as I crossed the room to collect her sketchbook and pencil and returned them to her. I sat on the other side of her on the couch, running my fingers over the embroidered silk. I was sure I had never touched cloth as expensive as this in all my days. The simple layout of the house gave the appearance of modesty, rather like Amadou Barry, but one could see in the quality of its appointments that the family did not maintain a more opulent house only because they chose not to.

"I might believe anything *now*," she went on darkly, pressing the sketchbook to her chest. "I might believe my own father and mother handed my dear cousin over to wicked magisters under false pretenses, knowing they had bound themselves years ago to a contract that actually called for *me* to be handed over to the mage House."

"Did you know?" I whispered, fingering a perfect rose made of tiny red stitches.

"Can you possibly imagine I would have stood by meekly and let them sacrifice you in my place had I known?"

Tears burned. "No," I choked out. "I never did believe it, not for all this time."

She grasped my hand. I twisted the bracelet she had given me off my wrist and placed it back onto hers, the mark of our compact. Thus we made our peace.

"We were both duped," she raged, turning the bracelet around and around her wrist. "Lied to. Used. I am so angry I could—"

Her expressive face sheared through so many emotions so quickly that it was dizzying.

Rory leaned forward. "You could *what*? I am all ears."

"It was a figure of speech, you wretched idiot," she said with the same dismissive scorn she heaped on her sisters when they annoyed her. "There's nothing I can do but sit here and be grateful for these very fine and high-placed and fabulously wealthy people who have been so generously willing to offer a sad, impoverished lowly Barahal shelter, food, and a bed."

She turned quite, quite pink, as with shame.

"Bee!" I said.

She jumped to her feet and strode to the window, her back to me. "I know nothing of what you have suffered, and yet here I am speaking only of my own mild difficulties. I'm terribly selfish."

Astonishingly, she burst into tears. Real, raw tears.

I ran to her and hugged her, and she pushed me away and cursed so frightfully that I laughed. She wiped her eyes and threw one killing look toward Rory, who had closed his eyes and was pretending to not be there.

"Bee! What happened?" I demanded.

"No, you tell me first," she cried. "Tell me what they did to you!"

"I'll tell you everything, but I want to hear your story first so I can start making a plan."

She set a palm on the perfectly polished glass of one of the windowpanes. The garden, in winter, wore its green yew hedges as its brightest tone; leafless fruit trees lined a path toward several round graneries partially obscured by willow hurdles set around them like a stockade. Beyond lay stables and laundry. The high stone boundary walls were obscured by trimmed evergreen yew trees, guardian against magic. For a house in Adurnam, they had a lot of land.

I waited, and she began.

"You can imagine what happened after the magister hauled you away that night. Mother and Father did not sleep. A few chests were packed with clothes, necessaries, and Father's private correspondence."

"What happened to the package Andevai—the magister— gave to Uncle?"

"They burned it first thing, all of it. They threw that book you found on the fire, too."

"*Lies the Romans Told*?"

"Yes. But when they weren't looking, I pulled it out and hid it behind Uncle Daniel's journals. Which they left behind."

"They left behind the journals? How could they?"

She shrugged. "We left the house before dawn and went straight to the harbor. A Kena'ani captain was obliged to offer us passage when Father invoked the old custom of motherhouse. While we waited in a cabin on the ship, Mama and Papa told me the truth. Thirteen years ago, a contract was forced onto the Hassi Barahal clan by Four Moons House. The magisters held evidence that the Barahals had spied for Camjiata during his campaigns while at the same time selling information to the princes and mage Houses allied against Camjiata. In exchange for keeping the evidence of this double-dealing a secret, the magisters had the right to take possession of the eldest Barahal daughter at any time before she reached her majority. Me, Cat. It was me they wanted, not you."

"I know."

"How could Mama and Papa think I would ever forgive them, once I found out?"

"Bee..."

"Let me finish. The tide turned and the ship sailed. I sweet-talked the harbor pilot into smuggling me on board the pilot's skiff when he returned to harbor. The ship could not turn against the tide, so they went on to Gadir without me. I hope they think I cast myself overboard and *drowned*!"

"Bee!"

"I don't mean it! Not for the girls' sake. I left a note. I didn't want Hanan and Astraea worrying. They were so scared, for I had to drag them from their beds and make them dress in the dark in the terrible cold. Shiffa and Evved and Cook went, too, but I knew Pompey and Callie remained behind. I walked home. But you know, Cat, there was almost no food left in the root cellar, and coal enough for only a week, and no money at all. I can't imagine how we were meant to survive the winter had we not been forced to flee!"

"But—"

"Pompey went back to his family in the country. I gave him some things he could sell, for I thought it only fair he should have a severance wage. Callie has nowhere to go, you know. She's got no kin. I couldn't turn her out on the street, so we sold off a few things Mama and Papa had left behind. Once I was certain we had sufficient coal to heat the kitchen and grain to keep two of us for some months—for Callie knows exactly where to find the cheapest victuals at the tradesmen's market— then I went to the academy and asked to speak to the headmaster. I asked him to contact Four Moons House for me so I could exchange myself for you."

"Bee!"

"But first he made me describe the ceremony to him, the one we witnessed, when the jelly was brought in."

"It's *djeli*," I said. Then: "But you were sent upstairs. You didn't witness it."

"I peeked! After I described it, he told me that the law allows the head of the house to dispose of any minor under his rule at his pleasure, which means Uncle had a perfect right to marry you off against your will while you were still underage. Worse, a marriage chained by magic cannot be severed under any circumstances except by the death of one of the people involved." She caught my wrist in a bruising grasp. "They tried to kill you, didn't they, Cat? *Didn't they?*"

My voice was a hoarse whisper. "Yes."

"But you escaped those hateful mages! You escaped, Cat, and you came back. I knew it was what you would do."

She was flushed and magnificent, refulgent with indignation and pride. As if the sorcery of beauty had called, the door opened and Amadou Barry, Roman legate, stepped into the chamber. Seeing her, he halted as if he had slammed into stone. The chamber could have erupted into a blazing storm of fiery flying pigs, and he would have had eyes for only Beatrice.

"You are not wanted," she said imperiously, with a flick of her hand.

He opened his mouth, closed it, and went out. The door closed with a snap behind him.

"Well, there's a change of heart," I said, reflecting that Andevai would have argued instead of retreating. "Once, you did little else but moon over his handsome eyes and pleasing manners."

"I do not see him. I do not recognize him."

"You're so flushed I think I am going to have to fan myself. What happened?"

"She loves him, she loves him," said Rory in exactly the tone thirteen-year-old Hanan would use to tease her older sister.

She crossed her arms and glowered at him. "Who do you think would win, dear cousin, if it came down to battle between you and me?"

He laughed without stirring in the least, entirely unaffected by a stare that would have obliterated any other man. "You're delectable when you're angry. I could just eat you up."

"You could just try," she retorted. "You remind me of that little beast Astraea, unrepentantly spoiled."

"And you remind me of my younger sister—not Cat, but the other one—the one who is tiresome and self-absorbed and who never shuts up, yowling day and night for attention."

I broke in before the duel got ugly. "Bee, he's not joking. He could eat you up. Now tell me what else the headmaster said."

"He told me that by no means should I return home. That Four Moons House would likely come after me. He sent his dog—"

"His dog?" asked Rory, licking his lips.

"His assistant, the albino from the east," she said impatiently. "Anyway, the dog went scouting and came back to report that soldiers wearing the livery of Four Moons House had stationed themselves outside our house. So the headmaster offered to protect me. You can imagine my surprise when he summoned Amadou Barry. Who is no student. He's an agent working for Rome."

"He's a legate."

"Yes, that's how the headmaster addressed him." Her lips quirked up in an ironic, even sarcastic, smile. "And because I am very clever, I discovered that Legate Amadou Barry is the one who brought that book to the academy."

"*Lies the Romans Told*? Why would a Roman legate possess that book?" But I recalled Shiffa's words. "Unless it *was* a codebook. Written by a Barahal. You don't think—?"

"That he came to the academy to ingratiate himself with Barahal girls? Whose parents might know something of it?" She fluttered her lashes, all honey, and then smiled a cruel smile. "I told them Papa burned it."

"How did you come here?"

"I had little choice. The headmaster kindly informed me that not even a mage House will invade the residence of a family connected to the nobility of Rome. Yet you may suppose that however safe I am here, however well I have been treated, I am but a pretty bird in a pretty cage. I endured it because I knew I had to stay out of the hands of the mage House until you returned."

I looked at her narrowly. "That can't be the only reason."

She flushed. "Yes, I got to see Amadou every day, and speak with him familiarly, every day. So I bided here quite peacefully and even eagerly as the weeks passed, knowing there was a separate watch posted by the headmaster's loyal dog on our house to make sure Callie was not disturbed. To keep an eye for your return. And then"—she trembled—"and then he kissed me."

Rory grinned. "The man stinks of love for you, darling."

"Don't be crude, Rory," I snapped.

"Nothing can go on here without his aunt—he calls her 'Mother'—hearing of it," she murmured. "She spoke privately to me. It was the kindness that was the worst of it. I was a very fine young woman, she said, but it was certainly impossible that a young man who was on his mother's side the grandson of a prince and on his father's side a grandson out of the Valerii—"

"The patrician Valerii?" I cried.

"Not only that, the Valerii Messalans."

"By the way you are steaming from your ears, I believe this term means something to you that it cannot mean to me," remarked Roderic languidly.

"Descendants of the Roman consul and commander who obtained the only significant victory Rome ever claimed over Qart Hadast," I said, pressing my hands to my breast. "They are the worst enemies of the Kena'ani. Also, they never marry outside their patrician clans."

"It seems they do. Amadou's mother was born into a princely Fula lineage. His father's father was also of noble Fula birth.

They are bankers, too, hugely wealthy. *He* is the one who married a Roman woman of the Valerii gens. But I don't really care about that, Cat. The war with the Romans happened so long ago. His aunt made it very clear, in so very kindly a manner, that we Barahals were *beneath* them. Any alliance between us could not be contemplated. And then he...*he*...Later he found me, and he spoke such ardent words to me that I became quite dizzy. He offered me a flower marriage, as if I would entertain for a single moment the idea of sleeping in his bed for one year only afterward to be cast off like a common prostitute, for you know that is what people think of us Phoenician women. I told him just what he could do with his insulting offer. Then he apologized most profusely and spoke most bitterly of how unforgivable his own behavior had been and how he had never meant to offer me an insult but was only overcome by his feelings for me."

"Oh, Bee," I whispered.

Roderic whistled softly.

"There. I've said it, and I did not die." She choked on the words, wept gustily, and finally began to laugh in the way crying people do, who cannot help but find their own sobbing ridiculous. "Oh, Cat. Then the worst thing was that the next night, I dreamed about you and Cold Fort. I had informed Legate Amadou Barry that I certainly would never again speak one single word to him beyond what was absolutely necessary to the customary pleasantries of greeting and departing. I had to eat my words and go to him and ask him for such a tremendous favor, to ride off on what he must have imagined was a pointless chase after a cloud-headed girl's stupid dreams."

"And he said?"

"How I hate men! He said yes instantly and asked if there was anything else he could do to serve me if only to make up for the insult he had not meant to offer me. But now you are here, and that is all that matters. So, I'm done. Do you have a plan yet? What happened to you?"

I nodded at Roderic. Like a soldier taking an order, he rose and went to lean against the door so no one could barge in to interrupt our cabal.

"The mansa's troops are after me; it's true. I think the best thing to do is let the Barry family shelter us until the solstice. Once you gain your majority, Four Moons House has no contractual hold on you."

"If they want me that badly, they'll find a way to get me, don't you think?"

"Yes, and we'll need a plan for that, too. But maybe after the solstice, the mansa won't feel obliged to kill *me*, which prospect I selfishly admit pleases me no end. If the Barry family will shelter Rory and me with you, then we have two days to rest—"

Roderic raised a hand, beckoning silence. His lips curled back and his shoulders tensed, as if he were about to hiss. "Cat, this doesn't smell good," he murmured.

I looked at Bee, who was still at the window. Her brows twitched down. I slid over to the door beside Roderic. We had entered the house through the front door onto a long entryway similar to the design of the house in which I had grown up. Indeed, we'd left our coats and cloaks there. I pressed my cheek against the door and heard the front door shut and an exchange of surprised greetings in the entryway.

"I expected you sooner than this, Marius!"

"So I would have come, had my cousin not detained me. I don't like it, Amadou. My cousin says we are required to give Four Moons House what they want in this matter."

My blood ran cold in my veins.

"We must hand both young women over to the magisters?" asked Amadou.

"There's terrible news. Camjiata has escaped his island prison."

Bad news can strike with the deadly precision of a knife stabbing up under the ribs. In the entryway, Amadou Barry gasped aloud.

"The story goes that the girl may be crucial to efforts to track him down before he calls together a new army," continued Marius.

"Catherine Hassi Barahal?"

"No. The other one."

"But Four Moons House is trying to kill Catherine Barahal."

"Do you know what my cousin, the prince, said to me? For you can be sure I said those exact words to him. He said"—here Lord Marius's voice changed, as an actor's does when playing a different role; in this case, he spoke in a reedy, nasal tenor meant as a satire—"'one death cannot count against the tens of thousands who will come to grief if Camjiata rises again.' And do you know what I said to him, Amadou?"

"You said," interrupted Amadou, "that someone else could marry Beatrice who could keep her safe and secure."

"I certainly did not! The sooner you purge yourself of this infatuation, the easier you'll sleep at night. I said, that accepting the need for a mage House to secure the lass through magical binding, don't they have other cold mages in their house who can marry her without having to kill the first one?"

I grabbed Roderic's wrist and tugged him over to Bee as I spoke. "I'm coming to think this business of marriage is tremendously dangerous for young women. We have to get out of here."

"Oh, good," said Roderic. "I was getting bored. I can cause a distraction."

Bee set her hand on the latch. "What manner of distraction?"

"You won't believe it," I said.

"You'd be surprised what I would believe," she retorted. "I *have* actually read your father's journals, you know."

"He's not my father." I did not mean the words to come out so defiantly.

She looked at Roderic. "Be spectacular, Cousin." The latch opened easily. Like everything in this house, it was well crafted and fastidiously tended. In the entryway, the two men were still arguing in low voices. From outside came the *tik-tik* of bare branches disturbed by a rising wind. Dusk, and then night, would hide us, but it would also become bitterly cold.

"We'll draw attention without cloaks or coats," I said, fingering the handle of my cane, now trembling with the hidden hilt of the ghost sword as night approached. "I have coin left, but what use is that to us if we freeze?"

Bee secured the sketchbook in her bodice. "Callie showed me where there's a night market for cheap clothing. I also know how to get over this garden wall." She swung a leg over the sill. "Let's go."

I looked at Rory.

"I'll track you down," he said.

I took hold of his hand. "They are soldiers."

He smiled, looking supremely satisfied with himself. "So were the others."

"Don't kill him," whispered Bee hoarsely. She grasped Rory's hands with her own. "Please don't..."

"Little cousin," he said, "if it displeases you, then I would not dare."

Bee nodded, slipped over the edge, dropped into the garden, and ran for the shelter of the nearest hedge.

"Rory," I said, but the words were like whetted steel, too sharp to speak.

"I will keep them busy only long enough so you have space to run. Then I'll run, too. But, Cat, if they were to cut my spirit from this flesh, I am not sure if I would perish in truth or merely return to my own land. You must not regret this. We are kin. I am bound to help you. Now go quickly."

I kissed him on each cheek, then slipped over the sill and, ghost sword in hand, dropped down onto a graveled strip that ringed the house. How long ago that night seemed when I'd clambered over broken glass at the inn. Clearly I was fated to be spending an inordinate amount of effort escaping out the back through gardens.

I did not look back as I dashed into the shadow of the hedge where Bee was waiting for me. At the yew trees, I laced fingers together and made a brace for her foot; she climbed. Once she braced herself in a perch, she pulled me up after. Branches dragged at my clothes. Leaves like the kiss of thin, cold lips pressed against my cheeks. As we surveyed our next move, a clamor erupted from the house.

She climbed up on my shoulder and heaved herself to the top of the wall. With her own weight as counterbalance, she hauled and I scrambled up beside her. Poised on the wall's crest, we scanned the dim expanse of the garden behind, the garden before, and the buildings—stables below and loft above—that abutted the mews.

If you can't go back, you have to go forward.

She braced herself across the wall, and using her arms as leverage, I lowered myself into the adjacent garden; she dropped, and I caught her. Within shrouding trees, a dog barked twice; a pair of mastiffs came whining out of the blur of night and sniffed at our hands.

"Which way?" I asked as she rubbed them behind the ears, and they whimpered in ecstasy.

"Out through this stable, across the mews, into the stable, and through the house opposite. They won't expect that." She touched her blessing bracelet to her lips. "Blessed Tanit, protector of women, be merciful to your humble and devoted daughters, and open all doors in our favor."

"Selah," I echoed. One of the big dogs turned its head to smell my outstretched hand, then dismissed me as a person of no interest because Bee was there to slobber over. "It's fortunate that dogs love you."

A musket went off, and then a second; each report made me flinch, but it was too late to help Rory now. Barking wildly, the dogs raced away down the wall. We trampled through fallow beds and fetched up against a tall and impenetrably thick hedge.

"Call those dogs in before the lady calls for them to be slaughtered!" a man called from the other side of the hedge.

"Yes, Maresciallo," said a lighter, younger male voice.

Not ten paces from us, a gate opened and a figure strode through, whistling sharply toward the barking dogs, by now lost in the shadows at the end of the garden near the house. Bee and I grabbed the gate before it could swing shut. I peered across the open space on the other side of the hedge, where a single lamp had been lit and hung by the stable entrance. No one was in sight. We dashed to the stable.

The pleasant smell of horse manure, hay, and warmth wafted out to us through an open door. Two men were talking, but not close by. I slid into a dark space warmed by a pair of hearths and lined with stalls and the big breathing presence of horses. Bee followed me. We kept to the shadows and moved fast. The men were talking on the narrow stairs that led to the loft, only their trouser-clad legs visible. One called to someone above who was, evidently, trying to see into the house next door to discover what had caused the commotion and musket fire. The massive double-gated doors leading into the mews were closed but unbarred, and I pressed Bee back before she could grab the latch. Someone was on the other side. The latch moved, and we shrank back into the corner, Bee behind me and me nothing more than the shadows and the unswept straw and the plaster of the wall as a young man dressed in servant's livery charged in from outside, yelling.

"Nothing in the mews, Maresciallo. But a fierce lot of noise!" He trotted past us to the stairs.

We slipped through and out into the dark mews and straight across without pause to the stables on the other side. They were shut tight, and when I pressed my cheek against the latch, I could feel they were chained. There was no way in.

Bee was already moving toward the dead end of the mews, and just as she reached the next stable entrance, one of its doors was flung open. She flattened herself against the wall as a man strode into the mews and crossed to the stable entrance of Amadou Barry's aunt's house. It was all the chance we needed.

We slid inside and sped through the musty stables, where we felt the presence of not a single living thing, not even a rat. Just as we coursed out the door that led into the garden, a voice from the loft spoke, inquiringly, in a lilting and somewhat nasal language I had never before heard. Emerging into the garden, we heard shouts, but they were not close by. They weren't on our trail yet. I heard no more musket shot.

A straight path graveled in white pebbles led from the stables to the back of the house. On a modest portico lined with four slender stone columns, glass-paned doors, shuttered and locked, faced the garden. Bee pulled a pin from her hair and coaxed one to open. We entered a paneled sitting room, its furniture shrouded in muffling covers, the air bone cold and the fireplace so dead I could not taste any memory of fire and ash. The room had two doors.

"I can't see," Bee murmured.

I guided her through the maze of furniture to the door opposite the portico and leaned against it. In the chamber beyond, no fire burned, but I felt a shallow breathing presence so faint that if both rooms had not been so quiet, I would have missed its tremor.

I tapped her shoulder, and she crept with me along a carpeted runner to the other door. As I set my hand on the latch, it turned. The door caved open, and we faced a woman holding in her right hand a five-branched candelabra with all five candles alight and, in her left, a small book, pages open. She had the most interesting features, Avarian in the length and fold of her eyes but with a round, moonlike face and eyes so dark they seemed black. Indeed, she looked something like the scarred foreign woman I had seen in the County Members inn in Lemanis, only she had age on her shoulders, a grim set to her mouth, and wore spectacles with one lens of clear glass and another that looked so frosted as with the crackle of ice that she could not possibly see through it.

"Oh!" said Bee, clapping a hand to the top of the sketchbook as if she had meant to theatrically pound fist to bosom. "You frightened me, la! I came to see the maester. He invited me, you know." She tittered inanely. "We met at Surety Gardens, for you know they say a man is sure to meet an obliging woman—"

The woman closed the book with such a snap that both Bee and I jumped. She gestured imperatively, imperiously, and as if ensorceled, Bee and I meekly followed her to the next door, which was already open and leading into the chamber I had just avoided.

The walls, lined with shelves, were insulated with books.

There was no fire in the hearth, but despite this, the chamber was perfectly warm, its heat the splendid calm of sun-warmed rock. Three dogs lay on a rug, alert but eerily silent as they watched us enter. A pair of lamps set on side tables burned sweet oil, their glow illuminating an upholstered chair in which sat an ancient and very frail man. He wore a light red and gold silk jacket over loose trousers and a pair of black house slippers. His white hair was bound in a braid that trailed over his shoulder. His face was thin, and his hands were as bony as claws. Indeed, he looked far too weak to rise, but when he looked up at the pair of us trembling on the threshold, his gaze stunned us into immobility.

With a sharp inhalation, Bee stiffened, her fingers tensing on mine. "I recognize you," she said in a low, almost pained tone. "I saw you—I saw this library—in a dream."

"Of course you did," he said in a labored hiss, as if gruel had filled his lungs and made it hard to breathe. "I have waited, all these years, as all creatures wait for death to approach them."

As he spoke these words, he looked away from Bee to me. His blue eyes had the blaze of fire, like echoes of the lamps but far more penetrating, able to pierce the stygian depths. Then he blinked, and I staggered and caught myself as from a fall.

He said to Bee, "I knew you would come." His words were like a spell. She walked as in a trance across the carpet to his chair.

"Bee!" I said, although I could not move, not even to lift my cane, which suddenly weighed like lead in my hand. My eyes watered as though I were standing too near a bonfire.

To my utter and heart-stopping astonishment, she knelt before his chair. He kissed her forehead as gently as a father kisses the brow of his child when he sends her out into the cruel world, knowing she will meet bitter disappointment and sharp pain before she has any hope of finding happiness and peace.

She looked up, her face aglow in the lamplight, so beautiful that it was as if he said the words out loud—"so beautiful"—only I heard no utterance. He bent farther yet, and for an instant I saw a different face, a younger face so wild and strong and striking, as if years and decades had unwoven from his skin.

He touched his lips to her lips, scarcely more than a butterfly's kiss. A touch. A breath, given from him to her. He drew back. Bee's eyes flew wide and she collapsed in a faint.

"Bee!" I cried, but I could not move.

On the floor, Bee took in a hard breath; she rose to her feet, staring at him, but she said nothing, as if he had stolen her voice.

"Now I am released," he said. "I have given you my heart's fire to help you walk your dreams in the war to come. Go quickly. Take Montagu Street to Serpens Close. There, at the back past the well, you will find a stair that will lead you under the old guildhall to a path alongside the Duvno Stream. After that, you are on your own, for beyond that I cannot see. When the soldiers and mages come calling, as they will shortly, my servants will have departed, and I will be dead."

The servant's candelabra dipped before us, as with a bow, and we stumbled away down the hall to the front door. The woman opened it, and when we passed over onto the threshold, she shut it behind us without a word. Bee and I stood shivering on the steps, his words like knives in our hearts. A clatter of feet and hooves drummed a swift rhythm as, away behind us, the pursuit began in earnest. Blessed Tanit. What had happened to Rory?

I groped for and grasped Bee's hand. "Who was that?" I whispered.

She drew in a shuddering breath and found her voice.

"I don't know."

29

In the confines of Serpens Close, we discovered a stair that led, just as the old man had said, to a path along Duvno Stream, a bricked-in sewer whose stench was leavened only by the steadily dropping night temperature. We hurried for some way along this path and left it to make our way through deserted streets to humbler districts and eventually the festive sprawl of the winter market on the shore of the Solent River. Here we bargained for winter coats, the kind worn by women who must work out of doors through the fierce winter chill, and cloaks to go over them to double as blankets. Bee traded her elegant frock for sturdier garb, and we stood in the cold street and shivered, heads bent together and my hand on the hilt of my ghost sword in case anyone accosted us.

"We need legal help," I said. "What about those trolls I met?"

She looked askance at me. "You met trolls? Spoke to them?"

"I liked them, Bee. So would you have. But I don't know where their offices are. We can scarcely go searching this time of night. We have to find somewhere to hide until the sun goes down on solstice eve. Tonight, tomorrow day, the next night, and the next day. That's all."

"Then what? Beat off our pursuers with your cane?"

"I don't know, but our first goal is to get you free of the contract."

"What do you think happened to Roderic?" she whispered.

I wiped my eyes, unable to speak.

So at length we settled into the smoky supper room of a tavern, where we shared a bowl of millet and goat's meat stew at a corner table so out of the way that a stout oak pillar cut off our view of the door into the common room. In this forsaken corner, there was plenty of smoke but little enough heat. Out there, people were eating and drinking and conversing merrily, as folk did who weren't running for their lives. We had, of necessity, come into the somewhat more expensive supper room, but despite the late hour, it was packed with noisy folk keeping late hours. I demolished our first helping and began working through a second while Bee picked past stringy goat's meat and yellow turnip seeking what was not there.

"The old man said he was waiting for me," said Bee.

"Maybe. Or maybe he was an old lecher and thought it a likely story to draw you in for a kiss."

I had expected her to recoil at the thought of being kissed by a dying man who must have been ninety if he was a day. I had even hoped perhaps to squeeze a chuckle from her. Instead, she pinned my wrist to the table.

"No. He said I was death coming to meet him." I had forgotten how deep her gaze was. Men stuttered and collapsed at a glance from her eyes. Right now, I thought she looked as if the weight of the world's misery had fallen on her shoulders. "He said he was giving me his heart's fire to help me walk my dreams in the war to come. I'm frightened, Cat. What did he mean?"

"I don't know," I said. "Eat something."

She released my wrist and scooped up a spoonful of brown gravy. With a frown, she stared at a shred of wilted green mint floating in the liquid, then drizzled the spoon's contents back into the bowl. "I'm not hungry."

"We have to keep up our strength. If not for yourself, then think of Rory, who may have sacrificed his life for us."

She sighed and, after wiping her eyes, began to eat. "You never told me what happened to you, Cat. The tale would make the stew go down better, I'm sure."

So I told her. As the story unfolded, she ate with more gusto, and her bowed shoulders began to straighten as if my words nourished her.

"Can that be true? That the male who sired you is a creature of the spirit world?" she demanded, a little too eagerly. "Like an eru or a saber-toothed cat?"

"What else can I think?"

"It does seem likely, but awfully strange. And how would they have managed the . . . the deed?"

"In the usual way, I would suppose. Not that you know anything about that."

"No more than you do!" She grinned, then bit a finger, thinking. "Still, if it's true, do you think we could cross into the spirit world and hide there?"

"If I knew where to find a crossroads. If you could even cross with me."

"The magister crossed."

"He was raised among hunters. Didn't I mention that? It's a dangerous place, Bee."

She frowned. "And this world is not? Tell me, Cat, did all that coin you now possess come from him?"

"Yes."

Through narrowed eyes, she regarded me shrewdly. "Did he *like* you?"

"Yes, certainly he must have, because that is how young men show young women they like them. By trying to kill them."

"But you said he said afterward that he was sorry."

"He never said that!"

"Maybe not in those exact words. But he said—"

"Leave it! I do not ever again want to talk or think of Andevai Diarisso Haranwy."

"How quickly you snap, for someone who claims to be undisturbed by the flies buzzing all about her."

"Somehow, that makes me feel like a steaming pile of fresh manure out in a field."

She smirked.

"Our pardon." Two men reeled up like gasping fish. They wore the respectable clothing of apprentices and clerks, and the younger had dressed his up with a bright orange and brown dash jacket. Because of their pallor, it was easy to mark the flush of drunkenness in their cheeks. I shifted my sword to my right side so I could if necessary draw it quickly.

The younger one straightened his jacket and then addressed us. "You fine gels look like you have an empty cup, which we would gladly fill."

Bee skewered them with a glare. "Was that meant to be poetic or merely crude? You may move on."

"No reason to knife a man just for asking!" They departed, unsteadily, and made their way to a table crowded with young men who greeted them with the hoots men shower upon the unfortunate. A few blew kisses in our direction. I thought about how much we were like the table and the wall, nothing to bother looking at, nothing at all, and they turned back to their conversation and, I hoped, forgot about us.

Bee was carving lines in the smears of gravy left on the bottom of the bowl. "How could he do it? Use the vision of a woman who was walking the dreams of dragons to plot a military campaign?"

"Who? Camjiata? Do you ever see Camjiata in your dreams?"

"How would I know? I've never seen him except in carica-
tures. Some make him squinch-faced, hunchbacked, and spittle-
ridden, while others claim him as mighty and black-haired.
Rather like you, now that I think on it, so perhaps you are
secretly his love child."

"I am not—" Words caught in my throat. I stuck a spoonful
of stew into my mouth and chewed to make them go back
down. It was no stranger a notion than the other possibilities.
"Anyway, how would an imprisoned man know about you?"

"Couldn't someone who walked the dreams of dragons dream
about someone who walked the dreams of dragons? If he had a
wife who dreamed, she might have told him."

"If she was a diviner. But diviners are notoriously imprecise.
And I'm not sure what that has to do with walking the dreams
of dragons."

She looked up, resting the spoon on the bowl's rim. "You said
that when a dragon turns over in its sleep, the world changes."

I shuddered. "Yes, in the spirit world. I saw it happen."

"What about in our world? You called it a tide. Wouldn't that
tide run through this world, too, somehow? If things are connected, as you say."

"I just don't know, Bee."

"What do you think dragons dream of, Cat?"

"Plump deer who run exceedingly slowly."

She pulled out her sketchbook from the knit bag we had purchased to carry a change of drawers and shifts and a few other
necessaries. She paged through the sheets: Some were drawn to
capture historical events, like the Romans kneeling before the
armies of Qart Hadast after they lost the Battle of Zama. Others were pure fancy, like the poor folk falling from balloons. But
others, I now realized, represented scenes from her dreams,
when it seemed she had truly dreamed things that had not yet
come to pass: the ramparts of Cold Fort; the bookshelves and

dead fireplace of the library in which we had met the old man; my hand pressing down the latch of the balcony door in the academy lecture hall. A tall man standing framed by the lintel of a door; I did not know him but I was sure I had seen that face recently.

"If they know what Camjiata looks like, and I have sketched him in a recognizable place in my dreams and maybe with some means to identify the day or season, then the cold mages and the princes—who hate each other but hate Camjiata more— might have a chance to find him. Wouldn't they?"

I whistled softly. "I never thought of that."

"But why, then, could the agents of the Prince of Tarrant and the mansa of Four Moons House not have come to my parents and asked with a pretty and a please to pay for my services? Maester Amadou was certainly willing to pay for my kisses!" She flushed, glancing toward the table of clerks and apprentices who had begun singing a song likening the city council members to high-priced and coldhearted whores who lifted their skirts only for the wealthy and never for passion or justice. "'Greetings and peace to you, Maestressa Barahal,' they might have said, 'for you have the very means by which we may capture the wicked Camjiata, the Iberian Monster whose armies wrought such devastation across the lands. And for your services we will meanwhile lavish gold upon your family so they can pay their debts and buy new curtains to replace these much-mended and very shabby old ones.'"

"They might," I agreed. "But they had evidence the Hassi Barahals were spies for Camjiata. So that answers that question. Anyhow, having met the mansa, I am certain that once he determined he wanted as well as needed you, he'd not be willing to share you."

She tucked the book into the bag. "So no matter what happens, we will still be at the mercy of people who can force us to do their bidding just because they have powerful kinfolk, and money, and soldiers."

"In't that the truth!" cried the innkeeper as she swept in on the wings of Bee's final words. She poured mulled wine into the tin cup we were sharing. "Always it is lords and mages who grind us under their well-shod feet. Shoes that were made by the likes of us, weren't they? Yet we are tossed a pittance and told to be grateful for the work, while they parade in the avenues and rest on finest linen and crow in the city council. Who hears us?"

"Indeed!" replied Bee emphatically, with raised eyebrows. "They have curbed our mouths with bridles and bits! Thus are we silenced."

"The very words of the Northgate Poet!" said the innkeeper. "I took you for radicals. For you clearly aren't nightwalkers. If you don't mind my saying so, you ought not be out so very late. Not with your looks, and on such a night with a picketing planned."

Bee and I glanced at each other.

"I thought it would have started already," said Bee, batting her eyes in that invitingly innocent way she had.

The innkeeper was a stout, healthy woman old enough to be our aunt. She smiled warmly on us in the way older women do when you remind them of their daughter. "Och, no, lass. Word just came round early today, that tomorrow morning, the Northgate Poet means to go sit on the council steps and refuse to eat until the city council agrees to seat council members elected from the populace."

"That's a radical notion," Bee said, eyes widening with real surprise.

"No different than what happened in ancient days, in old Rome, so the poet has declaimed. Them who can read, can read it on broadsheets being posted. Maybe you saw the one we nailed up by the door. In old Rome, plebeians had their own tribunes and their voices were heard. So you can sure we in the city mean to go picket by the steps in support of the poet's hunger strike. It's just that the prince does not like crowds and is threatening to call a curfew. He'll not touch the poet, of course. But he may strike at us! So folk are building up their courage for tomorrow's picket by drinking, and drinking men are like to have wandering hands, if you take my meaning."

"That's just what happened, maestra," Bee agreed with the smiling alacrity that made people adore her. I kicked her beneath the table, to warn her that she was overdoing it, and she trod so hard on my foot the pressure brought tears to my eyes. "We sneaked out because we wanted to see the protest. But now we're frightened, and it's too late to walk home."

"Phoenician girls, aren't you?" asked the innkeeper with a sigh of resignation that made her ample bosom heave beneath the stained apron she wore over her winter jacket and skirts. A man called a name, possibly hers. She glanced toward the door that opened into the common room and flagged the man standing there, husband or brother perhaps, with a wave. "How like your sort to educate their girls in books and neglect common sense. What are your families thinking to let you go walking alone? I suppose it's just as possible you climbed out the window and never asked permission."

I choked down a mildly hysterical laugh, thinking of our flight into the garden. But then I thought of Rory and covered my eyes.

"There, there, lass," she said pettingly. "All will be well. You come back with me into the kitchens. My kitchen girls share a bed in the scullery. They'll be up all night, for I don't expect this crowd will leave until dawn, and then for the council square. You can sleep there."

"That's very kind of you." Bee reached into her sleeve for our coin. "How much for your trouble?"

The woman had a frown so deep and unexpected on an otherwise good-natured face that it was like a hard frost falling in the middle of summer. "You paid already for drink and meal. This other I do for my daughters' sake, so it would fall poorly if I took payment. I only ask you go straight home in the morning and give up this rash adventure. Bad things happen to girls out on the streets on their own. Anyway, it's no good for my reputation to have you sitting here. I've had more than one drunken man ask me about the pair of you in that leering way men have. As if I manage the sort of establishment where I offer up girls as well as ale!"

"We ask forgiveness if our presence here has caused you any sort of trouble," said Bee in her most unctuous tone. "We never thought we'd run into men who...who put their hands where they aren't wanted!" Her blushing innocence would have shamed the most persistent suitor. I rolled my eyes, but the woman melted as rivers thaw beneath a glowing spring sun.

"Best come now. The drunker men get, the less likely they are to hear you say no."

I gathered my ghost sword, and Bee took up the knit bag, and with our coats and cloaks over our arms and the eyes of half the men in the room on us, we meekly followed the woman into the back, past the ale room where a lad was pumping out ale from barrels into pitchers and setting them on a table for the servers, and on into the steaming clatter of a kitchen at full boil.

Two kitchen girls were chopping and grinding at a big wooden table, while the cook was managing the fireplace and its joints and kettles. All were too busy to do more than nod at us with the glancingly curious expressions of people who would find you a seven nights' wonder if they were not so tired. I was chastened by their industry, and they still had more than half the night ahead of them. A lad hurried in lugging a bucket of coal and set it down by the fireplace.

"Is there anything we can help with?" I asked.

"Och, no," the innkeeper said, not unkindly. "You'd just get in the way. Go on through into the scullery."

The scullery had a cheery fire blazing in the fireplace and a fair amount of heat radiating from the copper where water was heated in a huge tub. The stone sink with its big wooden bowl for washing sat unattended. Most of the sideboard was taken up by stacks of dishes, but at the far end rested six painted masks almost ready for the solstice festival. Bee went to look at them as I crossed to the curtained alcove to the right of the fireplace and peeked in to the bed behind. It looked amazingly inviting, with sheets recently laundered and ironed, an unexpected nicety.

"All ready for solstice night except for the blessings," said Bee.

I went over to examine the masks. One was a fox, and one was a cat with whiskers sticking out from the wood, and the other four were round, humanlike faces with two painted black and two painted gold and decorated with snake-trail patterns in white and red. The shapes were decently done by a craftsman, bought in the market, but the decoration showed more enthusiasm than artisan's skill.

"We can paint in the charms," she went on. "It would be a small gesture of thanks, for the offer of a bed on this cold night."

"Would that be right? Usually people go to a temple scribe to have it done."

"Why would it not be right? Usually they go because they cannot write. Maester Lewis once told me that anyone who knows the proper act can make the offering."

She fished out a little pot of ink and the quill pen we had purchased earlier with a blank journal book and other necessities. She had a neat hand, and I watched in fascination as she tucked the blessing symbols in among the cat's whiskers and almond eyes, and the fox's big triangular ears and whitened muzzle, and flowed the charms like ribbons through the more crudely painted patterns on the faces.

"There," she said. "Now I feel I have not taken without leaving something in return. It binds you, you know, to take without giving."

"Unless they plan to turn us in to the constabulary for a handsome reward."

"Have you heard any criers on the street announcing our escape? Now that I see these crowds, I wonder if they can even risk it. The crowds are already agitated at the prospect of the Northgate Poet going on a hunger strike, so how do you think the mob will react to news that the militia and cold mages have allied to hunt down two young women? If I were the prince, I would send out spies and seekers to hunt very quietly."

"You would hire Barahals, you mean."

She grimaced as she cleaned the tip of the quill pen. "Yes, exactly. Barahals to hunt Barahals. Then they would close in and take us without anyone being the wiser that we were being hunted."

"Maybe. But I admit, I'm very tired. I'm willing to take the chance to rest tonight. We'll take turns on watch."

But after we took off our boots and crawled into the alcove bed and decided on a turn of watch each, the clangor and bustle from the kitchen lulled us. Or maybe it was the sound of ink drying. We must both have fallen hard asleep, for I woke to silence and no idea how much time had passed. I heard not even the pop and rustle of fire. With the curtain drawn, we lay in darkness except for a line of light where the curtain's edge did not quite meet the wall. Day had therefore come, but the inn, it seemed, now slept.

No. Someone waited in the scullery, a presence notable for its measured but not precisely calm breathing. A chair scraped softly as it was moved. Bee lay between me and the wall; I hooked a finger at the curtain's corner and twitched it back just enough to see out.

Andevai Diarisso Haranwy sat in a chair with his back straight, his feet flat on the slate floor, and his hands in loose fists on each thigh. He looked like the kind of academy student who pays close attention in class not necessarily because he is actually interested but because he is determined to do well. There was no fire; I heard no sounds of life, nothing. Just him, sitting there with his greatcoat slung over the chair's back, and Bee's steady breathing behind me, and a cat's questing meow from out of doors.

"I was raised in a hunter's village," he remarked to the dust motes swirling in the frigid air, "and furthermore, having followed you through the spirit world, I am more visibly chained to you, magically speaking, of course, than might otherwise be the case." He touched a gold locket hanging at his throat, which he had not been wearing the last time I had seen him. "Also, I have a strand of your hair. In case you are wondering how I tracked you down."

He paused.

Naturally I made no reply. Honestly, I could not understand why he would suppose I would be stupid enough to say anything. Also, he wore a jacket in the oranges and browns favored by working men, only his was so particularly tailored to his build that few working men could ever have afforded such style, and the fabric was such finely woven damask that it shimmered in a way to make a person wish to trace its shape on his body. His boots, if somewhat smudged by the dirt of back streets, had the gloss of finest leather, in fact, they were utterly gorgeous with a creamy black finish. In other circumstances, I would have been struck dumb in admiration.

This was not one of those times. I was merely speechless with anger at my own self for being careless enough to get caught.

"As it happens," he went on, "you are being hunted through the city by the allied forces of the mansa of Four Moons House and by the militia and constabulary of the Prince of Tarrant. That they have not yet found you is only because an unlawful assembly has gathered at the council hall square this morning. Naturally the prince has had to mobilize his militia there to protect the city from disruption. Even so, I have come to the unfortunate conclusion that you will be apprehended if I do not assist you."

Bee popped up over my back. "Do people really talk like that?" she demanded as she swept the curtain out of my hand and opened it wide.

Seeing Andevai, she said, in an altered tone, "Oh."

"So at this point," he concluded, without appearing to have heard her, for although his gaze briefly took her in, he fixed on me, "I feel obliged because of past missteps to render aid."

His complete lack of surprise in seeing Bee gave me the sudden uncomfortable idea that he had already been over here to part the curtains and see us sleeping. I did not like to know he had watched me while I was not only unaware of his presence but also unable to even think of defending myself. I grabbed my sword—it was again a cane—and sprang up from the warmth of the bed into the chill of a chamber inhabited by a cold mage.

"*Misstep*? Is that what you call attempted murder? Or perhaps you meant a misstep because you did not succeed?"

He rose, making no effort to draw his sword. "I cannot expect you to forgive me, Catherine. That is not why I am here—"

"It seems obvious even to me, with my sleep-befuddled brain, that you are here as part of the hunt. You cannot expect us to surrender without a fight."

"I don't expect you to surrender. Were you even listening? I've come to try to put things right—"

I laughed scornfully. "Ha! It's far too late for that! It was too late the day you forced the Barahals to hand me over."

"I did not *force* the Barahals to hand you over. I was sent to marry the eldest Barahal daughter, with no further instructions and, I might add, no knowledge of why or how the original contract had been made. I did what I was told."

"Tried to kill me!"

"Cat," said Bee in her reasonable tone. "Oughtn't we to hear him out?" She rose, straightening and smoothing her rumpled gown. "You said yourself he expressed regret for the action. Also, it is obvious he could have killed you while we were sleeping. But he did not."

"My thanks." He studied Bee. "This is the eldest Hassi Barahal daughter, isn't it?"

Even in disarray, curls half smashed on the side she'd been lying on and utterly tangled everywhere, modest gown somewhat askew and a pinch of sleep blearing her fine eyes, Bee was entirely and astonishingly adorable. Everyone always said so.

He shrugged dismissively and shifted to glare at me. "Did it ever occur to you, Catherine, that I might begin to wonder why the mansa sent *me* to destroy the airship?"

"The airship!" squeaked Bee.

"Why would the mansa send me to marry the Barahal daughter, when so much is at stake? If she is so valuable, why not marry her to one of the magisters born into the house, not some village boy they all look down on? Why would the mansa tell me so little before he sent me out? Why would he not even tell me the single most important thing, that the diviners believed she would walk the path of dragons? The mansa never spoke one word of that to me. That I know anything about the dreams of dragons is because I had begun my training as a hunter, and the first thing a hunter learns about the bush is that when dragons shift in their sleep, a tide washes the spirit world and obliterates everything in its path that is not warded. Given the risk involved, why would they only give me my orders and send me off? Is it because they knew I would be unquestioningly obedient as I have always had to be as I struggled so hard to meet their expectations and fulfill my promise and protect my village?"

"When you put it like that," said Bee, "it is puzzling."

"*Must* you agree with *him*?" I cried, for I am sure I would never have switched sides on her with such alacrity.

"Cat, I do not like him any more than you do, for he did try to kill you, and that I can scarcely be expected to forgive. But when you consider the situation rationally, it is puzzling."

"Thank you," he said, looking very irritated and very handsome.

No, of course he did not look handsome. I was merely exhausted from the exigencies of the last few days and made vulnerable to trivial considerations because I was worrying about Rory. One sees strange things in such a state of mind. One might think *anything*.

"I have been forced to come to the conclusion," he continued, "that the mansa considers me *expendable*. In rather the same way, I suppose, that the Hassi Barahal house considered you expendable, Catherine."

"Is this an effort to make me feel sympathy for your situation by comparing our plights?"

"Yes." Then he looked startled, as if that was not the word he had meant to say. "I meant, no, not at all."

I had not realized Bee had so many smirks in her. She looked at me in the most annoying way possible, blinking thrice as though to send me *a message*, which I ignored with a frown I hoped would blister that knowing smile right off her lovely face.

"Go on, Magister," she said in a tone that invited confidence. "I, at least, am listening."

He had a way, I had come to recognize, of drawing himself up with shoulders braced and chin lifted that made him look exceedingly arrogant, but however vain and arrogant he actually was, there was more to that look than met the eye. "You have no need and certainly no desire to feel sympathy for me, Catherine."

"That's right, I don't," I agreed with a cruel smile. "By any chance is your shoulder paining you?"

"It has healed," he said curtly. "Catherine, I am just trying to explain why you should consider trusting me."

"What has become of the innkeepers and their staff?"

"I found the inn locked up and deserted. Leaving you entirely unprotected, I might add, and quite asleep. I expect they went to the council square to swell the ranks of agitators."

"If the inn was locked up," said Bee, "how did you get in here?"

"I expect he shattered the lock," I said before he could answer.

"Can he truly do that?" Bee asked. "I mean, that's what people say cold mages can do, that you can measure their strength by their ability to shatter iron and extinguish fires, but—"

"Yes, he can really do that."

Her eyes widened as she examined Andevai with an expression that could have been awe, anxiety, or admiration. "Oh."

"Are you done speaking for me?" he asked with a sarcasm I'm sure I'd not earned.

From the other room, a clock ticked over.

As if the clicking of its mechanism were a signal, a hazy thud sounded somewhere outside. Andevai tipped his head back to listen. Bee looked a question at me. A series of rumbling reports rolled like distant thunder.

"Are those muskets?" whispered Bee.

A thunk struck at the front of the inn, causing both Bee and I to skip backward. We heard hacking blows, a man's curse, and the clatter of metal chains spilling to the ground. A door groaned. Feet tapped on slate, and voices spoke from the common room.

"Whsst! Have all the fires gone out? Didn't you bank them properly, lad?"

"I did, maestra!" was spoken indignantly.

"Hush!"

Several people were sniffling or weeping, their gasps flavored with fear.

"Get up, then, to the roof. Keep an eye out. Girl, stop your crying. It does no good." Footsteps split off to pound upstairs.

"That lock was shattered," the man's voice spiked, "but then the door sealed with no lock, like it was frozen shut."

"Not so loud. You two, get the door shut and barred. Julius, you come with me. We left those two girls sleeping in the back. Hurry!"

The innkeeper and her man burst into the scullery, she holding a rolling pin and he an ax.

Andevai turned to face them, but he did not draw his sword.

The innkeeper's eyes widened as she took in first the fireplace's cold ashes, all heat sucked from them, and then Andevai. No one could mistake him for anything but the scion of a wealthy house, yet her tone was more blunt than respectful. "We want no trouble out of cold mages, Magister. It's the prince's corrupt council we're protesting."

From the common room came the squeak of tables being shoved, and thumps as they were turned on their side.

"You shall get no trouble from me," said Andevai. Yet he did not budge, as if, I suppose, he thought he was protecting us from *them* in a manly and courageous fashion.

Booms shuddered the air, and we all flinched as a shattering fusillade of pops resounded from nearby. A shrill echo of screams and shouts followed.

The innkeeper lowered her rolling pin. "This is no refuge for a high and mighty personage of your sort, Magister."

Two young men appeared, panting and sweaty, gripping iron pokers from the fire. "The militia has gone to war against us!"

The woman nodded grimly. "All we can do is lock our doors and tuck our heads under." Another set of reports made a staccato rhythm, interspersed with cries and more screams. "If there's blood on the streets, then there is worse to come."

"Bloody princes!" cursed the man.

"The beast has been roused," cried one of the young men defiantly. "So cries the poet!" The poker in his hand shook as he trembled, watching Andevai as if he expected him to lash out to punish him for such radical words.

Andevai said nothing, nor did he move.

"What beast?" Bee asked. "What do you mean?"

"Many are angry," said the innkeeper, "but now we have found our voice."

As if to emphasize the truth of her statement, muskets fired yet again, closer now, thunder echoing in a closed tin. In their wake swelled a rising tide of voices whose pure intensity reminded me of the hum and ring of the dragon's turning in the spirit world.

Bee stepped out from behind Andevai. "Maestra," she said politely, not begging, "that's a fearsome noise outside. Might we shelter in the inn until the tide has passed?"

The woman sighed as she looked at Bee. Everyone always did.

"He cannot," she said, as if she thought *we* had invited him in or that *we* were his companions. "Even if I wished to, which I am sure I do not, I dare not offer shelter to a cold mage. Were he to be found here, they'd burn down my inn."

"Not with me in it, they can't," said Andevai in a tone that made me either want to kick him or to laugh. Because it was true.

"Can you defend yourself against knives and shovels and axes and scythes and whatever other instruments they will bring to pull down these good timbers and you to lie crushed beneath them?" she asked, not belligerently but not meekly, either. She passed the rolling pin into her other hand and signaled to the two young men to go around us and out the door that led into the side yard. "How many can you fend off before they over-whelm you? Are you willing, Magister, to let strangers die—me and my people—by forcing them to shelter you, who have entered this house without invitation or permission? Whatever you are, I am sure I wish no harm to you in particular as long as you leave alone me and mine. But I will not risk my people and my livelihood for you. No offense meant."

Remarkably, he endured this speech without the least sign of emotion, no cracked glass, no shattered cups; perhaps he was accustomed to the right of older women to scold him.

"I will depart, maestra, if you will be so kind as to tell me how to get out of here without running straight into the mob."

"Out the back and through the yard, there's a gate into the alley."

The rising tide had indeed grown to the roar of a once-slumbering beast now roused. I felt their outrage through the soles of my feet.

Andevai pulled on his greatcoat and walked to the door. With a hand on the latch, he turned to address Bee. "This I meant to tell you before we were interrupted, Maestressa Bara-hal. Five days ago, your father returned to the Hassi Barahal house. The mansa's agents had already secured the house in expectation of capturing you or Catherine if you returned there. They took your father into custody instead. I thought it right to warn you that his presence in Adurnam may be used to draw you in. By no means should you go home to try to free him before the solstice, because the mansa himself has come to Adurnam to track you down."

He clicked down the latch.

"I regret whatever trouble I have caused you," he said to the innkeeper, and with this he opened the door and vanished into the yard behind the inn.

Bee moaned, sagging against me. "Papa came back to find me! And he's now in their clutches! What will we do?"

"If Rory were here, we might manage a rescue between the three of us." But to speak his name forced me to contemplate that he might have been killed. A brother found, and then so swiftly lost. How careless of me! I sucked in a harsh breath, grabbing Bee's hand as I searched for words, although I did not know how to comfort either of us.

The sound of breaking glass sprayed like shards over us, followed by a smashing crash as an impact hit the front door hard enough to make the entire inn tremble.

A howl rose like wolves scenting blood. "Death to mages!"

"Burn them who suck the life from our children!"

Bee yanked her hand out of mine and bolted, pushing past the innkeeper and her husband.

"Bee!" I shouted after her.

"I won't allow kindness to be repaid with destruction!" she cried, and ran into the kitchen, out of my sight.

Ba'al protect us! I ran after her. The innkeepers followed at my heels through the kitchen and the ale room and the empty supper room into the black-beamed common room. Bee stood behind a table, facing the front of the inn. One of the doors was cleaved in two, planks snapped and gaping, and a long casement window lay half in pieces on the floor and half in jagged patterns still affixed within what remained of the frame. Outside, a surly crowd of men crowded forward to surge in, but it seemed Bee's presence, staring them down, had arrested the forefront in the act of clambering across the damaged sill.

"By what right," she cried, "do you invade this peaceful house?"

"A boy says he saw a cold mage come in here."

"There is no cold mage in this building!"

The power of Bee's voice caused them to look over their shoulders and address remarks to the men pressing behind them. This shoving, restless crowd was inflamed by drink as much as by anger. I stepped up beside Bee, wishing my cane were a sword and not, in daylight, just a cane.

A man with a ripped coat and blood on his face called, "Aulus also says he saw the cursed cold mage shatter the lock and go in! And then when he ran after to check, the door had been frozen shut!"

"We mean to go in ourselves and see, maestressa," said a burly man wearing a blacksmith's apron. "Just step aside, and no harm done to your pretty face."

I grabbed Bee's wrist before she could run forward and do something rash like slug a blacksmith. Glancing around, I did not see the innkeepers, but I heard footsteps ascending the stairs. Bee and I were alone against the mob.

"I will not allow you—" began Bee.

The boom of repeated musket fire cracked over her words, and we both ducked. Down rolled the thunder of hooves, screams and shouts and voices aflame with panic and rage. The crowd before us dissolved like salt stirred in water as two ranks of mounted militia wearing the green Tarrant jackets galloped up the street with swords flashing and muskets smoking. We watched helplessly through the fractured casement as men went down beneath the bright blades. The blacksmith hit the mullions and collapsed across the sill. A lad, blood bubbling up through his hair, staggered, screaming, toward the window and fell before he reached the safety of indoors. The crowd scattered; the soldiers rode on, leaving the reek of fear and destruction behind them.

Then Andevai was in the room, striding past me to the window. He grabbed the body and heaved it out. He grabbed up big shards of glass from the floor and held them up to jagged edges. The temperature in the room dropped so precipitously that my eyes stung and my mouth went dry, teeth chattering. He knit the glass together, bent to pick up larger pieces, spinning out an icy frame in which to hold it.

I dashed forward to grab up shards and hand them to him, to make the work go more quickly. On the street beyond lay the two bodies before the window, and three more within view, two sprawled lifeless while a third, a man wearing a cap trimmed with a red ribbon, dragged himself along the cobblestones like a rat with broken hindquarters. Two women ran out from a building and hauled the red-capped man inside their door, him whimpering in a way to set me so on edge that I had to gulp down a sob.

"Why are you doing this?" I said, finding a measure of calm in our pointless and rather idiotic task.

"Broken things must be fixed," he said. "Also, if the front is closed up, looters and thieves are less likely to come inside."

"I mean, why follow us back here?"

"Because you didn't come after me when I left," he said. "And I heard the shouting and the crash."

"You could have walked into a killing mob."

"Yes."

It was so cold standing next to him that I might as well have been immersed in a snow bank, but I kept bending and handing, bending and handing, and the effort kept a core of warmth in my body. He remained intent on the glass, spreading in its patchwork frame back across the gap more quickly than I would have believed possible. I could not discern what he was doing without a mirror to watch him in, but somehow he was able to knit the glass together by tracing the breaks with a hand.

"Why?" I asked.

He spoke without looking at me. "I made a promise to myself that if I was not going to kill you, then no one would."

"Very noble I am sure." Musket fire popped in another street, startling me so badly I dropped a thick pane of glass, which broke in half at my feet. The street before us lay empty under a gray sky. "Then why delay by fixing this window? If folk see you here, or recognize your work for cold magic, the innkeeper and her people will suffer."

"Catherine, the militia just rode past. We can't go out quite yet. Anyway, people blame cold mages for everything. Cold magic is so commonly used to improve life that folk take it for granted."

"It *is*?"

He rushed on without having heard me. "How few understand that cold magic saved most of them from a life of constant petty war and raiding. That it is the mage Houses that have secured them from the tyranny of princes."

"Only to substitute their own tyranny. You're the son of slaves, Andevai! Bound for generation after generation to serve a mage House. Whether bound by princes or mages, what difference does it make to those who want freedom?"

"What is freedom?" he asked bitterly, "and who is truly free? We are all bound by what we are, and where we come from."

"Maybe," I said slowly as I considered the turn my life had taken, the lies I had been told, "because we do not look farther than where we have been told to look. Perhaps it would all appear very different if we weren't afraid of what we are. Or what we might become."

He had cut his hand, blood smeared across one palm as he stared at me. He looked as if I had just struck him. I was rather struck myself. The words had come out, although I'd had no idea they were waiting on my tongue.

What was I most afraid of? Beyond the prospect of being hunted down and killed.

I was most afraid of being alone and unwanted.

"Cat, come look at this."

I turned. While Andevai and I had been working at the window, Bee had evidently run back to the scullery to fetch our things. She stood bent over a table piled with our coats. Her sketchbook lay open as she drew with quick, measured strokes on the page. "I didn't have time when we woke to think about what I'd dreamt last night, but now it's flooding back. Under the gaunt ribs of a whale...no...sheets of fabric and twisted metal...scorched wood...They're looking for something, digging in the wreckage...." The words emerged in ragged bursts, as if she were running and thus out of breath. "A man, tall, wheat-haired. With a mustache? I have never met him, but he knows you, Cat. He's standing with a troll...laughing...."

"Brennan?" I said.

Abruptly, Bee's hand stilled. Her eyes rolled up, and a shudder ran straight down through her body. She spoke in a deep, masculine voice, raspy with age. *"The airship."*

I had heard that voice before, from a dying man. I stared at her, my skin prickling as with ice, and yet it was a pressure of warm air that pushed in through the remaining gaps in the casement, bringing with it the reports of musket fire and the churning roar of the riot gathering force in distant streets.

Andevai's hand touched mine. The warm moisture of his blood trickled onto my skin. "Is there something wrong with her? That's not her voice."

For a moment, the touch of his hand and the comfort of his

presence seduced me into tightening my fingers over his as I looked at him. "I think she's talking about the Rail Yard."

He stood very close, his expression not arrogant at all but focused, disciplined, and direct as he stared at me. Only at me. "What do you want me to do, Catherine?"

Kiss me.

I yanked my hand out of his and strode across the chamber. I grabbed Bee just as she shuddered and shook herself, tongue flickering out of her mouth in a way that was not quite human.

"Cat, the airship," she said hoarsely in her own voice. The cold had cracked her lips, and she licked away a spot of blood. "Look. The snow. A thread of smoke, there. A festival wreath. It might be today. Look how short the shadows are. They'll be there when the sun's at its highest. We've got to go."

"Of course." I shut my eyes and envisioned a map of the city. We stood in the district called Cernwood Fields, and if we made our way through the Bitters and across Dog Isle past Eastfair Market...

"I know how to get there," said Andevai.

"You don't even live here," I objected, opening my eyes. "You're from the country."

"I studied maps. Your face is bleeding, Catherine."

Bee shoved my coat into my arms. "You can argue later."

I laughed. I am sure I sounded on the edge of lunacy, soon to be howling at the moon, as I tugged on coat and gloves. We pushed through the wreckage of tables and the splintered door. As we paused on the street, deserted but for the four sprawled and bloodstained corpses, Andevai absentmindedly licked the wound on his thumb. I gingerly brushed my gloved fingers over the cut on my chin, which I had thought healed over. A drop of blood beaded on the leather from the reopened cut, and although I had not meant to, I raised my hand and touched my blood to my lips. The blood he had drawn.

"Are you sure," Bee said, "that we can trust him, Cat?"

I looked at Andevai. He looked at me, not with arrogance or pride but with an expression whose intensity I dared not fathom. He lifted a hand, to indicate that I must cast the lots to judge his fortune.

I said, "I suppose we're about to find out."

30

The inhabitants of the district of Cernwood Fields had gone to ground, shutters and entrances closed, although here and there we saw a gate or a door cracked ajar as if to offer a haven for folk fleeing the soldiers. We struck a steady loping pace down the main street and thence into side streets, pausing at each intersection to consider where the worst sounds were coming from. In our winter coats we appeared nondescript, even Andevai. At intersections, we discovered shops with broken windows. We surprised men patching a shattered casement with planks of wood, but once they had a good look at us, they set back to work.

We had to walk some miles northeast to reach the Rail Yard, and soon enough we left the troubled central streets behind us and strode through a frigid morning. An odd quiet gripped us; Bee said not one word, and with Andevai in our company, I could find nothing to say. He remained silent, seeming half absent, as if his concentration were elsewhere.

The usual morning crowds about their business were nowhere to be seen, only a few people like us scurrying on their way with heads down. A pulsing roar of human voices punctuated by the reports of musket fire faded as we made our way through the somber warehouses on Dog Isle to the bridge beside the long roofs of Eastfair Market. My eyes began to sting from a bitter tang in the air. Folk at the market gates called after us, asking what we'd seen. We hurried around to the market's rear where laborers off-loaded coal cars and men changed out horses and brought in new teams. Beyond Eastfair Market, the lowland plain began its gentle rise toward the steep Downs and high Anderida. Thirty years ago, according to maps in my uncle's study, this had been countryside. Now three mills built of brick and timber stood one after the next along a line of rectangular ponds and a channel of the Sieve hemmed in by stone banks. Waterwheels groaned where water trapped in the murky ponds raced down toward the channel. Chimneys coughed smoke whose sooty weight swirled over lanes of squalid housing. I tasted the stench of human waste, sweet rot, and hot, gritty ash. Although we were at least half a Roman mile from the nearest of the mills, the sound of the machines made a heart-battering clatter that filled the air. Despite unrest elsewhere, the factories were spinning.

Pausing to catch our breath, we stared over the hard angles and smoky pallor.

Andevai spoke in a low voice, as if the sight pained him. "If you want to go to a place where the mansa will feel some reluctance to follow, that is the place."

Surprised, Bee glanced at him, and she caught my eye and raised her eyebrows.

I shrugged and began walking again. Yet my thoughts spun over and over as I considered the busy combustion of factories and the fire-withering heart of mages.

The Rail Yard was a field of tracks sown from the burgeoning rail system that, in concert with canals, wound down from Anderida to haul coal, timber, and iron to Adurnam's port. Workshops and stables crowded one side of the Rail Yard, but we tramped past them to the high brick wall that surrounded the industrial yard. Its iron gates were chained and its guard posts abandoned.

"How do we get over?" Bee asked, surveying the impressive walls and gate.

"I can break the lock." Andevai searched through the heavy wreath of chains for the lock as I drew Bee back, remembering the force of the shattered cup. After a moment, he laughed and began to haul lengths of chain through the iron railings. A crudely cut lock thumped out of the lacework to the cobblestone pavement. "Someone was here before us."

He shifted the gate open enough for us to slip through, then closed it and looped chains back through. Parallel to the wall ran a series of long, low workshops with big doors, all chained closed. Some of the roofs were half caved in, and most of the windows were shattered, as if a man had walked the length of each building and smashed each individual pane with a sledgehammer. No one had swept up the debris exploded over the dirt.

I looked at Andevai. "Did you do that?"

"How could—" demanded Bee, and then closed her mouth.

A clink of dropped metal falling on metal came quite distinctly from beyond the workshops, followed by a curse in a male voice.

I raised a hand for silence and gestured that they should stay hidden. Then I padded down a lane between empty workshops toward the open space beyond. I drew on my glamor and became brick and dirt and broken glass, the battered surroundings of an industrial yard inhabited by the ghosts of projects abandoned because of destruction. A twisted hulk sprawled across open ground. Its vast ribs curved as high as the surrounding roofs, and flaps of shredded skin stirred in the breeze. Within the ribs mounded more fabric in coils and rumpled hills like the collapsed internal organs of a whale. Pockets of hard snow had settled into crevices and corners, making the remains sparkle. Although torn and burned, the airship's skeleton had a graceful beauty.

Rats scrabbled in the wreckage: Three figures huddled around a fractured wood-framed basket, the remains of the gondola. A man plied a shovel; a woman knelt and picked through a heap of debris, trying to free something. The third figure had a troll's plumage, and although its back was to me, it had turned its head so far around it was looking right at me. No head should be able to turn that far. I shuddered, and then, at last, I recognized them.

Fiery Shemesh! Chartji, Brennan, and Kehinde.

Chartji raised a hand in a gesture humanlike if odd in its rhythm, meant to beckon me forward. Then—thanks be to gracious Melqart—she turned her head back properly round to watch what Kehinde was doing.

I ran back to my companions.

"Come, quickly. They're here! Just as you said, Bee."

Andevai had his back to me, and his head positioned in the normal way, but he gestured in the direction of the main gate. "I'll stay here."

"Are you afraid to see the results of your handiwork?"

"I know what it looks like."

"How can you know what it looks like? You were at the inn when the explosion hit."

"Say what you will and think what you must, Catherine," he said with so much force it seemed my lips prickled as though freezing into ice. Bee shivered, eyebrows drawing down dangerously as she frowned. "Someone must stay here to keep an eye on the gate. If I whistle, that will be your signal to run."

If ice had touched me a moment before, I was now flooded with hot alarm. "Has someone been following us all along?"

"It's not what I see. It's what I sense. I can feel threads of cold magic for some distance around me. The mansa is in Adurnam, and he is on the move—which means he is personally searching for you and Maestressa Barahal."

"If you can feel the, ah, threads of the mansa's movement, then can he not feel you in kind? Track us by following you, if he suspects you are with us?"

"He will be able to sense my magic." He bit his lower lip, white teeth furrowing the lip as he studied me. I did not like that look. It reminded me of our hands touching, our fingers entwining, at the inn. I felt heat flood my face as I blushed.

He looked away sharply. "You're right. It would be best for me to mark a trail back through the city as a decoy, although it is unlikely the mansa suspects I am trying to aid you." He examined the gate as though to memorize the number and ornamentation of its iron finials with their resting eagles and coiled snakes. "It's doubtful he will suppose me to have so much initiative. Or be rebellious." His sour words surprised me. Before I could reply, he went on thoughtfully, finger and thumb tracing the trim line of his closely shaven beard to his chin in a way that was terribly distracting. "Or I could rejoin the mansa and try to lead him away from you until nightfall tomorrow brings the solstice, and thereby Maestressa Barahal's release from the contract."

"Surely a mage House can force my cooperation with or without a contract," said Bee. "Kidnap me. Take me prisoner. I have no one to protect me. My family could not manage it even when they were here."

"It's true," he agreed, "that folk without support or means are at the mercy of those who have the weapons, or the magic, or the followers to coerce them. My village knows that well enough, for it is how we became slaves. What he will *not* have is a legal contract to force your compliance. But if you do not choose to become part of Four Moons House, then you must find some other power to become client to."

Bee looked at me. "I would rather sit in a cage and starve myself to death than share the bed of a man under the terms I was so insultingly offered!"

"Of course you would!" I agreed. "We'll find another way. With Tanit's blessing, we'll reunite with Rory."

Andevai glanced at her and then sharply at me. "Who is Rory?"

"A kinsman."

"Oh. Well. Thus you prove my point. How is anyone to survive without the protection of a powerful patron or the support of your kin?"

"Surely we have laws to which we can appeal," I said.

I turned as Chartji ambled into view, feet crunching on debris and her head bobbing slightly. Her crest was raised, its plumage startlingly bright in the crisp air, in a season where colors were usually so muted.

"Did someone have a question about the law?" She wrinkled her snout to mimic a human smile, but the expression produced a rather more threatening visage.

Bee recoiled, taking two steps back. "That's a *troll*," declared Bee in passionate tones.

"Bee!" Her rudeness appalled me. "This is Chartji. I won't trouble you with her full name, which I have been assured we would not understand in any case."

More of her extraordinarily impressive teeth came into view as her smile sharpened and her crest stiffened.

I went on quickly. "She is a solicitor at the firm of Godwik and Clutch, with offices in Havery, Camlun, and Adurnam, although I've been told she is originally from Expedition. This is my... cousin... Beatrice Hassi Barahal."

Bee had the grace to look embarrassed by her unfortunate reaction. "Salve," she said awkwardly.

Quickly, to smooth over the chasm of bad manners, I indicated Andevai. "And this is my... my..." My tongue froze. My lips turned to stone.

"I am Andevai Diarisso Haranwy," he said, coolly enough.

"I believe we have encountered each other before. Greetings of the day to you, Chartji. May you find peace."

"And to you," said Chartji. She then began speaking in what I guessed was an older dialect, the one I was pretty sure Andevai's grandmother had spoken.

Andevai's flaring eyes revealed his startlement. Then he flashed a grin. A grin! Had I ever seen him smile with such delight? The troll and the cold mage ran right down through a series of exchanges whose rhythms sounded very like the usual local greeting but whose tones had an appealing music I could not duplicate. Chartji did not miss a beat, and Andevai looked—

Blessed Tanit! I was like a runaway wagon careening down a hill. His charming smile did not alter our situation one bit. With the day passing and our plight as unsettled as ever, I broke in.

"My apologies, but we ought to move farther away from the gate."

"I take it you are here illegally, just as we are?" said the troll.

I walked up the alley between two workshops, and the others followed. Both Andevai and Bee pulled up short when we came into sight of the wreckage, the gaunt ribs, the listless folds of torn fabric skin, and the shattered spars and planks of the gondola amid a dusting of ash and shattered tiles and bricks and who knew what else? Maybe the dust of human bones.

Bee intoned a phrase under her breath, an old Kena'ani curse whose hard consonants made me shudder. Ablaze with wrath, she turned the full force of her indignation on Andevai, for it had to be said of Bee that although petite in stature, when roused she seemed as vast as the heavens.

"*You did that?*" she cried. "It was so beautiful! How could anyone want to destroy something so beautiful?"

I thought for an instant that a blizzard would blast down from above and bury us in ice, but instead, Andevai looked straight at me.

He said, in an odd tone, "Because they were commanded to do so, and thought they must obey."

If the earth could have swallowed me then, I would have been grateful. Even my ears were burning, and Bee was struck dumb; and Chartji graciously said nothing, so the world was reduced to his intent gaze and my churning, roiling contradictory emotions like the insatiable whirlpool said to drag down ships in the sea-lane that is the only egress to the fortress of Atlantis.

He went on, as sharply as if he were furious. "After all, I have changed my mind. It is best I leave now. I will find the mansa and do my best to lead him away from you on a false trail. I'll do what I can to protect you. Fare you well, in peace."

He walked so abruptly away, out of sight, that I had not even time to part my dry lips.

"Cat," said Bee in the voice she usually used to inform me that she had spotted a spider dangling from a slender silk thread directly above my head, "is there something you are not telling me?"

"There's nothing I'm not telling you!"

I marched over to where Brennan and Kehinde were digging. Brennan paused with a foot upon one flange of his shovel and grinned.

"A happy day it is to see again an old friend." He offered a hand in the radical's greeting, and I shook it and released it to greet his companion.

Kehinde got up from her knees with what looked like a spanner in her left hand and a blackened spar the length of her forearm in her right. "Catherine Hassi Barahal! Salve!"

"Salve! If I may ask, what on earth are you doing?"

She assessed the debris at her feet: a chunk of metal and charred wood they had only just excavated from beneath snow, dirt, and ash amid the ruins of the canvas and wood gondola.

With a sad smile, she said, "Recovering my press. I'm hopeful that if we excavate enough of the parts and can find the blue-print, which I am assured was placed in a water- and fire-tight container, we can have a replica crafted here in Adurnam. We have already made contact with several machinists sympathetic to the cause who are eager to attempt the task."

"A press?" I surveyed the extent and composition of the debris. I could not see how a printing press could possibly fit within the space they were digging, much less be conveyed across the Atlantic Ocean on an airship.

She pushed her spectacles up the bridge of her nose with a wrist and thereby smeared a grainy layer of soot along dark skin. "It's what they're calling a jobber press. A new invention from Expedition. It is powered with a foot treadle"—she waved the charred spar in her hand, which I could see was like a short plank of wood—"and is quite small, which is a remarkable innovation, for it lends itself to work within the various secret societies—"

"What manner of secret societies?" I asked, still attempting to see what she saw in the tangled mess in which she and Brennan had been digging. A metal wheel, as big as a cart wheel, lay half uncovered, propped up on a metal cylinder and a flat sheet of blackened metal.

Brennan laughed. "If we could speak of them openly, they would not be secret, would they? A press is a means to print pamphlets and broadsheets to educate the population. About, for instance, the ancient right of the populace to elect their own tribunes, what we might call 'council members' in these days. Or to disseminate copies of Camjiata's legal code, so people can find out what rights had been offered them and then snatched away after the general's defeat. But a press is bulky, hard to hide, impossible to move quickly, and easy to place a stamp tax on. This is something different."

Bee stepped forward. "May I?" she asked Brennan, taking

the shovel before he could respond with anything more than a startled look at her flushed face and mussed curls. She poked along the curve of the metal wheel and followed a line only she could see out about four strides. There, she used the shovel to lever up a battered tube about the length and thickness of my arm.

"That must be it!" cried Kehinde.

"If there's a blueprint in there," I said, "it surely can't have survived the conflagration."

She set down treadle and spanner. "It's lined with asbestos fabric beneath layers of oilcloth. We knew there was a risk that the airship might be assaulted."

"Did anyone . . . *die*?" The words fell hollow from my tongue, like the dead shades of real words. "In the explosion?"

Brennan looked at me, and then toward the alley down which Andevai had disappeared. He looked at Chartji, and her crest flattened, then raised. She cocked her head to the right, snout lifting, and made a show of flashing her claws in a language using body and feathers and hands and expression to speak. All this he interpreted, but such language, the show she made with her posturing and gesture that he understood, could as well have been Greek to me.

"We weren't here in Adurnam when it happened, of course," he said. "We only arrived a few days later, after we made your acquaintance, Catherine. Word on the street is that all the watchmen were accounted for, including two who claimed to have been drugged, although a later proceeding charged them with drunkenness. As for the crew, they were not in the yard at the time but celebrating at a nearby tavern. There remains a persistent rumor that the remains of a single body were recovered by the authorities, but the council proclaimed the yard off-limits and have had it chained off since that day."

"Why are you here today?" Bee asked. "And not some other day?"

Brennan smiled wryly. "We know people, who know people. When we reached Adurnam, certain people I was introduced to, introduced me to the Northgate Poet."

"The man who started his hunger strike today?"

"That he sat down this morning on the steps and that we came here to dig is not quite a coincidence. With the prince's militia busy dealing with unrest, we knew we could search unobserved."

"For a time," added Chartji. "We need to move quickly."

Kehinde exclaimed as, having unwound the crumbling outer bindings, she uncapped the tube and drew forth the tip-most end of papers so brown they were but one step from curling into dust. She impatiently pushed her spectacles back down to the tip of her nose and perused this scrap end over the lenses.

"Salvageable!" she uttered in tones so fraught they would have seemed at home on the stage. "Brennan! It's what we prayed for!"

His expression brightened. His grin, like sun, shone on her.

Her eyes widened, as if in surprise to hear herself. Her lips pressed together, and she looked away from him. After gently pushing down the fragile blueprints, she capped the tube. "Chartji," she said in a crisp tone, handing the tube over to the troll. "You guard this." She grabbed the spanner from the ground. "We must pull out every part of the press we can carry."

"We can help," I said, caught up in her eagerness.

"Cat," said Bee. "Ought we not keep moving?"

"What *has* happened to you?" Brennan asked, hand still on the shovel. "Last we saw of you, you and that fine figure of an arrogant cold mage were fleeing the Griffin Inn with an angry mob from Adurnam on your heels. Which, I might add, is when we first got the news about the destruction of the airship."

"Let me tell you while we dig."

They were clever listeners and asked all the right questions at the right time. I left out many details I was not yet willing— might not ever be willing—to share, but I laid out the main narrative precisely and with feeling. Bee dug with a vengeance into the debris, heedless of splinters, shards, and soot.

"I am not at all surprised to hear that a mage House would engage in such an unsavory enterprise," exclaimed Kehinde, placing the platen from the press into one of the leather sacks they had brought with them. She straightened. "But I admit, I am stunned to hear their claim that Camjiata has escaped!"

Brennan whistled lightly in agreement. "That's put the lion among the cattle."

"I think the mage Houses meant to keep it secret," I said. "But they were forced to tell the truth to the Prince of Tarrant and his people."

Brennan glanced at Kehinde and then at Chartji. Kehinde nodded and the troll bobbed her head. "So shall we keep it secret, until we have a better idea how best to use such precious information."

"Who are you, anyway?" Bee surveyed Kehinde and Brennan with a critical eye, then paused, more briefly, on Chartji, color high in her cheeks. "Who do you work for? Who has hired you? Who is your master?"

Brennan chuckled. Kehinde sighed and set back to digging.

Chartji said, "Our tale is simple, Maestressa Barahal. We work without a master and without hire."

"More than that," added Kehinde, still digging. "We dispute the arbitrary distribution of power and wealth, which is claimed as the natural order, but which is in fact not natural at all but rather artificially created and sustained by ancient privileges."

"We're radicals," said Brennan with a laugh for Bee's grimace at the matter-of-fact way in which Kehinde delivered this revolutionary and convoluted sentiment. "And we've come by it honestly, each by our own path."

"Now," said Chartji, the word followed by a brief trill. "Are we done here?"

"We're done," said Kehinde, hoisting each of six sacks in turn with a startled "oof!" "We can't carry more than this. We must hope it is enough to reproduce the mechanism."

"I should hope," said Brennan, "that our own machinists are fully as clever as yours in Expedition, Chartji."

"So we shall see," she said with another of those toothy grins. "I never quite know what to expect from you rats." She turned to me. "What, then, Catherine? What of your legal question?"

"Can you protect us from Four Moons House? Physically, I mean? Can you defy them? Or would it endanger you and your own goals?"

"I'll give you honesty," said Brennan. "We can't defy a mage House. If they got their hands on us, they would destroy us."

"Kill you?" said Bee in a low voice, glancing at me.

"Magisters and princes are notoriously intolerant of folk who defy them," he said. "The law firm has remained beneath their notice. So far."

"Why did you say that about Camjiata's legal code?" I asked. "He was a monster."

"He was a radical, in his own way," said Brennan. "A selfishly ambitious man, so we're taught, but if you look at his legal code, you'll see he understood he could succeed only if he offered rights and privileges to the common people that their masters had long denied them. Do not be sure the stories you hear about the war are all true."

"I'm not," I said, too quickly, and then I said, "I'm not so sure any longer of what I know."

His approving nod made me smile and look down.

A whistle, high and strong and shrill, pierced the air like a flung javelin.

"That's my nephew," said Chartji. "Cover your ears."

We did so. A swift exchange of whistling took place between Chartji and the unseen nephew. She was not whistling through lips, as humans would do; did her nostrils flare? Where was the sound coming from? With a last liquid phrase, she signaled and we lowered our hands.

"Mage troops coming," she said. "Time to go. Do you come with us?"

"Not yet," I said as Bee nodded. "We'll put you in too much danger."

They gathered sacks and tools and made hurried farewells.

Chartji turned to me a final time. "You'll find the Adurnam offices of Godwik and Clutch in Fox Close." She added, in the language of the Kena'ani, gesturing to include Bee, "Peace upon you and in all your undertakings."

Then they were gone. Bee and I were left staring at each other in the shadow of the shattered airship's ribs.

"I've never before exchanged words with a troll," she said in a choked voice. "Yet the creature seemed quite unexceptionable."

"No doubt because she is a personage of sensibility and intellect. About you, I admit, I retain a great deal of doubt. Don't you think we'd best *get moving*, before we're discovered by whatever that whistle warned against?"

We hurried down the alley, pausing to overlook the gate with its loosely wrapped chain. I caught a glimpse of our companions crossing the rail lines before they cut behind a distant brick warehouse. Where was the nephew? Just how far had the whistle carried?

Bee used her shoulder to shift the gates. She squeezed through the gap and under the loose chains. I heard a steady thunder of hooves, and I grasped Bee's wrist and pulled her to the right along the high wall.

"We can't go back the way we came," I said. "If I do not mistake my ears, a host of mounted troops approaches."

She shook her arm out of my grasp, but only so she could trot alongside me more easily. "Do you think it's really possible we can find a place to hide overnight in one of the mills?"

"In that racket? I should be surprised if we could not. Who, after all, is likely to be sneaking *into* the factories?"

"Radicals meaning to inflame the workers."

That her lips were set grimly did not surprise me; we were, after all, in a desperate situation. "Is there something wrong with radicals?"

"Don't you think so?"

"Considering the Hassi Barahals have been accused of spying for Camjiata—"

"Really, Cat. Who supposes Camjiata to be a radical? He was a general!"

We fled around a corner just as the first rank of a troop of horsemen arrayed in the splendid turbans and knee-length jackets of a mage House appeared before the Rail Yard. I doubted they had seen us, but fear lent wings to our feet. We held our skirts away from our legs and ran into an overgrown field of dead grass and abandoned waste. Where a few scrawny trees gave shelter, folk had used the cover for their commode, so besides the cinders and smoke and clatter and hum, there was also a stink rising so strong it seemed we plunged straight into Sheol, if Sheol looked like a factory district whose chimneys thrust as spears into a cloudy sky smeared with cinders and ash. A rickety wood bridge crossed a stream whose water oozed sludge. A dead rat was caught in the weeds, rigid with indignation, no doubt, at having drowned. Since rats could swim as easily as they could scuttle, I wondered if it was the poisonous water that had killed it. Its corpse made me think of Rory, and my steps faltered.

"Hurry!" Bee picked her way across the bridge. A horn cried behind us. Farther off, a series of shrill whistles chased into the distance, but as we hurried up a stony path between heaps of discarded brick and wood so in pieces it wasn't even worth scavenging, the troll signals became drowned beneath the pulsing hum of the three mills.

"Should we keep running?" Bee shouted. "Up into the hills?"

"No! We'll be easier to catch in the countryside. I think Andevai is right. We'll be hardest to track in the machinery."

"Then where?" Soot streaked her face; she had lost her bonnet, and her hair spilled over her shoulders in an unruly mass of black curls.

Blessed Tanit! I could not help myself. I began to laugh.

"What?" she cried.

"I suppose I'll be the one who has to spend tedious hours combing out those knots and tangles!"

"Oh, Cat!" She embraced me so tightly I grunted in pain. "How I missed you!"

I sniffed hard and pushed her away. "Of course you did! Who else has the patience to comb out your hair?"

Dressed as we were, we did not look so strange walking along the dingy row of houses, each with a door closed to the world and a pair of steps leading up to it. A woman with two very young children at her skirts slouched past us with a basket weighing heavily on her arm; once, perhaps, you could have seen its straw weave, but now it was blackened by coal dust. The children were very thin, and all were shod in crudely carved wooden shoes. Yet she in her shabby clothes was as neatly made up as she could make herself, and she took a moment from her weary errand to nod in a friendly way.

"Chance you be Missy Baker's cousins?" she asked. "Down in Wellspring Terrace? She's expecting a pair of lasses from the country, up for the work."

"We're not," said Bee at her most confiding, with a smile that could melt suspicion into sweet candy. "Is there a hiring office here?"

"Toombs Mill is full up, as well I know," said the woman. "That's yon first mill, there. You may check at them others, Calders and Matarno. I don't know aught of them, except it's a fair long walk to get there."

We thanked her and walked on, past men pushing wheelbarrows filled with rags and another leading a donkey pulling a covered cart whose concealed cargo stank so badly we had to cover our noses. Toombs Mill was a great beast of a building, fully four stories in height, with a dwelling house attached on one side like a small child to a stout parent, and at the far end a long low wing that I guessed housed the weaving shed. The din of its machines chased us along past a wharf where idle men watched us with the kind of stares that made us walk faster. These men with starving eyes had about them a sallow-cheeked desperation that made the villagers of Haranwy, despite the ties that chained them to Four Moons House, seem the more fortunate. Yet how could I judge? Why should laborers live in such deplorable conditions and entire villages be chained by custom and law to a master? Weren't both terrible things?

On we walked past a dye works with its pungent odor and thence along a lane of dreary one-story brick warehouses. The steady roar of the mills serenaded us.

"This racket will drive me mad!" cried Bee.

"Aren't you mad already?"

She essayed a punch to my shoulder, but her heart wasn't in it. The day's walk and last night's escape were taking their toll even on her resilient frame, and the constant ringing, thrumming clatter was surely enough to unsettle the firmest resolve and drum into oblivion all coherent thought. We walked the length of Calders Mill and onward toward the twin stacks of Matarno Mill, at the end of the race.

Men winched bales out of a barge and loaded them onto a flatbed wagon. Bales of finished cloth had been stacked on another barge for the journey downstream. Dusk turned the water black; even the last glancing rays of the sun could wake no glistening shimmer on that foul liquid. A pack of scrawny boys fished from the bank, shivering without coats. Two braced themselves each on a crutch; one was missing his right leg below the knee, the trouser leg tied off with a bit of string.

A long, low howl scraped the air like a wolf marking its prey. A second, shorter blat replied, and a coughing *toot-toot-toot* roused briefly and wheezed to a halt.

All my life in Adurnam I had heard echoes of these calls from the comforts of the Barahal house. Only now did I see what they announced.

The rhythmic scratching brawl of the looms stepped down piece by piece. Within the queer alteration of sound formed by its cessation, the ringing clamor of the mules fell silent, and slowly the din settled and the ground ceased humming beneath my soles until all I heard was a buzzing in my ears. In the fury's wake, an avalanche rumbled into life. A man unlocked a chained set of double doors on the ground floor of Matarno Mill, and workers spilled forth like stones and dirt racing down a cliff in an unstoppable tide. They wore wooden clogs rather than the leather shoes we could afford, and the noise made by feet striking stone, wood, and earth washed all before it. But most striking was their silence. You would think that after a day hammered by noise and unable to exchange a single civil word in a normal tone, folk would be ready to chatter about their thoughts and hopes and gossip. By the worn and exhausted faces flooding past us, I could see that no one had the strength to speak.

Just before the first wave reached us, I looked at Bee, and Bee looked at me. We needed no words to share what must have been obvious to both of us. It simply had not occurred to either of us that the mills would shut down for the night, because they relied on daylight for their workers to see. Then the wash hit us, men and women and children in faded and mended clothing, the women with their hair covered by scarves and faces pallid or ashen, depending on their complexion. So thin they were, faces pinched, hands trembling; one young woman was rubbing her right ear, and a man with stooped shoulders leaned heavily on a comrade, as though he were about to faint. A boy no older than Hanan passed, his gait made awkward by the evident pain caused him in his right leg, for he grimaced each time that limb pressed into the ground. A very small girl passed holding a bloody rag to the back of her head and crying, although not one soul paid the least attention to her.

Bee pushed forward against the tide, and with an elbow here and a shoulder there, we pressed through the crush toward the mill's doors, where a pair of foremen watched as the workers departed. In such a commotion, it was easy enough to be what I was not. I was not walking *into* the mill but rather was part of the outward flow; Bee was twisting her bracelet, as if anxious about a missed tryst, no one important. Hidden within the glamor of misdirection, we got inside the stairwell; very dim it was, with no windows and only one lamp burning midway between each floor. The clomping of many feet echoed in the stairwell as folk pushed down.

Shoved against the brick wall, we swam like birds against the current upward, for laborers from the upper floors were only now coming down. At the first landing, we slipped into a vast, low room with big windows where the encroaching dusk gave us little enough light to see by. Brushes were hung from a rack on the wall. Spinning mules stood in their ranks, fiber pulled in long threads but now still. Bee knocked her knee against a wheel, and I jammed my toe when I kicked a runner lying so low along the floor I had not expected it. White flickers of lint drifted and warmth lingered. Dust tickled in our nostrils. A bloody knot of human hair lay on the floor.

"Did you see how young those children were?" whispered Bee.

Footsteps clumped behind us. We turned.

A night watchman with a lantern and a knotted whip walked in. "Here, now, off you go, girls! I've no time for your malingering! We're closing up!"

We hurried away down the long room to the opposite door, by now drowned in gloom, down the cold, silent stone steps, and again outdoors. Out back, connected to a one-storied annex, rose the engine house, where the engine still hissed and wheezed. A pair of watchmen stood by the door, talking and laughing. Bee grabbed my arm and tugged me with her as she marched to the door. As they looked up to see her, she bobbed her head and rubbed her hands as if nervous.

"Begging your pardon," she said in a soft, un-Bee-like voice, "but we're come up from the country for we were told we could get jobs here."

"What kind of job were you thinking?" asked the younger man.

The elder gave a frown. Bee burst into tears.

I said, "Oh, please, we're good girls. We were sent up to live with our cousin on Wellspring Terrace and take a job here, for there's no husbands for us at home. But she died, and her husband said a terrible thing to my sister, like he meant to...to mistreat her. We've just enough coin to make the trip home, but nothing for a roof tonight, and it's so cold, and we're so frightened."

Bee bleated out another anguished sob.

"All we ask is one night. In a safe, warm place, like you'd hope for your own sisters and daughters."

"Probably that bastard Tom Carter," said the elder. "For his wife died three months back. Some say he shoved her down the stairs, and her pregnant! The baby died, too."

Bee wept noisily.

"All right, then," continued the elder with a sigh, "and don't you go being disrespectful," he added, with a stern nod at the younger man. To us, he said, "I'll tell them to let you lie on the floor just inside the door. But how much sleep you'll get I could not say, for it's a cursed din."

"Do they keep the furnace lit all night?" I asked, hoping he would say yes.

"Yes. It's easier that way than drawing it up each morning." He opened the door.

And, indeed, inside the stone walls of the engine house it was smoky and noisy and hot, but it was combustion, and if anything would hide us from the mansa, it was combustion.

We curled up against a wall, out of the way, in our coats. The workers in charge of the furnace ignored us. It was smoky, and noisy, and hot, but we slept.

31

A horn blast woke us before dawn. The hard planks had bruised my right shoulder, and my neck ached from lying crooked all night. My stomach felt hollow, and worst of all, the smoke and heat had parched my lips until they were flaking. The older watchman appeared as, from far off, a roll like thunder rose.

"Best you get moving, then," he said in a loud voice above the steadily increasing rumble. "May the gods watch over your travels."

Bee got quickly to her feet. "My thanks to you," she said with real gratitude, and she kissed him smartly on the lips, which made him flush and then smile. We hurried out into icy dawn, where the silence was shattered by the clatter of hundreds of workers surging along the streets, entering the factory doors, and clomping up the stairs in their wooden shoes.

We joined the stream, going up one floor to the long room with the spinning mules. I grabbed a pair of brushes from the bar, and Bee and I set to work brushing beneath the thread as more workers streamed into the spinning hall. They looked as weary in the gray pallor of morning as they had under dusk's gentle glow.

"Here! You two!" A man with a weathered face and a scar across his nose called us out. "Who are you?"

"Maester told us to start by brushing," said Bee. "Was it wrongly done, maester?"

"Out with you," he said. "You don't belong on my floor."

"But the maester told us—"

He raised a hand in which he carried a knotted whip. "Before I have cause to use this on you!"

We scuttled toward the door. Fortunately, he turned away as, with a hiss of steam, the gurgle of water, and a clunk, the workings began turning over. A low roaring bass and a high, bell-like ringing combined to create a humming clamor. Scarcely had we reached the door than we heard the pop of the lash and a child's shriek, but we dared not turn around. We paused on the landing, shivering, for it was cruelly cold, and we were stiff and hungry and our voices more like croaks from being so dry.

"Now what?" Bee asked. Even with a brick wall between us and the spinning hall, I could barely hear her.

"Let's go up! We must pray that the mills' voice and the combustion that powers the machines will conceal us from the mansa."

We climbed to the next floor and peeked in to another wide room of spinning mules. The clamor and constant movement; the men and women tending the machines; the children on a constant plodding track between threads needing to be pieced while others crept beneath the wheels, sweeping up lint and dripping grease with their hand brushes; the simple exhaustion of every soul there: all this protected us from scrutiny. No one had time to look our way, not until a foreman strolled down the center aisle with a whip in hand, his restless gaze raking the ragged children in case one might sag to grasp a breath of rest. The heat was beginning to rise, and a mist of pale fiber dust floated with it so with each breath I began to feel the urge to cough.

Bee nudged me. The foreman had seen us.

We retreated, and thence up again on the deserted stairs to the top floor. Just beyond the landing we discovered a blind corner, a stub end of the stairs on which we could sit in darkness, for there were no windows in the stairwell, and chafe our hands against the cold as the mill roared beside us. The vibration ground into our bones. Beyond all that, I could still feel and hear the other two mills besides, a clashing, dinning storm so relentless that it enveloped you like a blizzard. We breathed lint and tasted cinders, and Bee cradled her cheeks on her palms with her fingers covering her ears as if that could banish the tumult. Nothing could, just as nothing could banish the tumult of my thoughts.

How foolish to believe sunset would free us. Four Moons House might have no contractual power over Bee once she made twenty, but they could easily squash her vain attempts to maintain her independence by using their influence, wealth, and magic to force her into a cage, or even a new contract, of their choosing. What independence had we, really? Without money of our own and without influential patrons, we might soon find ourselves scrabbling for work in the brutal factories or standing in our rags at the door of a mage House or prince's dun begging to be taken on as a client, our lives and labor forfeit, in exchange for their protection. Had we sacrificed Rory for nothing? Was the outcome already determined?

I did not hear or see Bee's tears; I smelled them and I felt them, and so I threw an arm over her shoulders. For hours we hid, concealed by the busy turbulence of the mill that, like a huge beast, lived oblivious to our insignificant existence, two tiny sparks amid its oceanic vastness. We dared not speak, lest we be discovered, and we could not speak, because we could not hear each other. Cold, hungry, thirsty, tired, and exhausted, we sat in a shivering stupor. There was nothing we could do but survive this day.

And then I felt a change in the humming pulse, a tremor in the air, a shift in the harmonics of the conjoined hum of the three mills.

I grabbed Bee's arm, my hand tightening. She gulped down her tears and straightened. I did not think she could hear what I could hear. Not above Matarno Mill's tumult.

The music and beat of distant Toombs Mill was faltering, and the counter-rhythm it played into the whole stuttered and failed as the entire mill went silent. Dead.

I stood and pulled Bee up behind me, hit the stairs running, down and down, and we hit the great double doors, slammed right into them, but they were locked and chained from the outside. I hammered at them with my fists until Bee yanked me away.

"What is it?" she shouted. "What is—?"

Calders Mill began to die. With my head pressed to the doors, I heard the change fall in the same way one sees light shift before a storm, lowering, darkening. Silence can herald peace, or it can herald death.

The hooves of many horses beat a pattern on the dull earth; their noise drummed up through my feet and into my heart. Folk were shouting, yet at such a remove I could not hear their words; I could only feel the tide of the mansa's power approaching us like a katabatic wind blasting down off the ice.

There had to be another way out of the mill.

We started back up the stairs. The lamps flickered and went out. In icy darkness we climbed, saying nothing, for there was nothing to say. We needed our breath to run.

Below, the lock on the outside doors shattered with a splintering explosion, and the machines on the ground floor shuddered, and sputtered, and lugged to a halt. We burst through the doors into the spinning hall, with its machines set transversely to the windows to make the most of the light. Oddly, as we ran for the door on the far side, jumping over runners, stared at by the workers, shouted at by the foreman, I was reminded of the tables in the academy's library, set transverse to the tall windows. There, for the first time, I had seen Andevai, although I had not known who he was or that our paths would collide so fatefully.

Bee reached the door before me and yanked hard on the lock fixed to the latch. The thrumming that pervaded the structure began to thin and fade as the mansa mounted the steps behind us. Somehow, a hairpin had remained stuck in Bee's curls. Without a glance behind her—for who needed to look when we could feel the machines shudder and die at his approach?—she pulled the hairpin from her hair and set it into the lock mechanism, her expression fixed with concentration and her eyes closed.

As the machines fell silent and the wheels ceased, children crept under the threads to hide, and women and men turned to stare at the opposite door. Whip raised, the foreman advanced on that other door, ignoring us. He halted dead as a man stepped over the threshold and into the hall.

The mansa had come.

His was a presence one could never forget after meeting him: tall, imposing, and utterly commanding. A woman dropped to her knees, sobbing. His gaze, across the length of the hall, caught me. Pinned me.

"Got it!" said Bee triumphantly.

With a snick, the lock opened. She flung open the door. We bolted, and I slammed the door shut behind us, then leaped down three steps at a time after her, down into a black pit, for the lamps had all gone out.

On the stairwell's ground floor, we had a choice of three doors. I yanked at the doors leading outside, but they, too, were locked and chained. We could go back through the ground-floor hall of the mill, where we knew his soldiers had entered, or out through the weaving shed that was attached as an annex to the main building. In the weaving shed, looms still clattered, the floor humming beneath our feet as the machinery vibrated in full spate.

The door, unlocked, opened easily and we plunged over the threshold into a long, wide building whose timber roof was inset with windows. People bent over their work, oblivious to our entrance, unaware of the changed tenor of the mill, subservient to the deafening roar whose rhythms fell like a dance around us. Bee's mouth moved, but I could not hear her. Far, far away, down the length of the shed, stood a double door, our last hope for escape.

The machines closest to the stairwell shuddered and coughed, missing their beats. The engine in its adjoining house thudded and hissed and whined as the magister's descent down the stairs killed the fiery heart of its combustion. The laborers did begin to look up then. A woman wiped strands of hair from a sweaty forehead. A man stood poised with shuttle in hand, looking confounded and bewildered. We ran the length of the weaving shed—a good, long way—as the looms one by one fell silent behind us like voices smothered.

We ran, but it was already too late.

The far door opened and armed men wearing the fine jackets and bearing the bows and spears of mage House troops walked through. They halted, blocking our escape. Midway, we stopped and surveyed the walls of the structure. The windows were too high to reach. I turned, and Bee turned beside me, as the mansa and his attendants swept into the weaving shed. The last looms thunked and shushed in a kind of choking *clut-clut-clut* as they wheezed out their death rattle.

We had nowhere else to run. Even if I might hope to conceal myself and sneak past them, I could not conceal Bee. And I would not abandon her. Never.

"Bee," I said in a low voice, "if you grab a spanner and climb up on one of the looms, maybe you can reach and break one of the windows and climb while I rush him."

"Cat, I can't reach."

"But he'll kill me and force you to marry Andevai. Or himself!"

"He can try," she said ominously.

"He has the right. It's in the contract."

"I'm beginning to wonder what that troll would say about the legality of that contract, if it was forced on the family when they were under duress. As I'm sure it must have been."

"Too late to ask her now. If you run while I attacked—"

"With what? Sarcasm?" She took my hand in hers. "We'll face this together."

The mansa was a storm whose strength could not be evaded. He had a breadth of shoulder that made him fill whatever space he stood in, and a bold, striking face whose lineaments were stamped by both his Celtic and Afric forebears. He wore his silver-streaked black hair in many small braids tied off with tiny amulets. He was a man to respect, but also to fear, as we must fear him, because whatever else he might be, however fair a ruler of his House, however wise or capricious, intelligent or heavy-handed, in his command, he had already demanded my death.

He was not, I suppose, a man accustomed to having his will crossed.

I tightened my grip on my cane, yet I could see no means by which I could force a way through for us, not even if it were night and my sword alive in its spirit form.

As chaff parts where a current flows, the laborers shrank away from their stations to huddle against the wall. In such circumstances, what could they hope for except to behave as rabbits caught in the open by a roving hawk: freeze, and pray to the gods to let the predator overlook them.

Bee and I stood alone in the middle of the shed to face him and his attendants: the djeli, Bakary, who looked more weary than victorious; two men in nondescript clothing who might have been House seekers, and a pair of cold mages. The older cold mage I had never seen before, but the young one was the man who had attacked me at Cold Fort. Six soldiers escorted them.

There was one more. There was Andevai, pushing to the front to stand next to his master.

He had betrayed us after all.

A dull, dead emptiness engulfed me. Bee's hand tightened on my fingers, but the pain of her grasp could not rouse me out of this soul-sucking extremity of despair. I had allowed myself to hope, but he, too, had betrayed me

Who had I been, to think I could defy a mage House? Me, whose name was not even a true name, for I was not a Hassi Barahal; I had scant memory of my mother, Tara Bell, and had until a few days ago no knowledge at all of the creature who had evidently sired me, a father who had never acknowledged nor shown the least interest in me. I was nothing more than an afterthought, a piece of refuse to be glancingly tossed to one side. At least as a sacrifice I had some use in the world. I shook off Bee's hand and stepped in front of her.

"Here is the eldest Barahal daughter at last," said the mansa with more gravity than anger, in the tone of a man who regrets the necessity of creating an unpleasant scene but accepts that the situation is one that has been forced upon him. "We are not too late. Andevai, kill the other one."

"No."

I thought a machine had exhaled or that the steam engine in its housing beyond the shed sighed a last protest. Yet in the world beyond these walls, no voice cried, no wheels rumbled, no child laughed or wept.

The mansa looked at Andevai, and the temperature in the shed dropped precipitously.

"No," said Andevai calmly in answer to whatever command he had seen in his master's gaze.

A voice—impossible to tell who or where among the onlookers—sobbed softly.

"*No*," Andevai said for a third time.

The mansa looked astounded.

"Andevai," said the djeli, in the tone of a schoolmaster, "consider what words you speak before the mansa."

"I have considered them. If we prosper only through the suffering or death of another, then that is not prosperity. I will not do it."

The mansa's anger crashed over us. Wires snapped; a windowpane cracked, although no shards fell. Not yet. And yet, I was no longer afraid.

"What is this defiance?" asked the djeli. "The slave does not command the master."

"It is wrong to kill her. I won't do it, and I won't let you do it, Mansa."

When the mansa spoke, he did not shout. Likely that would be beneath his dignity. "The child of the children of slaves cannot know the taste of wisdom. His kind do not know wisdom, because they gave up their honor long ago."

Andevai said, "I am no longer ashamed of where I come from, although the House made sure to tell me over and over again that I should be grateful to be allowed to enter where I was not wanted. I should never have been ashamed. I just did not see that before. You need me, Mansa."

The young mage sniggered but swallowed his laughter when the mansa raised a hand.

"Do not believe for even one breath, child of slaves, that I need you more than you need me. I brought you in when you were a ragged, barefoot, ignorant youth."

Suddenly every person in that wide space was slammed to their knees as though felled by a hammer blow. Every one, even the other two cold mages. All, except the mansa, and the djeli. And Andevai.

"Strong," remarked the mansa. "But not strong enough."

I knelt on bruised knees, not sure how I had come from standing to kneeling, for the blow had hit so hard I had no memory of it. Bee gasped for breath beside me.

Andevai and the mansa faced each other like two men embarking on a duel of honor. Magisters wield cold as blacksmiths wield heat; this secret they have held to themselves for generations. Already the temperature in the room was bitter, but now it plunged, and the metal of the machines groaned. The windows shattered with a snapping crash, and their shards rained like edged ice onto the silent looms and the sobbing onlookers, poor trapped souls. Bee's teeth were chattering, and her lips were white. I tried to rise, but a bone-deep numbness pervaded my bones, and I could not move.

Tides of cold magic pulsed and ripped around us. Invisible to the eye, they throbbed in the air like unvoiced thunder until I could only hope for lightning to strike and put me out of this misery.

But it did not. Something else happened instead. In my left hand, the hilt of the sword bloomed.

Cold magic had woken it. Cold steel cuts cold magic. I twisted the hilt and unsheathed the sword. Its glittering edge flared, as bright as snow under the glare of the winter sun, almost blinding. Bee gasped, and then choked, as if she'd been stabbed, but it was only the cold striking so deep it would soon kill.

Neither magister moved. Rigid, they fought in a realm outside ordinary vision.

With cold steel in my hand, I rose and cut my way forward through the currents of magic. Icy swells slapped me, made me stumble, made my mouth ice and my feet lead weights, but my blade sliced a path, and I drove forward into the maelstrom.

How it felt to them I could not know; I was not a cold mage. But the mansa looked up, looked over, looked startled. His hold loosened. There came as in the eye of a violent storm an eddy as his attention shifted briefly away from Andevai.

Andevai glanced toward me. He raised a hand in a gesture copied from the mansa, and he said, in exactly the same preemptory tone he'd used in the inn in Adurnam on that long-ago night when we had first met, "Down!"

I dropped to my knees and ducked my head.

The cold hit like an ax blow, flattening me with a single, brutal cut. My chin slammed against the floor, and all breath was punched out of my lungs.

After a moment of stunned incomprehension, I discovered myself lying flat on the cold floor, pain lancing through my chin. Therefore, I was still alive.

A stunned silence muffled all sound except for a vague muzzy humming, half heard as in the distance. I raised my head cautiously as the cold eased. Only two men still stood: the djeli and Andevai.

The mansa had been driven down to his knees.

Andevai's voice was cool, almost conversational. "You brought me in when I was a ragged, barefoot, ignorant youth because you could not ignore what I am, Mansa. I have been reminded every day in Four Moons House of where I came from and exactly who my people are and how my village stands in relationship to the Diarisso lineage. All that is true. But you will be better served by me if I am a willing magister than an unwilling one. There are other Houses. Are you sure I am not cold-blooded enough to abandon my village? For I think it must be clear to you now that if I decide to go, you cannot stop me. You want what is in me, since none among the other young men are what I am. And I want what you can teach me. So we each have something the other wants."

The mansa climbed to his feet and, with a composure I had to admire, brushed off his robe before addressing the djeli. "My canoe has run to ground on the sand. Yet he is brash and insolent, and speaks out of turn to his elders."

"Steel cuts steel," remarked the djeli. "Do you wish the sword to rest in your hand, Mansa, or be held by another?"

The mansa's silence seemed answer enough. He could not bring himself to say what must be obvious to everyone: that Andevai's display of power had surprised even him. For all I knew, it had surprised Andevai himself.

Rising to hands and knees, I looked behind me. In fact, I had come barely four steps although it had seemed like a mile. Bee was crumpled on the ground, her face an awful ashen color, as if she was close to fainting. I scrambled to her, but she pushed up with unexpected strength and sat back on her heels, resting her forehead in one hand while she gestured with the other to show she was all right.

"Show your generosity and magnanimity by letting Catherine live," continued Andevai. "Negotiate a new contract with the Barahal family on what terms you and they think fair for what protection you can offer and what gain the eldest daughter may achieve thereby. Show that Four Moons House can be a true ally, not a power that forces its will on others because it can."

"You know nothing of the situation," said the mansa impatiently. "The girl is a danger, but hers is also a necessary gift in such disordered times. We must possess her so others cannot take her. For you can be sure there are others who have agents seeking her."

The steady hum had begun to resolve into a melange of voices, coming from outside and growing louder. Back by the walls, laborers lay on the floor, trying to remain unnoticed as the light withered and the shadows grew. At the doors, the soldiers brushed themselves off with commendable briskness, as if they were accustomed to being hammered down every day and almost killed with marrow-sucking cold. Of the two mages, the older one was shaking his hands as if flicking off unseen beads of water, while the younger, who had recovered more quickly, wore a remarkably sour expression as he stared resentfully toward Andevai. For his part, Andevai stood with his head slightly bowed, showing the humble respect of a student for his teacher—although the lift of his shoulders suggested a more complex stance.

In my hand, my sword had returned to its daylight state. A whisper of breeze stirred like the memory of summer. From my knees, I eyed the two doors and the shattered windows, wondering how we could make a break for it.

A crow came to rest on the lip of one of the broken windows, claws gripping the frame. It dipped its inquisitive black head and peered in with its bright black eyes to see what it could see.

Bee, looking up, saw the crow. Her expression and color changed, as if she'd just recognized something. She rose as stiffly as might an old woman, shook herself, and set her lips together in the determined frown that always presaged her worst explosions.

"Bee!" I said fiercely.

She faced the mansa as the didos once faced the hated Romans: proud and queenly.

"I am not mute." Her clear voice filled the space. "If you have business with me, Mansa, then speak or be silent."

I tightened my grip on my cane, sure that this time she had gone too far.

The mansa shifted his gaze from Andevai, with his bowed head, to Bee, with her challenging stare. She met him look for look, and the grim press of his mouth softened. His eyes crinkled to reveal unexpected laugh lines. Then the cursed magister chuckled in that condescending way older men do, who are amused by the antics of downy goslings or who find young women attractive.

The light overhead changed consistency, or maybe that was just her look darkening as a familiar stormy expression transformed her face. "How can you imagine I would stand by while my beloved cousin's life is threatened? While she is pursued through no fault of her own merely because you are angry that you did not get what you wanted? Am I to think this is the act of a man who wishes to do what is right in the eyes of the gods, or rather the act of a man who is angry that he did not get what he wanted the instant he wanted it?"

"Maestressa," began the djeli hastily, "to address the mansa without an intermediary—"

"No, Bakary. I'll speak to her with my own mouth." His smile faded as he, like all of us, heard the growl of a crowd approaching, shouts raised in a chorus I had heard before:

"Away with the oppression of princes and mages! We'll rule ourselves!"

"Take your choice. Freedom or fetters!"

Bee said, "My cousin and I are leaving. These laborers will go with us, unmolested."

The mansa looked torn between amusement as at a charming child's antics and annoyance at her defiance. "No one here can interfere. Four Moons House has a legal contract, made by your elders, that gives your person into our House should we at any time choose to take possession of you. Any court and any jurist will rule in our favor."

From far away, farther it seemed in that moment than the remembered days of a childhood whose happy security I could never again embrace even in my memories, I heard Adurnam's bells speak. The bell guarding the temple of the god Ma Bellona, who is valiant at the ford, raised his voice as herald to the crossing from day into night. The sister bells by the river, at the twin temples of Brigantia and Faro, sang out a response in their sopranos.

Bee's smile flashed triumphantly. "But the gods have ruled otherwise. The bells ring in sunset, and therefore the solstice. I am now twenty, Mansa. Your contract is void."

32

In the icy twilight, the mansa called cold fire, its eerie glimmer making monsters of the bulky machinery that surrounded us. The laborers caught inside with us murmured in fear.

Bee did not tremble. "I have by law attained my majority. I am thus released from the contract Four Moons House forced on the Hassi Barahals. However, by the laws of my own people, I remain under the guardianship of the Hassi Barahal family. If you wish to discuss a new contract, then you may send representatives to the mother house in Gadir to open negotiations for some manner of agreement between them, you, and me."

"Pretty words from a pretty girl, but they are foolish as well as ignorant." His words fell heavily. "Do not doubt, daughter of the Barahals, that you will be pursued by people far less merciful than I am. Do not doubt that there are more people in the world who suspect you exist than you can possibly know. Others will discover you soon enough. The Barahals cannot protect you. You cannot stand against both prince's court and mage House."

Bee drew her sketchbook out of the knit bag and held it in her right hand, and his gaze fixed on the book, and his eyes widened as if he guessed what lay within. She spoke. "You are not my master, and you do not rule over me. Nor do you know what I have seen. Do you think you can force me to talk?"

"There are ways to enforce compliance."

"Yet you might more easily negotiate in good faith. Whyever would you not, when that avenue is open to you? Put me in a cage, Mansa, or sit me across a table. I think you can imagine in which chamber I will prove more cooperative. I can go on a hunger strike just as the poets do. As the Northgate Poet has, in the council square, to force the Prince of Tarrant to listen to his words and to listen to the grievances of the populace. What makes you think I'm not courageous enough to do the same thing?"

Our audience of laborers raised their heads at these words. The soldiers shifted restlessly, for the threat of a public hunger strike was enough to make any powerful lord anxious. Outside, the rumble of the crowd grew more ominous, a few voices crying out, "Burn them!"

The mansa's cold fire burned more brightly, as if fueled by his anger. But his voice remained soft. "What makes you think the Prince of Tarrant and I cannot simply sweep you up and haul you away? That we will not, for the good of all people?"

"You hear the crowd gathering outside. Do you think they will let me be taken prisoner so easily? The people in that crowd will favor my cause over yours. Do you doubt it?"

"The mob will trample you an hour after they raise you up. If they raise you up and do not simply swallow you whole."

She raised her chin. "And how, Mansa, is that different from how you and your allies intend to treat me?" Turning, she gestured imperiously to me. "Catherine, come. We are going now."

I glanced toward Andevai, who looked up to meet my gaze. Something in his look made my heart race, or perhaps it was only the realization that Bee truly meant to defy the mansa, to dare him to stop her in front of witnesses he could easily have killed afterward. No one need ever know what transpired here except his own loyal followers. And Andevai.

She turned her back on him and marched, head high, to the far door in the shadows. Andevai nodded at me, as if to say he would protect our backs. My heart was thudding, like repeated hammer blows; I was almost dizzy with them, with him. I was unsteady, but I gripped the hilt of my sword. And I followed Bee. The soldiers stepped back from the door as if she had commanded them to open a path for her. The mansa said nothing.

Not until we reached and shoved open the heavy door.

"Very well, maestressa." He did not raise his voice. He had so much power that he need never shout. "My soldiers will escort you to your family's house, where your father bides. They and the prince's militia will guard the house so none disturb you. This night and tomorrow are festival days, not an auspicious time to engage in negotiations. On the day after solstice, the Prince of Tarrant and I will call to begin discussions. Do you think that a reasonable compromise? Ah. Listen!"

The thunder of horses' hooves and the hallooing of cavalry guardsmen announced the arrival of more soldiers. The growling voice of the crowd began to shatter into a hundred voices as their resolve crumbled and people began to scatter.

The mansa's smile mocked Bee's brief triumph. "As I expected, the prince's militia has arrived to disperse the crowd."

I covered my face with a hand, bracing for the sound of terrible mayhem, but instead the rush of shod feet sprayed in every direction as people fled into the drowning night. The militia rode up and took places surrounding the mill. I uncovered my face. Flakes of snow drifted down through broken windows overhead like the last drowsy remains of lint.

"Reflect on this, stubborn girl," the mansa said. "I am a reasonable man. You, and this girl you call cousin, and even this rebellious young mage I have harbored, have convinced me that perhaps it is time to consider a different sort of arrangement. Yet I must always do whatever is necessary to safeguard my kin and my House. As for you, Maestressa Hassi Barahal, you are in more danger than you comprehend. I can protect you. You will not get a better offer than mine."

Bee's brow creased as she stared at the mansa. "What does it mean to walk the dreams of dragons?"

With the cold fire illuminating his face, it was possible to see his slight smile, like a man contemplating a sweet, much anticipated and soon to be consumed. "That's something we will have to discuss privately, you and I." Then he looked at Andevai, and his lips curved into a frown. "Andevai, you will see they are delivered safely to the house and a guard set under the supervision of Donal." He indicated the older magister. "After which you will return immediately to me."

Andevai paused—quite deliberately, I am sure—before he answered. "Yes, Mansa."

Light sparked, then swelled smoothly from a pinprick into a disembodied, floating lantern as Andevai walked down the hall and, bathed in its light, halted before us. It was an impressive and even flamboyant display of magic, however trivial it might seem to him.

"So, Catherine, I am commanded to escort you and Beatrice home."

Her home, but no longer mine. Yet I could not say that to Bee. Not now. Not yet.

In fact, I could say nothing at all. Standing so close to him, I was struck dumb.

Fortunately, Bee was not. "Our thanks," she said grandly.

She walked out of the weaving shed. Outside, she scanned the torchlit ranks of militiamen as if hoping, or fearing, to see Amadou Barry among them. If he was, we did not see him. "How are we to get there, Magister? I cannot ride in these clothes."

Andevai was a magister of exceptional power, able to call cold fire, weave illusions, raise storms, and wield cold air like a hammer.

But he was also a country boy born and bred, and he had not the least idea of how to go about finding a hackney cab in the city on Solstice Night under a curfew. We did, however, and we found a lachrymose fellow with horse and cab lurking by East-fair Market who took one look at the soldiers and the gold coin offered him and agreed to convey us.

We kept the shutters open as we went. Andevai rode up by the driver. The mage House soldiers surrounded us, with the other magister riding at the rear as if to protect us from attack from behind. The city did not slumber so much as it waited with held breath for the ravening beast to pass. The prince's troops were out in force everywhere, patrolling the street on horseback and on foot; because of this, no roaming packs of young men sang and clapped songs or importuned harried householders for a swallow of mead. This year, the solstice festival, also known as the Feast of the Unconquered Sun, would pass without merrymaking.

Even with curfew's heavy hand emptying the streets, fires had been lit in pots and braziers on every corner. In the squares, bonfires blazed with a few huddled attendants keeping watch. The solstice fires had to burn to hold off the long night, to give strength to the beleaguered sun so it could follow these lamps and rise again in the morning. As tiny as candle flames, beacon fires shone at the crests of distant hills; closer to us, fires withered and almost died before flaring up after we passed.

Bee said in a low voice, "There must be something else we can do, Cat."

"It was a magnanimous offer. It astonished me."

"It was a condescending offer. Not much different than Legate Amadou Barry's. The mansa has dropped his net on us already."

"Maybe," I said. And then, hearing the soldiers outside speaking of cats, I whispered, "Hush."

"Nay," one was saying to his companion in country accents, "they surely said it were a saber-toothed cat. Full grown, it were, that's what I heard. Black as night, and as fierce as a summer storm." He laughed. "It got into the prince's menagerie, ate a peahen and the lady's prize pug dog before it got out again, and no one to stop it."

Bee grasped my hand as my heart staggered and stopped and congealed to lead in my chest, and then bolted into a full gallop. I laughed, pressing a hand to my mouth.

"Poor dog," said Bee. "Although I hate those filthy peahens in the park. But it makes you think, doesn't it? We are not without resources."

I lowered my hand. "What are you thinking?"

"Fire is their weapon," she said.

"Whose weapon? The mob's?"

"No. The radicals. They mean to burn away the old order. Think how sheltered we've been, Cat. How little we know. How many times we walked past the Northgate Poet without the least idea he meant to face down the prince. We're not beaten yet. How shall we start?"

"I think we should start by getting a hearty supper, a bath, and a good night's sleep."

She laughed, and then we cried a little just in sheer relief. After, we sat in mute amity, watching the silent city pass and listening to the clop of horses' hooves as our driver wielded reins and whip, and our stern escort of soldiers and silent cold mage guided us through the city and at last to Falle Square, the place that had once been my home. Gaslights faded as our company drew alongside and then swelled back to life after we passed.

"Look," said Bee. "There's a light in Papa's office window."

Seeing the candle, my heart grew dark. We disembarked on the porch. Andevai escorted us to the door. It opened before we could knock to reveal an astonished Callie.

"Maestressa!" she cried, seeing Beatrice. Then she recognized me and took in the magister, and she stood back without another word to let us pass inside.

"Wait here," said Bee. "Let me go up alone to my father. Callie, can you put together some manner of supper? And heat water for a bath? We'll just use the copper tub in the kitchen." She went up the steps. Callie hurried into the back, leaving me with the cold mage in the entry hall.

The first time I had seen him, I had thought him vain, arrogant, and conceited, and far too well aware that he was a powerful magister from a powerful mage House who walked through the world with a handsome face and expensive, well-cut, and flattering clothing. Nothing about him had changed, except maybe he had dug down and discovered the kernel that was his essential self, which was still vain and arrogant and a magister. But that was not all he was. I could see his resemblance to his grandmother in the steady regard of his gaze.

"We are still married, Catherine," he said. "I will not abandon you. Or sacrifice you, as the Barahals did. Neither will I force you to come with me, as so many selfish magisters have done to the women of my village."

I wanted to argue with him, to declare that I had escaped him once and could do so again, but after all, Bee and I had not escaped Four Moons House. So I remained silent.

Falteringly, he went on. "It became plain to me that my village helped you escape out from under my nose on Hallows Night. They did it because they chose to honor guest rights above their own safety. I cannot do less than they did. So I have my own offer to make you. If you wish, you can make a home with my kinsmen in the village. They will take you in and treat you as a daughter. Or, if you wish"—here he paused to take in a resolute breath before going on—"you can come with me back to Four Moons House."

"After what happened in the mill, you're returning to Four Moons House?"

"Catherine! Of course I have to return. Do I have to list the reasons?" He raised a hand to touch the gold locket he wore at his neck, realized he had done so, and fisted the hand as he lowered it. His next words were delivered in a clipped tone. "But of course you cannot wish to come with me, after everything that has happened."

When it is very cold, it is easy to feel heat flush your cheeks. "I thank you for your kind offer, Andevai Diarisso Haranwy," I said in as level a voice as I could muster. "I am well aware you took great risk on yourself and your blameless village when you decided to help me. What happened before is therefore gone, forgiven, dismissed, and we are quit of it."

"Does that mean you forgive me for even one breath considering that I might be obliged to kill you?"

If it were possible to blush harder, I am sure I did so, because he stared at me with such a look as made him seem much better-looking even than he likely thought himself, and it is very bad to encourage young men into believing you find them handsome. "Yes. But my answer must be no. To your offer, I mean. I have to find my own way. I have to find out who my kin really are. I remain grateful to the honor with which your kin treated me. As for the other, I do not belong at Four Moons House. But I thank you, for being what are you, which is a man of honor, one who respects me."

I would never see him again, because we must go our separate ways. There could be no consequences for one impulsive act. And I had to admit the truth, because truth is the kernel of everything: I was curious to know what his lips tasted of. I was hungry.

So I took a step forward, I raised my face to his, and I kissed him.

It is hard to imagine that cold mages might have heat. In the instant of my lips touching his, he was ice, and in that instant I thought he was offended or aghast and in the next I realized he had simply been startled. Because he grasped my left arm with his right hand and cast his left arm around my back and drew me against him. And he kissed me back.

A kiss can be like the world turning over. It can be like the tide of a dragon's dream washing through the unseen world that is hidden to mortal eyes but that nevertheless permeates our being. It can be hot and cold together, as vast as the heavens and yet specific to the pressure of hands and the parting of lips. It raised more intense feelings than I had expected, like being engulfed in a storm of lightning. And in being more, I felt lessened when clumsily we broke apart and each stepped back in confusion. My face was in flames. He looked so rigidly and overbearingly imperious that I knew he must have been powerfully affected.

"Catherine!" he said. "Surely you see—"

"Andevai, you are a cold mage of rare and unexpected potency, as you told me often enough. I do understand why you feel you need to return to Four Moons House. You've opened the mansa's eyes to your worth. But I would never be content or welcome there. Nor do we know each other, or owe each other anything except what was forced on us. So why be burdened with me? You didn't try to kill me. You changed your mind. You did what was right."

The moment stretched into a while. Cold fire gleamed softly over the threshold of a house no longer spelled to keep out intruders, because the Hassi Barahals had abandoned it. As they had abandoned me. Then he shook his head as if shaking off an irritation.

"To have done what was right must be enough." His tone was formal, even harsh. "Peace upon you, Catherine, and in all your undertakings."

"Peace upon you and in all your undertakings," I echoed stupidly.

He went to the door, and I grasped the railing and retreated two steps up the stairs toward the first-floor landing. Then I turned back.

"Andevai."

He had the door open already, but he halted at once and turned. To kiss a man, and enjoy it, is not to love him. I did not love him. How could I? I barely knew him. But I was stunned by what I saw in his face: hope; shame; that thrice-cursed pride that, after all, was part of what drew the eye to him; hurt; humility; even, maybe, a measure of peace—a very human and appealing mix of emotions. It was as if I were seeing him for the first time.

"There is one thing that still puzzles me," I said, but the thought of going on was overwhelming, and I hesitated.

"Do not think that after all this, I am afraid to hear anything you may be afraid to say," he said, a bit irritably.

I lifted my chin. "All right, then. You are always very precise when it comes to magic. So I've observed. And you really, really don't like to get things wrong. So when you saw there were two young women, that day you came to this house, why did you not even ask about my cousin?"

His crooked smile made my heart turn over. "All right, then. I'll tell you." He paused, as if gathering courage, before he forged on. "When I saw you coming down the stairs that evening, it was as if I were seeing the other half of my soul descending to greet me."

I stared at him, but he was perfectly serious. The words set off an avalanche in my head: memories, flashes of things he had done and not done, said and not said.

"No going back from that, is there?" he added, as if to himself. Somehow he had relaxed, because a certain calm permeated him, like the calm that comes over the sailor when she has cast off from shore and the tide is bearing her out come what may. "So if you tell me now, Catherine, right now, that you never again wish to see me in any capacity, under any circumstances, I will never approach you again."

Unfortunately, I could not speak. I simply could not say one word. Any word.

"Ah," he said softly, which was not really a word but a reaction. And the cursed magister smiled coolly in a way I would have told him was very irritating indeed, if I could have talked. "I'll have to come back, then, when you've recovered enough to tell me what you really think."

He turned and walked out, taking the light with him, and my voice, and all my capacity for thought or movement.

From the shadows of the first-floor landing above me, Bee said, "Blessed Tanit! Spirits cleaved from one whole into two halves! The cold mage has taken a fancy to you, Cat, although I can't imagine why the way you kept at him with your claws. Still, he struck quite a romantical pose, don't you think?" I could see in the dusky dimness as, above me, she clasped hands to her heart in the manner of an actress striking a pose in one of the festival tableaux. "Commanded to kill her, he pursued her. Pursuing her, he fell in love with her! Or should that be, falling in love with her, he then pursued her? Yet he defied the heavens and his master to win her. And then, being heartless, she rejected him."

I no longer found the air cold at all. Indeed, the unheated entryway with the door standing wide open seemed quite steamy. "Have I ever mentioned how tiresome you are?"

"More than once!"

But this time it really was too much. I really was not joking. I walked out of the house, halting on the stoop to watch half of the company ride away, Andevai among them. He glanced back once. That was all. I could watch the course of his progress by the way the gaslights faded and flared.

When his party left Falle Square, there were still soldiers waiting at the house, but I ignored them. I crossed the street, my feet crunching in a dusting of snow. I opened the gate into the park and walked to the stone stele, the votive with her full lips, broad nose, and braided hair. I knelt, although the ground beneath my knees leeched all warmth from me. I raised a hand to touch the sigil the guardian held in her carved right hand: the sigil of Tanit, protector of women. I had nothing to offer except my thanks for our deliverance, but on this night, that was enough.

33

"Cat!"

Uncle's voice made me stiffen. Without looking at him, I climbed to my feet and took in an unsteady breath as I found that sudden rage blinds more easily than darkness.

"Catherine," he said, his voice breaking on my name, "I beg you, forgive us."

I said nothing. I heard Bee's silence beside him.

"Or if you cannot forgive us, then at least allow me to tell you what happened thirteen years ago. Let me tell you what we felt was best kept secret for all these years."

I was not sure what I would have done if it had not been so dreadfully cold, if it had not been the dead of night on the longest night of the year, and if I had not been so very, very hungry and thirsty, and filthy on top of all else. If I had not just kissed a man who had told me I was the other half of his soul. But winter, and kinship, binds chains on you. It is not so easy to turn your back on everything you once thought you knew.

He said, "I have his final journal. The one we kept hidden from you."

Such simple words, to hurt so much. I covered my face with my hands.

Bee said, "Come inside, Cat. Just to get some hot soup and a change of clothes at least. Those really stink. A heavier coat, and your good gloves. A bath, which you need. A fire and mulled wine. A warm bed just for tonight. Please. I'm sorry I said those stupid things."

I had done it all for her. Who else did I have to do anything for?

But weren't these very thoughts a lie? A saber-toothed cat roamed the city. An eru had called me "cousin." I still had my ghostly companions: *Daniel Hassi Barahal, Tara Bell, and child*.

I walked past my uncle and accompanied Bee back into the house, back into the magnificently warm kitchen where Callie greeted me shyly. I heard the soldiers enter to take possession of the ground-floor parlor and the front and back entry. The magister announced his intention of taking an upstairs bed so they could light fires in the chambers below. Fortunately, they stayed out of the kitchen. They left us alone.

We sat down at the heavy wooden table where we had often helped Callie and Cook prepare food. I took a spoon in my hand and began to eat the comforting soup, broth of chicken flavored with leeks, parsley, turnip, carrot, and precious chunks of meat. My uncle sat down on the bench on the other side of the table. I could not know what he saw in my face. His was drawn gray with anguish. His black hair was uncombed and undressed, an untidy mop of tight curls. I had never had curls. My long black hair was as straight as if it had been ironed. Just like Rory's.

In the end, as if reluctantly, he began to speak.

"We were never close, Daniel and I. He was only two years younger, but we could not have been less alike. He was always quarreling with everyone, challenging them, questioning every remark and all the proper ways we had of doing things. He was restless, difficult, nothing like me. It made sense for him to travel, gathering information. I just wanted to make the family prosperous and secure again, and to be secure myself. I married

Tilly at the family's urging, in order to consolidate lines of connection between the Adurnam branch and the Havery branch
of the Hassi Barahals. She and I have always worked hard. We
get on well together. I did my duty to the Barahals, and so I
waited in expectation for Daniel to do his duty, as all of us are
meant to do. Then he came home with *her*."

"Her?" asked Bee quietly.

"She was hideous. A monster."

I kept eating, because I had to eat to be able to listen without
screaming at him.

"Hideous?" asked Bee in a tone both high and strained.
"What ever can you mean?"

"She was a soldier, one of Camjiata's Amazons. A terrible,
brawny woman with uncouth manners. She had injuries—terrible
injuries. Her left leg was damaged, so she limped everywhere
and supported herself on a cane. I suppose it must have bothered her, who was once strong enough to march from the Mediterranean basin to the Baltic Ice Sea. Her left arm ended at the
elbow in a stump with a flap of skin sewn together. Blown off
by artillery, so she told us. She joked about it! I cannot even bear
to repeat the japes she made. The left side of her face was man-
gled. Her eye was missing, scarred shut. Burn marks and scars
down her cheek and jaw. And yet she would stop and stare at
herself in every mirror she passed. She had no sense at all of what
was appropriate."

I kept eating, one spoonful at a time. I remembered how
strong her arm was, and how I always thought that she smelled
as I supposed a soldier would: determined, a little sweaty, and
fierce in a way that had always comforted me. That, and her
words of warning. That was my mother.

"I could scarcely manage to look at her, and yet Daniel treated
her as if she were the most beautiful woman he had ever seen."

"Maybe because he loved her," said Bee.

"Oh, I am sure he did. He liked sentiment. He loved nothing more than looking noble."

I choked on a lump of soggy carrot.

"Did she love him?" Bee asked in a toneless voice.

"A good question! Camjiata's Amazons were required to be celibate. Absolute fidelity to the general. So when she turned up pregnant, she was arrested and imprisoned. The penalty was that she should remain in prison until the child was born. Then she would be executed and the child raised in an orphanage or, if it was healthy and comely, fostered out."

Trembling, I set down my spoon.

"Daniel was in Lutetia during the big council called by the general to write that radical civil code he meant to impose on Europa. She must somehow have gotten a message to him, asking for help. She knew him from that cursed ice expedition. And from before as well."

"From before when?" Bee asked.

"They first met when they were young, before she went into the army, before Camjiata was a general, when he was just Captain Leonnorios Aemilius Keita fighting in a war between feuding princes."

How was it I had never heard this tale?

"I think that's why she begged Daniel for help, because of the history they shared. Tilly said Tara adored Daniel. I never saw it myself. Perhaps the bards and jellies would sing of it and call it love, if love is a tragedy."

"It's *djeli*," I said. "I wish you people would use the word correctly."

"You just said you could scarcely bear to look at her, Papa," said Bee, more softly than before. She glanced at me. "So maybe you did not see what you did not want to see."

"I am not a sentimentalist. Does it matter, anyway? Only to Daniel, who almost destroyed the family by agreeing to help her. He took her to the Hassi Barahal house in Havery first, you know, right after she gave birth to Catherine. They made him bring her to Adurnam, because it was farther from the front lines. Camjiata's war had by then engulfed Europa. It was dangerous to shelter a deserter. Either Camjiata's agents would get wind of it and come to fetch her back for trial and hurt some of us in the process, or the authorities would get wind of her presence and accuse the family of spying."

"But we are spies," said Bee. "The Hassi Barahals have always been spies."

"We are not spies. We began as travelers. Like all of our people, we had to make a living, so we became merchants in the field we knew best—that of gathering information and passing it on. To be accused of harboring a spy is very different in the eyes of the authorities. It makes it look as if we have taken sides."

I picked up the spoon with a trembling hand. I hadn't finished my soup yet. I had to finish my soup.

"Aren't we supposed to take sides in such a case," demanded Bee, "by supporting your family no matter what?"

"Tara Bell was not our kin! The child she gave birth to was not even Daniel's child! He admitted as much, for you can see Catherine looks nothing like us!"

I raised my eyes to his face, and he looked away. I stared at his face, so familiar and even in its way beloved; he was the man who had taught me how to read. He was not a particularly affectionate man, but I had always thought him a good one: loyal, hardworking, funny at times, faithfully devoted to the Hassi Barahals.

I was not wrong about him. I was just not a Hassi Barahal.

"What happened then?" I asked hoarsely.

"Then Camjiata's dreams of empire came crashing down around him. The Houses destroyed his wife's mage House for turning traitor to their kind. His army was defeated. The allies took him prisoner. They dared not kill him, for that might have further inflamed a discontented populace. So they imprisoned him in a secret place rumored to be an island in the Mediterranean. Then Four Moons House came to us with proof that we had sold information to Camjiata's army."

"Had you?" Bee asked.

"There exists no proof that we did anything of the sort," he said.

"Because you burned it," I whispered. "Andevai handed over the proof in exchange for me. You burned it right then as he was driving away with me."

"We had no choice," he said stiffly, "but to agree to the contract Four Moons House forced upon us, or we would have been ruined. Destroyed, like Camjiata. Why they wanted you, Beatrice, they never explained. When do magisters ever need to explain themselves?"

Andevai had explained himself. But he was not like the others.

"Have you ever heard the phrase," Bee asked, " 'to walk the dreams of dragons'?"

He shook his head. "Is it from an old bardic poem? Or a jelly's tale?"

I rose from the bench. "Why did Daniel and Tara leave Adurnam with me?"

The lamps hissed. The fire crackled. Callie sat on her stool by the hearth, not even pretending not to listen.

He met my gaze, and I suppose I had to respect his willingness to do so. He looked older than his years, and he looked weary, but I was no longer sure he was sorry about anything.

"Four Moons House came to us and demanded the eldest Barahal daughter. Bee's freedom and life were at risk. So I went to Daniel. Tara was pregnant again, you know."

I was frozen, unable to move or speak or even, really, to think at all. *Pregnant again*, with a child who would have been my younger sibling. A baby brother or sister I would never know.

"I took on the responsibility. The others were too afraid. I went to Daniel. I said, 'You'll have another baby, a child to love and raise. Let us take Catherine—she's a bastard, anyway; she's not even yours—and give her to the mage House in Bee's place'. Next I knew, they had packed their things and left."

My legs gave out. I sat, and fortunately, the humble bench held me as a mother surely holds its child, supporting it when it falters.

"'A bastard, anyway'?" said Bee in a hard, cold voice. "Is that really what you said?"

"Someone had to be willing to tell the truth! Make the hard choices!" He went on, shaking his head as if harried by the buzzing of bees or the anger of the whispering gods. "Next thing, we got word of the ferry accident. You were brought back alive, but they were dead."

"Did you ever see their bodies?" Bee asked.

He stared at the fire. "Oh, yes," he murmured, his voice a scrape where memory rasped. "The recovered bodies had been laid out in a warehouse. Daniel had an old scar on his shoulder. And Tara...well...there could be no mistake."

He began to sob, as if the sight were as fresh as the day it had happened.

After a while, he wiped his eyes and blew his nose in a handkerchief. Then he fished in his coat and brought out a journal, perfectly ordinary, covered in bound leather and tied shut with a green ribbon. He set it on the table in front of me.

I reached for it but drew back my hand before I touched it. "What of the other missing journals? Were you hiding them, too?"

"We don't know what happened to them. Not even Daniel

knew. He did his best to direct them to the Barahals, but you never know what will happen on any journey, do you? Things get lost." He stood. "I leave at dusk tomorrow. The tide turns at midnight, and we take ship for Gadir to join Tilly and the girls. I've been advised to sell this house. It has already been purchased."

"By whom?" demanded Bee.

"By Four Moons House. The offer came at the Prince of Tarrant's request, which means it is a command one cannot refuse. Beatrice, you'll come with me, of course. And you, Cat. If you will come with us, we will ask your forgiveness and you will be part of us."

I said nothing.

Bee said, "Papa, you seem not to understand something. The mansa and the prince do not intend to allow me to leave Adurnam."

"How can that be? The contract is void!"

Bee's expression was as blank as uncut stone, a smooth face that might conceal any object or emotion beneath if only a carver knew how to release what lay hidden within. "You really don't understand, do you? That's why they're buying the house. To keep me here, in a familiar, comfortable cage. Don't you see it? By sacrificing Cat, you didn't save me. All you did was sacrifice everything she thought you and Mama meant to her."

"I've asked for her forgiveness. Cat, do you forgive me?"

I searched for a voice and found one, although I was not sure I recognized it as mine. "Did she ever tell you who sired me?"

He shook his head with a grimace. "She never told anyone anything. To think of all that valuable information she must have had, for she knew Camjiata well, you know. And yet she refused to tell us anything, even though we could have sold that information and made our lives a cursed sight easier. Still." He broached the words as if they were painful. "I suppose she felt loyalty of a sort, even to a commander she had deserted. There's something commendable in that."

I could not bear to look at him. Instead, I spoke to the wall. "I know you did what you thought you had to do. I know you did it out of concern for Bee, and you may even regret the pain it has caused me. But my parents would not have drowned if you hadn't driven them away. I'm not ready to forgive that yet."

"How like Daniel you are," he muttered. "So intransigent."

"Is she like Uncle Daniel, or not like him, then?" Bee's gaze had a regal scorn that surprised even me. She looked so calm and spoke so evenly that it was difficult to see how furious she actually was. "You cannot have it both ways. You betrayed not just Cat, not just your brother and my aunt Tara, but also me. You betrayed the Barahal daughters, all of us, and sons, too, the ones you never had. You betrayed the honor of our house. You acted just as the Romans always claimed we Kena'ani did. I'm ashamed."

"We were forced into a corner. We only did what we thought we had to do. What else would you have had me do, Beatrice?"

She shook her head. "It's done. Now all you can do is go to Gadir. Take better care of Hanan and Astraea than you did of Cat. For Tanit's sake, Papa, don't let Astraea get away with being such a little brat. And take Callie, if she'll go. For she's alone here."

"Callie?" he said, so startled at this request he forgot his tears.

"Do you want to go?" Bee asked Callie. "I know you've nowhere else to go."

With her flyaway pale hair pulled back severely but wisps straggling everywhere, and a mended shawl pulled tight around her narrow shoulders, Callie looked fragile, but she was not weak nor was she stupid. "I don't know what to expect in Gadir, truly, but I've been cold and starving on the streets of Adurnam, and I never want to be so again. But if you and Maestressa Cath-erine must stay, then won't you be needing me here?"

"There will be other arrangements," said Bee. "You must go with him. And now, I admit, I am terribly hungry, and I would like to eat."

With a halting step, Uncle left the kitchen.

Callie took the bowls, ladled more soup in, and set them down with a cup of mead. She checked the lamps and retreated to her stool. I did not ask her to leave. This was her room, not ours, and, anyway, it was warm and removed from the cold mage and the soldiers. I heard them moving about in the front parlor and entry hall, speaking in low voices. Bee picked up her spoon and ate her soup. Then she drank the mead, first her cup and, after a while, mine.

I stared at the journal.

Long I stared. Hope tasted of ashes in my mouth.

I had come too far to give up now.

I untied the ribbon, and I ran a hand down the creamy leather and, with a held breath, opened it. I knew his writing, with its long tails and flowing curves. So easy to read.

I read as the lamps burned, and as Bee watched me, and as Callie waited, for servants must learn to wait, it being their duty to do so whatever their personal wishes might be.

Tara has risked much and never faltered in her duty. She has seen awful things. She has blood on her hands. She is scarred by the wars.

He did not mean only physical scars.

I will protect Tara always, however I can. What happened on the ice does not matter. The child will be my child. I will protect her no matter the cost. I have promised Tara that, and even if I had not, it would make no difference, for my little cat is my sweet daughter, the delight of my life. How I wish I had known far earlier how one can lose one's heart to something so precious.

My tears fell on ink long since dry. He had written this so many years ago.

Tara lost one arm to cannon fire, and the other is crippled such that she cannot really care for the baby. She makes light of it in front of others—soldiers' humor—but I am the one who holds her at night when she screams, reliving the battles in her dreams. I am the one who reassures her that the child will love her for the courageous and beautiful woman she is, not for her two arms or her two eyes.

Blessed Tanit, do not let my heart break.

That ass Jonatan came to me with a disgusting proposition, which I absolutely will not countenance. Giving up my girl for his, as if mine were worth nothing, which I am sure she is to him. I protested. I offered ways to bargain with the magisters. I even offered to steal the cursed documents back. He threatened me in that unctuous way he has. Said the family would turn us out if I don't cooperate. "Is some other man's bastard worth this to you?" he asked me. So despite Tara's condition, despite the health and vigor she has regained simply by remaining in one stable place for so long, we must leave. It is a mercy that Camjiata has been captured and his army dissolved. I am not sure where exactly we can find refuge, but at least we can hope to travel there safely.

Only they had not traveled safely. He and my mother had died. It's just they hadn't meant to. They had been running away to go make a life elsewhere. With me.

How many times must I repeat myself, I wonder, trying to explain it to people who do not want to hear? She is my daughter even if not of my breeding. What is breeding, after all, except a moment's release? Isn't the raising more important? I will cherish my little cat always.

But my heart broke anyway, and Bee put her arms around me, and I wept.

34

And so dawn comes, and it is bitter, and it is sweet. I had a father after all, even if he was dead. I had a mother whose courage was greater than I had ever imagined. They had loved me enough to try to make a life for me, even if it had not worked out, because Lady Fortune is more powerful than frail human plans.

But that didn't mean Bee and I were ready to surrender.

Solstice day passed quietly inside the house. We heated water and bathed in the scullery, Callie standing watch. The magister walked a circuit of the upper floors. The cawl protecting the house had faded with Aunt Tilly's departure, but the magister spun some manner of cold magic to seal the window latches shut. The soldiers kept to the ground floor, guarding the front and back doors. Uncle readied his single bag, weeping all the while. Callie we asked for a favor. At dusk, a hackney cab rattled up, the horse stamping in its traces.

"It's here," I said, for I had been watching for it.

A young soldier opened the door, trying to be polite or perhaps to impress Bee.

Uncle was entirely deflated, a balloon unable to stir as the wind rose.

"Beatrice," he said despairingly.

"I'll write every month so you know I am well. That's all I can promise. Give my love to Hanna and Astraea. Best you hurry, so you don't miss the tide."

"Uncle," I said, choking back tears, "give my love to the girls. Tell Aunt—" I could not go on. I had loved Aunt Tilly so.

I did kiss him then, after all, not in forgiveness but in regret for what we had lost. Bee offered a formal kiss to his unshaven cheek, like a dido showing distant favor to an unloved but hard-working courtier. With bowed shoulders and bent head, Uncle crossed the threshold with his bag. Callie followed him, carrying one light carpetbag and three heavy ones. We made our farewells, and she nodded at us to show that she understood her part in this: Once they had left the house, she would insist on stopping at Tanit's temple to make an offering of grain to the priests, so they might pray for Tanit's blessing and a safe journey. Not even Uncle Jonatan would refuse that.

The cab rolled away. The soldier shut the door, glanced at Bee, and then away.

We went upstairs to the first-floor parlor, where we had profligately lit the stove with the last of the coal and the chamber with our last two beeswax candles. We settled in the window seat, she with her arms hooked around her bent knees, tucking them close to her chest, and me with my father's journal, number 46, on my lap. The knit bag, now our only possession, sat on the cushion, its bulge enveloping her sketchbook, the singed copy of *Lies the Romans Told*, and the journal Uncle had given me last night.

"I was thinking," she said.

"Dangerous at all times, and with a tendency to cause pain in those who are unaccustomed to such exercise," I remarked.

But then I opened journal 46 to the end, to the conversation between the young natural historian and the lieutenant while the aurora borealis played its changes across an arctic sky. Knowing now what I knew, the words fell entirely differently. How could I have missed the hints in their chance comments and asides? They had known each other before this; it was so clear from their joking manner, the quick rejoinders, the shared knowledge of things they shouldn't have known so easily about each other. A new perspective gives a person new eyes. Knowing what I now knew about Andevai—

"Cat! Are you paying attention? You look a little flushed. I *said*, perhaps we'd be better off to go to the academy and throw ourselves on the mercy of the headmaster."

Startled, I retreated behind a glower. "The one who handed you over to Legate Amadou Barry? I think not."

She sighed. "No, I suppose not. I'm just exhausted by thinking of having to haul Uncle Daniel's journals across Adurnam." Abruptly, she sucked in breath so hard I looked up and followed her gaze out the window and over Falle Square. "Fiery Shemesh! What's this?"

A black coach rumbled down the west side of the square, pulled by four horses as pale as milk. My heart leaped in my chest, or it would have, if I'd had a heart, which Bee so often accused me of lacking. But after all, it was not the coach I thought it was: This vehicle bore a crest of four moons—crescent, half, full, and new—and its coachman was a heavyset man with black skin and its paired footmen a matching set of blond Celts. The horses were ordinary horses with brown specks flecking their gray coats. Their hooves fell solidly on stone. I wondered if I would ever see the eru and the coachman again.

Four Moons House had come to claim its new property the moment the festival was over. The coach drew up before the house, and the footmen hopped gracefully down to open the door and pull down two steps. The man and woman who climbed out were not cold mages but wore the serious garb and tidy demeanor of accountants and housekeepers, stewards come to take possession and take inventory. Seeing them emerge, I felt a dull ache in my heart. Was it sadness at losing the only home I remembered? Selfish disappointment that Andevai had not come himself? Relief that I did not yet have to figure out what to say to him?

We rose as the stewards were shown in. They were reserved and polite.

"I am Maestra Fatou," said the woman, "and this is my cousin, Maester Conor. We are come at the mansa's order to take over the running of the household. Also, he did not think it appropriate for two young women to live alone without older female companionship."

"Of course," said Bee. "Our thanks. We're a little nervous of the soldiers, I admit."

"Have they shown you any disrespect?" she asked sharply.

"No, no," said Bee in a tone that suggested otherwise. "We have been locking ourselves in here at night. We sleep here, for no fires will light on the second floor, with the magister sleeping up there. If you don't mind, could we wait until morning to show you the house? You may take the cook's room downstairs, by the kitchen, where there's a fire, or bunk with the soldiers in the dining room below us."

They left, and we made ready. We sat in darkness and silence and warmth, waiting for the midnight bell. When the lonely tenor cried the night watch across the city, I took Uncle's keys and unlocked the door into his private office. We padded in, and I unsheathed my sword and sliced through the cold magic that bound shut the latch. We paused, listening, but no alarm stirred the house; the magister was asleep and would, we hoped, note nothing until he woke. Bee positioned herself by the window where, weeks ago, an unwanted visitor had climbed in unannounced and unasked for, slipping through the protective cawl. I went downstairs in my slippered feet, carrying a lantern lit with the last beeswax candle. I pretended to trip and stumble as I came to the back door.

The mage House soldiers were well trained. They were

perfectly awake: two inside and two outside. I held the lantern up right into their faces, to confound their night vision.

"We forgot to take a chamber pot upstairs," I said. "I've got to use the latrine."

They opened the door, and I quickly shone the lantern light in the faces of the outside pair. I made a business of exclaiming over the bitter cold, and my slippered feet, and how I had forgotten my cloak, and should I go back and get it, and on in this vein as I listened for the faint creak of Uncle's office window opening above and the fainter creak of the stout branch on which Bee was climbing out to the wall. We'd climbed that path before. We Barahals were trained to be spies, after all.

When I was sure she had gone, I used the latrine and made my way back to the first-floor parlor. I locked myself in, pulled on boots and coat, secured the knit bag with its books around my torso, stoked the fire, and made up lumpy figures beneath the feather bed we'd thrown over the window-seat cushion. Then I went into Uncle's office and locked the door between office and parlor. The office door leading onto the landing was already locked from inside. If we were fortunate, they would not think to break down the doors until morning.

With my ghost sword slung tightly over my back, I climbed out and crouched on the wide branch to close the window behind me. Some instinct or training or sound alerted the guards standing out back, and they glanced around and up, but I was part of the tree, nothing more than a skeletal winter branch, a little stouter than most, but nothing to notice. Nothing to see.

Bee and I met in the mews. We avoided the gaslit thoroughfares and made our way through the cold winter night, me at the front with my good eyes and my ghost sword to mark the path, Bee following tightly in my footsteps with an ordinary cane of her own to sweep the street for obstacles. We found our way to the Blessed Tanit's temple near the academy, whose gates remained unlocked in every season and at all times of the day and night. Three bags, Callie had been instructed to give them. One was full with the last of the grain from our larder, given as an offering for the priests. The other two held my father's journals and a few other items crammed in with them: four silver candlesticks, four beeswax candles, and some stockings, shifts, and underthings that had been left by Aunt Tilly when the family had fled. What coin we had, we'd sewn into our bodices. The priests slept soundly in their winter cottage; I had no trouble retrieving the two bags, except for their weight.

It was a cursed long and struggling walk hauling them across the dark city. Winter's cold deadened the night. Fortunately, no festival debris littered the streets to trip us. The balloon rides, the ice fair with its food booths and games, the processions to the temples, the public banquets at which beggars snatched from the filth of the streets would preside over the only good meal they would eat all year, all had been canceled due to the riots. The prince's curfew kept criminals and rogues at home this night. Militia patrols, however, were out in force. We would hear the clop of hooves and see yellow torchlight gleaming around a corner, giving us time to shrink back into a shadowy alcove or rubbish-strewn alley to hide.

"I feel like someone is following us," Bee said in a low voice as we crouched on the steps of a locked and barred chandler's shop, waiting for a clot of six Tarrant soldiers to decide that they did not want to loiter in the intersection ahead. "Do you really know how to get there? We've never been to that part of town before. Are you sure they'll help us?"

A cold wind chased down the street and kissed my nose and lips like a flirt. Or a cold mage. "I'm not sure of anything," I said, shivering. I was tired and much too chilled, and my arms hurt even though we were swapping off carrying the bags. "But

I know the radicals have no love for cold mages or princes. If anyone can help us now, surely it's lawyers."

"You set your sights too low," said a male voice.

We both started up to our feet, and I had my sword unsheathed in an instant. The blade's faint glow was enough to illuminate a young man leaning insouciantly against the shuttered windows next to us, his shoulders bracing up the wall and his arms crossed over his chest as he watched the mounted patrol down the way confer by the light of their blazing torches.

"Rory!" I said, and although I whispered his name, the swelling in my heart was more like a shout.

"Don't pet me until you put that thing away," he said just before I meant to fling myself at him for a celebratory embrace.

"Cat," murmured Bee, "I thought you were exaggerating about your cane turning into a sword. Also, the blade gleams."

"It's cold steel," I said, sheathing it with the mysterious twist that sheathed the blade as into a sheath that existed only in the spirit world. Then I hugged him. "Oh, Rory, I was afraid I'd lost you. But I didn't. And you even found clothes!"

"Hush," said Rory. "They're still hunting me."

We waited in silence until the patrol rode on. Then we started to walk, and in truth, I felt much stronger and less cold now that the three of us were reunited.

"How was the pug dog?" asked Bee tartly.

"Too fatty," he said, "and the peahens had all those feathers. That was nasty. It never bothered me before I wore this skin. By the way, Cousin Beatrice, as I promised, I did no lasting harm to either of the fine lords. Or to any humans, really no more than I had to." He touched right hand to left shoulder.

"You're hurt," said Bee. "You need tending."

I could not see him grin, but I knew he grinned; the flavor of the air changed. The night felt brighter and the bags less heavy.

"You want to lick the wound?" he asked.

"You're disgusting!"

"Why is that disgusting? Doesn't everyone do that?" He looked at me. "And don't think for one moment I'm carrying either of those bags. What do you have in them? Stones?"

"Books," said Bee scornfully. "Books, books, books."

"Not a single one I am willing to part with," I retorted.

Even had we trudged without the burden of books, Fox Close was quite a long way south and east across the city, close against the excise office and the customs embankment and near the quays. It was in a district inhabited by people who would not have been welcome to live in the houses around Falle Square: foreigners, radicals, technologists, and solicitors. The cocks had crowed by the time we staggered onto Enterprise Road, although the brilliant gaslamps lining the street—the very latest in design—still burned with a remarkable cheer that lifted my spirits and fed a flare of hope to my weary heart. Bee stared and stared, for there were a lot of trolls—and men, and a few goblins not yet burrowed into their daylight dens—coming and going into offices and coffeehouses and shops, all of which were already open and bustling, as if to make up for lost time after yesterday's festival closings and the riots the day before.

"There is Fox Close," I said, indicating a humble lane tucked away between a tavern and a coffeehouse but equally busy if one judged by the foot traffic pouring in and out of its throat.

As we made our way down the lane, the gaslights began to hiss and fail, but it was day's arrival, not that of a cold mage, that shuttered them as the gas was turned off. Ahead, on the right side of the lane, hung a newly painted sign, visible in dawn's light. The script painted on the sign was pin-perfect, orange letters shining against a feathery brown backdrop: GOD-WIK AND CLUTCH.

"I hope this works," Bee muttered.

We hauled our bags up to the stoop and earned a few curious

looks but no offers of help. I plied the knocker. We waited. Rory sighed, looking ready for a nap. I licked my lips, and then was sorry I had done so, for my lips were so dry and cracked that my tongue released a smear of blood. Bee adjusted the fit of her gloves on her fingers. I untangled my cane where it had gotten caught in a fold in my skirts.

The door opened, and a troll looked at us, cocking his head first to one side and then the other to get a good look with each eye. He wore a drab jacket that set off astonishing scarlet and blue and black plumage and crest, truly spectacular.

I found my voice from the pit where it had crawled in to hide. "May the day find you at peace," I said, a little hoarsely. "My name is Catherine Hassi Barahal. This is my cousin, Beatrice, and my brother, Roderic. We're here to see Chartji. The solicitor."

"You're that one," he said in words so eerily without accent they did not quite sound proper. "Chartji warned me."

"Warned you?" I could not get a full lungful of air in, for my chest had gone numb.

"'Let her in quickly shall she come standing at the door.'" The troll hopped back and gestured for us to enter, baring his sharp teeth in a manner that made Rory yawn threateningly and caused Bee to take a step back. By which movement, she revealed our luggage.

"Oo!" He bent forward and peered at the two bulging bags with their brass clasps. *Things!*"

"Who's at the door, Caith?" Brennan came out from a back room, wiping his hands on a grimy cloth. He saw me and grinned. "Catherine! And your charming cousin, Beatrice. And another companion, I see."

"My brother, Roderic," I said.

"Well met, indeed! Did you tell them to come in, Caith? Give them a cup of water?"

"Things!" said Caith. "Even some shiny things. Two brass clasps and a sword."

Startled, I looked down. Daylight had veiled the sword, and even to me, in the first weak glimmer of dawn, it appeared as an ordinary black cane.

Brennan said, "Please step inside at once. Caith, close the door behind them."

The urgency in his tone propelled us like a ball shot from a musket. We hurried in and dropped the bags in the hall as Caith shut the door and locked it with a pair of heavy chains.

Brennan said to Rory, "I'm Brennan. Caith, did you remember to introduce yourself?"

"Oo!" The troll shifted his fascinated gaze away from the brass clasps to look first at Brennan and then at us. His crest flattened and lifted and flattened again. "My pardon! Caith. Not my full name, but assuredly yours. I am what you would call it the clutch cousin sibling child..." His head swiveled uncomfortably far around, to beseech Brennan evidently.

"Nephew," Brennan said. "Not an egg sibling child, but a clutch sibling child."

"Ah, I see," I said, although I had not the least idea of what he was talking about. Caith twisted his head back around to face me and displayed his teeth again. It was clearly an effort to mimic a smile, however disturbing he looked, like he was ready to eat us up. So I smiled in return and addressed him politely. "May you find peace on this morning, Caith."

Caith led us to the back. In what had once been a sitting room, Kehinde knelt among the pieces of her press, which were spread out in a pattern I could not read. She was so absorbed in moving pieces around to see where they fit that she did not even look up.

Old Godwik was seated at a desk, pen in hand, but he looked up at once. "The Hassi Barahal in her mantle! What an exceptionally pleasant surprise! Let me crow on the rocks at sunrise! And this…the cousin, I presume. And…" He gave Rory an exceptionally piercing look. "Interesting. I've not seen one like you before. Well met. Please enter our nest."

Belatedly, surprised by his words, Kehinde looked up. "Catherine!" She smiled.

Brennan lugged the two carpetbags into the room and set them against the wall. A moment later, Chartji walked in, claws stained with ink and carrying a bowl of water in one hand.

"Catherine!" she said. "And your clutch sibling Beatrice! And did I hear this one called brother? I thought you might come."

"We have a proposition to make you," I said without preamble. "Our services, in exchange for yours. We believe that if anyone can help us get out from under the power of magisters and princes, you can."

"Drink first," said Chartji. "That's the proper way. Then we'll talk."

As we passed around the bowl, a knocking came again at the door. Caith's footfalls pattered down; chains rattled softly. The hinges creaked slightly as the door was opened.

After a pause, he called in his uncannily pure voice, "Brennan! There's a rat here who says you're expecting a messenger. He says a rising light marks the dawn of a new world."

Brennan said sharply, "Get him in fast and shut the door." Then he stepped out into the hallway. With a frown, Kehinde pushed her glasses up the bridge of her nose and followed. Bee, who had been drinking, handed the bowl to Rory. She grabbed my wrist and tugged me after them. We all spilled into the hallway to see Caith stepping back from the door as a pair of men surged in. I knew them! Hard to forget those faces: They were the two foreigners I had seen in the inn in Lemanis. They carried themselves very differently now. No longer diffident, they prowled like scouts, gazes ranging over our faces and up the stairs. The young man clearly did not recognize me, although he stared too long and too admiringly at Bee. The older man looked twice at me with obvious recognition, then frowned as Rory strolled with a threatening grace out of the back room, followed a moment later by a limping Godwik. On the stoop was the woman dressed as a man, the third foreigner I'd seen in Lemanis, but after glancing inside, she jumped back down to the street.

A man walked up the steps and into the entry hall. He caught Caith's gaze and gestured. Obeying this wordless order, the young troll closed and chained the door. The door's lintel framed the newcomer: He was a tall, broad-shouldered, black-haired man about Uncle's age, and he wore a shabby wool great-coat and a faded tricornered hat rather the worse for the wear. The clothes did not make the man. He might have worn rags, or he might have worn robes of gold, and either way, he would be the first person in any chamber you would notice, no matter how large the crowd.

I had seen him before. Only not like this. Before, he had hidden the true crackling strength of his gaze and the coiled power of his presence.

The man and Kehinde were eyeing each other with the look of dogs who aren't sure whether they will become friends or attack.

"I expected a courier," she said. "An ambassador, to open talks between your people and mine."

"I am my own ambassador," he said with a lift of his chin that had more power than a grand flourish. "As I must be, in these troubled times."

"Truly," said Brennan, a little curtly, "I would have expected you to arrive with more of a retinue."

"Numbers breed attention," said the man. "You understand why I must avoid attention, here in the enemy's country. However, be assured I have many agents already in the city."

I knew him.

He looked at Bee and nodded, as if they had already met, although that was impossible. "You must be the eldest Hassi Barahal daughter, just as Helene told me. Black curls, she said, very young, quite beautiful, and with as much subtlety as an ax."

Mouth agape, Bee pulled her sketchbook from the knit bag and opened it to the page with a sketch that matched his person, and the door's frame, exactly. He'd rendered her mute.

But his gaze had already moved on. To me.

"And you must be Tara Bell's daughter. It was so strange to see you that day when you climbed into the wagon in Lemanis. I thought you must be hers, for you look just like her, except for the hair and the color of your eyes. The youth's presence with you confused me, you calling him your elder brother. And it was too early to meet you. Helene was never wrong about such things."

I blinked. "You're Big Leon. The carter's cousin. We last saw you at Crane Marsh Works in the middle of Anderida. And these two, and the woman outside…a party of five and their mules and wool. What? Were you the one who was sick and about to die?"

"The authorities became suspicious. We split up, and I came ahead, carried by the wings of those who have remained loyal all these years to the cause."

"You walked into Adurnam alone?" demanded Brennan. "With all the mage Houses and every prince in northwestern Europa hunting for you? That seems rash."

"And irrational," said Kehinde thoughtfully. "We could turn you over to the Prince of Tarrant for a significant reward."

"But you won't. For you see, I am never alone. The hopes and ambitions of too many people are carried on my back."

"You're Camjiata," I said.

He had a way of tilting his head that made it seem he was about to laugh but had decided not to. That made you want to have a chance to laugh with him, if only you could find a way to surprise that laugh out of him and earn the praise of having amused him. "Of course I am Camjiata. Who else would I be? At last, after the patient work of many years and many hands, I am free."

Chartji stepped forward, offering the traditional bowl of water.

He doffed his hat politely, drank it all in one thirsty gulp, and wiped his lips with a sleeve. "And now we have business to do, and no time to wait."

"Did you come looking for me?" said Bee breathlessly. I could not tell if she was terrified, or exhilarated, or making ready to punch him in the face. "Did she tell you how to find me? Your wife, I mean? The one who walked the dreams of dragons?"

"Yes. It was the final thing Helene said to me before they killed her. She told me that the eldest daughter of the Hassi Barahal clan would learn to walk the dreams of dragons. Find her, she said, because you will need her, as you have needed me." He lifted his right hand in the orator's classic gesture, and we all stared, waiting for his next words, because a person could not help but stare at him. He commanded our stares. "That's what puzzled me on the road, you see. Because Helene said that the eldest Hassi Barahal daughter would lead me to Tara Bell's child."

"B-but I'm Tara Bell's child," I said, and everyone looked at me.

"Of course you are," said Camjiata. "You could be no one else but who are you. So must we all be, even Helene, who knew that the gift of dreaming would be the curse that brought death to her. Yet even then, even at the end, the gift compelled her to speak. For those were Helene's very last words, the very last words I ever heard her say."

He paused. And I waited. We all waited. A log shifted on an unseen fire somewhere in the house. Beyond the closed door, the rising light brought the city of Adurnam to life with a new day.

"She said, 'Where the hand of fortune branches, Tara Bell's child must choose, and the road of war will be washed by the tide.'"

"A fanciful turn of phrase," said Kehinde, "but as I have a pragmatical turn of mind, can you tell me what you think it means?"

He smiled as if, having meant to catch our interest, he had nevertheless not lost his ability to enjoy the pleasure of knowing he had done so. "Why, the depths of the words are easily sounded. She meant that Tara Bell's child will choose a path that will change the course of the war."

He looked at me. They all looked at me.

"Which means you, Catherine Bell Barahal. Because that child is you."

Look out for the second book in
The Spiritwalker Trilogy:

COLD FIRE

by Kate Elliott

Acknowledgments

A few years ago, my three children (all then in high school) and their friends Jamie Blair and Stephen Blocker asked me if I wanted to world build with them, and thus we began collaborating. Out of collaboration sprang stories, and eventually *Cold Magic*, during the writing of which they offered, and I asked for, suggestions, advice, ideas, and corrective so that in some ways this is far more a collaboration than any kind of novel conceived and written by me alone. Also, they read scenes and drafts multiple times, and we discussed plot points and background details. This project would not exist without them. Of course, they wouldn't exist without me (oh, and their dad, but whatever, honey, we love you, but the "shower of meteors" idea just didn't work with the backstory we'd already set up), so I guess they and I are finally kind of even?

So, to Rhiannon, Alexander, and David: you're my favorite kids ever. Love you, yr Mom.

Awesomely valuable beta readers and research consults and advice givers (don't blame them, though, if there's something in the text that seems wrong or mishandled—it's my fault, not theirs). Listed in no particular order (and I'm missing someone, to whom I apologize in advance):

A'ndrea Messer, Michelle Sagara, Darcy Kramer, Katharine Kerr, Amanda Weinstein, Melanie Ujimori, Naamen G. Tilahun, Kari Maund, N. K. Jemisin, Edana MacKenzie, Andrew Vitro,

Theodore Vitro, Robert and Bernice Littman, Jeanne Reames, Karen Williams, Sherwood Smith, Constance Ash, Catherine Wood, Rebecca Houliston, Cynthia LeCount Samaké, Barou Samaké, and Jay Silverstein.

Ann Marie Rasmussen got articles for me I could not access myself, usually with titles like "The Quarternary History of the English Channel: An Introduction."

My thanks to my agents, Russell Galen and Danny Baror (I know they're just doing their job, but I still appreciate their work above and beyond).

And, of course, a special and fulsome thanks to the fabulous Orbit crew.

About the Author

Kate Elliott has been writing stories since she was nine years old, which has led her to believe either that she is a little crazy or that writing, like breathing, keeps her alive. Her previous series include the Crossroads trilogy (starting with *Spirit Gate*), and the Crown of Stars septology (starting with *King's Dragon*). She likes to play sports more than she likes to watch them; right now, her sport of choice is outrigger canoe paddling. She has been married for a really long time. She and her spouse produced three spawn (aka children), and now that the youngest has graduated high school, they spend extra special time with their miniature schnauzer (aka The Schnazghul). Her spouse has a much more interesting job than she does, with the added benefit that they had to move to Hawaii for his work. Thus, the outrigger canoes. Find out more about the author at www.kateelliott.com

SPIRIT GATE

Book One of the Crossroads Trilogy

**IN A WORLD TORN APART BY WARFARE AND
BETRAYAL, A NEW DARKNESS HAS RISEN**

For hundreds of years the Guardians ruled the Hundred, but these
unearthly beings have faded from human sight and no longer
exert their will on the world. Only the reeves, patrolling on
enormous eagles, still represent the Guardians' power. But there
is a corruption in the land that not even they can control, and
fanatics are devastating villages, towns, and cities in a drive to
annihilate all who oppose them. No one knows who leads them or
why, but they leave ample evidence of their brutal strength
and cruelty.

Outlanders Anji and Mai are on the run with a company of
dedicated Qin warriors, when they meet an unusual reeve.
Together they could take on the devouring horde; and they must
make the attempt, or the land will certainly be lost. But a young
woman sworn to the Goddess may hold the ultimate key . . .

www.orbitbooks.net

SHADOW GATE

Book Two of the Crossroads Trilogy

HER DYING VISION HAD SHOWN HER THE NEXT
WORLD – BUT HER SPIRIT HAD NOT MADE THE
JOURNEY.

Marit was pretty sure she had been murdered. She vividly recalled
the assassin's dagger but she woke alone, sprawled on a Guardian
altar, with more questions than answers.

The Guardians once ruled the Hundred, but disappeared in ages
past, leaving reeves to manage the peace. But Marit finds this
peace shattered as an army ravages the land. Its leaders walk in
shadow, wearing the cloaks of lost Guardians. As she searches
for meanings in a changed world, Marit finds her old love Joss
and the Outlander Anji struggling to maintain order. But her
own enemies are drawing close. Marit tries to untangle the
web of betrayals that connect her murder with the razing of the
countryside, but she can't run forever. She will be found and there
will be choices: complicity or death.

orbit

www.orbitbooks.net

TRAITORS' GATE

Book Three of the Crossroads Trilogy

CHAOS AND DESTRUCTION RULE BENEATH THE BANNER OF A TWISTED STAR

Reeve Joss is struggling to defend a country ravaged by twin armies led by warped Guardians. Joss's men now patrol a land of burning villages and homeless refugees as he tries to separate traitor from friend; while his thoughts still stray to Zubaidit. But this temple-trained assassin is focused only on her target, Guardian Commander Lord Radas. His death would benefit them all, yet Guardians are immortal and now use their powers to twist the hearts of men.

Joss is also disturbed by dreams of Marit. His lost love has become a feared Guardian herself, but rejected their corrupt temptations to seek others of her kind. She prays some remain uncontaminated by the blight cursing their land – and that it's not too late to fight.

www.orbitbooks.net